ACCI...
EMI...

ACCIDENT AND EMERGENCY

Caroline Anderson

Josie Metcalfe

Sharon Kendrick

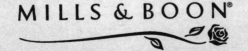

MILLS & BOON®

*MILLS & BOON and MILLS & BOON with the Rose Device
are registered trademarks of the publisher.
Harlequin Mills & Boon Limited,
Eton House, 18–24 Paradise Road, Richmond, Surrey, TW9 1SR.*

ACCIDENT AND EMERGENCY
© by Harlequin Enterprises II B.V. 2000

The Spice of Life, Loud and Clear and *Casualty of Passion* were first
published in Great Britain by Mills & Boon Limited
in separate, single volumes

The Spice of Life © Caroline Anderson 1993
Loud and Clear © Josie Metcalfe 1996
Casualty of Passion © Sharon Kendrick 1995

ISBN 0 263 82427 6

111-0001

*Printed and bound in Spain
by Litografia Rosés S.A., Barcelona*

Contents

Caroline Anderson's nursing career was brought to an abrupt halt by a back injury, but her interest in medical things led her to work first as a medical secretary, and then after completing her teacher training, as a lecturer in medical office practice to trainee medical secretaries. She lives in rural Suffolk, with her husband, two daughters, and assorted animals. She also writes for Mills & Boon® Enchanted™.

Other titles by Caroline Anderson:

THE SPICE OF LIFE

by

Caroline Anderson

For Annie
who gave me the carrots in the frilly
and lots, lots more. Bless you.

CHAPTER ONE

KATHLEEN HENNESSY was spoiling for a fight.

She had just spent a weekend at home in Belfast dutifully admiring the latest Hennessy grandchild and enduring countless little digs about good Catholic girls and settling down to raise a family instead of racketing about the world enjoying herself—as if it was such a sin to enjoy life, for God's sake, she thought angrily, and anyway six years as Sister in the accident and emergency department of the Audley Memorial in Suffolk hardly constituted racketing! Anybody would think she was a promiscuous little tart, the way her family reproached her for her single status. . .

All except Maria. She understood—mainly because she was only twenty-six and already had four children and another on the way. She had had such a promising career as a physio, Kathleen thought crossly, and now she was trapped at home with her children while her husband powered quietly on up the career ladder, leaving her behind.

And nothing wrong with it at all, if that was what was right for you, but it wasn't right for Maria, and it sure as eggs wasn't right for Kath!

She turned her little car precisely into a parking place in the hospital car park, climbed out and slammed the door. Damned dictators! Why couldn't they just understand that she didn't want to be married and settled with umpteen kids and a mortgage up to the sky and no life to call her own?

Selfish, they'd called her. OK. That was fine. So she was selfish. Perhaps that was why she worked the hours she did in the most gruelling part of the hospital, picking up the pieces—literally, sometimes—and putting them back together if possible, consoling distraught relatives if not.

'They probably think I'm still carrying bedpans all day!' she said to no one in particular, and locked her car door with a vicious twist.

As she did so she glanced towards the entrance of A and E, checking automatically for Jim Harris's car—except it wouldn't be there, she remembered with a twinge of regret. Jim had left, moved on to London and was heading up a new Rapid Response Unit there in connection with HEMS, the Helicopter Emergency Medical Service.

She wondered what his replacement would be like. Well, they'd find out soon, she thought, glancing at her watch, and then stared in amazement as a heavy black motorbike cruised lazily into the consultant's slot and stopped.

'Well, of all the nerve!' she muttered, and, yanking her keys out of the door, she shoved them into her bag and marched across the car park, head held high.

'Excuse me, you can't leave that there!' she said firmly, and looked him straight in the eye.

Her first mistake. Even through the streaky visor she could see that he had the most mesmerising eyes—laughing eyes—laughing at her. She looked hastily away—and found *her* eyes glued to a body that had no business being so magnetically attractive.

He was still sitting astride the bike, balancing it with his long, lean legs tautly encased in black leather. Hell, the whole man was tautly encased in black leather! His body flexed as he hauled the heavy bike up on to the centre stand, and her heart jerked and accelerated to a steady two hundred beats a minute. Well, that was what it felt like.

Ridiculous! She dragged her eyes up and watched as, unhurriedly, he stripped off his heavy gloves and laid them across the bike before lifting his helmet off and balancing it in front of him. His hair was dark, almost black, rumpled by the helmet but unruly anyway, and a heavy stubble covered his jaw, lending him a rakish and piratical air. His lips were firm and sensual—and twitching.

Ignoring the kick of her heart as she met his eyes again without the intervention of the visor, she tried again.

'You can't leave your bike here, it's the consultant's parking space! If he's needed urgently and he can't find anywhere to park, he could waste precious minutes while someone's lying dying for want of his attention!'

A dark, slender brow arched tauntingly above the laughing grey eyes. Holy Mary, he had lovely eyes! She forced herself to concentrate.

'Aren't you being rather melodramatic?' he said in a deep, cultured voice with a deceptively lazy lilt to it. It made her toes curl just listening to him, and perversely that made her even angrier.

'No, I'm not, and if you knew the first damn thing about Accident and Emergency you would know I wasn't!' she snapped.

He inclined his head in a cheeky little salute and

grinned. 'I concede to your superior knowledge, Sister,' he murmured.

Oh, that voice!

'Good,' she said, and was disgusted to notice that *her* voice was softening. She firmed it up. 'So, please move your bike.'

His lips twitched. 'I really don't think——'

'Are you going to move it, or am I going to contact the hospital security staff and get them to move it for you?'

The smile blossomed on his lips and, lifting his hand, he coiled a lock of her hair around his finger, drawing her closer. 'You know, Irish,' he said softly, his voice like raw silk sliding over her senses, 'with a temper like that you really ought to have red hair. . .'

For a full second she was too stunned to move, but then she slapped his hand away, and, drawing herself up to her full five feet four, she glared at him furiously.

'That just about does it!' she hissed. Spinning on her heel, she stalked away with her head in the air.

In the midst of the morning rush-hour his laughter drifted after her, curling round her senses and inflaming her still further.

She marched into A and E, slapping the swing doors out of the way with the palm of her hand, and turned smartly into the cloakroom. Two nurses in there straightened away from the walls, murmured, 'Good morning, Sister,' and faded into the corridor.

Kathleen turned and studied herself in the mirror. 'Red hair, indeed!' she muttered. 'Rude man.' In fact, there was a trace of red when the sun was on it, but she didn't want to dwell on that at the moment! No, it was plain old dark brown, cut in a blunt bob at her

chin, easy to keep neat and tidy—unlike his wild tangle
that was almost black, except at the temples where it
was streaked with grey.

To match his eyes, she thought, and her own lost
focus as she remembered the strange way the colour
had seemed to change as he laughed. Like pebbles
underwater, flickering with the light.

Yuck. She'd be reciting poetry next!

Her own eyes were a muddy green, and just now
they were spitting fire, like a little cat. In fact it was a
wonder there wasn't smoke pouring out of her ears!

But, my God, he did look good in all that leather
gear...

She turned away from the mirror with a sound of
disgust. Imagine getting turned on by a biker! He was
probably smothered in tattoos, for heaven's sake! She
ruthlessly suppressed a little shiver of curiosity. Perhaps her family were right; maybe it was time she
settled down.

She took her frilly cap out of the locker and skew-
ered it to her hair with the pins, adjusting it until she
was satisfied that it was absolutely correct. Nothing got
past Sister Hennessy that wasn't correct—including
That Man!

She glanced at her watch and pulled a face. There
wasn't time to report the bike to the security staff
before hand over. She left the cloakroom and went to
her office, took the report from the night sister and
then went out of the office towards the nursing station.

However she didn't get there. One of the nurses she
had seen in the cloakroom was standing in the middle
of the corridor, flushed pink and grinning like an idiot,

while That Man lounged on one leg in all his taut leather and chatted her up.

Enraged, she marched up to them.

'I'm sorry, sir, but you aren't allowed in this area. It's staff only. Nurse, are you here for a reason?'

The girl blushed even pinker, and stood up straight. 'Oh—yes, Sister. I'm starting on A and E today.'

Kathleen eyed her up and down. 'Are you, indeed? Well, you'd better come with me. The exit's that way, sir,' she added pointedly, and then marched the nurse into the CSSD store.

'Right, young lady, there are a few things you need to know about how I run this unit, and the first is that my nurses don't loll around in the corridors indulging in idle chatter with strange men!'

'But, Sister, he asked me——'

'I don't want to know what he asked you! I've already had trouble with him today. The best thing you can do is keep out of his way until I get rid of him. Right, this place is chaotic. I want everything cleared up and sorted out before the rush starts again, all right? If you think we're getting low on anything, I want to know, please. I'll send another nurse in to help you. Here's the check list.'

And she swept out, heading for the phone again.

There was no sign of him now, thank goodness. Security said they'd send someone over right away, and she busied herself for the next few minutes with the half-dozen patients in the waiting area.

There was a nasty sprain which needed an X-ray, a query appendix for the surgical reg and a couple of cuts and other minor injuries which needed cleaning up and suturing.

Mick O'Shea, the surgical registrar on take and one of her old SHOs, breezed in as she was cleaning up one of the patients with a cut hand.

'Top o' the mornin' to you, Sister Hennessy!' he sang, cheerful as ever, and she shot him a black look.

'Good morning, Dr O'Shea,' she said repressively.

He pretended to look chastened, and inspected the cut with great care.

'Just a couple of wee stitches—sure you can manage, Sister?'

'Probably a great deal better than you,' she replied with a sugary smile, and after a reassuring word to her patient, she led Mick out into the corridor.

'Your patient's in here,' she said shortly.

Mick stopped her with a hand on her arm.

'What's eating you today?'

She gave a strained little chuckle. 'It shows?'

He grinned. 'Only to an expert in family relationships—and I know you were away for the weekend!'

Her chuckle relaxed. 'I've been home—got lots of grief about not being settled down with fourteen children——'

Mick laughed. 'Why under God do you imagine I never go home?'

They shared a commiserating smile, and Mick put his arm around her shoulders and gave her a friendly hug. 'Of course you could always marry me and blame the lack of children on my war wound——'

She spluttered with laughter. 'What war wound?'

He grinned cheekily. 'Poetic licence, m'darlin'! We'd make a lovely couple, don't you think? Can't you just see your mother in a pink floppy hat with cherries on it? How about a quick kiss to seal the pact?'

'Put me down, you lecherous old goat!' she said with a laugh, and, pushing him away, she straightend up in time to see That Man emerge from Jim's old office with Ben Bradshaw, the senior registrar.

He had obviously showered, the almost-black hair falling in damp curls over his broad forehead, and he had changed into casual trousers and a shirt. The stubble was gone, and he was even wearing a tie—well, nearly. It hung round his neck, the knot well below the open collar of his shirt, and in the vee she could see the cluster of damp curls at the base of his throat. He looked almost respectable—and very, very sexy. He was also in the wrong place again. Kathleen opened her mouth, and a lid drooped over one of those fabulous grey eyes in a wicked wink.

'We meet again,' he said with a grin.

'Morning,' Mick greeted him. 'Good weekend?'

That Man shrugged. 'Not bad—bit windy earlier. Good thermals, though.'

Thermals? As in underwear? Never! Kathleen glanced sharply up at Mick. 'Do you know him?'

Mick nodded, and Ben Bradshaw stepped into the yawning void. 'Have you met Sister Hennessy yet?' he asked.

That Man's full lips twitched. 'Yes, we have—er—spoken,' he said, and the smile won and tipped the corners of his lips, bringing an enticing little dimple to one cheek. He held out his hand. 'Jack Lawrence,' he said, and if the floor could have opened up and swallowed her she would have been delighted.

As the fiery blush mounted her cheeks, she shook his hand briefly, desperately hoping for a miracle.

Holy Mary, she thought, all these years I've been a good girl—can't you do something?

Apparently not. The floor stubbornly resisted her prayers and imprecations. Jack Lawrence released her hand and turned to Ben.

'So, how's the rest of the weekend been? Sorry I had to desert you yesterday.'

'Oh, not a problem. There wasn't anything too drastic.'

'Good. So, Sister Hennessy, how would you like to offer me a cup of coffee so we can get acquainted while these two young men carry on with their duties?'

Her mind flailed. 'I—I have somebody to suture——'

'Ben, would you? I think Sister Hennessy and I need to have a chat. We'll be in my office.'

And that was the end of that.

She followed him numbly, still praying for that elusive miracle as they went into the staff rest-room and collected two cups of coffee and then out again, back down the corridor to the consultant's room—his room.

On the way her mind ran over their conversation in the car park. One thing in particular sprang to mind. 'If you knew the first thing about Accident and Emergency——' Oh, Lord, let me be dreaming...

He opened the door for her, closed it behind him and indicated the chair, then lounged against the window sill and grinned. 'Would you like to go first?'

Oh, sure—and say what? She almost laughed. 'Not really—I'm still trying to swallow the rest of my feet,' she confessed ruefully.

He chuckled, a wickedly delicious little chuckle that

sent a shiver down her spine. She set her coffee down before she slopped it all and met his eyes defiantly.

'Why didn't you say something?'

He smiled slowly. 'Such as?'

'Well—I don't know—anything. "I'm your new boss" would have done nicely. You just stood there and made a complete fool of me——'

He shook his head. 'Oh, no, Irish, you did that all by yourself.'

She blushed again. 'You could have said something,' she repeated stubbornly.

'Yes, I could, you're quite right. It was unkind of me. I apologise. '

She shot him a keen look, quite sure he was laughing at her, but his face was sober and his eyes were gentle now.

'You didn't look like a consultant.'

'No.'

'You should have said——'

'I should. You didn't really give me much chance——'

'Rubbish! You had every opportunity!'

He shrugged and grinned. 'I suppose so, but it just seemed like a bit of harmless fun—and you know, Irish, you're beautiful when you're angry.'

She was speechless.

The phone rang, and he reached out a long arm and hooked it up. 'Lawrence.'

He listened for a moment, a slow smile spreading over his face, and then held the phone out to her.

'Security for you—something about a motorbike in the car park. . .'

* * *

Kathleen supposed there was some comfort to be gained from knowing that nobody had ever died of humiliation. Doubtless in later years she would be glad of that, but for now she was too embarrassed to care.

It wouldn't have been so bad, of course, if it had only been him, but there was that second-year nurse whom she had accused of loitering with him in the corridor—that was going to take some fancy footwork to get out of without loss of face. Oh, well, at least she wasn't Japanese. Good job too, as there wasn't a handy sword to fall on. She didn't somehow think a stitch cutter would do the trick quite so well!

In the end she screwed up her courage, took the girl into her office and apologised. 'I made a mistake,' she admitted. 'I didn't realise who he was, and with the security problems hospitals have been having recently, you can't be too careful.'

The nurse smiled. 'I didn't know who he was, either, but he asked me where he could find you, and I told him I didn't know, and he said "Are you new too?" and then you arrived and. . .' She trailed to a halt. 'He didn't look—well—like a consultant, did he?'

Bless her, Kath thought. 'No, Nurse, he didn't, but he is.' She glanced at her name badge. 'Amy, have you done any work on Surgical?'

She nodded. 'I did some time with Sister Lovejoy last year, and I've done some orthopaedics.'

'And how did you get on?'

She nibbled her bottom lip. 'OK. I had a bit of a problem with Mr Hamilton when he first arrived—I did something rather stupid and he was furious, but the patient was OK and he was great after that. Sister Lovejoy was ever so kind to me over it.'

Kathleen groaned inwardly. That was all she needed, a nurse who made mistakes.

'Well, Amy, if you aren't sure about anything, you ask, OK? We can't afford to make mistakes down here. I think you'd better work with me for the next few days, or if I'm not here, then with one of my staff nurses. Right. Do you know what triage is?'

'Um—is that putting patients in order of priority as they come in so that you don't leave people to bleed to death because they're at the end of the queue?'

Kathleen winced and grinned. 'Sort of. You're on the right lines. It really comes into its own when there's a big emergency involving lots of people. Then the triage nurse is perhaps the most important member of the team. It's a tremendous responsibility, and challenges all your skills and training, but it also depends a lot on gut instinct. OK, now we're going to go and have a look in the waiting-room and at the notes, and do a bit of triage there. If they're all on a par, we take them on a first come, first served basis. Anyone with a suspected heart condition or serious bleeding or a major fracture or head injury comes first, though, and every time an ambulance brings someone, they get seen immediately in the trolley area.'

She took Amy down the corridor. 'Here we have the cubicles for the walking wounded or minor cases, then the trolley area for the major cases, and then the resus. room for the crisis cases. Then down here we have a couple of day beds for patients who need to rest under observation for the day following treatment but who don't really justify admission, and then over here we've got the two theatres for major suturing and cleaning

up, and then down there at the end the X-ray and
plaster rooms.'

Amy nodded, her eyes like saucers, and Kathleen
remembered the first time she had worked in A and E.

'Don't worry, you'll be fine. I'll look after you.'

They checked the few patients in the waiting-room,
and Kathleen got Amy to sort them into priority,
talking through the decision-making process as she did
so.

'Fine,' she said when Amy had finished. 'No problems there. But don't worry, you wouldn't be asked to
do it alone yet. The triage nurse is always qualified and
experienced, but it doesn't hurt you to see how it's
done.'

It was, in fact, a ridiculously quiet day with a steady
trickle of bits and pieces, an ideal day to find one's
feet.

Unfortunately it meant that there wasn't enough for
the consultant to do to keep him out of her way, and
every time she turned round she almost fell over him.

'Are you checking up on me?' she demanded half
way through the afternoon.

'Now, Irish, you know better than that,' he said with
a cheeky grin, and left her alone for a few minutes.

Then there was a call on the red phone.

'OK,' Kathleen said. 'We've got someone coming in
on a blue light, a young man who's fallen under a train.
Could be an attempted suicide, we don't know. Anyway, there's considerable loss of blood, massive lower
limb and pelvic damage and some chest injuries. We'll
need plasma expander, and samples immediately for
cross matching. Better have some O neg. sent up for
immediate use as well. Right, let's move.'

They prepared the resus. room, and when all was ready they informed the patients still waiting that they might have a slight delay due to an emergency that was being brought in. There were the usual grumbles, but they faded instantly as the ambulance backed up to the entrance, doors already opening.

He was screaming, the high-pitched, nerve-grating scream of agony that always turned Kathleen's blood to stone, and the waiting-room fell into shocked silence.

They wheeled him rapidly into Resus., Kathleen snapping out instructions right, left and centre, but as they peeled back the blanket to examine him, even Kathleen after all the years she had been working in A and E was shocked at the extent of his injuries. Both his legs were severed completely, the right one mid-thigh, the left up at the hip. His head was cut and bleeding, and his jacket was torn and damaged, indicating possible chest injuries. His right arm was also lying at a funny angle and was probably dislocated or fractured.

Amy Winship took one look at him and disappeared quietly through the door, and Ben Bradshaw winced. Only Jack Lawrence appeared quite unmoved, glancing dispassionately at the damage that Kath revealed with her scissors. There was blood everywhere, more of it by the second, and nothing they did seemed to stop it. His left leg was particularly bad, the vessels refusing to co-operate. They slowed it to a steady well, but it wouldn't stop, and through it all there was the awful screaming.

'For Christ's sake get an anaesthetist down here and shut him up,' Jack Lawrence grunted, and moved to his head, checking his pupils automatically. 'Have we got any ID?'

Kathleen shook her head. 'No, nothing. The ambulance men checked his clothes.'

'Damn. We need to get his relatives in fast.'

She raised an eyebrow. 'You don't say?'

He grinned ruefully. 'Any sign of a surgeon? And we need cardiothoracic and orthopaedics, too.'

'Before or after the mortuary technician?' Ben said under his breath.

Kath glared at him, and he shrugged.

'Just being realistic, old thing.'

'Well, don't bother—and don't call me old thing. Just do your job, please. Have you stopped that bleeding yet?'

He shook his head. 'It's leaking from the abdomen— I think he needs a bit of surgical attention.'

Kath shot him a dry look. 'You guys are really sharp today, aren't you?'

Jack was inspecting the young man's chest dispassionately, watching the ragged rise and fall of the ribs as he dragged in a breath between screams, and he shook his head thoughtfully. While he ran thorough hands and eyes over his shattered body, Kathleen started cleaning up the chest area ready for the heart monitor after checking the IV line that was running in Haemacel and taking blood for cross-matching, dodging round the radiographer who had brought the portable in and was taking X-rays.

When his chest was clear, she put on the pads for the heart monitor, frowning slightly as she did so at the feel of the chest wall under her hands. As she watched his breath jerked in, and a large section of his chest wall moved in instead of out.

'Flail chest,' she said quietly, and Jack nodded, drawing her to one side.

'The lung's collapsed, I think. Probably where he was hit by the train. His pelvis is shot to hell, too, and judging by the feel of the abdomen, he's got massive haemorrhaging.'

Kath nodded. 'So why is he still alive?'

'God knows.' Their eyes met and tracked together to the heart monitor. 'He's not doing too well, is he? I think we need an echocardiograph. Can you get the cardiographer?'

Not that there's a great deal of point, Kathleen thought to herself, but we may as well go through the motions.

While she phoned the switchboard and requested that they page the cardiographer, Michael Barrington the orthopaedic SR arrived and glanced at the shattered stubs of the young man's femurs.

He swore, softly and succinctly. 'Got any X-rays yet?'

Jack nodded. 'Yes, they're just being developed.'

Michael pursed his lips. 'Done a real job on himself, hasn't he? Anyone know why?'

'No. We don't even know if it was an accident yet.'

Their eyes flicked to the monitor. Their patient was still alive but his condition was deteriorating visibly. The anaesthetist, Peter Graham, had arrived and managed to dull his pain. Now he merely lay and moaned, but at least he was no longer screaming.

Amy popped her head round the door to tell

Kathleen that they had found some ID on the track
and the police had brought his parents in.

'His name's Steven Blowers. They want to see him.'

Kathleen exchanged glances with Jack, and he shook
his head.

'Put them in the interview-room and give them a cup
of tea. One of us will be out in a minute,' she told the
young nurse. 'Oh, and Amy? Say nothing.'

Amy nodded gratefully and retreated.

The X-rays appeared and Michael ran a critical eye
over them.

'Ouch. Do you want me to interpret, or is it aca-
demic?' he said quietly.

Jack's mouth lifted in a wry smile. 'Probably. We'll
see what the cardiothoracic guy has to say.'

When he arrived moments later, he took one look at
the X-rays and shook his head.

'You jest, of course?' he said drily. 'Look at this
shadow here—probably a bulge in the heart or the
aorta behind it—the kid's a goner. He'll never make
the anaesthetic, and even if he did, who wants to be a
bloody cripple? Oh, well, we can only fail. Let's have
him up in Theatre.'

He sauntered out, whistling, and Kathleen met
Michael Barrington's eyes. They were like chips of
blue ice, his lips compressed into a thin line.

'Call me if you need me in Theatre—but I'd just as
soon Tim Mayhew did it—I don't trust myself near
that bastard.'

And he turned on his heel and stalked away, his
limp almost imperceptible.

Jack raised an eyebrow. 'What's eating him?'

'He's a bloody cripple,' she said succinctly.

'What?'

'He has an artificial leg. He went to assist at a passenger train derailment last year and got trapped in the wreckage. We had to amputate part of his leg to free him.'

'Ah. . .'

Just then their patient moaned and opened his eyes. Kathleen was there instantly.

'Steven? It's all right, you're in hospital. Can you hear me?'

He licked his lips and nodded slightly. 'Messed it up, didn't I?' His voice was a mere thread. 'I thought it would be quick,' he went on painfully. 'Let me go— please, let me go. You don't know what this is all about.'

She squeezed his hand. 'Do you want to tell me?'

'Danny,' he whispered. 'My fault. . .gave Danny— HIV.'

'Oh, Christ,' someone muttered behind her. Kathleen closed her eyes. The room was a bloodbath, all of them were covered, and their patient was HIV positive.

Great. Oh, well, it had happened before, doubtless it would happen again. As far as she was aware, no one had cut themselves or pricked themselves with a needle.

Behind her she could hear Jack calmly telling everyone to go and shower and change and come back in full barrier gear.

She could see blood on Jack's cheek and on his arm above the gloves. God knows where it was on her.

Steve groaned again, and the nurse in her took over.

'Your parents are here, Steven. They're waiting to see you. Do you feel up to it?'

His mouth twisted in a bitter little smile. 'You mean I'm going to feel better?' he whispered.

It wasn't really a question. Kathleen lifted her head and met Jack's eyes pleadingly. He nodded.

It was time to be honest.

'You've got severe chest and abdominal injuries, as well as the injuries to your legs.'

'Will I die?'

She was struck by how blue his eyes were as they bored into her own—blue and clear, like the sky. What a bloody waste.

'I'm afraid it's quite likely.'

'Don't be—afraid. It's OK, really. It's what I want. . .'

His eyes flickered closed, and he licked his lips. 'Love a drink.'

'I'll get you some iced water.'

She found a nurse and sent her for it, and then held the cup and dabbed his lips with a swab dipped in the water.

'Thanks.' His voice was weaker. Kathleen didn't think they could afford to wait any longer.

She met Jack's eyes, and he nodded. 'I'll get them.'

'Thanks.'

As he moved past her, she took a clean swab and wiped his cheek.

'You could change your coat first.'

He glanced down and gave a short, humourless grunt of laughter. 'Yes, I think you're right. Put a blanket over him.'

He was only gone a minute, and when he returned,

it was with a couple in their fifties who were holding hands as if they were desperately hanging on to reality.

They were obviously shocked by his condition and lost for words, but he shocked them further with his.

'Never been what you wanted—I'm sorry. Never meant to hurt you,' he whispered.

Kathleen swallowed a lump in her throat, Ben coughed discreetly and Jack busied himself at the X-ray box.

The phone on the wall rang softly, and Kathleen answered it.

'Theatre's ready for him,' she said quietly.

Jack nodded and took a step towards Steve where he lay surrounded by his family, and then everything seemed to happen at once.

The monitor shrilled, Steve moaned, his mother gasped, and everybody leapt into action.

'Pressure's dropped right away,' Kath said quietly.

'Damn, he's arrested,' Jack muttered, and flung the covers off his chest.

Kath snatched up an airway and tipped back his head. 'Ben, come and bag him while I get the drugs.'

She handed the airbag to the registrar while Jack pressed rhythmically on the patient's sternum. 'What do you want, IV adrenalin, calcium and atropine?'

Jack nodded. 'And adrenalin into the heart. Let's not mess about.'

Someone suggested to his parents that they should leave, but no one had time to show them out.

She handed Jack the syringe with the long needle, and he slid it neatly between the ribs and into the heart while Kath injected the other drugs into the giving set in his arm.

'OK, let's check the monitor.'

They glared at the screen, willing the line to flutter into life, but the trace remained persistently flat.

'Come on, damn it!' Jack muttered and thumped his chest again. 'Now!'

Nothing.

'Try again?' Kath said quietly.

Jack let his breath out on a sigh and shook his head. 'His aorta's gone. It's pointless. Damn, damn, damn. . .'

He removed his hands, stripped off his gloves and stepped back, only then noticing the stricken parents still standing near the door. He lifted his hands helplessly.

'I'm sorry—we did everything we could.'

'Oh, thank God it's over,' his mother said unsteadily, and then the tears overflowed and ran down her pale cheeks.

Kathleen carefully covered the shattered body with the blanket, but left his face uncovered. Relatives hated to see a sheet over the faces of their loved ones. It was illogical, but quite understandable, and she respected that. Sticking her head out of the door, she summoned a nurse and got her to take the young man's parents back to the interview-room and give them a cup of tea.

They cleaned themselves up quickly, instructed all the others to shower again as thoroughly as possible in view of the AIDS risk, and then went into the interview room to talk to Steve's parents.

Jack was astonishing. All day long she had wondered how he had managed to bamboozle his way into a consultancy, but first the calm, unflappable way he had dealt with Steve and now here, with the devastated relatives, Kathleen had an opportunity to see at first hand the qualities that set him apart as a consultant.

He talked through the whole drama again with them, explaining the various problems their son had had, discussing the probable outcome of each of his injuries had he survived, and then, when there was no doubt left in their minds that he should have died, he gave them even more.

'Whatever problems you've had in the past, remember that he loved you, and you loved him. No one can ever take that from you.'

It was a calculated tear-jerker, but delivered with great sincerity, and Kathleen found her own eyes misting over.

She escaped to her office as soon as the Blowers' left, grabbing herself a cup of coffee on the way. Seconds later there was a tap on her door and Jack came in.

'Are you OK? You looked a bit shaken up.'

'Oh, yes, I'm fine. It all adds variety. You know what they say—the spice of life, and all that. . .'

Her voice cracked and she cleared her throat.

He gave a grim little smile. 'If you say so, Irish. Got any of that coffee left?'

She handed him the cup and he swallowed the remains with a gulp.

'Home, I think. Fancy a drink on the way?'

She remembered their inauspicious start, and her somewhat ungracious behaviour during the morning. Perhaps it would be an opportunity to smooth things over, to apologise again and make a fresh start.

Her mouth was opening, the reply ready, when there was a tap on the door.

'Ah, Mr Lawrence—there's a young man who'd like to talk to you. His name's Danny Featherstone. I think he's a friend of Steven Blowers.'

He nodded at the receptionist. 'Put him in my office. I'll be along in a tick.'

He turned back to Kathleen and shrugged.

'Sorry.'

She took a deep breath.

'Maybe later?'

He shook his head slightly. 'Some other time, perhaps. I don't know if I'd be very good company tonight after all. I'll see you.'

And with that, he was gone.

CHAPTER TWO

THERE was a strange car in the consultant's slot the following day.

Kathleen found herself heaving a sigh of relief. If he had come by car, then she wouldn't have to endure the sight of him in all that black leather gear looking like something from Star Wars. All he needed was a sweeping black cloak. . .

She hauled herself back to reality. Damn the man. He was persecuting her, and he didn't even know it! She hadn't been able to sleep at all the night before for thinking of him, and some of her thoughts had been unprintable.

But then, yesterday had been a funny old day, clouded as it was by the memory of Steve Blower's traumatic and tragic death and the image of Jack comforting his parents. It seemed inconceivable that the man who had teased her so unforgivably in the morning had been so filled with compassionate understanding later in the same day. She had had him pegged as an emotional lightweight, probably good at his job in a technical sense but untroubled by messy feelings.

Instead, he had proved himself to be capable of great human emotion. Odd, that. Jim had been good with relatives, but Jack had some extra dimension to add to it.

She had pondered on it all night—that and the image

of his laughing eyes and the way his full, firm lips tipped so readily into that wickedly sexy smile.

Just a flirt, she chastised herself, and probably a married flirt for all that. After all, he must be pushing forty at the very least to be a consultant in A and E, although he didn't look it by any stretch of the imagination.

Well, only the once, when Steven Blowers had died and he had looked up at the parents, and then a curious bleakness had stolen over his face and drained the life away. Then he had looked older.

With a sigh, she got out of the car and locked it, walking deliberately by his car to peer curiously inside.

It was a very ordinary car, a middle of the range Ford in deep blue metallic with a roof-rack on it and the back full of—ropes? How odd.

She made her way into the department, greeting all the staff with a smile and a friendly word. Amy Winship was on earlies, and flashed her a grin.

'Morning, Sister.'

'Good morning, Amy. Is Mr Lawrence in his office?'

'No, he's gone to get some breakfast. He arrived at four, apparently. There was a pile-up—they called him in.'

She nodded. Yes, he would certainly earn his keep in this job, she thought drily.

She went into her office and took the report from the night sister, then swung cheerfully into her routine.

She was busy taking off a back-slab and replastering a fracture when Jack appeared, sticking his head round the door and grinning.

'Morning, Irish.'

She shot him a black look and squeezed the water

out of a bandage viciously. 'Good morning, *sir*!' she said pointedly.

His grin widened. 'Having fun?'

'Absolutely. Want to help?'

He shook his head. 'You're managing just fine, I'd only get in your way. I'll watch, though.'

And he did, propping himself up against the wall and chatting lightheartedly to the patient while she wound the plaster bandage round the broken wrist.

'There,' she said with a smile when she had finished. 'We'll let that set for a little while, then X-ray it again to check that it's nicely lined up. OK?'

The patient, a woman in her forties, nodded. 'Thank you both. It feels much better already than it did yesterday.'

Kathleen forced a smile, showed the lady to the waiting area outside the X-ray room and went back to clear up her mess.

'Thank you both, indeed!' she muttered.

'I did talk to her to set her at her ease,' he justified mildly.

Kath snorted. 'She was already at her ease, *sir*, and while we're on the subject of putting people at their ease, my name is Sister Hennessy!'

He grinned, totally unabashed. 'I'll try and remember that, Irish.'

She wondered if she would lose her job if she tossed a sodden plaster bandage right at his grinning mouth.

Probably, but by God, it would be worth it!

A brow twitched. 'I wouldn't,' he warned softly.

She lost the battle and laughed. 'Now, would I?'

'Quite likely!'

She met his eyes, searching for any lingering trace of

the bleakness she had seen the night before, but there was none, only undiluted wickedness flirting with her senses.

Well, he was wasting his time because as far as he was concerned she had no senses left!

She wiped the sink down viciously. 'Can I do anything for you?'

He chuckled. 'Now that's a thought to play with!' he said softly.

'Damn it, Jack Lawrence——'

She turned, the soggy, dripping plaster bandage in her hand, but he was gone, only the last swoosh of the swing door left to show he had ever been there.

She sighed and shook her head. Aggravating man. She mustn't let him take the rise out of her like that. He just seemed to find it so infuriatingly *easy*!

She caught up with him later in the staff-room, cracking jokes about second-rate coffee.

'So,' she said, 'how did you get on with that young man's friend last night?'

His face lost its sparkle. 'Ah, Danny. Well, he was very distressed, as you can imagine. They'd been lovers for some time, apparently. A few months ago they had a row, and Steve stormed off and went nightclubbing in London for the weekend. He caught HIV from a casual encounter, didn't realise and they patched up the row. The rest, as they say, is history.'

She shook her head slowly. 'How sad—what a dreadful waste.'

'One of the dangers of casual, unprotected sex. If you're going to live that life, you have to learn to do so responsibly.

'You don't have to engage in casual relationships,' she replied, more sharply than she had intended.

He arched a brow. 'Tut, tut, Sister Hennessy. Your Catholic upbringing is showing.'

'And what if it is?' she retorted, her chin lifting.

He met her eyes reprovingly. 'We're here to help, not to pass judgement. It's no business of ours to referee lifestyles.'

'But that's nonsense! I wouldn't hesitate to tell an overweight, unfit man that he was putting his health at risk. Why should I be allowed to give him dietary advice and not be able to advise a young person not to engage in indiscriminate sexual activity?'

He grinned. 'You don't tell an overweight man not to eat, you tell him what he can eat *safely*. *Ergo*, when you give advice on sexual behaviour, you don't say, "You mustn't", you say, "Do it like this"—likewise junkies. You have to give them clean needles and good habits, not moral outrage and prohibition.'

'Who in the hell is talking about moral outrage?' she demanded, her voice rising.

He just grinned wider, bent forwards and dropped a kiss on her startled lips.

'Beautiful,' he murmured absently, and walked away, leaving her riveted to the spot, astonished.

'Well, well, well—I do believe our dear Sister Hennessy is speechless!'

She glared at Ben Bradshaw, dragged some air into her deprived lungs and marched swiftly down the corridor into her office, shutting the door firmly behind her.

Then she let out the breath and sagged against the desk. Dazed, she lifted her fingers and rested them against her lips. They felt—tinglingly alive, soft and warm and swollen, aching for—for what? For more?

With a whimper of disgust and confusion, she sank into her chair and stared absently at the mound of paperwork. Damn him. Why did he have to do that? As if he'd known she'd spent all night wondering about the feel of his lips on hers, about how it would be if he kissed her.

She'd never expected rockets to go off and stars to shoot in all directions—leastways, not from just a casual brush of flesh against flesh. . .

She suppressed a shiver. Damn him. There had been nothing casual about that kiss. Brief, yes, and outwardly innocent, but my God, packed with promise!

Well, it wasn't about to happen again!

She got to her feet, checked her cap in the little mirror on the wall and marched out into her department.

She rapped on his door, swung it open and stood in the doorway, not trusting either of them if it was shut.

He raised his eyes from the paperwork on his desk and leant back in the chair, a lazy grin on his face.

'I suppose you want an apology?' he said unrepentantly.

'Don't you ever—ever!—pull a stunt like that again!'

The grin widened. 'Sorry—didn't you enjoy it? Perhaps next time——'

'Didn't you hear me?' she returned, her voice torn between a growl and a whimper. 'There will be no next time!'

'Pity. I was rather looking forward to it.'

She glared at him. 'You're incorrigible.'

He shrugged, a laughing, arrogant, almost Gallic

shrug. You would have thought it was a compliment, she thought crossly.

'I try to be.'

'Well, don't. This is my department, and I won't have you lolling around here undermining my authority——'

'My dear girl, nothing I could do could possibly undermine your authority,' he drawled lazily. 'The entire department cowers at the sound of your voice. I should have thought a little evidence of human frailty would merely enhance your reputation—and the association would do mine a power of good!'

She snorted. 'Your reputation would be greatly enhanced if you took yourself seriously!'

Something changed in his face then, some fleeting spectre that drained the life from his eyes and left them cold and hard.

Then he smiled, a dangerous, cynical smile.

'Life's too short to take it seriously, Irish. You should learn that, before it's too late.'

And with that he picked up his pen and returned to his paperwork, dismissing her.

She was in the staff lounge making herself a drink when he came in half an hour later.

'Coffee?' she asked, more as a reflex than anything. He shuddered and shook his head.

'Think I'll pass. Actually, I wanted to talk to you about yesterday. What's hospital policy on HIV testing after an incident like yesterday?'

'I don't think we have a policy. It's never been a problem before. If someone knows they've been contaminated by a needle or a knife, for instance, then I think the testing certainly is available.'

'But not otherwise?'

She shook her head. 'No. Why should it be necessary? I mean, I don't think anyone took any risks, and we were all wearing gloves anyway because of the state he was in—I would be worried that it would make people panic unnecessarily. You know, rather like getting an adverse smear test, and before you know where you are you've convinced yourself you've got cancer when it was probably just a lousy smear and they didn't get enough cells. Do you understand what I'm saying? I don't think we should threaten people's conception of their immortality unnecessarily, and I'm perfectly certain we're all quite safe.'

He shrugged. 'It was just an idea. Professionally, if I felt there was a risk I should want to know that I was clear so I was certain there was no danger of me passing anything on to a patient or a future partner. I mean, if you did contract it, wouldn't you want to know?'

She met his eye determinedly. 'Of course, if I felt there was a real risk, but I wouldn't pass it on anyway. I'm extremely careful at work and I don't have indiscriminate sexual relationships.'

He laughed softly, and it tickled up her spine. 'Your rosary's showing again, Irish. I didn't say anything about *indiscriminate* sex. Take Ben, for example. He's married. I gather his wife's pregnant. Now how would he feel if he contracted the virus from a freak accident at work and gave it to his wife and child just because we had failed to test him?'

Kath stared at him, stupefied. 'Maggie's pregnant? When?'

He grinned lazily. 'Well, I hardly liked to ask him *that*!'

She clicked her tongue irritably. 'You know what I mean. . .'

'Ask him—I'm sure it's not a secret.'

'I wonder why he hasn't said anything?' Kath mused.

'I think they only knew this morning, and you've been so busy being cross——'

'Huh! How would you like it if you were sexually harrassed?'

He grinned again. 'Try me.'

She drew herself up and sniffed. 'Don't be absurd. Why would I want to do that?'

'Because you're curious? Because you're secretly dying to press that delightful body up against me and find out how it feels?'

He was so close to the truth that she flushed and looked away. 'Please,' she muttered in a strangled voice. 'You're embarrassing me.'

His deep chuckle curled round her insides and squeezed. 'I'm sorry. I'll leave you in peace with your atrocious coffee.'

Her head came up. 'Jack?'

He stopped and looked back over his shoulder. 'Hmm?'

'About the testing—do you really think it's necessary?'

'In this case, no, but I think we should keep an open mind if anyone asks. I doubt if they will, but just keep your ears open.'

She nodded, and with a wink, he was gone, leaving

her dealing with her curiosity about how his body *would* feel pressed against hers, and the slow recognition that the coffee was, indeed, atrocious.

'Who is he, do we know?'

The ambulanceman shook his head. 'Collapsed in the park. Nobody knows him, no ID. Passer-by saw him and reported him—thought he was drunk. He was unconscious when we got to him.'

'Right, thank you, Sid.'

Kathleen bent over the unconscious patient and sniffed. No alcohol, but he was clammy and grey, and quite likely hypoglaecaemic. There was a pin-prick hole in the tip of his left thumb, and she nodded. Diabetic, gone into a coma from low blood sugar. She left the cubicle to find a blood test kit, and came back to find the new houseman, Joe Reynolds, ordering head X-rays and a neurologist's opinion.

She rolled her eyes and wondered how to tackle it. Young doctors were usually only too willing to take advice, but every now and again you got one like this lad, who clearly was all at sea and didn't know how to light the flares!

'Not a bad idea,' she said, 'considering he's probably banged his head when he passed out. Diabetics often damage themselves, don't they?'

He looked faintly startled. 'Diabetics? Does he have a Medic Alert bracelet?'

'I have no idea, but he——'

'Well, then, I think it would be safer to assume a neurological cause such as CVA, don't you, Sister?' he said loftily.

'Certainly, *Doctor*, if you say so,' she replied sweetly,

containing the urge to crown him for his patronising ignorance. After all, how long would it take to do a blood test with a Haemastix strip? Thirty seconds? What he was planning would tie half the hospital up for the entire morning!

Jack was busy, dealing with a nasty fracture, so she went to the nursing station and picked up the phone. 'Page Dr Marumba for me, could you?' she asked the switchboard. Seconds later she was connected to the consultant physician.

'Are you busy, Jesus? I wonder if I could offer you a cup of coffee in my department within the next couple of minutes?'

There was a deep chuckle from the other end. 'My pleasure, Kathleen. Problems?'

'You might say that.'

'Be right down.'

'Bless you.'

She put the receiver down and went back into the cubicle. 'Should we take some bloods for chemistry, Dr Reynolds?' she asked mildly.

'Ah—good idea, Sister. Perhaps you'd like to do the honours?'

'Certainly.' She withdrew fifty millilitres of completely unnecessary blood from the patient's arm, filled up the appropriate bottles and then put a blob on the treated strip and glanced at her watch.

As she finished she heard Dr Marumba's deep, cultured rumble in the corridor.

She stuck her head round the curtain and winked. 'Nearly done here, Dr Marumba. Could you give me a minute?'

'Sure.' The tall man elbowed his way past the curtain

and peered at the patient. 'Interesting—looks like hypoglycaemia, doesn't it, Dr Reynolds?'

The SHO's jaw dropped. 'Ah—um—well, it's certainly a possibility, sir.'

Jesus nodded. 'Oh, yes, see the strip—blood sugar way down. Well spotted. I see Sister Hennessy's done all the necessary tests for you. Well done. Glucagon?'

'Ah—well, yes, I——'

'Good, good. Well, I mustn't hold you up. Perhaps I'll come by for coffee another time, Sister. I can see you're busy here with Dr Reynolds.' He brushed past Kathleen, and the orthodontic miracle of his smile flashed against the rich ebony of his skin. His wink was wickedly conspiratorial.

'I'm sorry about the coffee,' she apologised, working hard on her straight face.

'Forget it—it's better upstairs, anyway.'

'Not you, too!' She turned back to Joe Reynolds and smiled innocently.

He returned the smile warily. 'I guess I owe you an apology, Sister.'

She let her smile mellow. Poor boy, he had no idea his downfall had been engineered. 'Think nothing of it,' she told him. 'I've been doing the job for years, don't forget. Experience counts for a lot, Joe. OK, what next?'

He opened his mouth, shut it again and grinned sheepishly.

'Glucagon?'

She waited.

'Um. . .'

'We'll go through it together, shall we? Then he can go and rest in the day ward for a while.'

The relief on Joe's face would have been comic if it hadn't been so worrying. Yet another one she was going to have to watch like a hawk, she thought wearily. Between him and Amy Winship, they were well staffed with idiots at the moment.

Oh, well, it would give her two bodyguards if she didn't ever let them out of her sight. That way she might have some protection against Jack Lawrence and his hyperactive lips!

It worked till Thursday, but then Amy was on days off and Joe had a cold. Inevitably it meant that she and Jack were in closer proximity, and it threatened to push her sanity over the brink.

Though why it should, lord only knows, she thought. What is it the man has that's so darned appealing?

Charm, her alter ego told her. Lazy, sexy, masculine charm—bucketfuls of it, coupled with a certain vulnerability that showed every now and then. Unfortunately it was a potent combination, and there was no known cure.

By about two-thirty she had run out of ways of dodging him. They had a patient with multiple lacerations of the face and neck following a fall through a window, and he needed extensive suturing. Never having seen Jack suture, she wondered if she ought to call the fascio-maxillary surgeon over from the Norfolk and Norwich, or if she could, indeed, trust Jack to do a decent job. Their own fascio-max man was on holiday that week or the problem wouldn't have arisen.

She decided there was only one way to deal with it, and that was directly.

She found him in his office.

'How's your suturing?' she asked without preamble.

'My suturing? Pretty good—why?'

'We have a patient with multiple lacerations of the face and neck and our fascio-max is away—I was just wondering if you were good enough,' she replied bluntly.

He smiled—which was just as well. He could have flipped, having his professional competence challenged like that.

'I think she'll be safe with me,' he said mildly.

'He.'

'Even better. I'll practise on the jaw-line—then if it isn't good enough, he can always grow a beard to hide it.'

His voice was so bland she really wasn't sure if he was joking, but having asked and received an apparently satisfactory reply, she decided she had no choice but to go with him.

'He's in Cubicle Four.'

Jack nodded. 'I'll have a look, but then I think we'll move him into Ops if I think it's justified. I'll need a good work light.'

He went in to the patient, a man in his thirties, and smiled a hello.

'I was enjoying that cup of tea,' he said mournfully.

The man attempted a smile. 'Sorry, Guv. Made a bit of a mess, haven't I?'

'Just a shade. Still, soon have you sorted out. I think we'll move you into a little theatre we have down here for just this sort of thing, OK? I'll get the nurses to move you and get you comfy, and I'll have a bit of a wash and change. See you in a tick.'

By the time Kathleen had sorted the patient out and

found someone to give his wife a cup of tea and explain what was happening, Jack was back in Theatre, clad from head to toe in green theatre pyjamas, with a J-cloth hat and a mask.

'Good, ennit? Just like the telly,' he said to the man, and received a lopsided grin for his pains. 'You know, you really ought to do something about that razor you've been using!'

The man chuckled. Kath knew what Jack was doing, unobtrusively trying to assess the range of movement and any possible nerve damage indicated by loss of mobility in any of the facial muscles.

She relaxed. Already gowned and masked herself, she drew up the lignocaine and opened the suture packs.

Three hours later Jack tied the last suture and stood back to survey his work.

'Bee-ootiful.'

It was. Oh, the patient looked a mess, but Kath had seen the enormous care that had gone into the alignment of each suture, the meticulous attention not only to the innumerable tiny little muscle fibres, nerves and blood vessels but to laughter lines and wrinkles to ensure that the tissues were realigned as closely as possible to their original position. He sealed the whole area with plastic skin to prevent infection, and then stripped off his gloves and stretched.

'Thank you, Doctor,' the patient said a little stiffly. He was going to find it rather difficult to talk for a few days, Kathleen realised.

Jack smiled warmly. 'My pleasure. I'm afraid you won't be Miss World again, but you'll do. All adds character. Come back in a week for a check-up and to have the majority of the sutures out, or earlier if they give you any trouble or get infected. Try and keep them dry, and take the painkillers we'll give you for the first few days. How did you get here?'

'My wife drove me.'

He nodded. 'Good. Well, get her to take you home and look after you. You'll be off work for a week. Sister will give you a certificate, and you'll need a follow-up next time you come if you're still a bit sore. Hopefully you won't need it.'

With a cheery wave he left them, and Kathleen helped the man to his feet and put him in a wheelchair.

'Don't want you collapsing on us—not good for the department's reputation,' she joked lightly, and wheeled him round and handed him over to his wife.

She found Jack in his office, leaning on the window with a cigarette in his hand.

'You smoke!' she said in horror.

'Only under duress. That was a long old job. Thanks for your help.'

'You're welcome. You did it well. I'm sorry I asked you if you were good enough.'

He chuckled. 'Your privilege, my darling girl. I hope you aren't going to find me anything else to do tonight.'

'Why, tired?'

He grinned. 'No, I was hoping you'd join me for that drink.'

She was caught without defences, her mind still playing with the idea of being his darling girl.

'Ah—drink?' she said helplessly.

'Yes, you know, as in go into a pub and order something in a glass and eat a few nuts and so on.'

She wasn't sure about the 'and so on', but there

didn't seem to be any way out of it without being churlish.

'Um—perhaps just a quick one...'

'Am I treading on anyone's toes?'

'Toes?'

'Yes, toes. As in, some resident lover or whatever—perhaps Mick O'Shea?'

'Mick?' She was startled.

He shrugged. 'You were all over each other on Monday morning.'

'Oh, that—no, Mick's a friend.'

His brow arched delicately.

'Truly! I've known him for years.' She eyed Jack suspiciously. 'What about you? I don't suppose you're married?' she said bluntly.

He threw back his head and laughed. 'Are you crazy? Why would I want a wife?'

She shrugged. 'I don't know. Why would anybody want a wife? I'm sure there are all manner of reasons.'

He chuckled. 'None good enough for me, I'm afraid. Never again.'

'So you're divorced?'

He nodded.

'I'm not going to bed with you.'

He blinked, and caught the smile before it got away. 'Of course not.'

'I mean it!'

He grinned wickedly. 'What d'you think I'm going to do, drag you behind a hanging basket and rip your knickers off?'

The image was so outrageous that she giggled. 'All right. What time?'

'Seven-thirty? Do you want me to pick you up?'

'On that bike? No way, *José*. Just tell me where.'

'Rose and Crown, Tuddingfield?'

She nodded. 'OK. I'll see you there at seven-thirty.'

Deciding she was crazy, she made her way back to her room, collected her things and was just about to leave when a man carrying a young boy walked up to the doors.

He looked a little lost, and Kathleen went up to him.

'Can I help you, sir?'

'Oh—it's my son—he's got cystic fibrosis, and my wife's gone away for a few days with a friend for a break. I thought I could cope, but they sent him home from school and I just can't seem to shift the stuff off his lungs.'

Indeed, the child was rattling and bubbling, coughing weakly and obviously in great discomfort.

Kathleen put her arm round the man's shoulders and led him in.

'Come round here with me, and we'll find a physio to take care of things for you. What's his name? Do we have any notes on him in the hospital?'

'Anthony Craven—yes, you've got stacks of notes. I'm sorry, I feel such a fool. I was sure I could cope but the CF clinic people had all gone home by the time I realised I couldn't manage——'

'Look, don't worry, it really isn't a problem. I'll get a physio. You sit in here with Anthony and I'll be back in a tick.'

She put him in the cubicle and went back to the nursing station to phone the physiotherapy department.

After a few seconds she glanced at her watch in disgust. It was just after six, long after the time she should have gone off duty, and that was exactly what all the physiotherapists had done. She would have handed over to one of her colleagues, but somehow she just felt this case needed her personal attention.

She called the switchboard and asked them to page the physio on call, and was told she was in ITU with a patient and likely to be tied up for at least half an hour.

She cradled the phone with more force than strictly necessary, just as Jack Lawrence strolled past in his black leather gear.

'Problems?' he asked.

She glanced up. Nothing compared to what her heart did when she looked at him like that. He was long overdue for a shave, and the combination of the dark stubble, the tousled hair from the theatre cap and the warm smell of leather was a potent combination.

She shook her head. 'Not really. I want a physio for a kid with cystic fibrosis, but she's down in ITU and won't be free for half an hour.'

Something happened in his eyes then, some kind of inner battle. It was evidently resolved, because a sort of gentle resignation settled over his features.

'Where is he? I'll do it.'

'In Three, but are you sure you know——?'

He laughed, a short, strained little laugh. 'You really don't have any faith at all in me, do you?' he said, and his voice sounded strangely sad. 'Trust me. It isn't something you easily forget,' he added enigmatically, and with that he turned on his heel and strode back down to his office, emerging a moment later back in his normal working clothes.

The harassed father was only too glad to hand over

as Jack tenderly lifted the boy, laid him on his side over some foam blocks and firmly but gently percussed his chest.

Kath watched, mesmerised. He seemed to know just where to tap, and how hard, and how long for, and bit by bit the boy's lungs cleared and he began to breathe more easily.

When he was finished he sat the boy up and tousled his hair. 'OK, son? Come back in the morning and we'll sort you out again.'

And with that he was gone, back to his office to re-don his leathers.

Kathleen emerged from the cloakroom with her things just as he was walking past, and she went with him out of the door. He didn't break his stride or slow down, and she practically had to run to keep up with him, but something in the set of his jaw worried her.

He stopped by the bike, taking his helmet out of one of the panniers on the back, and then swung his leg over the seat, straddling the machine easily.

'Are you OK?' she asked finally, when it was obvious he wasn't going to acknowledge her presence.

He looked up. 'Of course. Why shouldn't I be?'

His eyes had a distant, cold remoteness she hadn't seen in them before, and she knew instinctively that something was very wrong.

Before she could say any more, he settled the helmet down over his head and fastened the strap. Then rocking the bike off the centrestand, he walked it back out of the space and starting it with a throaty roar, he left her standing there.

It was sheer, blind gut instinct that made her go to the porter's lodge and lie.

'Could you give me Mr Lawrence's address? He's left something here and I know he'll want it—I thought I'd drop it in to him. I have to go out that way tonight.'

He flicked open a card index, scribbled an address and phone number and handed it to her.

'Thanks, that's great.'

The old porter grinned and winked and opened his mouth. Kath ran before he had time to air his suggestive remark.

She was at the pub in the village at seven-thirty, but she was pretty sure he wouldn't show. There was no sign of either his car or the bike, and she waited until eight-fifteen.

Then, her heart in her mouth, she went into the pub, located the public call box in the lobby and dialled the number the porter had given her.

It was picked up on the fourth ring by an answerphone. She listened to his voice, waited for the tone and then cradled the receiver gently.

She knew he was there. Something—that same gut instinct that made her get his address alerted her. She looked at the address. Lone Barn, Finningham Lane, Tuddingfield. Well, she was in Tuddingfield, and she'd seen the turning off to Finningham. All she needed now was Lone Barn.

Thoughtfully, she went back out to her car, got behind the wheel and drove slowly out of the village, turning down the narrow, winding lane to Finningham.

She saw it almost immediately, the black wooden structure in sharp relief against the evening sky. Lone Barn indeed. It was set in the middle of a corn field, and she turned between the tall stalks of corn and followed the track up to the barn.

There were no lights on, but the bike and car were there, parked in an open-sided barn, and the door to the house was hanging open.

She wiped her damp palms against the skirt of her dress and drew a deep breath, then got out.

'Here goes,' she muttered to herself, and walked slowly up to the door.

CHAPTER THREE

HE KNEW she was there long before he saw her. He had been dimly aware of the sound of an approaching car, and there was only one person who would have bothered to seek him out. She would have had to charm his address out of the porter, but she wouldn't have had any trouble doing that. Lord, no.

He lifted his head.

Dear God, she was lovely. Sweetly pretty, in her full flowered dress that hung in soft folds around her slender legs. The slanting sun was behind her, and as she stood there in the doorway he could see the outline of those smooth, slim thighs through the fine fabric. His gut clenched, and he forced his eyes up to her face. Her eyes were huge, almost luminous in the shadowy light.

He drew a deep breath and reached for the tumbler of Scotch beside him.

'You didn't turn up,' she said in her soft, lilting voice.

'You didn't expect me to.'

'No.' She crossed the room and sat opposite him in the ratty old armchair. 'Nice place.'

He glanced around, conscious only of her. 'Mmm.'

'I like the brick floor, and all the wood. It suits you.'

'Earthy and unfinished. It'll be better when I've finished unpacking.'

Their eyes met, and his slid away. Damn, he wanted her.

'Are you very drunk?'

'I'm working on it.'

'It won't help, you know.'

He took a hefty swallow and crashed the glass back down. 'You're out of order, Irish.'

'I don't think so. I think something's eating you, and I think you ought to talk about it.'

'I don't want to talk about it. I want to sit here and get stinking drunk and forget.'

He lifted the glass again but it was empty. He lit a cigarette instead.

He could hear her sharply indrawn breath, the effort it took not to comment. Good, he thought, if I really work on her she'll go away and leave me to it.

'Do you know what I really want? You—your body, hot and naked and writhing under me——'

'You won't drive me out, Jack. Anyway, I'm quite safe. You haven't got any hanging baskets.'

He chuckled despite himself. God, she had guts. Or perhaps she just didn't realise how close to the edge he really was. . .

'Damn it, Irish, go home,' he said wearily.

'No. Let me make you some coffee.'

'I don't want coffee, I want to be alone—savvy? By myself. I don't want you here. Please leave.'

She was in the kitchen area now, divided from the rest of the downstairs by a row of cupboards that ran out at waist-height halfway across the room. She eyed him over the top.

'Where do you keep the coffee?'

'You don't give up, do you?' he said bitterly.

'Not easily,' she said blithely. 'All those years of training.'

She found the coffee without his help and put the kettle on.

He ground out the cigarette and watched her, the burning need in him too fierce to ignore. She had switched on the light and as she walked back towards him, he could see her legs again through the dress. Her soft fragrance drifted towards him, light and yet intoxicating, summer flowers and sun-warmed skin. God, he wanted her.

'Here.'

She held out the coffee but he didn't take it, not daring to trust himself if he reached towards her.

He closed his eyes wearily, but his eyelids acted only as shutters for his eyes, not his mind. He could still see her quite clearly, the outline of her legs, the soft rise and fall of her breasts with her gentle breathing, the way she looked at him, like a rabbit with a rattlesnake, half afraid and yet too fascinated to run.

He heard the coffee-cup as she put it down, then the soft swish of her skirt as she crossed the room and sat on the chair again. The light movement of air drifted her scent across his face, and he sucked the air in greedily.

'Talk to me.'

'No. Go home.'

'I don't think you really want me to.'

His eyes opened and he glowered at her, despairing. 'You don't know what I want.'

'Need, then. Whatever it is, you need to talk to someone. I'm here.'

'I'd noticed,' he growled, and dropped his head back

against the cushion. Why wouldn't she go home? She'd slipped her shoes off and had her feet tucked under her bottom, her legs demurely covered by that gauzy dress, but it was too late, he'd seen. . .

'Drink your coffee.'

'Damn it, I don't *want* any coffee!' he snarled, and she blinked.

'OK, don't drink it. I don't care.'

Their eyes met, hers wary, his angry and resentful, defensive. He felt trapped, cornered.

She wriggled in the chair and he caught a flash of silken thigh before she settled again. His body roared to life, hard and urgent, over-riding the pain. He shifted awkwardly, and her eyes flew to his lap and then up to his face, wide and slightly startled, like a doe.

'What's the matter, Irish? It's only basic human biology—nothing you haven't seen before.'

She looked away, flushing. 'Don't be coarse. I only wanted to help you.'

He was instantly ashamed. 'Look, I'm sorry,' he said heavily, 'but I don't need your help. What I need is to be alone.'

'So you can drink yourself into a stupor?'

'Yes, damn it, if that's what it takes!'

'To do what?'

He glared at her. 'Leave it, Kath,' he warned.

'No,' she said softly. 'Jack, I can't. . .'

She was breathing fast, her breasts rising and falling against the soft cotton, and suddenly he couldn't breathe, couldn't sit there another moment and watch her. . .

'For Christ's sake, get out,' he muttered, and levering himself out of the chair, he crossed the room in a stride and climbed the open stairs three at a time.

It was a mistake. He should have gone outside, grabbed the keys of the bike and taken off, but instead he was trapped and she was following him, her footsteps tentative on the stairs.

'Jack? Let me help you. . .'

She was either very stupid or very brave. He couldn't decide which. Pain and need were rising up in equal measure to swamp him, and he knew he didn't have what it took to turn away from her.

He threw himself down on the huge old bed and stared at the sloping timber ceiling. Oh, God, get her out of here, he prayed, but she kept on coming.

He felt the bed dip slightly under her weight, and he knew she was kneeling beside him. Her touch on his shoulder was hesitant, light as a butterfly, but it was enough.

With a deep groan he reached up and pulled her down beside him.

'Damn you, Irish,' he whispered hoarsely, and then his lips found hers and everything else receded.

Oh, God, she was so soft and supple, her body arching against his, trembling like a reed in the wind. She met his kiss eagerly, her hands tangled in his hair, and the last remnant of resistance snapped.

His hand slid up her thigh and found fine silk and lace in his way. And buttons. He despatched them and groaned again. So soft, so warm, so irresistible. He could lose himself in that sweetness, maybe even forget, for a while. . .

He wrenched his jeans down and moved over her, inhaling deeply. God, she smelt so sweet! Her hands were on his shoulders and she was pleading, but the words were a blur in the swirling mist of need and pain that engulfed him.

As he entered her he heard her cry out, and the sound inflamed him further, her soft whimpers slashing at the edges of his control.

So sweet, so tight—her slim, supple body writhed beneath him and he felt his control shatter into a million pieces. With a savage cry he drove into her one last time and felt the shockwaves pulse through him, draining all sensation and leaving a blessed numbness in which there was no more pain. . .

His chest heaving, he collapsed against her, the breath driven from his body, his heart thrashing against his ribs, and then slowly awareness returned, seeping into his dazed mind like ice-water, bring with it the pain and an overwhelming sense of self-loathing and disgust.

Dear God, what had he done to her?

He jerked his body away from hers and stood, dragging his jeans back up with hands that shook like leaves in a hurricane.

'Damn you,' he grated, and felt disgust like bile rising in his throat. 'Now are you satisfied?'

He heard a ragged sob, and then the bed creaked as she stood up.

'Jack. . .?'

'For Christ's sake, *get out*!' he roared, and after an interminable second, he heard her footsteps running down the stairs and then the sound of her car on the drive.

In the silence that followed he heard an owl hoot,

and then nothing, nothing except the harsh sound of someone sobbing.

'*Johnnie*!' he shouted, and the sound echoed in the stillness, bouncing off the walls and coming back to torment him.

Kathleen remembered nothing of the drive home, turning automatically into the parking area behind her flat and letting herself in with hands that shook so badly she could scarcely hold the keys.

She stripped off her clothes and dropped them where they fell, then ran a bath and climbed into it, scouring her skin over and over with a loofah as if she could wash away the memory of his body on hers.

Still trembling, she got out finally and wrapped herself in a huge towel and padded into the kitchen to put the kettle on.

God, what a fool! She should have seen it coming, should have realised she was pushing him too hard. She felt raw—not physically, except where she had scoured her skin in the bath, but inside, in her soul, as if he had reached in and desecrated some sacred part of her.

Rape.

It was a terrifying word, and yet he hadn't really raped her. Under different circumstances, even tonight, she would have been willing. . .

She laughed harshly. Willing? She had been aching for him since she had first seen him straddling that bike with such lazy arrogance. And yet, tonight, some demon that she didn't understand had driven him to an act she was sure he was now bitterly regretting.

Why had she left? She should have stayed with him,

told him she wanted to understand, held him in her
arms while he released the terrible pain she had sensed
inside him.

It had been in his eyes when he lay on the bed
staring rigidly at the ceiling, a terrifying, heart-rending
pain that cut her to the bone. And afterwards, for a
second she had felt him relax against her, his body
spent, his feelings so near the surface she could almost
reach out and touch them, and then he had wrenched
himself away from her and the defences had gone
slamming back up, shutting her out.

That was what hurt.

She absently brushed the tears from her cheeks and
sniffed. After all that, still he had shut her out.

'Damn you, Jack Lawrence,' she whispered. 'I won't
be shut out!'

She dialled his number with shaking fingers and got
the answerphone. 'Jack, please, pick up the phone. I
know you're there. I need to talk to you. Please pick it
up. I'm waiting. Jack, for God's sake——' Her voice
cracked and she took a steadying breath. 'Jack, ring
me, please!' She gave him the number, then put the
phone down, crawled into bed and waited.

'Morning, Sister!'

She smiled vaguely at the porter. 'Morning, Alvin.'

'Lovely day for it,' he continued cheerfully.

'Mmm.' For what? she thought bleakly. She took the
report, told them all where to find her if necessary and
shut herself in her office.

The bike was outside. He was here, somewhere in
the building, and sooner or later she had to face him.

Just now, assailed by a sudden attack of nerves, she hoped it would be later.

She misjudged him. There was a sharp tap on her door and it swung in, shutting quickly behind him.

She looked up and made herself meet his eyes. What she saw there left her cold.

He didn't beat about the bush.

'Kathleen, I'm sorry. I really don't know what else to say.'

She was silent for a long while, searching his face for a way forward, but it was shuttered and empty, all emotion banished. Was this the same man who had lost all control with her last night? No, not all control. He had released the pressure of his emotions in the only way a society built on a stiff upper lip had left him—but his control over his real feelings had remained even then. But what had caused that violent upsurge of emotion?

'I don't think I really want an apology, Jack,' she said calmly. 'I think what I really want is to know why.'

'How about because I'm a selfish, thoughtless, egotistical bastard, without any human decency?'

She shook her head. 'No, sorry, it won't wash.'

He laughed without humour. 'Damn it, you won't give up on me, will you?'

She sensed the frustration behind his remark, and backed off a little.

'I meant to help,' she said softly. 'If anything, I owe you an apology. I pushed you too hard. I'm sorry. . .' She reached out and laid her hand on his arm, and beneath her fingers she felt the corded muscle clench.

'How can you touch me?' he whispered harshly. 'Damn it, Kathleen, I raped you.'

'No, you didn't. Not really. I think I knew what was going to happen when I followed you upstairs. It was as much my fault as yours—probably more. At least I was sober!' She lifted her hand towards his face, and then dropped it. 'How's the head?'

He smiled ruefully. 'Lousy, thanks. I didn't have any more after you went.' He sighed. 'I owe you an explanation, don't I?'

Their eyes met and held, and gradually she saw warmth and respect creep into the granite depths.

'Tonight—can you come to the house? About seven? I'll cook you a meal.'

She hesitated, her heart pounding. What would happen, all alone with him in that isolated barn? Whatever had troubled him yesterday was still far from unresolved. Was she insane?

'You're quite safe.'

'You said that last night.'

He made a disgusted noise in the back of his throat and looked away from her.

'I know it's hard to expect you to believe it after what happened, but you can trust me. There are things at the house—things I'd like to show you.'

'Etchings?'

His mouth lifted in a token smile. 'Photos, mainly. Some drawings. Other bits and pieces.'

'OK.'

His eyes flicked back to hers, wide with disbelief. 'You will?'

She nodded. 'Is that a mistake?'

'No,' he promised fervently, and this time she believed him.

He walked back to the door. 'I have to go, Anthony

Craven's back for his physio. I said I'd do it, and I want to get some sputum samples for analysis to make sure he hasn't got a chest infection. And talking of infections, in case you're worried, you won't get anything from me—including pregnant.'

She stared at the door. Another page in the manuscript that was Jack Lawrence. She knew for a fact that he hadn't used a condom, so that meant he couldn't get her pregnant. Was that the trouble? Had Anthony Craven reminded him that he couldn't have children? Surely not. He had attended other children during the week, and been fine. And yet he had just said—she shook her head and stood up. Tonight. She only had to wait till tonight, and she would get her answers. But it was going to be a long day. . .

Not only long, but busy, filled with drama and tragedy, so that her own problems faded into insignificance.

She had been on the run since her conversation with Jack, a steady stream of nasty fractures and frightened children and anxious parents, and then, shortly after two, just when things began to settle down and she thought she might actually get some lunch, a car screeched up into the entrance and a man jumped out, flung open the back of the car and half dragged, half carried a woman towards the doors.

Kathleen called for help and ran to meet him.

'What's the matter?'

'She collapsed—said she had a pain, climbed off the ladder and passed out. We were decorating. Oh, God, is she all right?'

The porter arrived with a trolley and they lowered the woman on to it and rushed her into Resuscitation.

'Amy, get Mr Lawrence,' Kath instructed as they passed the bemused girl in the corridor.

'Yes, Sister.'

Kath heard her feet hurrying away, and snatched up the stethoscope. The woman's heart was still beating, but erratically.

'Is she on any drugs?'

He shook his head.

'Contraceptive pill?'

'No—I've had a vasectomy.'

'How old is she?'

'Thirty-seven—nearly thirty-eight.'

'And you're her husband?'

'Yes, that's right. My name's Thompson—Brian Thompson. My wife's Angie.'

Amy reappeared. 'Mr Lawrence is just coming.'

'Good. Thank you. Amy, take Mr Thompson and get all his wife's details from him, please, and then see if you can find any notes. Reception will help you.'

Jack arrived as Amy and Mr Thompson left.

'What is it?'

'Chest pain, sudden onset as far as I know, collapse—she's now arrhythmic, possibly fibrillating.'

All the while she was talking Kathleen was undressing the woman. Once she had stripped off her top clothes she slapped the monitor pads on and connected up the leads.

Jack whistled softly. 'What a mess! She's definitely fibrillating—I'd say she's had an MI.'

Kath nodded. 'Looks like it, doesn't it?'

'We'll give her a belt, see if that stops it.' He twiddled the dials on the defibrillator and told Kath to stand back. As he touched the paddles to the woman's chest wall, her body arched and flopped, and the trace immediately altered, settling to a normal sinus rhythm.

'So far so good. Can you take some bloods for chemistry, and we'll start her on streptokinase. Maybe that'll hold her. Who's on take today?'

'Jesus Marumba. I'll call him down.'

She moved to the phone on the wall and called the switchboard, asking them to page the physician, and then turned back to their patient.

She looked really grim—cold, clammy, grey. . .

She met Jack's eyes, and he shook his head. 'I wonder if she has any history?'

'Her husband didn't mention it, and you'd think he would.'

Amy slipped back in then. 'Records are sending her notes up now. Seems she's been seeing Mr Marumba for a few months. Her husband didn't know.'

Jack and Kathleen exchanged glances.

'What did you tell him?

She looked instantly alarmed. 'Nothing—I asked if he knew if she'd seen anyone in the hospital recently, before we contacted Records. He said no. I haven't spoken to him since—oh, except to say I'd find out what I could.'

Kath relaxed. 'OK, Amy. Well, she's still not really conscious, but he could come in for a minute, couldn't he?' Her eyes met Jack's, and he nodded.

'I'll get him,' Amy said, and vanished.

There was a sudden, yawning silence broken only by the slight hiss of oxygen to the mask over Mrs Thompson's face.

Their eyes were still meshed and Kath found she was unable to look away. The earlier remoteness was gone, replaced instead by a naked vulnerability that shook her.

'Did I hurt you?' he asked gruffly.

She looked away then, shaken by the memory of his body tangling so intimately with her. 'No,' she whispered. 'No, you didn't hurt me.'

She glanced at the monitor. 'That really isn't a very healthy wave,' she said in a slightly firmer voice.

After a second he shifted his eyes. 'No. We'll see what Marumba says.'

But he didn't get there in time. Seconds after Mr Thompson came back in with Amy, Mrs Thompson suffered a second, massive heart attack. Kath snapped instructions to everyone, and Amy wheeled Mr Thompson out and took him to the interview-room.

Despite desperate attempts to revive her, the trace remained stubbornly flat, until in the end they had to give up. Kath looked up at Jack in despair.

'She's thirty-seven. That's so bloody unfair!'

He sighed shortly. 'Life is. At least it was quick.'

'That's better than knowing, than having time to prepare?'

'You can never prepare. You think you can, but you can't. It's the finality of it. That's what gets you, no matter how much warning you might think you've had.'

He walked away, thrusting the swing door out of his way and striding off down the corridor towards his office.

Amy coughed. 'Um—her husband's in the interview-room, Sister.'

Kath looked at her blankly. 'What? Oh, right. Thank you, Amy. Could you stay here for a minute? I'll go and talk to him.'

She followed Jack out, glancing down the corridor after him. What had he meant? Because there was no doubt in her mind that he had been talking from personal experience.

Was that the problem? She glanced at her watch. Only three more hours to go, and she would find out.

She wore jeans and a sweatshirt that night—and then felt foolish because she knew he would realise instantly why she was covering herself from head to toe. She just felt it would help to establish some boundaries, and just then she felt they both needed space to get over the incident.

It hadn't stopped her putting on make-up, though, just a touch of eyeshadow and mascara, and a tiny puff of perfume at the base of her throat.

He was outside turning food on a barbecue when she drove up, and he lifted his hand and walked over to her.

She was glad they were outside, away from the scene of the crime, so to speak. She got out of the car and he stooped and brush his lips against her cheek. A little tingle teased her skin, and she was burningly conscious of the touch of his hand on her arm.

'Thank you for coming—I wasn't sure you would.'

'I said I would,' she reminded him, and he smiled wryly.

'I should have known better than to think you'd back down.'

She chuckled. 'That's me, in there to the bitter end, like a terrier. The only trouble is, I don't know when to stop.'

His thumb caressed her arm absently as he looked

down at her, and the smile left a lingering warmth in his eyes.

'Come and eat,' he said gruffly. 'I take it you aren't a vegetarian?'

'Well, it is Friday, and a good Catholic girl like me. . .'

He shot her a searching look. 'Are you serious? I can easily do you something else.'

She relented. 'One thing I'm not is a good Catholic girl,' she confessed with a smile. 'I'm under constant pressure from the family to settle down and raise a huge brood, but the thought just leaves me cold.'

He looked at her oddly. 'You should. You've got the right balance of humour and affection, and that wonderful warm openness. You'd be a terrific mother.'

She looked up, startled. 'I'd make a terrible mother—I have no interest at all in giving up my career to change nappies.'

'There's rather more to it than that,' he said with a vain attempt at lightness.

She frowned at him. 'Have you got children?'

That strange thing happened to his face again, the look she was beginning to recognise and dread.

'No,' he said shortly, and walked away from her back to the barbecue.

Oh, well. Two steps forward, three back.

She followed him and sniffed appreciatively. 'Smells delicious. What is it?'

'Chicken tikka. Can you keep an eye on it while I fetch the salads?'

'Sure. Anything I can do?'

He shook his head. 'What can I get you to drink?'

'Oh, just something soft, I have to drive later.'

'Mineral water?'

She nodded and watched him walk away. He was wearing jeans, like her, and a sweatshirt, and she almost laughed. They were both dressed the same, probably for the same reason, and yet it didn't seem to make any difference because all the action was in the eyes. Every time he looked at her, she came alive inside—except when he got that look, and then a little something died.

Patience, she counselled herself, and turned the chicken in the nick of time.

It was nine o'clock and they had been driven in by the mosquitoes before he broached the subject of the night before.

They were standing in the kitchen loading the dishwasher and putting the salads in the fridge when a picture caught her eye. It was a drawing, a crude pencil sketch of a person, untidily coloured in, in a simple pine frame, with the word 'Daddy' in bold writing beside the figure. It was hanging on the wall in the sitting-room but she hadn't seen it the night before.

For all its amateurish lack of style, it was vigorous and full of life, and she felt instantly drawn to it.

She waved a knife at it. 'Who drew that?'

He glanced up, and she instantly felt she was losing him again.

'My son.'

Here we go, she thought. Very carefully, very deliberately, she set the knife down on the worktop.

'I see.'

'Do you?'

'Well, no, not really. Tell me, Jack—talk to me, for God's sake.'

He nodded, and reaching out for her hand, he led her through into the sitting-room and sat down with her on the settee opposite the picture.

Then he began to talk, very quietly, in a curiously flat voice that showed her more clearly than anything else could how much he was holding back.

'His name was John. He was born sixteen years ago, and we realised that first winter that there was something wrong. I was doing my SHO in paediatrics at the time, and I had a word with my boss. He took one look at him, ran a battery of tests and told us he had cystic fibrosis.'

Kathleen closed her eyes. Now it all fell into place, the child Anthony Craven and his physio that Jack had done so competently, the way he had reacted. . .

'. . .anyway, with time it was obvious that he was going to need more maintenance than Gwen was prepared to give him. I came home from the hospital one day to find Johnnie all alone and desperate for physio, lying on the sitting-room floor crying his eyes out and starving hungry. There was a note from Gwen to say she couldn't take any more. She wanted other children, and by then I'd taken the decision never to have any more and had a vasectomy. We'd rowed about it endlessly, but I was quite determined. Evidently so was she. We heard nothing more from her, except through solicitors, and after the divorce was final, there was nothing.'

'What, *ever*?'

He shook his head. 'Not a word, not in all those years.'

'How old was he?'

'Not quite two.'

She could feel the tears pricking at the back of her eyes. 'Dear God, how could anyone do that?'

Jack shrugged. 'Lord knows. Anyway, I rang my boss, took some time off and my mother and father instantly took over, bless them. We moved in with them, although it meant I had a long journey to the hospital every day and I had to sleep there when I was on call, and we stayed with them until he was nine. He still spent every holiday with them, but I felt he needed more independence and so did they. Mum was getting on by this time and her own health wasn't excellent, and I moved to Manchester so we could be near the RMCH where they do a vast amount with CF. We hired a retired nurse to act as housekeeper and she did his physio when I wasn't there, and between us we managed to keep him going.'

He paused, and she waited, dreading the rest.

'Despite the aggressive treatment and the rigorous fitness programme we set up, he began to deteriorate. He got a chronic pseudomonas infection low down in his lungs, and he was having longer and longer spells in hospital. We'd talked about a heart-lung transplant, and he was on the list, but they never found a suitable match. He died three years ago. He was just thirteen.'

He fell silent, staring broodingly at the picture, and Kathleen closed her eyes to stop the tears from overflowing.

It's the finality of it. . .no matter how prepared you think you are. . . Poor man. Poor, poor, man.

She heard the hiss of a cigarette lighter, and opened

her eyes. He was leaning back, his eyes still fixed on the picture, and his cheeks were wet.

'I still miss him,' he said quietly. 'He was such a vital force in my life, and when he was gone, he took so much of me with him. I'd always known he was going to die, and so had he, really, but when it happened—it was a long time before I could really face it. I thought I'd come to terms with it, but that little lad yesterday...'

He rolled his head towards her. 'You just got caught in the crossfire. I'm sorry.'

She lifted her hand and touched his cheek, still damp where the tears had tracked, and bit her lip hard to hold back her own tears.

'I don't know what to say.'

'Don't say anything. Just let me hold you.'

He dropped the cigarette into the ashtray and held out his arms, and she snuggled into them and slipped her hands round behind him, hugging him tight.

She wasn't sure when the wordless comfort changed, or even if it did. Perhaps it just grew and matured until it took in all their emotions, but his hands began to smooth her back and shoulders, until in the end his fingers were threaded through her hair and his big, warm hands were holding her steady while he kissed her with mesmerising thoroughness.

She whimpered and shifted against him, and instantly he released her and straightened away from her with a ragged sigh.

'I'm sorry, I didn't mean to do that.'

She felt bereft, but a part of her still sane enough to try for self-preservation pulled her away from him and drew a deep breath.

'I suppose I ought to go home.'

'That might be wise.' His voice was husky, rough with passion, and scraped over her nerve-endings, leaving her tingling.

She stood up and walked to the door, not trusting herself to look back, and after a second she heard him come to his feet.

'I'll see you to your car,' he said gruffly, and followed her out, opening the car door and closing it after her deliberately.

She wound the window down. 'Are you going in over the weekend?' she asked, already missing the contact. She could feel the defences going up again, brick by brick, but there was no way of breaching them.

'No, I'm going away. I'll be in on Monday.'

The last brick slammed into place. Lifting his hand in a casual salute, he stepped back, leaving her no choice but to start the car and drive away with a casual wave. She made her way through the village and out the other side, then pulled over into a gateway by a field and cried her eyes out.

His defences might be intact, but hers were in ruins, laid waste by a man she hardly knew and yet loved with all her heart.

CHAPTER FOUR

KATHLEEN had always known, deep down, that one day she would meet someone she loved more than her career and would be ready to settle down with him to raise a family.

Now, with one of those obscene little twists that fate was so good at, the man chosen for her out of all those available millions not only couldn't give her children, but had no intention of getting involved in any permanent relationship, least of all marriage!

She had doubts, in fact, that he would even get involved in anything as routine as an affair! At least, not one with any possibility of being taken for granted.

It was a week before he even suggested they get together again for a drink, and that was lunchtime on Friday, at the end of his second week.

It was the usual Friday get-together, the alcohol-free lager and prawn salad session in the pub over the road, well within range of bleeps and so heavily attended by relays of medical and senior nursing staff. As such it hardly qualified as a date, but try telling her heart that!

She went, despising herself for her eagerness and unable to contain it, and watched the charismatic and social side of Jack at work with his colleagues.

He was a brilliant raconteur, with a wicked wit and a razor tongue, and he had them all in stitches. So different from the brooding and unhappy man of a week ago.

Would the real Jack Lawrence please stand up? she thought, and then smiled to herself ruefully. Both were sides of him, of course, not mutually exclusive, and only a fraction of the many-faceted man with whom she had fallen in love.

So she watched, and listened, and fell a little further, and when his bleep went she went back with him to the department and they worked side by side, communicating with a gesture or a word almost in silence, each anticipating the other's needs as they dealt with a little girl who had fallen out of a tree and broken both arms and one leg.

She saw other sides of him then, the skilled physician, the considerate colleague, and yet another side, the one gentle with their frightened little patient, reassuring and comforting her so that the procedures became less terrifying and more easily coped with. The patient stabilised and dispatched to Theatre, he tugged off his mask and grinned.

'We make a good team,' he said, and she glowed with pride and happiness.

She was screwing up the courage to suggest she cook him a meal over the weekend when he glanced at his watch.

'Ben's here, isn't he? Think I'll make a move. I have to get to Yorkshire tonight.'

'Yorkshire?'

He nodded. 'I'm pot-holing tomorrow.'

Her heart plummeted with the thought that he would be away again, and then hitched to a halt when his words registered.

'Pot-holing?' She controlled the squeak in her voice, and tried again. 'Isn't that dangerous?'

He grinned. 'Only if you're stupid. It's fascinating. I've got some fantastic pictures—I'll show you some time. Right, I'll just find Ben and then I'm off.'

She spent the weekend reading books on caving—or more correctly, she discovered, speleology—and it did nothing to set her mind at rest.

'Nuts!' she concluded, regarding a photograph of a filthy caver in wet-suit and helmet, wedged in a muddy slit about two inches thinner than he was. The slit was euphemistically called a squeeze.

She shuddered. What a way to die, stuck between two muddy rocks hundreds of feet under ground. She turned the page. There was a photo of a man dangling on the end of a hundred metres of rope, demonstrating SRT—single rope technique. One bit of string. 'Nuts,' she said again, and tossed the book to one side.

'Why did I have to fall for a suicidal maniac?' she asked herself, and cleaned the flat from top to bottom to take her mind off the image of Jack dangling on the end of a rope above a muddy slit somewhere in subterranean Yorkshire!

He was back on Monday, with a graze on one cheek and perky as a parrot. Perversely, she was cross with him for having survived when she had spent the weekend fretting. To cover the fact that she had far too many feelings altogether, she ignored him for the first part of the morning.

He collared her in the staff-room at eleven-thirty.

'Morning, beautiful. Good weekend?'

'Lovely, thanks,' she lied. 'You?'

'Great—superb conditions. I ache a bit—there were two quite long pitches to climb down, and getting back up is always harder!' He took a swallow of coffee and pulled a face. 'God, this stuff is disgusting. Is your car here?'

She nodded.

'Can we nip down to the catering suppliers at lunchtime and get a decent machine? I'd go, but the bike's still full of ropes and stuff from the weekend and I might not get it in.'

'You went on the bike?' she all but shrieked. 'To Yorkshire?'

'Of course! That's what it's for—speed, freedom and flexibility—and a hell of a lot of fun!'

And that just about sums you up, she thought wryly as the mischievous dimple came and went with his grin, but she wisely said nothing.

They bought a coffee machine at lunchtime, and it was an instant hit with all the passing staff who were called into the department during the course of the day.

'So, who's going to pay for the coffee?' she asked drily as she recharged the filter yet again during the afternoon.

He shrugged. 'I will—damn it, it's worth it. That other stuff was neat toxic waste!'

She wrinkled her nose at him and topped up the reservoir. 'Hmm. We survived on it for years.'

'Yes, well, you're obviously made of sterner stuff than me. It would kill me inside a month!'

'I doubt it—not if biking and pot-holing haven't got you yet. You must have a charmed life.'

He grinned. 'Just exciting. Calculated risks, appropriate safety measures, good equipment. It's like hang-gliding——'

'Like what?' she asked, her heart sinking.

'Hang-gliding—you know, when you——'

'—chuck yourself off a cliff in a pair of paper wings—crazy.'

'Hardly paper, and not usually off cliffs. Anyway, it's fun. Tremendously exhilarating, soaring above the countryside, free as a bird——'

'Yes, well, if God had meant people to fly——'

'—he would have given them wings. You should be good at it.'

She wrinkled her brow. 'Hmm?'

'Flying,' he explained, 'since you're chicken,' and ducking her fist, he left, flapping his elbows and squawking.

'I'll give you chicken, Jack Lawrence,' she muttered laughingly, and followed him out.

The following afternoon he invited her round for another meal. 'I could show you those caving photos,' he said, and she shuddered.

'Are you mad? Why should I want to look at pictures of you stuck in little cracks? No, thanks.'

His face closed up. 'Oh, well, perhaps another time.'

He turned and went back into his office, and she followed him hastily. 'Jack, wait! I didn't mean no to the meal—just to the photos of the caves. It gives me the creeps, that's all. I'd rather not see what you get up to underground.'

His face cleared, and his mouth tipped in a lop-sided grin. 'It's not so bad, really. Some of the caves are beautiful, but you don't have to look at them if you don't want to. It was just an excuse. I thought if I invited you round without one you'd say no.'

She looked up at him in amazement. 'Why should I do that?'

'Why?' He gave a low grunt of laughter. 'Perhaps a little common sense, after the first time?'

She flushed at the memory of their earlier intimacy, and laughed a little self-consciously. 'Oh, come on, Jack, we both know that was a one-off.'

'Was it?' he said softly.

'Yes,' she said firmly. 'I know you now, don't forget. You've got far too much integrity.'

'So what happened that time?'

She reached up and brushed the graze on his cheek. 'You were hurting, and I pushed you.'

'You didn't have to push very hard,' he reminded her, 'but you have my word, nothing will happen that you don't initiate.'

She laughed a little breathlessly. 'That's called passing the buck, Lawrence.'

He grinned wolfishly. 'Of course—there's always the chance you'll drop it! Seven-thirty?'

She answered his grin. 'OK.'

There was a tap on the door. Amy Winship stood there, all but wringing her hands.

'There's a person here who says he's taken an overdose. I didn't know what to do.'

'Fine—thanks, Amy, we'll deal with it. Put him in the wet treatment-room.'

They followed her out.

Their patient was a man in his late thirties, and Kathleen recognised him immediately with a sinking heart. He was a Valium addict who would try anything to obtain a supply of the drug—including pretending to overdose himself so he would be referred to psychiatry. Unfortunately for him, almost all the staff were on to him.

She turned to Jack. 'Leave this to me,' she said under her breath, and winked. Then she turned back to her patient.

'Hello, Jerry. Gone and done it again, have you, old son?'

He nodded and started to cry helplessly.

'It won't work, you know, and you know what I've got to do?'

He nodded and sniffed wetly. Kath sighed. 'Come on, then,' she said kindly, 'let's get you sorted out.' She tugged on a gown and gloves, and reached for the lavage tube, lubricating it. 'Lie down, my love, and open wide. That's lovely—swallow for me—well done.'

She deftly fed the tube down into his stomach, ignoring his gagging protestations, while Amy, following her instructions, filled two jugs with warm water and poured some down the funnel.

Kathleen was just lowering the end over the bucket when Jerry coughed and shot the entire contents of his stomach across the room—and all over her.

Behind her she heard a splutter of laughter, and turned with a glower to see Jack's retreating back.

Amy was biting her lip and trying not to laugh.

'Get a sample for analysis, please,' Kathleen instructed crossly, and with economy of movement she drained the tube, refilled it and flushed several times until the water was clear, and then withdrew the tube.

'There you go, Jerry. Now go home, be a good lad and don't do it again!'

'Can't I have some Valium, Sister?' he grovelled.

'No, you can't,' she told him firmly. 'Now out, please, so I can get cleaned up.'

'Sorry about that. . .' He waved vaguely at the room.

'Jerry, just go home and don't do it again.'

'I won't, Sister, I promise,' he lied.

Amy helped him up and showed him to the door while Kath stripped off her gown and gloves. She came back in, looked at Kath and her mouth twitched.

It wasn't a smart move. 'Get this place cleaned up, Amy, please,' Kathleen said firmly, and had the satisfaction of seeing the girl's face fall.

'Oh, yuck. . .'

Kath relented and grinned wryly. 'You should try wearing it! The frustrating thing is, he probably hadn't taken anything anyway.' She sniffed and grimaced. 'Shower, I think,' she muttered, and went out into the corridor. Jack was coming towards her, and flattened himself against the other side.

'You smell wonderful,' he said with a grin.

'Thank you.' Her smile was saccharine-sweet. 'And thank you for your help in there.'

He lifted his hands in a Gallic shrug. '"Leave this to me," you said.' His eyes tracked to her white lace cap, and the evil grin danced in his eyes. 'Um, Irish?'

She sighed. 'Yes?'

'You've got carrots in your frilly.'

There was nothing in reach to throw at him, unfortunately. With a wicked wink he ducked into the nearest cubicle, safely out of reach.

Torn between tears and laughter, she found herself a clean dress and frilly hat in her locker and went into the showers. One look at her reflection and laughter won.

'You're a cruel man,' she told him later, putting on a mournful face. 'Fancy laughing at a woman in that condition!'

'I thought the carrots suited you,' he said mildly. 'What with the red hair and all——'

'What red hair?'

'The red hair you ought to have.' He ducked automatically and grinned. 'What can I get you to drink?'

'Humph. I don't know why I waste time with you, really I don't. Could I have a white wine spritzer?'

He poured her a glass of white wine and tonic, plopped in two ice cubes and slid it over the worktop to her. He was standing in the kitchen, and she was in the living-room the other side of the units. She looked around her appreciatively.

'You've done a lot since I was last here.'

'Oh, not really. Just put up a few pictures and so on. I suppose I ought to organise some curtains, but I never shut them so it's hardly a priority. I'm not exactly overlooked.'

He walked round the end of the units and held out his hand. 'Come and sit down for a minute while the lasagne finishes cooking.'

He sat on the settee and tugged her down beside him, leaning over and sniffing her hair. 'You smell better, anyway.'

'Pig. A gentleman wouldn't have commented,' she told him sternly.

'Of course not, but then you know I'm no gentleman.'

He smiled, and then their eyes clashed and held.

She looked away first, her heart pounding. 'I won't be accused of leading you astray again,' she warned softly, and after a second he chuckled and relaxed back against the settee.

'Aw, shucks,' he said, and she giggled.

'Idiot. Where are these photos, then?'

'But you didn't want to see them.'

'Lady's privilege. I've changed my mind.'

'You're just trying to distract me.'

She grinned. 'Got it in one.'

With an elaborate sigh he unravelled his legs and stood up, crossing the room and squatting down by a pine dresser. He opened a door in the base and pulled out a huge stack of albums.

'Good grief—are they all caves?'

He laughed. 'No—there are lots of Johnnie. I never got round to showing you the photos of him last time.'

He showed her the caving ones first, and then they paused for supper before going back to look at the ones of his son.

Kathleen was worried that it would upset him, but he seemed quite relaxed, laughing over incidents and reminiscing out loud. The only low point was the last album, with a photo of his son in hospital. For the first time the laughter was extinguished from the little face so like Jack's, and in its place was resignation and courage, and a wisdom far beyond his years.

'I love that photo,' Jack said softly. 'I've got an enlargement of it in the bedroom. It was the last photo I took of him. He died early the following morning.' On the facing page, out of sequence, was an earlier photo of Johnnie laughing, his head thrown back, radiating life and energy. 'Whenever I get the blues, I look at this,' Jack murmured, his finger tracing the contours of his son's face. 'It reminds me that although his death was tragic, his life was full of fun and laughter. We had so many good times. No one can ever take that away from us.'

He sat quietly for a while, staring into space, and then abruptly shut the album and stood up. 'Walk?'

Not quite touching, they strolled down the drive to the lane and then along a little way to where a stream meandered under a little bridge. They stood on the bridge listening to the chuckling water, and after a moment Jack drew Kathleen into his arms.

'Will you scream if I kiss you?' he murmured softly.

In answer she lifted herself up on tiptoe and leaned against his tall, firm frame.

With a soft sigh his head came down and he took her lips in a gentle, lingering kiss. After a moment she moved away, her heart pounding. It would be so easy. . .

'I must go home,' she said, and her voice sounded strangled in the quiet night.

He squeezed her hand in understanding, and walked her back to her car.

'Thank you for a lovely evening,' she said, now strangely reluctant to leave.

'My pleasure,' he murmured, and for a second they stood there, regarding each other watchfully, the tension straining between them.

Only too conscious of the depth of passion simmering in him, and conscious too of her crumbling resistance and his vow that nothing would happen that she didn't initiate, she took a deep, shaky breath and got into the car, shutting the door firmly behind her.

He squawked and flapped his wings, and the tension dissolved in their shared laughter. 'You're a wicked man,' she said fondly. 'Goodnight, Jack.'

His smile was wry and full of understanding. 'Goodnight, Irish. See you tomorrow.'

She didn't trust herself to say anything else. With a smile, she started the car and drove swiftly away.

In fact it was Jack's sense of humour that kept her feelings in proportion during the next few days. Whenever the tension mounted, he defused it with a razor-edged comment, as often as not directed at himself, and so they were able to keep the rising tide of passion at bay.

Kathleen knew it was only a case of stalling for time, but every day that passed brought new understanding of this enigmatic man who had captured her heart.

He still irritated her with his casual dress, the sloppy tie hanging round his neck, the top button always undone, the lazy grin and teasing remarks in front of her colleagues, but as he teased them all she was in no way singled out. In fact, if he hadn't teased her, it would have been more obvious that there was some undercurrent in their communication with each other.

Professionally, though, she never had any cause to doubt his judgement or medical skill. He was fast, intuitive and decisive, his movements clean and minimal, his manner reassuring.

He often cracked jokes with patients to relax them, his easy camaraderie taking the edge off their fear without in any way compromising their faith in him.

It was the way she liked to work, and, watching him, she realised he was a master at it. Not only a master, but a natural comedian, because he found humour in seemingly impossible situations.

His wit was never cruel, but it was always horribly accurate and often wicked. Just how wicked she didn't realise until the next weekend, when she was on nights covering the regular night sister who was on holiday. Jack was on call, and they were passing the wee small hours of Saturday morning in idle conversation when the phone rang in the staff-room.

It was an unusually quiet night, and Jack had been called in earlier and had stayed not out of necessity but because, as he said, if he went home he would only be called out again.

Kathleen answered the phone, listened for a minute and asked a few questions, and then cradled the receiver with a groan. Jack's brow arched in enquiry, and she shrugged.

'Woman with a heavy period, demanding to see a gynaecologist before she bleeds to death. There's only one problem.'

'Which is?'

The receptionist thinks she's a man.'

An imp of mischief danced in Jack's eyes. 'Is that a fact? Well, well. . .'

He rose lazily to his feet and sauntered out into the corridor. 'Coming, Irish? I think this could be rather fun.'

'Oh, my lord,' she muttered, and followed him.

The 'lady' in question was heavily made up and dressed in a tight sheath of black and gold lurex that ended provocatively at mid-thigh. Her hairstyle was a bizarre pile of curls heaped somewhat haphazardly on the top of her head, and she was crouched over her stomach, clutching it most convincingly. The most remarkable feature, in fact, was the enormous pair of high-heeled shoes at the end of the spangled tights.

'Good legs,' Jack commented appreciatively. 'This

could be a real lulu.' He leant over the receptionist. 'That geezer in the dress—what's his name?'

She looked down at the computer screen. 'Queenie Butcher.'

There was a stifled snort of laughter from Jack, and Kathleen bit the inside of her cheek.

'Jack, you can't. . .'

'Watch me. Mrs Butcher, please,' he said clearly, and the creature rose to her feet.

'Ms Butcher, if you don't mind,' she simpered.

'I do beg your pardon—Mizz Butcher—would you come with me, please?'

Kathleen restrained the urge to roll her eyes as Jack led 'Queenie' to the little theatre at the back of A and E.

'Right, lie down on the couch and answer a few of these questions, and we'll see what we can do for you. When did your problems start?'

How he kept a straight face Kath would never know. She turned her back to him and fiddled with a trolley, and bit her cheek till it bled. Finally he ground to a halt and stood up.

'Right, Sister Hennessy, if you could prepare Queenie—you don't mind if we call you Queenie? Good—for a gynaecologist, I'll get Reception to page one for us. I think the lithotomy stirrups, please.'

And he left her to it!

Calling on an acting ability not required since her childhood, she covered her patient with a cotton blanket and then hitched up each leg in turn and strapped them into the lithotomy stirrups, thus trapping the hoaxer until the joke had run its course.

She went out and found Jack at the nursing station with Jake Hunter, the obs and gynae senior registrar.

'All set, Irish?' Jack asked her.

She gave a disbelieving laugh. 'Well, I did as you said.'

'Excellent. Come on then, Jake, let's give him a fright.'

'You are quite sure about this?' Jake asked dubiously, running a hand through his dark, floppy hair. 'I mean, I would hate to find she really was——'

'She really isn't, Jake,' Kathleen assured him. 'Not unless she's had a very nasty prolapse!'

He chuckled. 'OK. I'm game if you are. It's a shame Annie isn't on—a woman would be even better.'

Jack laughed. 'Come on, let's find out how far he's prepared to carry this through.'

But he wasn't. When they went back in, 'Queenie' was struggling to get his second leg out of the lithotomy stirrups.

Jack laid a firm hand over his shin and held him there effortlessly. 'What's the matter, Queenie?' he asked, his voice a river of silken reassurance. 'We won't hurt you. Why are you running away?'

In desperation he tugged of his wig and looked pleadingly at them. 'Look, it was just a gag, OK? No harm done, or anything—I had a bet with a friend that I couldn't con you.'

Jack grinned. 'Tell your friend he was right. You didn't even get past the receptionist, but I like the gear. Very pretty.'

Queenie almost preened. 'Well thanks, duckie. It's my show gear—I sing at a gay club in town. Any time you're passing, come in and have a drink. You never know,' his eyes ran over Jack's body lingeringly, 'maybe I could even be persuaded. . .'

Jack chuckled. 'Thanks for the compliment, but no, thanks. My current's strictly AC. For the record——' he released the leg and Queenie straightened up in relief '—I could call the police and have you arrested for wasting NHS resources on a hoax, but I tell you what, I'll settle for a donation to the Cystic Fibrosis Research Trust.' He grinned like a crocodile. 'Just to show how nice I really am.'

The man slipped off the couch, wriggled his feet into his enormous high-heeled shoes and tugged his wig on. 'Done. Here——' He rummaged in the pearl-studded evening bag and came up with a twenty pound note. 'Can I leave it with you?'

Jack plucked it from his fingers and grinned again. 'Most generous. You're too kind.'

'Any time, duckie.' Straightening his skirt, Queenie sauntered out, turning at the entrance to wink saucily at Jack.

He returned the wink, and Kathleen closed her eyes in despair.

'Mr Lawrence, you should be reported for demanding money with menaces.'

He slung an arm around her shoulders and grinned at Jake. 'Coffee?'

'I gather you've got a new machine.'

'Word travels,' Kath said drily. 'I'd better fill it up.'

They were still talking about the incident on Wednesday when Kathleen returned to work after her days off.

'Wish I'd seen it,' Ben Bradshaw said mournfully. 'Nothing like that ever happens to me. All I get is the blood and guts.'

'Ah, poor boy,' Kath teased. 'Never mind, there's a nice toenail in cubicle three you can go and remove to cheer you up.'

He wrinkled his nose fastidiously. 'Clean feet?'

She chuckled. 'Shouldn't think so—you don't get that lucky! Amy Winship's in there—she'll help you.'

He sighed and ambled down the corridor, whistling 'Hi-ho, hi-ho,' under his breath.

Kathleen went back into her office and found Jack in there, slouched in her chair with a cup of coffee in his hand. She took it from him and drained the cup.

'Lovely—thanks.'

He laughed and tugged her on to his lap. 'I was enjoying that—you'll have to pay for it.'

She squirmed and his arms clamped tighter. 'Don't do that, Irish, it's bad for my blood pressure,' he murmured in her ear. 'Now come on, pay up like a good little girl.'

She levered herself away from him with a hand on his chest and looked him dead in the eye. 'You don't want a good little girl, Jack Lawrence——'

'Oh, I do, but she won't co-operate.'

She froze for a second, caught by the magnetic intensity of those granite eyes, and beneath her palm she could feel the heavy beat of his heart.

The moment seemed destined to stretch on end-lessly, but then there was a sharp tap at the door followed by a gasp of embarrassment.

'I'm sorry—I——'

She leapt to her feet and turned round, fighting the blush. 'It's all right, Amy. Mr Lawrence was just going——' She shoved his feet off her desk and glared at him.

He unwound himself and stood up, grinned unrepentantly at them both and sauntered out.

Amy watched him go with her jaw dangling, then turned back to Kathleen.

'Um—Dr Bradshaw wondered if you could come. He growled something about my septic technique.'

'Septic or aseptic?'

She shifted uncomfortably. 'He said septic.'

Kathleen groaned. 'All right, Amy. I'll go through it with you again.'

Ben was right, Kath thought later. Amy's technique was abysmal. She carted all the junior nursing staff off during the afternoon for a training session in one of the treatment-rooms, and by the end of a vigorous drilling they seemed to have it firmly implanted. She just hoped it stayed there.

The other reason she had disappeared with the juniors was that it kept her out of Jack's way. Just as well for him, because she was hopping mad.

She saw him later going into his office and followed him.

'You——' she began, levelling a finger at him, and he chuckled and tugged her into his arms.

'Sorry, sweetheart.'

'Don't sorry sweetheart me! You're doing it again! Now put me down and for goodness' sake behave!'

He released her and stood back, eyeing her thoughtfully. 'You really are cross, aren't you?'

'Cross doesn't begin to cover it,' she told him furiously. 'Do you have any idea how embarrassing it is to be caught *in flagrante* with my boss?'

'*In flagrante*?' he laughed incredulously. 'My dear girl, you were sitting on my lap!'

She sniffed disapprovingly, and earned a chuckle for her pains.

'Oh, Irish, you are so lovely when you're mad——'

'Don't patronise me!' she stormed. 'I have worked very hard in this hospital to earn the respect of my colleagues, and in one fell swoop you've managed to compromise my integrity——'

'Hang on in there a minute, my lovely. I have done nothing—absolutely nothing!—to compromise your professional integrity, or to lose you the respect of your colleagues. All I've done is dent your holier-than-thou force-field a little bit. Lighten up, old thing. Why shouldn't we have a relationship?'

And that was the trouble, of course.

She looked up at him slowly. 'No reason at all, but we haven't, have we?'

After a second or two, he looked away. 'No. You're right. I'm sorry I embarrassed you.'

He was polite but distant after that for the rest of the week, and there was no suggestion that they should get together in the evening or over the weekend.

She was in one of the cubicles tidying up on Monday morning when he limped in.

'Hi.' He grinned sheepishly. 'Got a minute?'

'Of course—what have you done?'

'Hang-gliding—bit of an awkward landing. I often do it, but this time was a bit worse.'

She sighed. 'Let me see—sit on the couch and pull up your trouser leg. I hope your feet are clean?'

'Damn cheek,' he muttered, and hitched himself up onto the edge of the couch.

Very carefully she eased off his shoe and sock. 'Hmm,' she said enigmatically.

'Hmm yourself. What about poor old thing, let me give you a bit of TLC?'

'TLC yourself,' she snorted. 'Don't expect sympathy. Anyone daft enough to chuck themselves off a cliff——'

He squawked and flapped his arms, and she slapped his leg. 'Shut up and sit still. Do you want Tubigrip on it or not?'

'Yes, please, Sister. Sorry, Sister.'

She glared at him and he winked wickedly. 'I love it when you're rough with me,' he said huskily. 'Hit me again.'

'Jack, would you for God's sake shut up or I'll get Amy Winship and Joe Reynolds to come and deal with you!'

He shuddered and clapped a hand over his mouth, rolling his eyes theatrically.

She ignored him with difficulty and threaded a length of Size C Tubigrip on to the frame and then up over his ankle. 'There—how's that?'

'Tight.'

'It's meant to be.'

'So it is. Thank you, you're an angel.'

'Don't grovel, it doesn't become you.'

He laughed despairingly. 'What can I do? I'm not allowed to do what comes naturally——'

'Which is what?'

'This. . .' He reached out and tugged her into the V of his thighs, dropping his mouth to hers and taking it in a kiss that left her gasping for breath and so shaken she could barely stand.

She eased away and touched her fingers to her lips. 'You shouldn't have done that,' she breathed raggedly.

'You see? I can't win.' He slid off the couch, put on his sock and shoe carefully and limped out, leaving her slumped against the couch in despair.

It was another uneasy week, and by Friday afternoon she was longing for the end of the shift so she could go home and wallow in misery.

She went into the empty staff-room and helping herself to a cup of coffee, she sank wearily into a chair.

'Tired?'

She jumped and nearly slopped hot coffee over her skirt. 'Not really.' She watched as he crossed the room. He was still limping slightly, but much less than at the beginning of the week.

'Well, what is it this weekend?' she asked rashly, before her mouth came under control from her brain. 'Crawling down holes, or chucking yourself off cliffs?'

'Camping.'

'*Camping*?' she exclaimed.

He shrugged. 'The ankle needs to settle before I can go caving or flying again. I thought I'd go off and have a look at the north Norfolk coast, up near Blakeney.'

'Oh, it's lovely up there,' she said wistfully. 'You'll enjoy it.'

He hesitated a second, then met her eyes. 'Come with me.'

'What?'

'You heard.'

Her heart was pounding, her mouth dry. She knew what he was asking, and she knew what her answer would be.

'When do we leave?'

He grinned. 'Five tonight. And travel light—we're going on the bike.'

CHAPTER FIVE

BY A quarter to five Kathleen was having serious doubts about her sanity.

The inevitability of the next step in her relationship with Jack faded into insignificance compared with the sheer terror she was experiencing at the thought of going on his bike.

'I should have said no,' she muttered, looking yet again at the tiny pile of things she had accumulated. Were they suitable? Were jeans and T-shirt the right thing to wear, and what about her feet? Were trainers OK? She would need them over the weekend, God willing. Would they even get there? And what about a helmet?

She closed her eyes and dropped on to the bed, her heart pounding. Her hands were shaking, the palms damp, and she knew she couldn't stand to save her life. Every week there was a succession of motorbike accidents through the department, many serious, some fatal—she must be insane.

Suddenly she couldn't sit still any longer, and jumping up, she paced to the window of her sitting-room and peered out. Did she have time to run away? What if he hadn't left yet—she could ring him and tell him she'd chickened out, and he could flap his wings and tease her but at least she wouldn't have to—oh, hell, here he is, she thought, and watched as the huge bike rolled to a halt and he switched off the engine and hauled it up on the stand. It looked enormous, sleek and very, very fast.

I can't do it, she thought frantically, and then the bell was ringing and she had no choice but to open the door.

His face clouded instantly with concern. 'Are you OK? You're as white as a sheet.'

'Fine,' she said shortly. 'I'm all ready.'

He handed her a bag. 'Try these. They're my old leathers from way back when I was skinny. The jeans'll be a bit long and the jacket'll drown you, but at least you'll be protected a bit if we come off—oh, and I've got a lid for you to try. Hang on.'

If we come off, she thought despairingly. Lord, how can he be so casual about it?

He went back to the bike and unlocked one of the panniers, coming back with a colourful helmet. 'Here. Try it.'

She took it in shaking fingers and pulled it on, immediately feeling very closed in by the visor. He took her head in his hands and rocked the helmet, but it didn't move. He nodded his satisfaction and let go, and she wrenched it off and took a deep breath.

'No good? Is it too tight?'

'It's the thing over my face—I feel I can't breathe!'

'It's ventilated—here, look.' He showed her the little holes in the chin guard, and reluctantly she tried it again. He was right, she could breathe, but only if she closed her eyes so she couldn't see the perspex two inches from her nose!

She took it off again. 'OK. Let me go and try the leather stuff on. What else do I need?'

'Jeans, sweatshirt, shorts, undies, wash things—not

much. Have you got any boots? Knee-length leather ones, ideally.'

She frowned doubtfully. 'Winter fashion boots, with a low heel—will they do?' At his nod, she took the bag and went into her bedroom, pulling off her denim jeans and wriggling into the leather ones. They were loose around the waist and the legs seemed endless, but the hips fitted nice and snugly. The jacket was huge, but again fitted well around the hips and the cuffs had ajustable snap-fasteners. At least if she fell off she wouldn't lose all her skin——

'How're you doing?'

She opened the door, and he ran a critical eye over her before nodding. 'You'll do. Where's your stuff?'

She showed him the tiny pile on the bed, and he nodded again. 'Good. You're the first woman I've ever met who had the slightest idea what travelling light means. Right, sit down on the bed and give me your legs.'

She did as she was told, and with surgical precision he slashed four inches off the legs of the jeans. 'There.' He folded the knife again and slid it into a pocket. 'What have you got on under the leather stuff?'

'A T-shirt——'

'Not enough. Find a long jumper that comes well down, and tuck it in so you don't get a draught over your kidneys. I'll pack your stuff into the bike.'

He left the room and she tugged on a sweater and put the jacket back on just as he came back in.

'All set?'

She nodded.

'Right, let's roll.'

'What about sleeping-bag and tent and stuff?' she asked, stalling frantically now the time was here.

'On the bike. All I need is you.'

'Well, Jack Lawrence, you old romantic!' she teased with the last remnant of her sense of humour, and he smiled a slow, lazy smile.

'I can be. Come on, then. I want to get there in daylight.'

She followed him out, locking the door and slipping the keys into her handbag. 'Any room for this?'

'Sure.' He squeezed it into one of the panniers, and snapped it shut. 'OK, let's go. Here, I've put an inter-com into your helmet, so we can listen to music and if you want to talk to me, you press this button here— OK? Clip this to your jacket.'

He swung his leg over the saddle, rocked the bike off its stand and balanced it with his legs while she put on the helmet, tugged on the huge gloves and tried not to let him know she was panicking.

Suddenly his voice came over the headphones. 'Can you hear me?'

She nodded, and he grinned behind his visor. 'Press the button and say, "Yes, Jack."'

'Yes, Jack,' she mimicked saucily, and he laughed.

'Hop on, then.'

She swallowed and slid her leg over the saddle behind him, and he put her feet on the rests and told her to wrap her arms round him.

She needed no second bidding. She slid up close to his back, wrapped her arms firmly round his waist and tried to relax.

Pointless. He started the bike, eased it forwards and

suddenly they were tilting over as they went round the corner.

Her grip tightened as he accelerated, and after a moment or two he coasted slowly into the kerb and stopped.

'Are you OK?' he asked.

'Um—I'm just scared——'

'Press the button.'

'Oh. Right. Can you hear me?'

He turned round, took her intercom control in his hand and then gave her another lesson in operating the controls. 'Now,' he said patiently. 'What's wrong?'

She lifted her shoulders in a little shrug. 'I've never done it before.'

'OK. We'll go nice and slowly, and if you really hate it, we'll get my car and take that. OK?'

She nodded, infinitely relieved. Just a few minutes more and she'd be safe.

'OK, now try and relax and hold on to me. I'm not going anywhere—just go with my body.'

She nodded again, and he winked and turned back. Seconds later they were off again, and she shut her eyes tight, pressed her cheek against his back and clung on like a limpet. Soft music flooded through her helmet, and if she ignored the sensation of movement, she could almost pretend she was sitting at home. . .almost.

They headed north, and after a few minutes she began to think she might actually survive. Then they hit the main road and he opened the bike up and for an awful second she thought she was going to slide off the back.

Unthinking, she tightened her grip and felt him laugh under her hands.

His voice replaced the music in the helmet.

'Much as I love being crushed between your thighs, do you think you could leave me a little circulation? It's awfully hard to ride this thing with numb legs!'

Mortified, she released her death-grip on his waist and tried hard to relax her legs.

'Just go with the flow, Irish. There's nothing to it. You never know, you might even enjoy yourself!'

Fat chance, she thought in despair, but little by little, when nothing happened to unsettle her, she was able to relax more and in doing so became aware of all the little things she had missed before—the warmth of his back against her chest, the firm feel of his waist under her hands, the slight shift of his thighs against hers as he changed gear. Even the scenery began to enchant her, and the tug of the wind on her clothes became a pleasure rather than just another instrument of torture.

With a deep sigh, she snuggled against his back and settled down to enjoy the journey.

'You survived.'

She laughed sheepishly. 'I'm sorry—I had no idea I'd be such a dreadful wimp.'

His smile was sympathetic. 'The trouble is you've seen too much. There are too many idiots on the road, and they all end up coming through our department, but provided you're sensible and don't take risks either with yourself or your equipment, you should be OK.'

'Should be.'

He shrugged. 'Nothing's foolproof. Want some more food?'

She shook her head. 'No, I'm fine.' She looked around. They were on a slight hill on the edge of a little copse, and in the distance she could see the lights of boats on the sea. From where they were there wasn't a soul to be seen—certainly no other campers. 'How did you persuade the farmer to let us use his field?' she asked.

'Natural charm.'

She chuckled. Looking at his grin, she could well believe it. 'How much natural charm?'

The grin widened. 'Ten quids' worth.'

'Ten pounds——? But you could go to a campsite for far less!'

He shrugged. 'You want company?'

She shook her head. 'No. . .'

He stood up abruptly. 'I'll get the tent up. I don't think it's going to rain, but it's as well to be on the safe side.'

She frowned in puzzlement. 'Don't you sleep in it anyway?'

'Not if I can help it. It's like being zipped into a sponge bag—yuck. The best part about camping is the fact that you're out in the open. Seems crazy to me to shut yourself in.'

'Want a hand?'

He shook his head. 'You stay there, I'll manage.'

She packed up the remains of the bread and cheese they had had for supper, and then watched as he clipped poles together and hammered in pegs; within minutes the flimsy little structure was up and ready. It looked tiny, no more than an emergency shelter, which of course was all it was intended to be. Her eyes followed him as he unpacked the bike, and she wondered if he was just going to take it for granted that she would sleep with him of if he would offer her the choice.

Now what? he thought frustratedly. Damn it, why had he brought her here? He'd regretted the invitation as soon as the words were out of his mouth. He'd only ever taken Johnnie camping before, and had no idea how she would take to it. Probably scream if an earwig crawled into the sleeping-bag—and that was the other thing. Did he zip them together or just hand her one? Could he assume? Would she or wouldn't she?

Hell, he couldn't even ask, having told her the next time she would have to take the initiative, but if she didn't take it soon he was going to go out of his mind! Every time he looked at her he wanted her more. It wasn't just her body, either, though God knew there was nothing wrong with it. His own tightened in anticipation, and he swore softly under his breath. No, he wanted more than just her body, although what and why he didn't care to analyse. That was part of the reason for his edginess.

She was getting to him, wriggling past his defences and beginning to matter, and that was bad news. Even so, he found he couldn't walk away. Damn, why had he hurt her before? She was so sweet and funny, sharp as a tack and yet never unkind. In fact her only fault was her unrelenting interest in him, and like before he was helpless, devoid of the steely self-denial needed to walk away from her.

But how to tackle it? Last time had been so traumatic; what if he had put her off him for life? She would need such care and gentleness, and if it killed him he would give it to her, but the passion was raging in him until he could hardly see straight. He realised with a shock that he was nervous—as nervous as a randy adolescent on a hot date—and likely to be about as subtle!

Damn. He fished a cigarette out of his pocket and flicked the lighter. The end glowed in the twilight. She was watching him. What was she thinking? Perhaps he ought to take her home before he embarrassed both of them.

He drew deeply on the cigarette and stared out at the darkening sea. It was late now. He was going to have to make a move, one way or the other. Perhaps he would just hand her a sleeping-bag and offer her the tent. . .

Something was wrong. She didn't know what, but it wasn't like her to skirt an issue. She watched as he finished his cigarette, and then turned towards the bike. She heard him swear softly, and then he limped a little.

'Is your ankle still sore?'

'Only if I forget and twist it,' he said shortly, and pulled a groundsheet and two tightly rolled sleeping-bags out of the pannier. He spread out the groundsheet and unrolled the sleeping-bags, then paused. She saw him flex his ankle and wince, and she stood up and went over to him, kneeling down on the end of one of the sleeping-bags.

'Sit down, I'll rub it.'

'It's fine,' he said shortly.

'Jack, shut up,' she told him good-naturedly, and waited as he dropped on to the sleeping-bag.

She unzipped the boot and eased it off, then

unzipped the ankle of his leather suit and slid the leg up a little.

'It's swollen again—you haven't been resting it.'

Her fingers were gentle but firm, and he sprawled back on his elbows and watched her as she lifted his foot on to her lap and massaged all the tired muscles.

After a few minutes she bent her head and dropped a kiss lightly on his ankle, and then her hand slid up under the leg of the leathers and sensuously kneaded the firm muscle at the back of his calf.

She heard the sharp hiss of his indrawn breath, and then he bent forwards and drew her gently up into his arms. His breath was warm on her hair, and she could feel the trembling in his arms.

'Irish. . .?'

'I thought you'd never ask,' she whispered, and in the gathering darkness she heard a ragged sigh just before his head came down and blocked out the stars.

His lips were warm and firm and tasted of smoky coffee, and they brushed hers lightly, tormentingly.

She threaded her hands through his hair and kissed him back, and suddenly all the pent-up emotion of the past few weeks rushed up to engulf her.

She whimpered and he gentled the kiss, but it wasn't what she wanted. She arched against him, her hands searching desperately for his skin, and with a harsh groan he stood up and dragged her to her feet.

'Hang on,' he growled, and zipped the two sleeping bags together as fast as he could with shaking hands. Then those hands were unzipping and tugging and peeling off clothes as though they were on fire. Even so, it seemed forever before he drew her back into his arms.

The first contact of skin on skin was electric. His back was smooth and firm, hot under her palms, and the muscles rippled as she slid her hands down and smoothed them over the slight swell of his hips.

His arms went round her and eased her against his chest, and the brush of his body hair against her nipples made her cry out. Their legs tangled, and she cried out again as his thigh grazed between hers and rocked against her. Her lips found the soft skin in the angle of his shoulder, and her tongue dipped into the hollow of his throat, tasting the saltiness of his skin.

She could feel the pounding of his heart against her chest, and the pulse leapt under her lips. One large hand came up and cupped a breast, the thumb grazing one nipple as his head dipped and he drew the other into his mouth, suckling deeply.

A choked sob rose in her throat, and she felt his chuckle as he switched his attention to the other breast.

'Jack, please,' she whimpered, and he diverted his attention lower, stroking and taunting until she thought she would die.

Then he lowered her to the ground and shifted over her, and for a second it was like it had been before and fear touched her, but then his lips came down and brushed her mouth, and she was lost.

Her legs locked round his waist and she arched against him, pleading with him, and slowly, with infinite care, he eased into her.

It wasn't enough. After all this time, she wanted more—much more. He started to move, slowly at first and then faster in response to her pleas, and then suddenly everything disintegrated in a wild starburst of colour and sensation that left her shaken and helpless in his arms.

'Are you OK?'

His voice was gruff in the darkness, and she rolled her head towards him and reached up to touch his face.

'I'm fine—why shouldn't I be?'

He gave a low grunt of laughter, followed by an untidy sigh. 'I thought I might have hurt you—God knows I tried to be careful, but you seem to have this knack of wiping out twenty-five years of control and finesse with a single touch.'

'Twenty-five years? Lord, you started young!'

He chuckled. 'Not really. It was quite legal.'

She propped herself up on one elbow and looked down at his face in the starlight, her mind tangling on the mental arithmetic. 'You can't be forty-one!'

'Almost.'

She dropped back beside him. 'Amazing. You must be like a good wine.'

He chuckled again, and his fingers threaded through hers under the covers. They had taken refuge from the insects and the dew when sanity returned, and were lying gazing up at the stars.

Kathleen turned on her side and snuggled closer, resting her head on his shoulder. Her fingers trailed slowly over his chest, tangling absently in the soft curls. Lord, she loved him. Telling him would be a mistake, she knew that, just as surely as she knew he would never tell her what he really felt, but she knew.

Desire, yes, of course, or they would never have ended up like this, but also a reluctant fascination and a curiously protective tendency that she found both touching and revealing.

That love would come she had no doubt. Whether or not he would ever admit it was a different kettle of fish entirely.

His other hand came over and settled on her waist, the thumb drawing idle circles on her skin.

Turning his head, he brushed his lips against her brow in silent question.

Without hesitation, she lifted her mouth to his.

They woke to blue skies and glorious sunshine. Dressing quickly in shorts and T-shirts, they packed the gear away in the tent and Jack parked the bike in the trees, out of sight.

Then they set off over the fields for the nearest village, two miles away. They bought hot rolls and coffee in the little café, and ate them sitting on the sand dunes overlooking the sea, and then they wandered along the tideline searching for treasures.

Jack found a piece of driftwood, its gnarled form worn totally smooth by the action of the waves, and they decided it would look wonderful in his barn hung on the brickwork chimney-breast, so he carried it for the rest of the morning until they returned to their little camp at lunchtime.

They took the bike then and rode along the coast to Blakeney. They took a boat trip to see the seals, and in the evening they went back to the camp and lit a picnic-type disposable barbecue and ate burgers and sausages and fresh crunchy salad they had bought in Blakeney.

As darkness fell again they took turns to wash in the

tent, and then they lay together under the night sky and reached again for the stars.

She woke in the night to find him lying flat on his back, the glow of a cigarette lighting up his face as he inhaled.

'Can't you sleep?' she asked softly.

He was silent for a long time, then he blew out a long stream of smoke and turned his head towards her.

'Don't fall for me, Irish. This has been a great weekend, but it doesn't mean anything.'

She swallowed the hurt and told herself he didn't really mean it. He just didn't realise he loved her yet.

'Sure, and why would I fall for you?' she asked lightly, staring hard at the stars. If she could just keep them from swimming out of focus. . .

'You said you loved me.'

She was shocked. Had she said it aloud? God knew she'd thought it, but aloud?

'Oh, that,' she said dismissively. 'You don't want to take everything I say too seriously. It's just the heat of the moment. Anyway, I'm a good Catholic girl, remember? I've got to settle down and have babies, so you're quite safe. You're not in the least a suiable candidate.'

The cigarette glowed again in the dark, and he hitched himself up on one elbow and ground it out on the earth.

'No, I'm not,' he growled. 'Just make sure you don't forget it.'

'You're quite good in bed, though,' she added cheekily.

He gave a disbelieving laugh.

'Are you propositioning me?'

'Well, do you know, I believe I might be?'

His arms went round her and his lips found hers, and this time when the world fell apart and the sky came crashing down, she clamped her lips together and buried her face in his shoulder and said nothing.

'Well, you can't say he didn't warn you,' she muttered to herself during the course of Monday. Their 'great weekend' as he put it had come to a highly unsatisfactory end yesterday evening, when he had dropped her off at home, and after seeing her in, had ridden off with scarcely a word. 'Well, he said it didn't mean anything, so you've only got yourself to blame if you didn't believe him,' Kathleen told herself glumly.

Sunday had been wonderful, a lovely warm, lazy day, but since then he had treated her as just another member of the team, being quite natural and friendly and polite, but without any hint of intimacy.

In fact, looking back on it there had been no hint of any real intimacy over the weekend, except during their lovemaking. Then there had been plenty, both physical and emotional, but only then. It was as if that was the only emotion Jack allowed himself, the only time he let down his guard, and she sensed that it was almost involuntary and if he could have prevented it he would have done.

In fact, if anything he was even more remote and distant now than he had been before their weekend, as if he hadn't meant to let her get so close and was frantically clawing back space.

If so, the fates were playing into his hands. They had been busy in the department all day, a steady stream of non-urgent cases that kept her occupied and largely out of his way—until the middle of the afternoon, at any rate. Then a motorcyclist was brought in on a blue light, a dispatch rider who had been burning along the Norwich road and hit a patch of oil.

He was a mess, his left femur broken in at least one place, his right tibia and fibula shattered, his right shoulder dislocated and possible rib fractures.

Thinking of her trip to Norfolk on the back of Jack's bike, Kathleen's blood ran cold.

'Fat lot of use leather gear is to you under these circumstances,' she mumbled, and set to with her scissors to cut away his shredded clothes.

'Can we get the orthopaedic SR on take down here, please?' she threw over her shoulder, and then added, as an afterthought, 'and the neurologist?'

The team went smoothly into action as usual, only Kathleen's racing pulse betraying her inner horror. She wondered how much longer it would be before Jack was brought in in this sort of state, and how she would feel if he was.

Sick, was the short answer.

She made herself smile. 'Hello in there,' she said to him, and he groaned and rolled his head towards her. 'Can you tell me your name?'

'Graham—Glover.'

'Are you in a lot of pain, Graham?'

'Are you kidding?' he gritted.

She nodded. 'I'll get you something in a tick. Did they give you anything in the ambulance?'

'I dunno,' he slurred. 'If they did, it didn't work. . .'

Jack appeared at her elbow, winced and commiserated. 'Soon have you comfortable,' he lied easily. 'Let's have six units of whole blood cross-matched and run in some plasma expander in the meantime. I think

Michael Barrington's on his way down now—ah, the very man.'

Jack filled him in on the scanty information they had already obtained.

'Ouch—hello, old chap,' he said with a smile. 'I'm the guy with the job of gluing you together again. Have we got any X-rays?'

'No, he's going in now,' Kathleen said. 'I wasn't sure what you wanted, and I thought it was better to wait and get the whole lot.'

'OK. Let's take things in order—pain relief, X-rays, then we'll get that shoulder back in before we go much further. I think we'll need a full set, actually. I'm not sure if that leg's lying oddly because of the femur or the pelvis.' He turned back to the patient. 'Have you got any pain in your back or hips, Graham?'

He gave a feeble chuckle, and clutched his ribs with his left hand. 'Ow, damn. I don't know where it's coming from, and frankly, I don't give a monkey's.'

'OK. We'll give him seventy-five milligrams of peth-idine, get the shots and go from there.'

Kathleen injected the painkiller, and then he was wheeled off for X-rays.

They went into the staff-room and grabbed a coffee while they waited for the results, then they studied them together on the lightbox.

'Ow,' Michael said. 'Better get Theatre jumping, I think. Maybe need a fixator on the tib and fib, or put the right leg in a gutter for a day or two and see. I think I'll probably pin the femur, now we know the pelvis is cracked too. Don't want traction on it.'

Jack grinned at him. 'Another early night?'

He laughed. 'Don't. Clare'll kill me. Still, it's not for

much longer, then we're taking two months off to sail the Atlantic.'

Jack did a mild double take. 'Pardon?'

'Don't ask,' Kathleen advised. 'I thought you were bad, but this one's a menace. If it's impossible, he does it. Something to prove to the world, isn't that right, Michael?'

He smiled slowly. 'Well, to myself, perhaps. Still, it's a bit of fun.'

'What have you got?' Jack asked.

'Thirty-eight-foot sloop. My grandfather built her.'

Kathleen glared at Jack. 'You have enough dangerous hobbies,' she muttered.

'What, like the bike?'

She snorted.

'Talking of the bike, let's go and put that shoulder back. You any good at this?'

'Oh, yeah. Nothing like a good dislocation to cheer a patient up,' Jack said wryly.

Kathleen heard the yell from her office, and shook her head. He was quite unmoved, totally untouched by the man's obviously severe injuries. It could so easily have been him—or her!

She felt sick again, and sat down with a plonk. Didn't he care about his life?

The answer was simple. No.

And why? Because there was nothing left any more for him to care about, and if his attitude over the past forty-eight hours was anything to go by, he was keeping it that way.

She wondered without any real hope whether he would suggest they get together that night, and her level of optimism proved justified.

That he was regretting his impulse in inviting her to spend the weekend with him was obvious. What was equally obvious was that he had no intention of compouding his error with any further mistakes.

She went home—alone—and sat in darkness staring at the blank face of the television until eleven, and then she went to bed and stared at the ceiling instead.

CHAPTER SIX

TUESDAY was no better. Kathleen went out that evening and had a drink with a girlfriend, and got back to be told by one of her neighbours that the phone had been ringing.

Her heart leapt, but, rather than indulge her optimism, she rang her mother.

'Did you try me earlier?'

'I did. I've got good news—guess what?'

Kathleen sighed, ridiculously disappointed. 'Who's pregnant?'

'Patrick!' her mother announced with satisfaction. 'Well, not exactly Patrick, but Anne. The babe's due in January—isn't that wonderful? Of course, the cold weather's not ideal, but perhaps the next one will be a spring baby, and anyway the winters aren't so harsh these days what with heating and all—so, how are you, darling?'

'In love,' Kath told her glumly.

'Oh, darling, that's wonderful! Tell me *all* about him.'

So she did, sparing only the most intimate details.

'*How* old?' her mother asked, clearly appalled.

Kathleen sighed. 'Forty-one. Well, forty. Almost forty-one.'

'Oh. Well, if he's in good health I suppose that would be all right. After all, you're thirty now and no spring chicken yourself any more. So when are you bringing him home to meet us?'

'Mum, haven't you listened to a word I've said?' Kathleen yelled, and banged the phone down, tears of frustration in her eyes.

The doorbell rang, and scrubbing the tears off her cheeks with the back of her hand, she marched to the door and yanked it open.

'You!'

'I'm sorry—should I go away?' Jack asked a little too mildly.

'I wasn't expecting you,' she said ungraciously.

'I know—I tried to ring, but first you were out, then you were engaged.' He eyed her oddly. 'Are you OK?'

'No, I'm bloody well not!' she snapped.

She stalked away from the front door and it closed softly behind him. He followed her and cupped her slim shoulders in his big, comforting hands. Hah! I should be so lucky! she thought miserably.

'What's wrong, Irish?' His voice was soft, coaxing her. It did nothing for her temper. What's wrong, indeed.

'You are! You take me away for the weekend and then come back and act as if you've just met me at a friend's house for the first time! Damn it, Jack, after all we did——'

'I'm here aren't I?' he asked and his voice acquired an edge. 'I warned you not to take me for granted, Kathleen. I haven't got any ties, and that's the way I'm keeping it.'

She plonked on to the settee and it groaned in protest. 'I didn't think that meant you were going to pretend not to know me!'

'Oh, Kath——'

She snatched her hand away. 'Don't "Oh, Kath" me in that tone of voice! What's the matter—getting cold at night again?'

'Would you like me to leave?' he asked quietly.

'No! Damn it, no, I want you to stay! I just don't see how you can kiss and cuddle me in the department when nothing at all is going on between us, and then just as soon as there is, you switch it all off like a blasted tap!'

He sighed and lowered himself to the other end of the settee. 'I thought that was what you wanted! You went nuts when Amy caught you sitting on my lap—'

'Are you thick? That was entirely different! Sure, I don't expect you to make love to me in the corridor, but even when we were alone you practically ignored me!'

He ran his hand wearily over his face. 'I'm sorry. I guess I'm not really used to this sort of thing any more.'

'What sort of thing—talking to a woman after you've spent a weekend in bed with her?'

'Yes,' he said frankly, and it took the wind out of her sails.

'What do you do?' she asked in horror. 'Just walk away?'

'Usually—on the rare occasions when I take a woman to bed. Sometimes there's a second or third date, but not often.'

She was appalled. 'Jack, that's awful,' she said shakily.

'No, it's safe. That way nobody gets to depend on me, nobody gets hurt. I never intended to have a relationship with you. If you hadn't come round that night, none of this would have been allowed to happen——'

'So it's my fault if I get hurt? Fine. Just so long as I know.'

'Kathleen, don't be sarcastic——'

'I think you'd better go,' she said unsteadily.

'Oh, Kath——'

'Don't touch me! This is hard enough.' She sniffed and looked up at him through tear-filled eyes. 'Why did you come round, anyway?

His face was etched with tiredness. 'I wanted to see you. I was fool enough to think you might want to see me.'

'Oh, Jack, of course I want to see you. . .'

He opened his arms and she flew into them, burying her face in his chest.

'Take me to bed,' she mumbled, and he laughed softly.

'I thought you'd never ask!'

'That's my line——'

'Shut up. Where's the bedroom?'

'Oh, I love it when you're masterful,' she teased, and got a glower for her pains.

'Where?'

'Left, at the end.'

'Right.'

'No, left.'

'Irish,' he warned softly.

With a giggle she slipped out of his arms and disappeared through the door, turning off the lights as she went.

'Come and get me!'

He growled, groped his way down the pitch dark corridor and found her almost by instinct. Her little shriek was cut off with unerring accuracy by the simple expedient of covering her mouth with his, and she gave up her struggles and surrendered, her foolish heart only too grateful for the crumbs he offered.

And if her head warned her that he only wanted her for sex, her heart ignored the warning and opened itself joyfully to his tender passion.

She was very careful after that not to take him for granted, even occasionally making excuses to refuse his sporadic invitations, although it tore her to shreds not to be with him at every opportunity. Just as she didn't take him for granted, she made sure he couldn't take her for granted either.

She even started making other arrangements so she wouldn't just end up sitting at home staring at the phone and forcing herself not to ring him and say her plans had changed and she was free after all.

She had dinner with Ben and Maggie Bradshaw, and Oliver and Bron Henderson had a party which she attended, although she ended up bumping into Jack as she might have known she would, and going home with him for the night.

Occasionally she went out for a drink with Mick O'Shea, who was between girlfriends at the time and was happy to have Kathleen along as pleasant and undemanding company. They had known each other for so many years, since they had trained at the Royal Victoria, Belfast, that there were no secrets or illusions between them and she was able to tell Mick all her problems.

Then one day another mutual friend from their days at the Royal Victoria breezed into town and ended up on Mick's floor for a couple of nights.

They arranged to go out for a drink on the second evening, although Kathleen wasn't really looking forward to it as it was bound to turn into a 'What was the name of that blonde with the big chest?' sort of session and she would end up driving them both home and quite likely putting them both to bed!

And then, at four-thirty when she was just contemplating going off shift, a call came in on the red phone that made her feel cold inside.

Jack was standing beside her at the time filling in notes, and she quickly jotted down the address and the scant details they were offered, and turned to him.

'Toddler fallen out of an upstairs window and impaled himself on the railings. They want a flying squad.'

'Right. Ben!' he called, and Ben stuck his head out of a cubicle.

'We're off on a call—hold the fort, eh? Come on—we'll need to take some stuff—Haemacel, splints, airways, giving sets, saline—go and grab that lot while I find some coats for us.'

He ran down the corridor and Kath shot into the stores and grabbed the emergency bag and another unit of saline. He was back in seconds with Dayglo yellow coats.

'Here, put this on. We'll go on the bike—come on. Do you know how to find it?'

She glanced at the paper in her hand. 'Yes, I think so, but why don't we take my car?'

'No time, the bike's quicker. The traffic out there

will be building up already, Kathleen. Come on, you'll be fine.'

'I will?' Blindly, she followed him, and in the entrance she bumped into Stan, a burly policeman in black waterproofs who was just heading out of the department. 'Stan, just the fellow. We have to go out on a call—kiddy stuck on some railings. Can you give us an escort?'

'Sure—where to?' He took the paper, nodded briefly and ran out to his bike, firing it up instantly. Jack chucked her her helmet, stowed the emergency gear and fired up his bike, and in seconds she was clinging on behind him as the sirens wailed and they took off through the car park as if the hounds of hell were after them. She was surprised to see that he had the green flashing lights of a doctor set into the fairing at the front of the bike, and a siren that almost deafened her. It was her last coherent thought for some minutes.

Stan was away, cleaving a path through the traffic so that all Jack had to do was follow him. Simple, except that Stan was probably doing almost sixty through the centre of town! Kath was terrified, but there was no way she was going to fall off unless she took Jack with her!

Finally they reached their destination, to find a huge crowd of silent onlookers all standing back a respectful distance and watching in mesmerised fascination as a distraught woman sobbed and screamed for help. She was kneeling on the steps next to the old iron railings that ran along the front of the terrace, her arms supporting the naked body of her little boy, and she was trembling with the effort of holding him still.

The crowd had parted to let them through, and

Kathleen's fear for herself vanished as she took in the scene. The child had landed face down with his shoulders and arms across the railings, and the wickedly sharp spikes had pierced his tiny body in several places, mercifully passing each side of his neck. Incredibly, he was still alive.

Jack immediately commandeered two of the men to find a table and some pillows or something on which to rest the child's body, and with the help of a neighbour he managed to prise the terrified and exhausted mother away from her son.

Supporting his body with one hand, he quickly assessed him with the other. 'Right, he's still breathing. Let's get a line in fast,' he snapped.

It was already in her hand before he spoke, and by the time the men came back with the table and pillows they were running in normal saline through a line in his hand.

The ambulance arrived and the paramedics leapt out and ran up.

'How is he?'

'Still breathing—the spikes seem to have missed the main vessels in his neck, but the right brachial plexus may have copped it. Certainly his clavicle's gone. Possible head injury, maybe whiplash—he's unconscious at the moment. Hopefully he'll stay that way.'

Jack glanced up at Kath. 'Get an airway in, if you can. And we'll need pethidine drawn up in case he comes round—God knows how much. Work it out on his weight. I should say he's about twelve to fifteen kilos. He'll need a collar on just in case his neck's injured, but I don't know if you'll get it round the spikes. Where the hell are the fire brigade?'

'On their way.'

'Hmm. I hope they've got the sense to bring air powered cutters. I don't want him shaken to death, and we can't take him off these things. Can you get that airway in?'

Kath shook her head. 'No, he gags every time I try. I think he's hovering.'

Damn,' Jack muttered. 'I wanted him out of it. Give him the pethidine, then. Pity he didn't have clothes on, they would have cushioned his fall a bit. What the hell was he doing falling out of the window naked anyway?'

Stan, the policeman who had escorted them, had the answer to that. 'He was having a bath, and climbed to the end of the tub and fell through the window. The mother said she hardly took her eyes off him for a second.'

'Hmm. Well, you can't afford to at this age,' Jack grunted. 'Little kids are like quicksilver. How's the right radial pulse, Kath?'

She reached for the little wrist and laid her fingers against the inside. 'Very slight—less than the left, but it's still there. Perhaps the artery's just compressed.'

'Pigs might fly,' the paramedic muttered, and fastened the collar at last. 'Phew—let's hope that gives enough support.'

Jack ran a stethescope over the boy's chest and pressed his lips together. 'Right lung's collapsed—he'll need a chest drain if he makes it. Oh, at bloody last—the cavalry. Let's hope they get him out fast, or we'll need an anaesthetist.'

The fire brigade van pulled up in a flurry of flashing lights and the crew were there immediately assessing the job.

'Soon have him free—take about half an hour to cut through that lot.'

'You can't have half an hour,' Jack argued. 'Get another set of cutting gear and tackle both sides at once.'

The man opened his mouth to comment, shrugged and went back to the cab. Minutes later another team appeared and they worked alongside. Even so, it was painfully slow and the little boy stirred and cried out in pain.

'Give him a little more pethidine, Kath,' Jack said quietly. 'Say two milligrams. I want to get his arm off this spike to save having to cut it as soon as they've finished the rest. He can't hang on any longer. I take it Theatre's ready for him?'

Kathleen nodded. 'Oliver Henderson's on standby and he'll have Andrew Barrett in with him.'

Jack nodded briefly and returned to his relentless checking of the boy's condition.

At last he was freed, and gritting his teeth, Jack took the small forearm firmly in his hands and lifted it quickly off the last spike.

The child screamed and sobbed, and Jack's face, usually so impassive, twisted with pain. He reached out and stroked the little head. 'Sorry, son,' he murmured, and then the crew lifted him off the table, pillows and all, and strapped him into the ambulance.

Kathleen went with them, Jack followed on his bike, and they raced back with sirens wailing.

The surgical team were scrubbed and in Theatre ready, but Andrew Barrett, the paediatrician, was waiting for them as they pulled up.

He walked swiftly beside the trolley as they wheeled

it towards the Theatre lifts, and Kath told him as rapidly as she could what they had established.

'OK, he looks stable. Many thanks.'

Kath left them at the lift, and as the doors closed she caught a glimpse of him crouching down and talking to the little lad, his warm brown eyes kindly and concerned. She nodded. He was in good hands.

Jack was just arriving as she walked back into the department, and a police car drew up with the still-hysterical mother inside.

They led her into the interview-room, gave her a cup of tea and got her to sign the consent form—somewhat of a formality as the child was already in Theatre by this time, but at least that way they were covered in the event of any repercussions.

Then she and Jack placed the woman in the care of the duty staff and wandered down to the staff lounge to pour themselves the dregs of the coffee.

Jack flopped on to a chair and let his breath out on a sigh. 'Poor little bugger,' he said softly.

'He's alive—I reckon he'll make it.'

Jack dropped his head back against the chair and rolled it towards her. 'Yeah—maybe. God, those gawpers make me sick. Every time there's an accident, there they are, crawling out of the woodwork, eyes like saucers, lapping it all up. It makes me so angry—any one of them could have found something to rest that child on, but no, they all stand there in case they get blood on their hands and watch the child suffer——'

'Hey, Jack, it's just human nature.'

'Yes, well, there are times when I'm ashamed to be human if that's what it means.' He closed his eyes and dropped his head forward on his chest. 'I feel shattered—what time is it?'

'Nearly seven.'

'Fancy going to find something to eat?'

'That would be lovely. Do you want to nip home with me while I change?'

'Good idea.'

He unwound his long legs and stood up, arching his back and stretching. 'Come on, then, before I fall asleep.'

She drained her coffee, got her bag out of her locker and followed him out of the door. The traffic had almost disappeared and they arrived at her flat shortly after seven.

'What shall I wear?'

'Dunno—jeans? Nothing fancy. Come here.'

She went obediently into his arms and lifted her face to his.

'You did a wonderful job this afternoon,' he murmured between kisses, and she felt herself swell with pride.

'Thank you. You didn't do so badly yourself.'

He chuckled. 'You're too kind. Mmm. . .' His lips came down again and his hands slid down her back, urging her up against him. At once everything else receded, leaving them alone in a sea of passion.

His fingers dispensed with the buttons on the front of her dress and his hands, warm and firm and so, so clever, slipped inside and teased at the lace of her bra.

'Who needs food?' he mumbled against the lace, and his hot mouth closed enticingly over one nipple.

She sagged against him, her legs quivering, the blood

pounding in her ears, and grabbed his shoulders for support.

Suddenly his head lifted.

'Don't stop!' she wailed, but he held her away from him, his face taut.

'Doorbell,' he muttered.

'What?'

The bell rang again, and this time she heard it.

'Who is it?' he asked.

She shook her head vaguely, still trapped in the magic of his kiss. 'I don't know. . .'

'Get rid of them.'

She nodded, and tugging her clothes back into some sort of order, she went to the door.

'Hi—you're not ready yet!'

'Mick!' She clapped her hand over her mouth. 'Oh, lord, I'd forgotten!'

He ran his eyes over her dishevelled clothing and smiled. 'So I see. Well, who's it to be? Your old friend, or your new lover?'

She closed her eyes. Oh, damn, she thought, how would she tell him?

Jack spared her the agony of making a decision by appearing behind her, helmet in hand.

'Don't let me spoil your plans—the lady's all yours, O'Shea.'

And with a brief, hard kiss on her lips and a curt nodd to Mick, he was gone.

It was a miserable evening. Her thoughts were definitely not with her companions, and after a while they dropped her back at her flat and went on to a club together.

She changed out of her glad rags, tugged on old jeans and a sweatshirt and drove out to his house.

The lights were all off, but that didn't worry her. She knew he often sat in the garden in the dark and listened to the sounds of the night.

She parked the car and looked around, but there was no sign of him. His car was there, in the open barn, but the bike was missing.

She tried the back door and found it open, and going in she turned on some lights and made herself a cup of coffee. If the house wasn't locked, perhaps he'd gone to the pub to buy his horrible cigarettes or another bottle of Scotch to drown his sorrows—whatever, she didn't think he would have gone far.

She settled down to wait with a book on caving she found in his bookcase, but after a while she had to acknowledge he'd been gone longer than she'd expected.

Then she remembered he was on call, and used his phone to ring the hospital. Yes, he was in. There had been a gas explosion and there were several casualties. No, it was unlikely he'd be home for hours. No, she couldn't speak to him, he was with a patient.

She left his number with them and asked them to get him to ring, then made another drink.

When he called at a little before one in the morning, he was distinctly cool.

'What are you doing at my house?' he asked immediately.

'Looking for you—Mick and Terry have gone on to a club. You left in such a rush——'

He snorted. 'There didn't seem to be any point in a protracted farewell.'

'But, Jack, it wasn't like that——'

'Forget it, Kathleen. You're a free agent. How did you get in to the house?'

'Through the door, of course,' she told him crossly. 'It wasn't locked. I thought you were here at first, or just nipped to the pub or something.'

'Pub? It's one in the morning.'

'Yes, well, it wasn't then. Anyway, I soon realised you hadn't. What would you like me to do?' Wait for me, she wanted him to say, but of course he didn't.

'I've got my keys,' he said curtly. 'Just drop the catch on your way out. I won't be back before the morning.'

And he hung up.

Disheartened, she gathered her things together, locked the door behind her and drove home. Free agent, indeed! She was anything but, of course, but he wouldn't want to hear that. Oh, no. That implied commitment, and if you didn't have commitment, you could pretend you were free.

'Well, two can play at that game,' she said angrily. 'And anyway, who's taking whom for granted this time?'

Jack, too, was angry. Angry and frustrated and jealous as an ousted tom-cat.

OK, so her date with O'Shea hadn't turned out as he'd imagined, but the fact remained she had chosen her old college buddy over him—a fact that rankled for reasons he didn't care to examine.

Damn her! His body still throbbed in the aftermath of their interrupted lovemaking, and that too was irritating the hell out of him. He couldn't remember a time when going to bed with a woman hadn't dulled his interest, acting almost inevitably as a cure for his fascination.

But not with Kathleen. Oh, no, not with that aggravating, hot-tempered, sensuous little leprechaun. Far from slaking his thirst, all his weekend with her had done was whet his appetite and leave him with a desperate craving for more.

He had left her alone deliberately on that Sunday night, and again on the Monday, but by the end of Tuesday even his iron control had disintegrated in the face of his overwhelming need for her. Since then he had tried to stay away from her, and it seemed she was doing the same, which did nothing to cool his interest. Take tonight, for example—and just to turn the screw she had wound him to fever pitch before letting O'Shea in! Not that it had been difficult, he thought disgustedly. One touch and he was climbing walls for her.

An excess of teenage hormones, he told himself, lying desperately because the truth was too uncomfortable to face. He was still shocked that he had reacted so strongly when that jovial Irishman turned up. Damn it, O'Shea was lucky still to have all his teeth! Jack's fists clenched slowly until his knuckles stood out white against the tan.

She was getting to him, getting too close. What the hell was she doing at his house anyway?

He squashed the image of her curled up on a chair, feet tucked under her neat little bottom, waiting for him, her eyes drowsy and heavy-lidded——

'Damn!'

There was a knock on his door.

'Come in!'

It was one of the staff nurses. 'We could do with your help, sir, if you've got a minute.'

'Of course I've got a minute—what the bloody hell d'you think I'm doing here at this time of night?'

She blinked, apologised and quietly closed the door.

'Blast.' He looked down in surprise at his hands, and consciously straightened them, flexing the fingers to ease the tension. Then he left the room and went to find the nurse who had been the unworthy recipient of his evil temper.

He growled an apology, gave the poor girl a miserable parody of a smile and turned his attention to their patient. Behind him he heard someone mumble something about pre-menstrual tension, and a wry chuckle escaped him.

There was a collective sigh of relief.

By the following day Kathleen's temper had cooled slightly, but so had Jack's attitude.

Back to that, she thought wearily. Oh, well.

They were as busy as ever, and her mood wasn't improved by the fact that she had to juggle staffing rotas and the pharmacy budget.

'I suggest we just let them suffer,' Ben said cheerfully. 'Who needs painkillers? Let 'em scream.'

'Ben, you're disgusting,' she said with a weary smile. 'How's Maggie.?'

'Throwing up. Pregnancy isn't suiting her. I think she's going to give up work soon so she can take it easy. She was giving up anyway when the baby came, so she might as well go a little early.'

Kath laid her pen down and leant back, smiling at

him. 'Of course, with all that filthy lucre behind you you can afford to treat her like bone china.'

His mouth lifted in a wry smile. 'It has its uses.' He shifted awkwardly, then looked at her. 'How are you and the boss getting on?'

'Me and the boss?' she said innocently, struggling for air. 'OK. He's very competent.'

'Kath...'

Her composure crumpled. 'Ben, please, leave it,' she mumbled.

'Sorry—I didn't mean to pry.'

She gave a short laugh. 'There's nothing to pry into, Ben. We see each other every now and again, but we aren't joined at the hip like Siamese twins, you know.'

He chuckled. 'You ought to try it one day.'

She threw a paper cup at him. 'Go away and let me do my work, or we'll be running on one staff nurse and half an aspirin.'

And so she got through the week, surviving mainly on humour and philosophy, but occasionally resorting to sarcasm with particularly obtuse patients.

There was one woman who repeatedly used the unit as a GP's surgery. Kathleen had warned her countless times in the past, but this time she had had enough. The woman had a sore throat. Big deal, she thought, so have I.

'Is it very painful?' she asked briskly.

'Well, it is when I swallow or talk. I just need some antibiotics, really, I suppose, to clear it up.'

'How are your eyes?'

'My eyes? Fine.'

'Good. You see that sign up there? Could you read it to me?'

The woman glanced up at Kathleen, her face puzzled. 'Accident and Emergency.'

'Right. Which are you?'

'What?'

She took a deep breath. 'Have you had an accident?'

'Well, no, not really, it's just this awful pain in my throat.'

Kathleen was feeling the pain a lot further down, in the region of her tailbone.

'Is it an emergency?'

'Well, I—I suppose it needs treating fairly quickly.'

'Mrs Forbes, there are people in here who have got broken bones, or severe chest pain from heart trouble, or head injuries, or crushed limbs from industrial accidents. There are people who have been brought in unconscious for no apparent reason, who have had car accidents and been cut free by the fire brigade and rushed in for *emergency* treatment following *accidents*. None of them has a sore throat. Do you understand?'

'Well, yes, it could be a great deal worse——'

'And it would have to be before you require our services. Now perhaps you would like to go to your GP in the normal way and get him to deal with your throat.'

'But he's always so busy——'

'Mrs Forbes, we are busy. The average waiting time in here is nearly an hour. How long is it at your general practice?'

'Oh, at least half an hour——'

'So you could have saved yourself half an hour by going there.'

'But he always seems so tired and stressed.'

Kathleen could have screamed.

'Mrs Forbes, I am tired and stressed. My staff are tired and stressed. The medical profession as a whole is tired and stressed, and frankly, people like you don't help!'

'Well, there's no need to be rude!' the woman snapped, and snatching up her bag, she stalked off.

'Well, that was tactful,' Ben said from behind her. 'What's happened to our warm and sunny Sister Hennessy?'

'I'm tired and stressed, didn't you hear?'

Ben smiled sympathetically. 'You and me both. Let's go and have a cup of coffee and deal with this lot later. Judging by the look of them they aren't much worse than her. I tell you what, why don't you throw them all out and we'll have the day off?'

'Don't tempt me,' she said with a wry laugh, and picked up the next file. 'Hold the coffee. We'll get this lot moving and then stop. Mr Grieves, please? Could you come with me?'

By Friday she was unable to be philosophical any longer. She was lonely, and she wanted to see him. She wasn't alone. Several times she caught him looking at her unguardedly, and heat flared in his eyes, to be instantly banked as he brought it under control with his iron will.

But it was enough. She knew he wanted her, and even though it was only for her body Kath was so desperate for his attention that she was ready to settle even for that.

She hated herself for it, her pride and her need constantly at war, but finally by lunchtime her need won. She found him in his office. 'Jack?'

He stiffened at the soft sound of her voice, and his head lifted, his eyes carfully veiled.

'Yes, Kathleen. What can I do for you?'

I thought we were lovers! she wanted to scream, but she swallowed her hurt for the thousandth time and forced a smile.

'Are you busy tomorrow night? I thought I'd cook us a meal at my place. . .'

He stood up and paced to the window, his back to her. 'I won't be here. I'm off to Yorkshire tonight and I won't be back until Sunday afternoon.'

'Sunday, then,' she said, and damned herself for the note of desperation in her voice.

'I'll be late—God knows what time it'll be.'

'Well, why don't we leave it open? If you're back in time, come round,' she suggested, and hated herself for grovelling.

'OK, but don't bother to cook for me. I'll grab something somewhere.'

Well, she wasn't about to push her pride any further for him. She lifted her chin.

'Fine. Have a good weekend.'

'Thank you. You, too.'

Fat chance, she thought dismally, the prospect of two days and three nights without seeing him yawning ahead of her like the Grand Canyon. She left his office quietly, too raw to make a scene and attract attention, wanting only to crawl into a corner and hide.

The weekend was every bit as long and lonely as she had anticipated. The weather forecast on Sunday was for rain, and she thought of him riding his bike back down the motorway in poor conditions and had to revive her anger to stop from worrying herself sick over him. Instead she attacked her flat, scouring it within an inch of its life, and finally collapsed exhausted into the bath at five.

Not really hungry, she made a cheese sandwich and curled up in front of the television. She was just in time for the tail end of the early evening news, and her attention was immediately caught.

'. . .go back to Tim Styles at Ingleborough, Yorkshire. Tim, I gather you've got some news on the three missing pot-holers?'

Kath's heart slammed against her ribs, and she felt the blood drain from her face.

'Oh, no, it can't be him—he can't be there still. . .'

The picture cut from the newsreader in the studio to the rain-lashed Yorkshire countryside and a reporter standing huddled against the driving rain.

'In the last few minutes one of the party of missing students——' Kath let out her breath on a gust '—has made his way to the surface, and he has told us that there are still two men trapped below here,' he announced in the earnest voice of sepulchral doom so favoured by reporters at the scene of an incident. 'One man has apparently sustained a serious head injury after the belay on his rope failed and he fell fifty feet down a pitch to the rock floor.One of his companions has remained with him; a third, the one who sounded the alarm, is returning to the scene of the accident with the rescue team, which you can see gathering behind me.

'Conditions are not on their side. The rain which is making conditions up here decidedly unpleasant is as I speak seeping through the rocks and creating foaming torrents underground, flooding caverns and making passages impassable. There is one ray of hope—one member of the rescue team, himself an experienced caver, is a Casualty consultant from Suffolk who has volunteered to go down with the party to provide immediate medical assistance to the injured man. He's here with me now. Dr Lawrence, is there anything you can add?'

CHAPTER SEVEN

THE camera cut to Jack, fully equipped in Neoprene suit and helmet. Kath's heart stopped, and then started again with an untidy lurch. What was he doing there? He should be on his way home! He couldn't go down—didn't he know it was dangerous?

Then he was talking, explained what they hoped to do. 'The most important thing is to get medical aid to the injured man as quickly as possible. As with any sort of head injury, time is of the essence. It hasn't been raining very long, and the quicker we can move, the more likely we are to get them out before conditions deteriorate to the extent that the passages become impassable.'

'Is that likely? Do you know the area where the men are?'

Jack nodded. 'Yes, it's a pot I've been down many times—not the easiest; apart from a fifty-foot pitch we'll have to haul him up, there's a long sump we'll have to bring the injured man back through which could be tricky if he's unconscious or uncooperative. Also the main passage is a minor water course, but in rain like this it tends to swell. The more it rains, the fuller the stream will get and the bigger the problem, so really, time is the most important factor, especially as we don't really know what we're going to find when we get down there.'

'Can you give us any idea how long the rescue will take?'

He shook his head. 'Some time. It'll take us a couple of hours to reach them, and at least twice as long on the return, plus whatever time we have to spend getting the patient stable enough to move. As I said, the sooner we start, the sooner we'll have them out. In fact, if you'll excuse me, I believe we're ready now, so I must go.'

The reporter thanked him, and the camera tracked him as he trudged over to the other members of the team and they headed together towards a dark crack in the hillside. Then the camera returned to the reporter, who promised to keep the viewers updated.

The newscaster then switched to a trivial item about a cat who'd been rescued from the roof of the houses of Parliament, and Kathleen flicked off the set and threw her sandwich in the bin, her appetite gone.

What if he died? What if the rain increased and they were trapped underground by a flood that washed them away down one of those awful little squeezes? They would be lost forever, their bodies never recovered. . .

She clamped her hand over her mouth and caught the sob, then forced herself to breathe nice and steadily, in, out, in, out—she wouldn't panic. She wouldn't!

The phone rang, and she snatched it up.

'Hello?'

'Kathleen, it's Mick.'

She knew from his voice that he had seen the news too, and she had never been so glad to hear a friendly voice. 'Mick! What am I going to do?' she wailed. She could feel the panic rising again, but she was helpless to control it.

'Stay there, I'll come round. Put the kettle on.'

She did as she was told, moving mechanically, conscious of her heart flailing erratically against her ribs.

Mick came and made some tea and sat her down with a cup in her hands and tried to talk some sense into her.

'He knows what he's doing. He isn't going to take foolish risks.'

'Mick, going down there is a foolish risk—didn't you hear what he said?'

'I heard—and you know you'd go yourself if someone needed you.'

'Humph.'

'Humph yourself. He'll be fine. Drink your tea.'

'It's disgusting, you put sugar in it.'

'You need the sugar, you're shocked.'

'Rubbish, I'm just. . .'

He caught the tea before it toppled, and sat and held her while she howled her eyes out.

Finally she straightened up and glared at him balefully. 'That was all your fault. You shouldn't have been so nice to me. Now your sweatshirt's all soggy.'

'Hmm. I'll probably get rheumatism in my shoulder and nobody to blame but myself. That'll teach me to make tea for unstable women——'

He ducked the cushion and handed her back her cup. 'Finish this, love, and we'll wander down to the pub while it's not raining.'

She shook her head, feeling the dread clutch at her again. 'I don't want to leave the flat. There might be some news——'

'There'll be nothing for hours. Come on, a quick drink in your local.'

He was right, of course, she knew that, but she picked up the brandy Mick got her and downed it in one, then hovered on the edge of her seat until he gave up and walked her home.

They spent the evening with one eye on the television, playing cards and drinking too much coffee. There was a newsflash at nine to say that the rescue party had reached the injured man and were now returning to the surface, and then nothing until almost midnight.

Then, suddenly, the programme was interrupted by a newsreader who announced that the party had just reached the surface. They switched live to the scene, and Kathleen's eyes immediately picked out Jack crouched over the injured man and issuing instructions to the ambulance team. As soon as the ambulance pulled away the reporter made his way over to Jack.

'This is Dr Lawrence, who led the rescue. Dr Lawrence, what can you tell us about the condition of the injured man?' he asked him.

Jack looked up and wiped a grubby hand wearily over his face, streaking the dirt still further. His smile was wry.

'Much as I would love to claim all the credit, I must point out that my part in this rescue was very small indeed. The Yorkshire Cave Rescue Organisation is a very skilfully orchestrated operation, and they all know exactly what they're doing. Most of the time I was simply in the way. As for the patient, it's not my place to comment on his medical condition, except to say that he is still quite definitely alive and in the best possible hands.'

'What will happen to him now?'

'He'll be transferred to hospital for a whole series of tests and X-rays, and the results will determine the treatment he's given. He's had a very long and trying ordeal, and apart from his physical injuries he's had the cold and damp to deal with too, so his body's had a pretty severe challenge. Other than that, I'm afraid I can't comment.'

'Is he conscious?'

'I'm sorry, I can't comment on that.'

'The rescue took less time than you anticipated. Is that because the conditions underground were better than you'd expected?'

Jack shook his head and gave a wry laugh. 'No, rather the reverse. It was very wet, getting worse, and I didn't feel that the patient could tolerate sitting out flood waters, so we moved as fast as we could.'

'What about getting him through the sump? Let me explain for the benefit of viewers that a sump is like a U-bend in plumbing, permanently full of water, so that the only way through is to dive under the water. That must have been very tricky with a seriously injured patient.'

Jack gave a weary chuckle. 'Let's just say that the CRO have done that sort of thing before and it was all over very quickly! Now, if you'll excuse me, I could do with a bath and something to eat.'

The reporter signed off, and Kathleen stared at the screen as Jack's image was replaced by the film that had been running. She hadn't realised how tense she was until she heard that he was all right, but now she crumpled like a wet paper bag, laughing and crying and laughing again all at once, while Mick hugged her and passed her tissues.

He opened a bottle of wine he found in one of her kitchen cupboards, and they celebrated Jack's safety to the sound of Kathleen's tearful giggles.

'Are you OK now?' he asked after a while, and she nodded.

'Oh, yes. I was just so worried. . . I'm fine. You go on home. Thank you, Mick, you've been wonderful.'

He hugged her hard. 'You're welcome. I wish I had someone who cared as much about me.'

'Oh, Mick, there'll be someone. And if she's lucky, you'll love her, too.' She turned away, unable to talk any more, and felt Mick's warm hands pull her back against his chest.

'Oh, Kathleen, how could he not love you? Just give him time.'

She sniffed and pulled away. 'Mmm. Anyway, you'd better go, it's late. Will you be all right driving after that wine?'

He shook his head. 'Not really. I'll walk home and pick the car up in the morning.' He dropped a quick kiss on her cheek and let himself out, and she wandered round the flat, tidying up the bits and pieces and generally winding down.

Then, with nothing else left to do, she crawled into bed and slept fitfully, her mind filled with images of Jack's beloved, dirt-streaked face laughing into the camera.

She was woken at half-past five and listened for the sound that had disturbed her. A motorbike? Not Jack's. He would have rested up there for the night, of course, and would drive down in the morning. With a sigh, she snuggled down under the quilt again.

The bike was in his space when she got to work at eight. Stunned, she did a mild double take and almost ran into the department.

'Morning, Sister!' the nurses chorused.

She smiled vaguely at them and made her way to Jack's office. He was on the phone, and after glancing up briefly at her, he ignored her until he'd finished.

'You should be resting,' she told him then.

'I'm fine,' he said shortly.

'No, you're not, you're exhausted, and you aren't fit to work at the moment. Why don't you take the duty room and go and lie down for a couple of hours?'

He drew in a deep breath, paused for a second and let it out on a sigh. 'You're right. OK. But wake me at eleven, or sooner if you need me. Understand?'

He was cold and remote, shutting himself off from her completely. Pain, sharp and unexpected, swamped her.

'Yes, sir. I understand,' she said quietly.

She walked away, her head held high, and fought down the tears. Why do I care about you, you bastard? she thought miserably. God knows you don't deserve it! I don't know why I waste my time.

She took the report, went out into the department and threw herself into her work with tight-lipped determination.

Those who had seen her in this mood before faded quietly out of reach; others got their fingers burnt.

Amy Winship and Joe Reynolds, predictably, were among the others.

Amy failed to monitor someone's blood-pressure adequately and it was only because Kathleen bothered to check that a potentially life-threatening internal haemorrhage was detected in time.

As for Joe, who blithely missed a fracture a yard across, she could have pinned him to the wall with a scalpel, she was so cross.

'Take a sight test,' she advised tightly, and he flushed and apologised, which just made her more angry.

At quarter to eleven her old friend Jerry, the Valium addict, wandered in complaining of stomach pains and said he'd taken another overdose.

'Oh, Jerry, not today,' she groaned.

He peered at her owlishly, his eyes strangely sympathetic. 'No?'

'No—not unless it's for real.'

He nodded and walked away, and Kathleen closed her eyes.

'Jerry?'

He stopped.

'Come on, let's check you over anyway.'

She found a staff nurse to help her and they washed him out, finding nothing as she had expected, but she sent a sample of the stomach contents off for analysis anyway.

Then she took Jack in a cup of coffee.

He was lying on his back with the sheet round his waist, one arm flung up over his head, and she could see bruises all down the underside of his arm and down his ribs.

She set the coffee down on the little table and perched on the edge of the bed.

'Jack?'

He stirred and opened his eyes.

'Irish. . .what's the problem?'

'Nothing. It's eleven. I've brought you a cup of coffee.'

His eyes drifted shut. 'Thanks. Just leave it there, I'll get it in a second.'

His deep, even breathing told her he had fallen asleep again, so she slipped out of the room and left him to it.

Ben was in the staff-room. 'Jack OK?'

She nodded. 'I think so. He's covered in bruises all down his ribs—God alone knows what it was like down there. I've left him sleeping. What's afoot?'

'About twelve inches.'

She summoned a wry smile, and he relented. 'Nothing much. Joe's reducing a dislocated thumb if he can screw up the courage, and Amy's changing a dressing. I'm not sure I can bear to watch.'

She tutted. 'Amy's fine now. I've gone through her sterile trolley techniques until she can do them in her sleep, likewise all the other nurses.'

Ben snorted. 'She still manages to stick her fingers in the swabs with monotonous regularity, then she says 'Ooops!', grins and chucks them out and opens another pack.'

'At least she realises she's done it now.'

Ben rolled his eyes. 'That's better?'

The phone rang, and Kath picked it up. 'Sister Hennessy.'

It was ambulance control. They had been called out to a little boy who had been playing behind the family car when his father had reversed it out of the garage.

He had apparently sustained leg and head injuries, and was coming in, complete with hysterical parents.

'I gather they're in a hell of a state, so be prepared,' she was told.

She cradled the receiver. 'On your pins, Bradshaw, and you'd better get your wife down here.' She outlined the case briefly, and Ben winced.

'Aah! Don't know if Maggie can cope with that, she was a bit rough this morning. I'll see if Peter Travers or Andrew Barrett are around. We'll also need orthopaedics and neurology, and possibly a surgeon. Shall I wake the boss?'

Kathleen shook her head. 'No, let him sleep for now. We can always get him if we need him.'

They heard the siren and were at the entrance ready to take over as soon as the boy was carried out of the ambulance.

True to the controller's word, the parents were beside themselves, the mother sobbing and screaming accusations, the father grim-lipped and shaken, white as a sheet and obviously badly shocked.

She detailed Amy to take them into the interview room and give them tea and stay with them, and she and Ben went alongside the trolley into Resus.

The child, a boy of about two and a half, was unconscious and bleeding from a gash on his head. While Kathleen wired him up to a monitor and put in an intravenous line, Ben ran gentle fingers over the boy.

'Nasty head. Probably hit it when he fell. Abdomen seems OK. The right leg seems to be the worst—looks as if he was crouching and got knocked sideways by the bumper, then run over,' Ben said briskly. 'His foot's crushed, and the tib and fib are both broken. Heel too, I think. There's no degloving, anyway, thank goodness.'

Kathleen was just releasing the cuff. 'Normal—touch low, as you'd expect.'

Kath looked up and saw the paediatrician approaching. 'Morning, Andrew.'

'Morning. Oh, dear, poor little tyke. Where are the parents? I'd like some history.'

'Knocking hell out of each other in the interview-room, I think. I sent a junior nurse in there with them to referee, but I expect by now they've got her pinned to the wall,' Kath told him.

Andrew's brows twitched together. 'Who did it, then?'

'Father. Usual story—reversed out of the garage, didn't look behind, child playing on the drive.'

'Oh, God, why don't people learn from other people's mistakes?' the big man muttered, and bent over the child. 'May I?'

'Be my guest,' Ben said, and stood back out of the way while Andrew examined him gently but thoroughly.

'Seems fit enough—don't like the look of that head injury.' He traced the gash with a fingertip. 'Nasty bump—I think we need to look more closely at that. How are his pupils?'

'Still reacting, but a little uneven. I've ordered an EEG,' Kath told him, and he nodded.

'OK. Let's see what that turns up. I think we'll put him in special care when he comes out of Theatre.'

'Tim Mayhew's coming down to look at his foot. I gather Barrington's in Theatre already,' Ben added.

'Fine. Well, I'll go and see the parents. They're making enough noise to wake him up.'

Just then the noise increased dramatically, and was suddenly cut off again by a slamming door.

Amy appeared in tears.

'Problems?' Kathleen asked her.

'I tried to help,' she said, valiantly suppressing her tears. 'They didn't seem to want to know.'

'May I ask the thrust of the argument?' Andrew Barrett asked. 'It might save me from being shoved through the door like you.'

Amy ran a tearful eye over his not inconsiderable bulk and smiled damply. 'I'd like to see them try it!' She tipped back her head and took a deep breath. 'Mum says he should have looked first, Dad says if she'd been keeping an eye on him he would have been fine. Mum says he should have shut the door when he went back into the garage and he wouldn't have been followed. Dad says he did shut the door——'

'And Mum doesn't believe him. Typical. Don't worry, thanks for trying. I'll go and talk to them.'

'She also said if he'd gone like he said he was going to, this would never have happened and they would all have been a lot better off.'

Andrew made an O with his lips and nodded. 'Thanks.'

He left the room just as Jack appeared, his hair rumpled, his shirt half-tucked into his trousers, tie hanging round his neck. He glared at Kathleen.

'What the bloody hell's going on? It sounds like World War Three.'

'I should say that about sums it up,' she said drily, and turned her attention back to her patient, leaving explanations to the others. Hurt by his icy reception this morning, she was quite happy to avoid him.

She managed it until lunchtime, when he came into the staff room just as she was leaving.

'Any coffee left?'

'I expect so,' she said, and went to move past him. In doing so she jarred his arm, and he flinched slightly.

She gave him a narrow look. 'Are you all right? Do you want someone to look at you?'

'I'm fine, they're just bruises and the odd dent.'

'Did something go wrong?'

He laughed shortly. 'Let's just say I got in a tight spot.'

She looked away. 'I saw you on the television.'

He sighed. 'So did half the hospital, I gather.'

'I didn't expect you back until later.'

His mouth compressed into a hard line. 'No, I gathered that, too.'

She was puzzled. He had been so angry all day, but why? 'I don't understand. What do you mean? Am I supposed to have done something wrong?'

He let his breath out on a harsh sigh. 'Oh, come on, Kathleen, cut the crap. I saw O'Shea's car outside your flat this morning.'

She met his eyes, startled. 'It *was* you, at half-past five. I woke up, but I told myself it couldn't be you because you'd be in Yorkshire——'

'How convenient—was he there all weekend?'

She stared at him, stunned. 'You think—Jack, for God's sake! Mick's an old friend——'

'An old friend, or an old lover? Or don't you bother with the distinction?'

Anger took over from shock. 'Well, damn you, Jack

Lawrence, how dare you talk to me like that? He may not be as stinking, filthy rich as you, but he's worth ten of you any day of the week! At least he knows how to treat a woman!'

And with that she stalked off, head held high, and it was only later when she calmed down that she realised he still thought Mick had stayed the night.

'Well, tough,' she muttered. 'Let him think what he likes. Arrogant pig.'

Their contact after that was brief, professional and kept to the absolute minimum. It was impossible to avoid each other in such a hectic department, but fortunately the very business of it meant that any and every contact was necessarily fairly brisk.

And that suited Kathleen fine.

Her anger kept her going for the best part of two days, but then Mick bumped into her and asked how Jack was, and she told him, in words of one syllable.

'He thinks you stayed the night.'

Mick sighed. 'Damn, if only I hadn't had that wine and walked home—well, the man's a fool. Tell him that if there'd been any chemistry between us at all, I would have married you years ago and if he had any bloody sense he'd do it now—in fact, forget it, I'll tell him myself.'

Kathleen panicked. 'Don't you dare do any such thing, Mick O'Shea! You leave well alone, you've done enough damage. Anyway, it makes a useful armour.'

'Armour?' Mick was furious. 'Damn it, Kathleen, don't you go using me as a shield. If you want out of that relationship, you tell him. Don't hide behind me to do it.'

She sighed heavily. 'I don't want out of the relationship, Mick. It's just that sometimes—well, I don't even know if we have a relationship, and I don't want him thinking he can take me for granted.'

Mick shook his head slowly. 'You're trying to make him jealous? Forget it, he isn't that kind of man. If he can't have you all to himself, he won't want you at all. He's not a man who'll share his woman, and I don't blame him. I wouldn't be in a hurry to share you, either.'

'Huh. I don't frankly think he cares enough either way to worry. He was just annoyed because he came round and thought you were there.'

'At five-thirty in the morning? You're not telling me he'd ridden all the way from Yorkshire after the gruelling day he'd had, just to enjoy the pleasures of your delightful little body! Even Superman needs his sleep, Kathleen.'

She flushed and lifted her shoulders in a little shrug. 'God knows what he wanted. He isn't about to tell me now, anyway. Look, I'm going for lunch. You keep your nose out, you hear me? One word to him and I'll have you in a pot roast.'

Mick grinned. 'You and whose army?'

Kathleen shook her head and turned away, walking down the corridor towards the canteen. She didn't see Jack appear at the end of the corridor behind her, or see Mick lift his head and meet the level gaze.

Nor did she see Mick walk towards Jack, or see the expression in his eyes.

If she had, she would have turned straight round and come back, but she didn't, she kept on walking.

* * *

'I want a word with you, O'Shea,' Jack growled.

The man smiled lazily. 'Well, isn't that just a nice little coincidence?'

Jack opened his door and ushered Mick in with exaggerated courtesy. He wanted a cigarette. Damn it, his hands were shaking, but he had to know.

'I'm not sleeping with her,' O'Shea said quietly, 'nor have I ever done. There was a time I might have tried, back eight years or so, but there was never any chemistry. If there had've been, we'd be married now, because I love her, but not like that—not the way you love her.'

Jack's head snapped up. 'I don't love her.'

Mick's smile was slow and gentle. 'So why do you care that I was with her that night?'

Jack turned away and pulled a cigarette from his pocket, fumbling with his lighter. Damn the man, what was he saying? Was he with her or not?

'Were you?' His voice sounded like handfuls of gravel were stuck in his throat.

'I had been, earlier. I saw the news and went round to keep her company while she waited.' He paused, unsure how much to say. 'Oh, what the devil,' he said softly. 'She was in a hell of a state, Jack. She was so scared for you, and when she saw that you were OK, she just fell apart. I talked to her, we had some wine, and I walked home.'

Jack dropped into his chair and let out his breath on a ragged sigh. 'Oh, God. I thought—I knew she'd be worried, I didn't want to ring. For some reason I thought it would be better just to go to her so she could see I was all right.'

He paused, struggling for words. 'I know she loves

me—at least, I thought she did, and then I saw your car. . . She said you were worth ten of me.'

He forced himself to meet Mick's eyes.

'I can't give her what she wants from me, Mick. I wish to God I could. . .'

Mick laughed softly. 'She wants any damn thing you're prepared to give her, and that's a crying shame, because she deserves a hell of a lot more than that.'

Jack stood abruptly and turned to the window. Damn, why was everything out of focus?

'I know she does,' he said, and his voice was ragged. 'I thought if I stayed away from her. . .but I can't. I need her, but I can't love her——'

'You do love her.'

'No!' He shook his head, and repeated, softly, 'No. No, I mustn't. There's so much I can't give her—so much she deserves, so much she ought to have. I thought—perhaps if you two were—maybe she'd be OK with you.' He ran a hand through his hair, unable to deal with the sudden wave of emotion the conversation had brought with it. He took a steadying breath and turned back to face Mick, ticking off points on his fingers.

'Look, I'm divorced. She's Catholic. She'll be under pressure to get married, and there's no way I'm going to get married again, ever. I can't give her children, and she'd be a wonderful mother.'

'She doesn't want children, Jack.'

'She says.'

Mick sighed. 'She's a grown woman, I think she knows what she's talking about.'

'Maybe.' The phone rang quietly, and he picked it

up. 'Lawrence. OK, I'll be down.' He cradled the receiver. 'Sorry, I have to go. Look, Mick. . .'

Mick held out his hand. 'Forget it.'

Jack grasped the hand and shook it firmly. 'Thank you for being there for her.'

'Don't thank me, just get round there and talk to the woman.'

He made a non-committal noise, and Mick grinned.

'In your own time, of course.'

Jack returned the grin wryly. 'Of course.'

'Why do people always ring the doorbell when I'm in the bath?' Kathleen grumbled, and climbed out of the tub, grabbed a towel and ran down the hall. 'I'm coming, hang on—Jack!'

Flustered, she clutched the towel closer and gazed wide-eyed round the edge of the door.

'May I come in?'

'I was in the bath—give me a minute.' She shut the door in his face, too hurt and confused to allow him in until she was safely dressed.

She tugged on her jeans over damp legs, cursing and falling over on to the bed, struggling with the clinging fabric until she had them hitched finally over her hips. Then she grabbed a sweatshirt and tugged it over her damp hair, not bothering with a bra.

Refusing to allow herself the indulgence of looking in the mirror and repairing her make-up, she walked slowly back down the hall and opened the door again with trembling hands.

He was slouched against the wall, his helmet under one arm, and he shrugged slowly upright, his face impassive.

'May I come in now?'

'That depends what you want.'

'To talk to you.'

She turned away. 'Is there anything to say?'

He followed her in. She heard the door shut softly behind him, then the dull thunk of his helmet on the hall floor.

'Mick came to see me.'

She whirled round, her eyes flashing. 'Damn him! I'll kill him. I told him——'

'Irish, please let me talk.'

She looked up at him, and for the first time she saw emotion in his eyes.

'Sit down,' she said shakily, and took the chair. That way she could watch him, read his face, find out perhaps what he really meant. . .

He lowered himself on to the sofa and unzipped the top of his leather suit. She noticed his fingers were trembling, and her anger faded, replaced instead by a wild and optimistic hope.

'I was coming to see you,' he began, and his voice was low. 'I knew you'd have seen the news, and I wanted you to know I was OK. I knew you wouldn't be expecting me, but I really—I needed to see you, too,' he confessed, 'just to be sure I was still alive.'

She knew he was talking about the rescue now. So many times she had helped at the scene of an accident and felt the same need to be with people afterwards, just to be sure, as he said, that she was still alive.

'Was it really grim? You looked exhausted.'

He nodded. 'It was hell down there. There's a water-course that runs along the bottom of the passage, and you have to make your way along above this slit with

water pouring through it. Usually it isn't too bad, but
on Sunday the water was lapping at our ankles, and if
you slipped you could feel the current tugging at you.
If he hadn't been so badly injured we wouldn't have
even attempted a rescue until later, but he was in a
bad way, so we had no choice.'

'How bad was he?'

Jack shrugged. 'How bad can you get? Depressed
skull fracture, uneven pupils, ragged reflexes—and
more fractures than I care to think about. God knows
how he was still alive. The water was rising all the
time, and we had to seal him inside a waterproof bag
and drag him through the sump.' He paused, his eyes
firmly fixed on his hands.

'He got stuck—the stretcher caught on a rock. I was
with him, holding the drip inside the bag, and I had to
wrench him free and get out before we ran out of air.
That was grim. Then one of the team slipped in the
passage and went under the water. We were all roped
together, so we got him out, but it was a close thing.
He could easily have got a foot stuck and he would
have drowned. That was when I realised how much
you mattered to me.'

He looked up and met her startled eyes. 'I think I
love you, Irish,' he said softly, and his voice was gritty
with emotion. 'It doesn't change anything. I'll never
get married again, so don't hang around waiting for it,
and don't expect to have me at your beck and call,
because that isn't how I am. But I do want to see you
when I am around, and be with you.'

'When you haven't got anything better to do, you
mean?' she said sadly.

'No, Kathleen.' He stood up and began to pace, like

a restless lion. 'That isn't what I mean at all. I can't let you take over my life. I have to be independent. I can't allow myself to rely on anyone, and I can't cope with anyone relying on me. That has to be fundamental to our relationship, but it doesn't mean I don't care.'

Their eyes locked, and slowly she rose to her feet. God help her, she was doing something very foolish, but she couldn't walk away.

She held out her hand, and after a second he took it. Wordlessly, she led him to her bedroom and turned towards him, reaching for the long zip on his leather suit.

'Kathleen——'

She placed a finger on his lips. 'Don't talk. Just let me love you.'

She dragged the zip all the way down and eased the top over his shoulders, leaving his arms trapped behind him while she ran her hands lovingly over his chest. He was wearing a T-shirt, and she slid her hands beneath it and threaded her fingers through the soft curls on his chest.

She felt the groan against her palm, and smiled impishly, raking her nails slowly over his ribs.

His body shuddered, and then his tolerance disintegrated and he wrenched his arms free and wrapped them round her, holding her hard against him.

'Don't tease me, Irish,' he whispered, and his voice was a ragged thread.

She eased away from him and unzipped his boots, tugging them off before sliding the leathers down over his long legs. His T-shirt followed, and his briefs, then she pushed him towards the bed and stripped off her jeans and sweatshirt.

'Aren't you lying down yet?' she chided gently.

He reached for her, and then they were falling to the bed in a tangle of limbs and caresses and fevered kisses.

Their loving was wild and tempestuous, with no time to spare for tenderness or softly spoken promises. He was demanding, but so was she, both of them raging out of control, riding the wild storm that flung them helpless before it, clinging to each other as the only certain thing in a world gone mad.

Then he stiffened, harsh shudders racking his body, his head flung back as if in agony.

'I love you!' he gritted, over and over, the words torn from him, and Kathleen felt the world splinter all around her.

'Oh, Jack, I love you, too,' she whispered, and his arms tightened round her, holding her hard against his heaving chest, and she turned her face into his shoulder and wept.

CHAPTER EIGHT

THEY lay in the half-dark, lit only by the street lamps that shone through her open curtains, their legs tangled together, fingers linked on top of the quilt.

Kathleen was curled on her side watching him as he drew deeply on his cigarette.

'You ought to give that up,' she chided gently.

He grinned. 'Confucius he say the three best things in life are a drink before and a cigarette after.'

She giggled. 'I bet he never said such rubbish.'

'He should have done, then.' He stubbed it out and turned towards her. 'I got rough again; I'm sorry.'

Her lips curved slightly. 'Don't apologise, it was wonderful.'

He looked away quickly. 'Irish, don't look at me like that.'

'Like what?'

'With those great big eyes with love written in them in letters ten feet high.'

She pulled away, hurt. 'You can't make love to me like that and then expect me to carry on as if nothing's happened. I'm not one of your sophisticated women, Jack. You know I love you. I can't hide it and I won't. I'm sorry if it makes you uncomfortable.'

He rolled on to his back, one arm behind his head, staring rigidly at the ceiling.

'There's so much I can't give you. Marriage, children— so much you ought to have. Every time you look at me like that it just reminds me that I'm cheating you, short-changing you. I wish I could be what you want, but I can't. I'm sorry.'

'But, Jack, you are what I want——'

'No—no, I'm not, and I never will be.'

In the dim orange glow from the street lights, she saw a solitary tear trickle down his cheek and run into his hair.

'Jack?'

He turned to her blindly, his lips searching for hers and then clinging as their bodies met and meshed, their movements gentle now, their loving a balm to ease the sadness in their hearts. And when it was over and their tears had dried, they lay like spoons, curved together as if made for each other, and slept.

Kathleen had told Jack she couldn't hide her love. Over the next few days she was to find out just how true that was.

'Eh-up, Cupid's been at it again,' Ben Bradshaw said in a lousy Yorkshire accent.

'Well, Sister Hennessy, at last you fall victim to the mystery virus,' Jesus Marumba murmured with a wicked twinkle.

Only Mick said nothing, preferring for the good of his health to keep out of her way.

Of course, it wasn't made any easier by the fact that Jack was attracting a great deal of interest, anyway.

Andrew Barrett, the paediatrician, came down to the department on the Thursday morning to deal with an admission, and grinned at Jack. 'So, how's the big TV star today, eh?'

'Oh, for God's sake,' Jack said with an embarrassed laugh.

'Leave him be, Andrew, he makes a lousy hero. Coffee?'

'Thanks.' He settled into a chair with a big sigh and took a sip, then blinked. 'Gosh, this is better.'

Kath rolled her eyes. 'Not you too! How's the boy who was run over?'

He grinned. 'Driving us nuts. His foot's still elevated, so he can't fidget about, and that's tough on a little boy. No after-effects from that nasty bump on the head, though, and the parents have finally stopped fighting and started pulling together.'

'Oh, well, they say every cloud has a silver lining. How's the little chap on the railings?'

'Jeremy? He's fine. Going home tomorrow. He had a narrow squeak, that one.'

'Any permanent damage?' Jack asked.

'Don't think so. Possible slight nerve damage to the right arm—the brachial plexus was a bit chewed up, but he's been remarkably lucky. Bit concussed, of course, following the whiplash. He must have stopped falling pretty abruptly. Otherwise he was fine. Broken humerus and clavicle, again on the right. He'll need a bit of physio to sort that out when the cast comes off, but the chest drain was out after a couple of days, and his lung's working well.'

'Lucky.'

Andrew snorted. 'I'll say. That's another parent with problems, of course. The mother's on a bit of a guilt trip.'

'Of course,' Kathleen agreed. 'I don't know how these women cope. It would drive me crazy.'

Andrew smiled. 'Oh, I don't know. I love kids. Well, obviously, or I wouldn't be a paediatrician, but I'd be quite happy to have dozens.'

'How many have you got?' Jack asked.

'Of mine? None that I'm aware of,' he said with a grin. 'I'm not married. Never found anyone mug enough to have me. How about you? How many have you got?'

'Me?' Jack looked away, and then looked back. 'None—now. I lost my son three years ago to cystic fibrosis.'

Andrew's compassionate brown eyes registered shock, and then regret. 'Ah, hell, I'm sorry, I had no idea—forgive me for asking.'

Jack waved his hand. 'Forget it. Not talking about it doesn't make it go away.'

'Nevertheless, I trampled on a nerve. I apologise.' Andrew set his cup down and unravelled his long legs. 'Back to the grind. Thanks for the coffee, Kathleen.'

Kathleen watched him go. 'He's a nice man. Very quiet, but super with the kids. They all love him. It's a shame he's not married, he'd be a wonderful father.'

'What about you?' Jack said softly. 'You'd be a wonderful mother, but you aren't married either.'

'Well, for the first, as far as I'm concerned they don't go without the second, and for the second, I don't believe I'm about to be asked.'

She met his eyes steadily, and after a moment he turned away with a sigh.

'No—I'm sorry, Irish.'

She walked away, her heart heavy. Nothing had changed, except she could now admit to her love. The only difference was that they now spent some of their free time together, thus giving her even more opportunities to fall more and more deeply in love with him.

And she did, of course, despite all warnings to herself. He was away that weekend hang-glinding, and asked her to go with him. She refused, because as she said she had no urge to sit on a draughty hillside and watch him break his miserable neck.

In the event it was too windy to fly on the Sunday so he came back early and they spent the day in his garden preparing an area of lawn for seeding.

It was almost, she thought heavily, like being married, except that they weren't and never would be. His absence the previous day had brought that home as nothing else had. In a vain attempt to maintain her independence, she spent Monday and Tuesday nights at home—alone. It didn't work.

On Wednesday he came and found her just as she was finishing off applying a back-slab to a fractured wrist. After the patient had gone, he hitched one hip up on the couch and watched her clear up.

'Time on your hands?'

He smiled. 'Not really, I was just enjoying the view. I've missed you. Actually, I wanted to ask if anyone had said anything about HIV testing after our messy suicide.'

'Nothing to me, and I'm sure I would have heard. Ben certainly isn't worried, and I know I'm not, and Amy took herself out of range pretty swiftly.'

He chuckled. 'Wise, under the circumstances. Are you done? There's a woman waiting with a query fractured toe.'

He slid off the couch, wincing as he put weight on his foot.

'Is your ankle playing up again?' she asked sharply.

'Yes—and don't say a word!'

'Who, me? Would I? Where's this fracture, then?'

The woman had, indeed, broken her big toe. The fracture was clearly visible on the X-ray, and even Joe Reynolds could have seen it.

'My daughter told me she'd spilt nail varnish on my new bedroom carpet.'

'You shouldn't have kicked her so hard,' Jack said with a grin.

She laughed. 'Wretched child. I fell up the stairs running in my socks to clear it up. I'd just come in from the garden and kicked my wellies off when it happened.'

'How did you get here?' Kathleen asked her.

'My husband came home from work. Do you know what he said? Not "Poor thing, I'll be right home," but "Did you have your shoes on?" Self-righteous pig!'

Her husband laughed. 'Well, you never have shoes on. I've always said you'd hurt yourself one day. Perhaps now you'll listen to me.'

'You see?' she said, and rolled her eyes. 'Virtue personified.'

'Well, he can atone for his sins by waiting on you for a few days,' Jack said laughingly. 'I'm afraid it's going to be a bit sore, but as it's such an impressive break we'll put a garter strapping on to help immobilise it. Come back in a fortnight and we'll check its progress, but you'll find it takes a few weeks to really heal properly because we use that toe a great deal for balance.'

He left Kathleen to strap the toes together with a gauze swab between them to maintain the alignment, and then sent them off with a few coproxamol for the pain.

'Only eight?' Jack asked as they went.

'Think of my pharmacy budget,' she told him.

'The reality of medicine,' he said drily.

Their next patient, however, demonstrated the unreality of medicine. He was fitting, very convincingly, on the floor of the waiting area when she went back, and Joe Reynolds was hovering over him.

'Oh, not again!' Kathleen groaned.

'What?'

'Leave him to get on with it. He's a faker.'

Jack watched him for a moment, impressed, then winked at her and strolled off, whistling.

Joe was less convinced. 'Are you sure?' he asked anxiously.

'As the sun will rise in the east. Name's Harry Parker, a.k.a. John Hendy, Simon Smith and Peter Blake. He's an old friend. OK, Harry, up you get before you hurt yourself.'

The man hesitated, then clamped his teeth in a rictus and twitched off again.

'Harry! You're making a mess on my floor. Now get up, stop showing off and go home, please!'

The convulsions subsided and he seemed to go into a coma. Joe still looked worried. 'Sister, don't you think we ought to do an EEG? He's not responding to pain stimulus.'

She nodded. 'He's good. It's no good pinching his ear, you have to do something more dramatic, like kick him in the crutch.'

Harry curled up tighter and groaned, then opened his eyes. 'Where am I?'

Kathleen gave a humourless little laugh. 'Harry, we're busy. We don't have time to play games. Now get up, sit over there and you can have a cup of tea before you go home.'

He shambled to his feet and glared at her balefully.

'It worked last time. I got a bed for the night.'

'Are you back on the street?' she asked, immediately concerned.

'They threw me out of the hostel. I missed a night— well, I felt claustrophobic. Think I'll go back to London, more hospitals there. Got more chance of fooling them.'

She laughed. 'Why don't you try RADA? You've got a great acting career ahead of you if you could only learn a few more tricks.'

Joe looked slightly shocked. After settling Harry down with a cup of tea, she led Joe into her office and sat him down.

'Why would he want to do that?' he asked, clearly puzzled.

'Attention, a bed for the night as he said, something to do—he's a bright guy, but he lacks intellectual challenge. Fooling us gives him a buzz.'

'Well, he certainly had me fooled.'

She resisted the urge to say that wasn't difficult, and sent the poor boy off for lunch.

She went into Jack's office to find him on the phone.

He winked and waved her to a chair, then turned his attention back to the caller. After few moments he hung up.

'Humph.'

'What, humph?'

'Friend—chap at the Beeb. Wants us to do a part-recorded, part-live "Day in the Life of Accident and Emergency" thing.'

'What? Why us?'

Jack shrugged. 'Old Pals Act. He saw me on the television the other weekend. They had a hospital all lined up, and they've had to cancel because of staffing problems. I said I'd discuss it with you.'

'Oh, God—when?' Kath was totally bemused.

'Friday week.'

'Fri—oh, no. Not a Friday night! Are you nuts? All the drunks and the brawlers and the RTAs—are you crazy, Jack?'

'I haven't said yes yet.'

'Yet.'

'Yet.'

'Well, don't bother. They'll cause havoc.'

He leant back in his chair and grinned. 'Might be rather fun. They're very good, you know. They've done this sort of programme before, quite often. They won't get in the way.'

'No, well, they'd better not. I'm not having anyone underfoot. They get between me and my patients, at any time, for so much as a nanosecond, and they're out, I don't care what it does to their scheduling.'

Jack grinned. 'I'll pass all that on, shall I?'

'You do that!'

'I suppose you *are* on duty?'

'You bet your sweet life I'm on duty. No way half the BBC is coming into my department without my supervision!'

'I'll ring him back and say yes, then.'

She straightened. 'I never said that.'

That wicked smile played around his lips. 'No?

Quote, "No way half the BBC is coming into my department without my supervision," unquote.'

'Damn you, you're a manipulator, do you know that?'

He chuckled and picked up the phone. 'Better book yourself a haircut, Irish—oh, and have it dyed red to go with the temper. They're more likely to take you seriously then.'

She picked up a Biro off his desk and levelled it at him. 'They'll take me seriously, just you watch them!' She laid the pen down. 'I'll go and check the rota. Joe Reynolds and Amy Winship might just find themselves with a long weekend!'

She left the room to the sound of his deep chuckle.

The programme dominated the next week and half, to the exclusion of almost everything else including common sense. They had endless meetings with the producer and the reporters who would be covering the day, and Kathleen laid the law down with such charm and skill they almost didn't notice.

But, as Jack had said, they were professionals, used to working alongside other professionals without impeding their progress, and familiar with the intricacies of confidentiality and patient etiquette.

'No filming anyone who doesn't want to be filmed, and any flicker of sensationalism and you'll be out,' she told them on Thursday night, her smile for once absent.

They nodded agreement. 'We don't need to sensationalise,' the producer told her wryly. 'Usually we have to back off and tone down, because although the public have an insatiable appetite for gore, the camera crews get a bit queasy.'

She chuckled. 'Is that a fact? Well, Friday nights round here there's plenty to make you feel like that!'

Their meeting finished, the last details all sewn up, the crew headed for the door.

As they were leaving the producer paused and smiled at her. 'Don't worry, Sister Hennessy. We won't get in your way. The crew know what they're doing.'

She returned his smile slowly. 'Fine—just so long as they understand that I mean what I say.'

Jack looped an arm round her shoulders and tugged her up against his side. 'Don't worry, Bob, I'll lock her in her office if she becomes a nuisance.'

She laughed and punched him none too gently in the side. 'Nuisance yourself,' she scolded. 'You behave or *you'll* be locked up. Too much exposure to the camera already, that's your trouble. Think you're a celebrity or something.'

'Quite right, too.' He turned his head. 'Which is my best side, Bob?'

'The one without the black eye,' Kathleen said drily, and the team wandered off, still chuckling.

'Early start tomorrow,' Jack said. 'I'd better go back to my place—my suit's there.'

'Suit?' Kathleen did a mild double take. 'Did you say suit?'

He shrugged. 'Thought I ought to present the right image——'

'Oh, my God. . .' She rolled her eyes. 'Will we know you?'

He refused to rise to the bait, instead giving her a quick kiss on the lips and heading for his car. 'I'll see you in the morning—bright and early.'

She grinned. 'You bet—I have to get this place kicked into shape by eight.'

She ironed her dress carefully when she got home, and in the morning she climbed blearily out of bed at six to wash and dry her hair. Still she was in the department before seven to find the camera crew busy setting up unobtrusive lights in strategic places, and the cleaning staff putting the finishing touches to the floor.

She was accosted by a make-up girl who fluffed about with powder and asked her about eye make-up.

'I don't wear a great deal for work,' she explained, 'and I have no intention of going on air looking like a tart, so forget it.'

'Perhaps a little subtle shading?' she suggested diplomatically, and Kathleen surrendered.

'OK, but be quick, I've got a lot to do.'

'How's that?' the girl asked, but then the phone rang and there was no time to worry because they were swinging into action with the RTA, two victims of a car smash who came on a blue light with sirens wailing.

Kathleen and Jack ran to meet the ambulance, Kathleen taking over the bagging of one of the victims who had arrested in the ambulance.

They rushed him through to Resus, and got him going again, and while Kathleen put the monitor leads on Jack checked him for injuries and ordered X-rays.

It was only some time later when he was safely on his way to Theatre that they realised the whole lot had been filmed.

'Excellent,' Bob said enthusiastically, 'brilliant start to the day.'

Kath blinked. 'I wonder if our patient would agree

with you,' she said drily. 'I hope someone's at home videoing it for him.'

'Roll up, roll up for the Greatest Show on Earth,' Jack cried expansively, waving his arms around.

Kath flicked her eyes over his soft cotton shirt and cord jeans. 'What happened to the suit?'

He wrinkled his nose. 'I thought better of it. Not me, is it, really?'

She laughed and shook her head. 'Not really, but you might do up your top button and shove your tie up a bit—my mother's watching this.'

He rolled his eyes. 'Mine, too. I shall have such a lot to answer for.'

The day performed beautifully for them, right through to the evening, and then things started to go wrong.

They lost a patient, a young woman in her twenties who had thrown herself out of a car at speed to get away from her husband. It was messy and tragic and Kathleen wanted to cry for her, but the cameras kept rolling and she shrugged it off and carried on.

Later she caught up with Bob, the producer. 'That young woman—was that on live, or can we cut it?'

'No, it wasn't live—why do you want to cut it?'

'I just do,' she said stubbornly, and he agreed.

'OK. It's your department.'

'Thank you.'

She walked away, confident that the whole messy incident would be forgotten, but she was wrong.

True, they didn't show the filming of their frantic attempts to resuscitate the desperately injured girl, but they did show Kathleen emerging from Resus., tears in her eyes, telling the cameraman to get out of her way, and then they showed a brief interview with Jack where they discussed the case in scant outline, and also her reaction to the death.

'We tend to think we can do anything,' he said wryly, 'but we can't. We can only resuscitate, we can't resurrect. And yes, it hurts. You get mad, sometimes you cry, then you pick up the pieces and get on, because there's always someone else who needs you.'

She went and found Bob.

'You told me you were going to cut that.'

'We did.'

'No, you didn't. OK, you didn't show the gore, but you didn't cut it right out, either.'

He tried to reason with her. 'Kathleen, it was important——'

'What, to see me cry?'

'Yes.'

She glared at him, then sagged. 'I'm sorry. You're probably right. It won't do the public any harm to think we care about them, but I'm not used to being watched.'

'You're doing fine,' he assured her, and with a curt nod she went back to her work.

Amy Winship, severely threatened, was on duty and came to find her. 'Sister, that guy who threw up on you is here—says he wants to see you.'

'Oh, hell—where is he?'

'Cubicle Two.'

'Come with me,' she sighed, and twitched the curtain aside. A cameraman appeared at her shoulder. 'Not this one,' she said firmly, and he grinned and walked away.

She turned back to the man slumped in a chair in

the cubicle. 'Right, Jerry, what the hell are you up to, tonight of all nights?'

He gulped and shook his head slightly. 'Nobody will listen. It's just too much. Always, the craving—please, Sister. You've got to listen to me. I can't go on.'

'Have you taken anything?'

He shook his head.

'Look, Jerry, we're rushed off our feet. Come and see me on Monday, and we'll get you an appointment with a psychiatrist, OK?'

'It's too long.'

'Well, it'll just have to be. Now come on, we need this room.'

She watched him shuffle away, her heart troubled. Had she done the right thing?

'He looks really sad,' Amy said. 'As if, this time, it really is too much.'

Kath nodded. 'Watch him, Amy. Follow him, if you have to. I don't think he'll go far. Just keep an eye on him, talk to him if you want. But whatever you do, don't give him so much as a cough sweet!'

She went on to the next cubicle, a simple fractured thumb that even Joe Reynolds had managed to diagnose and set without too much trouble.

She passed Jack in the corridor and he winked at her. 'How're you doing?'

'OK. I had a go at Bob.'

Jack grinned. 'He told me. Listen, I want to grab some supper. Coming up?'

'What, and leave Amy and Joe without either of us riding shotgun?'

He chuckled. 'They'll survive.'

'Yes, but will their patients? Anyway, Amy's out

watching Jerry to make sure he doesn't do anything daft.'

'Jerry?'

'Carrots in the frilly—remember?'

The grin widened. 'Oh, *that* Jerry.'

'The very same. I just have a bad feeling about him.'

'Look, I'll go and get a couple of sandwiches and bring them back down. If you've got a minute you could fill up the coffee machine again, and I'll have a word with Jerry when I get back down.'

'OK.'

Just as she was turned away Ben called her. 'Got a kiddy with a nasty scald—can you give me a hand? We need some pethidine, I think, or even diamorph.'

She ducked into the cubicle, hardly conscious of the cameraman tucked into the corner. The child, a girl of about five, was whimpering softly, the skin of her legs and bottom already peeling.

The mother was distracted almost out of her mind. 'She must have decided to run herself a bath—I can't believe it. The water really isn't that hot, usually, but my other one was fiddling with the boiler earlier—he must have turned up the thermostat. Oh, God, will she be all right? I put her in cold water till the ambulance came, but I didn't know what else to do!'

Kathleen squeezed her hands quickly. 'That was fine. We'll get rid of the pain with some drugs, and then transfer her to the burns unit at Cambridge. She'll be OK. Don't worry.'

Ben glanced up from the child. 'Flamazine, Kathleen, I think, and paraffin gauze to protect her skin, then I think we need to get her moving. We'll give her diamorph, and we need saline to boost her fluids.'

He asked the mother the child's weight, worked out the dose and Kathleen went to draw up the drug and get the Flamazine ointment. Jack went past Resus and hailed her, and she popped out into the corridor. 'Can you check this with me?'

'Sure. I've got your sandwich. Everything OK?'

'Uh-huh. Just stick it on my desk, I'll have it later. Oh, could you ring Cambridge? Child for the burns unit — Ben's got the details, Cubicle Four.'

'OK.'

She double-locked the drugs cupboard and went back to Ben. 'Here we go.'

Very soon the child was calmer and they were able to cover the damaged skin and prepare her for transfer.

Sue, one of the reporters, followed them to the door and then turned to Kathleen. 'So, what will happen to her now?'

'Now? They'll clean her up, get lots of fluids into her because the main danger is dehydration, and then she may need skin grafts to repair some of the areas. Depends on the depth of the burns. Until a specialist has seen her, I wouldn't like to comment. Excuse me, I think I'm needed.'

Amy was hovering out of camera range, looking decidedly worried.

'What is it?' Kath asked her quietly.

'Jerry — he went into the men's a few minutes ago and he hasn't come out.'

'Oh, lord — I'll get Jack to check. Well done.'

She found him in her office eating sandwiches and downing the last of his coffee.

'Would you like to go to the loo?'

He blinked. 'Pardon?'

'Jerry. Just go and check on him. He's up by the entrance and I can hardly go in there, can I?'

Jack sighed and swung his legs off the desk. 'Eat your sandwich while you've got ten seconds. I'll be right back.'

She picked up the sandwich and took a bite, and then heard Jack's yell.

She ran up the corridor to the gents' loos and barged open the door. 'Jack?'

'In here—he's slashed his wrists. Get me some rubber straps, fast.'

'Here.' She tugged two strips of rubber tube out of her pocket. 'Never leave home without one,' she said with a grim laugh, and helped him drag the unconscious man on to the floor. 'Oh, help, there's blood everywhere—we need to get him in Resus. quick. Hang on.'

She stuck her head round the door and spotted a porter. 'Alvin? Get a trolley in here, quick. Amy, come and help.'

She saw a cameraman hovering, and glared at him. 'There's no room—unless you can fly?'

They hauled Jerry on to the trolley and ran down the corridor to Resus., the cameraman in hot pursuit. Sue was talking as they went, describing the scene, and Kathleen realised they were on air live again.

Still, there was no time to worry. They sat him up, hauled off his jacket and shoved up his sleeves, reapplying the tourniquets as quickly as possible.

'Get a line in, Kathleen. We need two units of Haemacel PDQ—Amy, jump.'

'PDQ?' she asked, clearly puzzled.

'Pretty damn quick,' Kathleen and Jack said in unison, and exchanged a grin.

'Oh—right.' Amy disappeared, and Jack shook his head.

Seconds later she was back, the Haemacel in one hand, a small white container in the other. 'I found this on the floor—I wondered if it might have fallen out of his pocket.'

Jack took it from her and turned it over in his hand. 'Ibuprofen. It's empty.'

'Would they do him any harm?'

'A hundred? Oh, yes—massive gastric bleed. Oh, damn. OK, Kathleen, let's pump him out.'

They connected up the drip, set it running and turned him on to his side. Amy, by now familiar with the routine, fetched a bucket and a sterile lavage tube from CSSD, and Kathleen ripped open the packet, lubricated it and passed it down his throat with ruthless efficiency.

'Coffee gounds—damn, he's bleeding. OK, we'll flush him and put him on forced diuresis. He'll need a catheter. We'd better get Marumba down here.'

While Jack and Kathleen dealt with the patient, Amy rang the switchboard and asked them to pass the message on to Dr Marumba.

Minutes later he turned up, briskly efficient, and ran his eye over the patient and the charts.

'Pressure's very low. We'd better have him in ITU I think.'

Jack nodded, his head bent over the worst of the wrists, suturing the ugly slash. 'I'm only doing the blood vessels; the tendons need a surgeon if he gets that far.'

'OK, we'll just dress it. What about the other one?'

'Just a dressing, I think. Perhaps butterfly sutures. This was the really clever one—probably the first. I don't suppose he had the strength in this hand to do the other very well.' He sat up and stretched, then stripped off his gloves. 'OK, take him away, that's all we can do.'

'Do we have notes on him?'

Kathleen rolled her eyes and slapped a dressing on his wrist. 'Half a rain forest,' she said drily. 'He's an old, old friend. Just take him away while you still can. I'll contact ITU and get a porter. Coffee?'

'No, I haven't got time. Later, perhaps.'

She phoned ITU, and then told Jesus that they were ready for his patient. 'Alvin, could you take Jerry down to ITU?'

Then she turned back to the reporter. 'Gory enough for you?'

Sue grinned weakly. 'Well done. I don't know how you cope.'

Kathleen gave a hollow laugh. 'Nor do I sometimes. I'll just have a mosey round front-of-house and see what's going on,' she told Jack.

He nodded. 'Try to find time for your sandwich, too.'

'Will do. See you in a minute.' She turned to Amy, who was clearing up the dressing trolley. 'Well spotted, Amy. If you hadn't found the bottle, he could well have died.'

She coloured, and her jaw sagged slightly before she recovered. 'Thank you, Sister,' she mumbled, and turned away, grinning like an idiot.

Oh, well, I've made somebody's day,' she said to herself as she walked briskly through the department, running her eye over the smooth operation of the unit.

Technically speaking, of course, she was off duty now and one of the night sisters had responsibility for the unit, but there was no way she was handing over until the camera crew went home.

Jack was on call anyway and had more reason to be there than her, but if anything that was an added incentive to stay.

There was a brawl going on in the entrance, and two policemen were clamping handcuffs on a couple of young men who were causing the trouble. A third, clutching a filthy rag to his face, was threatening them with all manner of retribution.

'You'd better watch your mouth, mate, or we'll have you, too,' one of the policemen advised him.

Kathleen felt a prickle between her shoulderblades and knew the camera was approaching. So, too, did the two boys in handcuffs, who immediately started swearing violently and accusing the police of unnecessary brutality.

Kath shook her head. 'Get them out, Stan, we don't need them in here. You, come with me. It's your turn to be a star.'

She towed the grumbling adolescent down the corridor and into a treatment cubicle. 'Right, sit down. Name?' She took his details, cleaned his face up and put a few butterfly plasters over the cut. 'It'll heal cleanly, so you won't have a scar to ruin your beauty. It was a nice, sharp blade evidently.'

'Glass—bastard bottled me.'

'You want to press charges?'

'Wot? 'E's me bruvver.'

'Charming family,' she muttered, and sent him on his way.

She turned to the camera and grinned. 'The things people do for entertainment round here on a Friday night!'

The cameraman winked at her, and she shook her head laughingly and went back out to Reception. There was no time for her sandwich, so she worked her way steadily through the next three cases.

She was just finishing with the last when there was a shout from Reception.

She ran round there and found a woman collapsed on the floor, blood oozing from a cut on her arm and another on her thigh. Her face was bruised and battered, one eye swelling rapidly, and she was mouthing, 'Help me, please help me,' over and over again.

Kathleen grabbed Amy and they lifted her on to a trolley and wheeled her into Resus.

The cameraman followed, but apart from telling him to keep her face out of shot Kathleen ignored him.

'Don't let him in here—keep him away from me,' the woman whimpered.

'Don't worry, pet, you're OK. We'll look after you. He won't get you here. What's your name?'

'Tracey—Tracey Ford. He isn't my husband. I live with him. There's the kids, too—I want them got away from him. I wouldn't have left them, but I thought he was going to kill me.'

'Go and find Ben or Jack, could you, Amy? And if the police are anywhere about, get one of them in here, too. Otherwise call them.'

She had the woman stripped and covered with a

blanket in moments, and bit her lip to contain her anger.

'How long's this been going on?' she asked gently as she cleaned up a nasty cut on the woman's arm.

Her face screwed up in a mixture of pain and self-disgust. 'Years,' she confessed. 'Years and years. He always promises, and then he's fine till next time—ow!'

'Sorry.'

Just then there was a crash and a roar from reception, and Tracey seemed to shrink with fear. 'That's him—oh,God, no, please!'

'Where is she, the whore? I'll kill her this time, she's gone too far, telling everyone. Where are you, bitch? Lying cow, I'll find you. . .'

The door crashed back and Kath turned to see a huge man, dressed in a pair of filthy jeans and a tatty old string vest and carpet slippers, swaying in the doorway and brandishing a lethal-looking kitchen knife.

Tracey screamed, and he lurched forwards.

'Oh, no, you don't!' Kath vowed, and, snatching up a stitch-cutter, she held it in front of her. 'You lay a finger on her and I'll kill you myself. Put the knife down.'

'Bloody IRA trash—get out of my way!' he roared, and lunged at her.

CHAPTER NINE

JACK was in the staff-room watching the programme live with Bob when he heard the racket in Reception.

Seconds later, the television showed a drunken gorilla brandishing a knife at Kathleen—his Kath!

'Bastard, I'll kill him!' Jack muttered, and tore down the corridor to Resuscitation, sending a dressings trolley flying.

He could see Kathleen in front of the treatment table, clutching a stitch-cutter like a lifeline, and as the man lunged at her he threw himself forward and grappled with him, falling with him to the floor.

Despite his drunkenness the man was still immensely strong, and there was a nasty moment when Jack could feel him gathering his strength, but then suddenly there was a dull thud and he went limp.

'Jack?'

Her voice was tentative, shaken, and he got slowly to his feet, searching her face.

'Are you OK?' he asked.

'Of course—are you all right?'

'Of course? What do you mean, of course? Damn it, he nearly killed you!'

'Well, he won't do any more damage for a while. I've knocked him out.'

Jack closed his eyes and sagged against the wall.

'Do you have any idea what I felt like when I saw you facing up to him with that silly little blade in your hand? Do you have any *conception* of what it felt like to know I was about to lose you?'

'Do I——?' Kathleen put her hands on her hips and squared up to him. 'Well, Holy Mary, Mother of God, you've finally seen the light! Do *you* have any idea how I've felt, weekend after weekend, knowing you're crawling down muddy holes or chucking yourself off cliffs? Not to mention every day of the week when you climb on that evil machine and ride off into the sunset!'

'That's different——'

'How is it different? It doesn't feel any damn different from where I'm standing!'

'You aren't fit to be allowed out,' he growled.

'Yeah, well, you and me both, then.'

'I mean it! You need a keeper——'

'Huh,' she snorted. 'Over my dead body!'

'Yes, well, you nearly managed that just now!'

'I did not!'

'You did—look at you! For God's sake, woman, he could have killed you!'

'So what's it to you? I thought I was a free agent?' she spat at him.

'Damn that,' he growled. 'I'm going to marry you and lock you up out of harm's way.'

'Oh, are you, indeed?' Her eyes flashed sparks. 'And with whose permission?'

'Yours, dammit.'

'You haven't asked me yet.'

'Well, I'm asking you now,' he roared. 'Marry me!'

'OK.'

'What?'

'But there are certain conditions.'

'Conditions?' His eyes narrowed. 'What conditions?'

Kathleen was enjoying his downfall, he could see that. She lifted her hand and ticked off on her fingers. 'One: you stop pot-holing. Two: you stop hang-gliding. Three: you sell the bike. Four: you give up smoking.'

He gave a short laugh. 'Anything else?'

'That'll do for now.'

'And what do I get in return?'

She grinned impishly. 'Me, in your bed every night.'

A slow smile spread over his face. 'Done.'

'You're a pushover, do you know that?' Her face crumpled slightly. 'Could I have a hug, please?'

He stepped over the recumbent body on the floor and swept her up into his arms, crushing her against his chest as his lips came down hard on hers.

Then, slightly bemused, he lifted his head and stared round at the cheering crowd that had gathered in the doorway. 'Oh, God,' he groaned, and rested his head against hers. 'I think I just proposed to you in front of most of Great Britain.'

She giggled. 'Good. You won't be able to wriggle out of it, then. Too many witnesses.'

'But you may want to.'

'No way.'

He kissed her again, lightly this time, conscious of the crowd and the cold dread that was touching him. There was something he had to do, and he didn't know if he could find the courage. 'We'll talk later.'

He straightened away from her and turned his attention to the man on the floor. 'I hope he's not been brain-damaged by that blow.'

On the treatment couch, Tracey snorted. 'If he is, they'll never tell the difference. Are you two really OK?'

Kathleen laughed and hugged her gently. 'Never better. I've been trying to pin him down for weeks.'

Jack grunted, conscious only of the icy fear that gripped him.

Suddenly the room seemed too crowded, and he stood up and glared at them all. 'Haven't any of you got any work to do?' he snapped. The crowd faded, and he turned his attention back to the unconscious man at his feet.

It took four of them to lift him on to a trolley and take him away for observation, with the police riding shotgun at his side, and then things gradually returned to normal—or as normal as they could given the extraordinary circumstances.

Kathleen was called to the phone and discovered her mother crying and laughing all at once, with all the family, it seemed, lined up behind her waiting to talk.

'I'll speak to you later. Of course I'm all right. All in a day's work. No, Mum, you can't talk to Jack, he's busy. I'll speak to Patrick tomorrow—no, Mum, I can't. Goodbye.'

She put the phone down and looked up at Jack.

'Busy, am I?' he said quizzically.

'Mmm—kissing me.'

'Uh-uh.' He backed off, the dread clutching him again. 'I'm through kissing you in public. Let's put this film crew to bed and then go home.'

She grinned. 'Sounds good to me.'

His heart wrenched.

It was some time before they were able to leave the hospital, and they went straight to Jack's barn. Despite the lateness of the hour, the phone was ringing when they got in.

'Ah—hi, Mum,' Jack said, and rolled his eyes at Kath. She smiled and went and put the kettle on, and listened as he wriggled like a worm on a hook. Finally she went and took the phone out of his hand.

'Mrs Lawrence? It's Kathleen. Don't worry, I won't let him get away. I'll be sure and get him to call you tomorrow. Goodnight.'

She grinned at him. 'See? Easy.'

He passed her the phone. 'So ring your mother.'

'No way! I'm avoiding her. Why do you think I'm here?'

'You're here,' he said softly, 'because we have to talk.' He set the phone down with exaggerated care. 'Nothing's changed, Irish.'

'Yes, it has,' she answered just as softly. 'We've both realised what we mean to each other. When I saw you struggling there on the floor with that evil man, I realised there was nothing I wouldn't do for you, or you for me. That's when I realised that I couldn't go on with this free agent nonsense. I need you, Jack, just as you need me. Without you, I'm empty.'

'Oh, Irish. . .'

He held out his arms and she flew into them, wrapping her arms tight round him and hugging him hard.

'Take me to bed, Jack.'

He fought it for a second, then gave in. 'My pleasure,' he murmured, and, lifting her easily into his arms, he carried her up the stairs and lowered her into the middle of the huge old bed.

He undressed her slowly, his eyes travelling over her skin as he revealed it, making it flush.

'You're so lovely,' he said huskily, and her throat had a great lump in it suddenly that threatened to choke her.

She reached for him, and he stripped off his clothes and lay beside her, taking her tenderly in his arms.

Suddenly he started to shake, his whole body trembling in reaction.

'I thought I was going to lose you,' he grated. 'I thought that bastard was going to run you through with that knife and take you away from me——' His voice broke and he dragged her closer, burying his face in her hair. 'Don't ever do anything like that again—promise me.'

'I promise. I just didn't think. He was going to kill her, and I was just—there, I suppose. Jack?'

'Mmm?'

'Make love to me, please?'

His hand reached up and brushed the hair back from her face, and then he was kissing her, his lips warm and gentle. She felt as if he was paying homage to their love, his every caress a thanksgiving, and for once the wildness left them alone so their loving was a thing of tenderness and healing, of joy and celebration.

Afterwards he held her gently and smoothed the tears from her cheeks, heedless of his own.

His sigh was heavy, though, and she felt it all the way through to her bones.

'What's wrong, darling?' she asked him softly, her hand over his heart.

'Oh, Kath, there's so much I can't give you. You deserve more,' he said heavily. 'Much, much more. Things haven't really changed, you know. I still can't give you children—well, only if we use IVF and they screen the embryos—always assuming my vasectomy could be reversed.'

She shook her head. 'I couldn't do that, Jack. I think *in vitro* fertilisation is wonderful for childless couples, but I could never consider that option for us. Perhaps I'm more of a Catholic than I thought, but the idea of all those discarded embryos—it makes me feel cold inside.'

His fingers threaded through hers and curled over his heart. 'But it's the only way I'd consider. Even if you don't carry the gene, one of our children or grandchildren or great-grandchildren might meet someone who did and repeat the tragedy of Johnnie all over again. I can't allow that to happen. Watching my son die was the hardest thing I've ever had to do. I couldn't do that to anyone else, however indirectly. And I'm too old to adopt, or foster. That means you'd be denying yourself the beauty and privilege of being a parent.' He swallowed hard. 'I can't do that to you, darling.'

She lifted herself up on one elbow and looked down at his, at his face drawn with sorrow and the love that would sacrifice itself for her selfishness—and so needlessly. 'Listen to me, please. I don't *want* to be a parent. The prospect of that responsibility terrifies me, and I know I wouldn't be content to sit at home all day with a baby. I'd go nuts. That's why I've never married. Everyone I've ever been serious about has wanted marriage *and* children, ultimately. I never wanted that before.'

'Before?'

She looked away, but he turned her face back with his hand.

'If we were able to, would you want my children?'

She met his eyes for a long while, then nodded. 'Yes—but because they would be yours, not because they were children. Because I know how much it hurts you not to have children.'

'But I have had a child, and although he's gone, that love, that joy will stay with me forever. And because I've known that love, I can't deny you the opportunity.'

'But I don't want the opportunity, Jack, can't you see that? I would only be doing it for you!'

He met her eyes steadily. 'There's always AID.'

'Artifical insemination by donor?' She gave a short laugh. 'No, thank you. I certainly don't want anybody else's child. Anyway, it's not as if my life is free of children. I'm an aunt nine—nearly ten times over, and we have an endless stream of children through the department. Any frustrated mothering instinct has plenty of scope there.'

'Kathleen, I——'

'Please, Jack. Your love is all I could ever need.'

He searched her face for endless moments, then his eyes filled. 'I give up. Damn it, I don't know why I'm trying to talk you out of it. God knows you're the only thing in my life to have any meaning since Johnnie died. That's why I crawl down holes and chuck myself off cliffs and ride the bike—it's been the only way I could feel alive, but since I met you I've come alive in other ways, ways I'd forgotten long ago. You've taught me to care again, and you've taught me that I matter, that my life is worth something. For a long while I thought it didn't matter if I lived or died, but you've changed all that. I don't have to run any more.'

He sighed and tugged her closer. 'Come here and hold me.'

She snuggled against his side. 'I mean it, Jack,' she said after a moment. 'You're all I need. Perhaps it's greedy to want everything. If I had to choose between having children and having you, it would have to be you. Nothing else could ever matter more.'

'I'm older than you,' he said quietly. 'You could be widowed young, and with no children or grandchildren to fill those lonely years.'

'I could fall under a bus.'

His arms tightened convulsively. 'Don't.'

'You know, with all these tragedies lining up in wait for us, we really shouldn't waste time.'

'Huh? Kath, what—oh, wow. . .'

She giggled. 'What was that again?'

He groaned and laughed. 'Damn it, woman, get up here.'

'Like this?'

He gasped and reached up to her, pulling her down against his chest, and then with a swift movement he turned her beneath him.

'Ooo, fancy stuff!' she teased.

'Be quiet and concentrate.'

'Yes, sir!'

Then there was no more banter, just a ragged silence, broken by sighs and whispers and breathless cries, until at last they lay still again, replete.

After a few minutes Jack groped for the bedside table.

'What are you doing?'

'Getting a cigarette.'

'Oh, no. Put them down.'

'Aw, Kath, come on——'

'No! No, no, no. No! Put them down. Now!'

He sighed heavily and dropped his arm back on the bed. 'You're a cruel woman.'

'Rubbish. Just looking after you.'

'But Confucius he say——'

'Never mind Confucius! I have other plans for you!'

Her hand slid down his ribs, and his eyes widened. 'I'll be exhausted!'

She grinned. 'Mm. Too tired to hold a cigarette.'

He flung his arms wide. 'I'm yours—take me!'

She knelt up beside him and looked down at his body, a satisfied smile on her face. 'You are, too.' Her smile faded, and she levelled her finger at him. 'If I so much as catch you *smiling* at another woman——'

He tugged her down into his arms. 'Don't be silly. If I'm too tired to hold a cigarette I won't be very likely to stray.'

'Hmm. That's true.'

He chuckled. 'Better start now, I've got amazing stamina.'

'The arrogance of the man. Prove it.'

Laughter danced in his eyes. 'My pleasure.'

Hours later he reached for the bedside table again.

'What are you doing?' Kath mumbled drowsily.

'Turning out the light.'

'No cigarette?'

'Uh-uh. I couldn't hold it. You're a wicked, wanton, resourceful woman, Irish.'

She giggled sleepily. 'See? Told you it would work.'

But he was already asleep.

Josie Metcalfe lives in Cornwall now with her long-suffering husband, four children and two horses, but when she was an Army brat frequently on the move books became the only friends who came with her wherever she went. Now that she writes them herself she is making new friends, and hates saying goodbye at the end of a book – but there are always more characters in her head clamouring for attention until she can't wait to tell their stories.

Other titles by Josie Metcalfe:

LOUD AND CLEAR

by

Josie Metcalfe

CHAPTER ONE

'No!'

She sat up in the darkness, the bedclothes tangled around her waist and legs. Her pulse was racing and her breathing was wildly erratic.

'Not again!' she moaned, pressing her hands against her temples as if she could remove with brute force the visions which filled her head.

She had fought so hard to stop this happening and for nearly two years she had believed that she had conquered it.

Now this!

She shivered as the sweat cooled on her skin, her cotton nightdress clammy against her breasts and over the discouraged slump of her spine.

As her pulse began to slow, the vivid details of the nightmare gradually faded until all she was left with was an after-image of torment.

To herself, she'd often compared it to the image she could see after she'd looked at something too bright, almost as if it were seared on the retina of the eye— only in her case it was burned into her mind.

Someone out there had managed to break through the shield that she had erected between herself and the rest of the world. Someone had made a mental connection, letting her experience their tearing anguish at first hand.

Who was it? Whose pain had she—?

No! She didn't want to know. That part of her life was over.

She shivered again as she glanced across at the numbers on her alarm. Still an hour before she needed to get up for work but there was no point in trying to go back to sleep now. She closed her eyes and shook her head despondently as the misery overtook her once more and her shoulders drooped.

She couldn't bear it if it all started again. This time it had been stronger than ever. Please God, it would be someone just passing through the area, she thought. Perhaps when they went back to wherever they came from they would take their dreadful suffering away with them.

The alternative was too awful to consider. She had spent too long and worked too hard to overcome it last time to contemplate having everything destroyed again.

Her lingering fear was like a small dark cloud in the corner of her mind when she arrived at the hospital.

'Hello, Em,' Charge Nurse Dave Maddox called. 'I hope you had a good rest yesterday because it looks like it's going to be bedlam here. It's a fine, sunny, bank-holiday weekend and the traffic on the motorway is already building up nicely. It won't be long before some lunatic causes mayhem just to keep us on our toes.'

'Thanks!' Emma pulled a face at him and he grinned in reply before continuing through the department towards the ringing phone.

Emma made for the staffroom to leave her jacket

and handbag, knowing that she'd arrived in plenty of time to change into her uniform.

A quick trip to the bathroom, to check that her rebellious hair was all tucked neatly under her cap, showed her a disturbing glimpse of her reflection and she leant towards the mirror, frowning at the dark circles showing through the pale skin under her silvery grey eyes. If it hadn't been for her thick dark eyelashes she would have been in danger of looking like a panda.

She smoothed a hand over the curl which had escaped, and subdued it with an extra pin, added to the armoury already holding the confining twist of hair, before she finally turned to leave the room.

'Have you spoken to anyone in the last couple of days?' Dave demanded when she rejoined him in the office.

'I went shopping yesterday morning—' she began.

'No,' he interrupted. 'From here, I mean. Have you heard about the new appointment? A three-month exchange with Tony Phillips. Lucky beggar's ended up in a big city hospital in America. Seattle, I think.'

'Someone new here? In Accident and Emergency?'

'Yes,' Dave confirmed gleefully, his hazel eyes full of his customary humour. 'The Professor brought him round himself, yesterday afternoon.' He'd used the nickname of one of the consultants. 'Had all the staff in a flap.'

'You're not kidding,' a second voice chimed in, and a slim arm looped over Emma's shoulder as Diane West joined them. She licked her lips lasciviously. 'You wait till you see him. He's absolutely drop-dead gorgeous. All mean, moody and magnificent.' She giggled as Dave went pale and then red, his expression pained, almost as if he was trying to stop her from talking.

'What's the matter, Dave?' Emma teased. 'You're not jealous that you've finally got some competition in the department, are you? Perhaps you're afraid we'll all fall madly in love with him on sight—?'

'I certainly hope not,' a deep, accented voice said somewhere in the region of her left ear, and Emma spun on her heel, to meet a pair of cold black eyes framed by the stark planes and hollows of the most sculpturally perfect face that she had ever seen on a man.

He's so tall, she thought, and blinked dazedly, her brain short-circuiting as she looked up at him.

He stood framed in the office doorway, so she could tell that he was at least eight inches taller than her own five and a half feet, with a whipcord leanness belied by the breadth of his shoulders. But it was his face that drew her eyes back—the golden olive tone of his skin, framed by jet-black hair lying flat against the contours of his skull and highlighted by the stark perfection of his fresh white coat.

'Staff Nurse—' his dark eyes pierced her '—are you just here for a social visit or have you actually come to work? There is a room full of patients out there, waiting for attention.' He took one step back into the corridor and disappeared from view as silently as he'd appeared.

'Wow,' Diane mouthed, and mimed a swoon.

'Our new colleague?' With feigned calm, Emma glanced down at the fob-watch pinned to the front of her neat blue uniform and confirmed that she was still nearly fifteen minutes early for her shift. She was grateful for the years of practice which had helped her to hide her fierce response to him. He'd been there for less than a minute, but his presence had been so forceful that it almost seemed to linger in the room after he'd left.

'Yup!' Diane confirmed in an imitation American accent. 'That's our Dr Wolf.'

'Oh, please, Di, it might suit him down to the ground but that's too corny for words! You'll have to think of another nickname.' Emma tucked a couple of pens into her top pocket with hands still shaking from the sudden surge of adrenalin, and turned to follow his uncannily silent footsteps out towards the reception area.

'Honestly, Em, that's his real name.' Diane's tone stopped her in her tracks. 'His name really is Adam Wolf.'

Emma paused long enough to laugh with delight. 'I'd heard that certain pressure groups in America were pushing for compulsory product labelling and warning notices on dangerous substances, but I hadn't realised they'd taken the idea quite so far!'

She was still chuckling at intervals as, with her usual good-natured calm, she coped with the usual early-morning rush of patients from the nearby town and its surrounding housing estates.

By half past nine she had already organised to send a child with a large, discoloured, egg-shaped lump on his head up for a precautionary X-ray, after his mother had described his spectacular discovery that he could climb out of his high chair. She'd also dealt with three assorted ankle injuries and a fractured toe, and irrigated an eye full of sawdust for an over-enthusiastic amateur carpenter.

Her next patient was a very shaky elderly woman who'd fallen while shopping, and she was just wheeling her towards a vacant cubicle to attend to her various scrapes and bruises when there was a cry for help behind her.

'Nurse! Somebody. . .!' The young woman who'd been sitting patiently with a fidgety baby on her lap was clutching the child frantically in her arms and racing towards the reception desk. 'My baby can't breathe. . .!'

Emma was the first one to reach her and plucked the struggling, red-faced youngster out of her arms and whirled into the emergency room, flinging questions over her shoulder as she went.

'Why did you bring him to the hospital? Was he having difficulty breathing?' To Emma's concern the child's face was taking on a blue tinge, the cyanosis showing her how severely his airway must be obstructed.

'No! It wasn't him. . . He was OK.' The poor mother's replies were almost incoherent. 'I only came here to bring my friend in because she had a fall. . . Oh, help him! Please do something. . .'

Her frantic words faded into the background as Emma concentrated fiercely on the child in her arms, her fingers flying to check his mouth for a small toy or any other obvious obstruction.

She was desperately conscious of his racing pulse and the terror in his eyes as she forced herself to focus, even managing to block out her awareness of the tall man who had just entered the room.

Suddenly she *knew* what was the matter and swiftly turned the child over so that he straddled her arm, with his head lower than his trunk. Quickly sitting down on the nearest chair, she supported his jaw and chest with her hand and rested the weight of her forearm along her thigh.

Four times she brought the heel of her other hand down smartly between his shoulderblades, then she rolled him face up on her lap to deliver four chest thrusts.

Before she could open his mouth to look for a small foreign body in his throat, he coughed violently and a small white button landed several feet away on the floor, to the accompaniment of an indignant wail.

'Good enough,' a deep voice murmured in a transatlantic accent, and Emma's concentration was broken. She'd known that he was there ready to help, but she'd also known, somehow, that he would allow her to do what was necessary without interference.

'Thank you. Oh, thank you.' The child's mother swooped to wrap the sobbing youngster in her arms, tears pouring down her own white face as she cuddled him against her shoulder.

'He should be fine now.' Emma stroked his silky curls and patted his little shoulder. 'If you take him through to the reception area I'll send one of the nurses to fetch you a drink while you catch your breath.'

She directed her out of the door and turned to retrieve the offending button, only to find it displayed on one lean male palm.

'How did you know what was wrong?' His voice was gentle but his dark eyes were piercing, probing.

'I...' Emma found her gaze hopelessly snared and her thoughts stumbled frantically. 'I saw the damp place on the mother's blouse where the baby had been chewing. . .the place where the button was missing. . .'

She tore her eyes away, suddenly afraid that somehow he *knew* that she wasn't telling the truth. It was totally impossible, but those eyes seemed so mesmerising. . .as if he could see into her head, as if he could read her thoughts.

'Staff?' a voice called from the corridor.

'Coming,' Emma replied, with a silent sigh of relief, and threw him a brief smile as she pushed her way through the doors to speak to one of the junior nurses. She gave a quick shudder as the door closed behind her, grateful to escape his presence. He was far too. . . too knowing. . .

'We've got a mum out here with a toddler who might have taken her grandmother's diuretic pills,' the young woman reported as she matched her swift pace to Emma's. 'She found her little girl surrounded by them but doesn't know how many she might have eaten.'

'Has she brought the bottle with her?' Emma thrust the enveloping feeling of uneasiness behind her as she concentrated on the next problem.

'Yes, Staff.'

'Well, phone through to the poison unit in London and they'll tell you what the best course of action is. Then come and let me know what they say.'

She knew that he had come to stand behind her, although he hadn't touched her, hadn't even made a sound. It was almost as though she was sensitive to him in some way, as if he was surrounded by some sort of energy field. . .

'We have similar poison-control centres in the States—about a hundred and twenty of them.' His deep voice sent a shiver down her spine and she turned slowly to face him.

'What part of America do you come from?' Emma found herself asking, not certain what had prompted the question. All she knew was that she couldn't bear to stand near him in silence.

Silence was dangerous.

When she allowed silence to fall it was harder to keep control. . .

'North-west,' he supplied, his dark eyes unwavering on her face.

'S-Seattle, wasn't it?' she stammered, desperate to keep the conversation going until she could find some way to escape.

He nodded. 'That's where I was working. Look, is there anywhere I can get a cup of *real* coffee?'

'Unlikely.' Emma chuckled briefly at the disgusted expression which crossed his face, and glanced down at the time. 'Look, I'm due for a coffee-break any minute now. I could make you a fresh cup of decent instant. . .'

She stopped speaking and bit her tongue, horrified to hear what she'd said. Where had the words come from? She didn't want to spend any more time with this man than she had to. He frightened her in ways she didn't understand.

'Contradiction in terms,' he said, with a scowl, breaking into her scurrying thoughts. 'There's no such thing as *decent* instant coffee but, if it's the only alternative to the grey dishwater I tried in the canteen this morning, lead on.'

As if he knew that she was looking for an excuse to get away from him and was deliberately foiling it, he turned to gesture politely for her to precede him along the corridor.

It was as he turned his head and the lights above struck blue gleams from his intensely black hair that, for the first time, Emma realised the thick, straight strands weren't just slicked back but were long enough to be tied at the base of his skull with a narrow leather thong.

She was sure that she hadn't made a sound at the startling discovery, but he turned his head sharply towards her as though she'd spoken, one eyebrow raised in a challenging arch.

'Something wrong?'

'Er, no.' Emma dragged her eyes away hurriedly and concentrated on reaching the staffroom. She could still feel the residue of heat in her cheeks as she pushed the door open and made her way to the kitchenette in the corner.

'How do you like it?' she threw over her shoulder, all too conscious of his silent presence in the room behind her.

'Strong and black, please.'

'Sugar? Or are you sweet enough without—?' She could have bitten her tongue off when she heard herself voice the teasing phrase, and the heat of embarrassment raced into her cheeks. What on earth was she thinking of, to say such a thing to. . .?

His sudden laughter drew her head round sharply and she was startled by the appreciative gleam in his dark eyes, his teeth very white and even against the coppery tone of his skin.

'Sweet enough without.' He threw the words back at

her, his smile lingering to soften the planes and angles of his face for the first time.

'Sorry it's only instant.' Emma held out the hand-thrown pottery mug. 'At least it's one of the better brands, and it always seems to taste less like cardboard out of these mugs.' She turned to add a splash of milk to her own mug then leant back against the counter to take the first sip.

'Take the weight off your feet while you've got the chance,' he murmured as he lowered himself into an elderly leather-look armchair and stretched his long legs out in front of him to cross them at the ankles. He slid down in the seat until his head rested against the back, his elbows planted on each arm of the chair as he cradled the bottom of the mug on the buckle of his plaited leather belt.

Emma perched on the arm of the matching chair, unable to relax. There was something about this big, silent man that kept her on edge—something almost predatory that made her as wary as if she were the potential prey of the powerful creature whose name he bore.

She tried to fix her gaze on the speckled blue-grey glaze of her coffee-mug but was unable to help the way her eyes kept straying towards him.

Each time she dragged them back to concentrate anew on the swirls and dips on the curving pottery, but each time she lost the battle, and she found herself measuring the length and power of the legs stretching out towards her, their long muscles barely camouflaged by the neatly pressed black trousers; under the cover of a loose-weave white linen shirt the taut concavity of his waist widened out into a deep chest and broad shoulders, all framed by the casual fit of the white coat splayed open each side of him.

When her disobedient gaze finally reached the corded length of his deeply tanned neck and the elegant symmetry of his face, she found his dark eyes waiting for her.

'You disapprove?'

The words were spoken softly but she had no difficulty hearing them or understanding the challenge they contained—it was almost as if they were reaching her brain without her needing to hear them first.

'Disapprove?' she repeated, her voice just a little unsteady in spite of her efforts.

What was happening to her? Was it the after-effects of the nightmare making her feel so off balance in his presence, or was it a result of the concentration she'd had to use to help the little boy choking on the button?

'Of long hair on men,' he pursued calmly.

'No!' she denied instantly as she relived her initial appreciation of how his hair suited him, then she coloured as she realised what her vehemence could imply. 'I mean...in this hospital we have various members of staff, including a Sikh and a couple of Rastafarians, with different ethnic origins and hairstyles...' She knew that she was babbling but somehow couldn't halt the avalanche of words.

'Once upon a time it would probably have caused a problem with the hospital authorities but the various equal-rights groups...' Her earnest voice died away as she caught the glimpse of humour in his dark eyes, a stray gleam of gold where she had expected only blackness.

'So,' he drawled softly, 'we both obey the rules and

keep our hair tied out of the way at work.' One corner of his mouth lifted in a wry smile.

Emma found herself gazing at him as she tried to imagine what he would look like when he let his hair loose. Was it fine and silky or thick and coarse? It was unlikely that it would spring into riotous waves as her own did when she took out the pins, but would probably hang either side of the lean planes of his face in straight dark sheets like. . .

'Oh!' She gave a slight gasp as recognition swept over her.

'Yes.' He nodded, his eyes darkly watchful. 'I'm what used to be called a Red Indian. Now they call us native Americans or American Indians.'

'What do *you* call yourself?' Emma challenged quietly, sensing his ambivalence over the direction of the conversation.

'Blackfoot,' he said, his voice filled with innate pride.

'Do you—?'

Before she could complete the question the door swung open and one of the younger nurses stuck her head round.

'Staff? Sorry to disturb you but you said you wanted me to report back when I'd spoken to the poisons unit. . .'

'Ah, yes.' Emma forced herself to concentrate. 'What did they advise?'

'They said to tell the mother to keep an eye on her little girl, but unless she started passing water a lot or feeling drowsy she would probably be fine.'

'Have you told her?'

'Yes, Staff.' She smiled and her eyes flicked briefly towards the silent occupant of the other chair. 'She was very relieved. Said she didn't know whether to hug her little girl or tell her off for worrying her so much.'

The door swished shut behind her as she returned to her duties.

'You believe in starting as you mean to go on?' His deep voice drew her eyes back to him as she was trying to think of a graceful way to leave the room without appearing to run away.

'In what way?' She swirled the last, rapidly cooling mouthfuls of coffee in the bottom of the cup, keeping her eyes on the patterns it made so that she wasn't tempted to look for the fleeting expressions crossing his face.

'The new breed of nurses,' he clarified. 'Highly trained professionals in their own right, able to take charge of many situations without needing direction from doctors.'

'In some fields the nurses are now more highly qualified than the doctors they're officially working under,' Emma agreed. 'Are you finding the situation very different here from what you left in—?'

'Staff?' Another head appeared around the edge of the door. 'Sister said to tell you she'd had to send Helen home with a migraine.'

'OK,' Emma smiled at the messenger and sent her on her way as she stood up. 'Damn,' she muttered under her breath. 'Now we'll really be pushed tonight.'

'Problem?' Adam Wolf straightened up to his full height and relinquished his mug into her outstretched hand.

'Only the age-old problem of too much work and staff off sick. . .' Emma rinsed the mugs out and upended them on the draining-rack before she turned to leave the temporary haven of the staffroom.

A long arm reached over her shoulder to push the door open and held it for her to walk through.

Emma flicked a shy smile up at him, unconsciously turning slightly as she passed him, to make sure that she didn't brush against him.

Over the years the manoeuvre had become such an ingrained habit of hers that she hardly realised she was doing it. As a child she had found it was the only way she could prevent herself from being mentally swamped by the feelings she picked up from other people when they touched her.

Suddenly she was swept by an overwhelming feeling of cold anger, and she became conscious that the powerful body beside her had grown rigid with disapproval. Even the air around them seemed to have grown chilly.

'You're quite safe, you know. It's not catching,' he snapped curtly as he glared down from his superior height, his tone caustic.

'What isn't?' Emma lifted stunned eyes towards him in total bewilderment. She shook her head, her thoughts suddenly a chaotic jumble, as if her brain was filled with static.

'The colour of my skin.' His eyes pierced her like twin lasers, his expression cold and hard as he turned away from her to stride down the corridor.

'Wait,' Emma called, but either he didn't hear her or he ignored the plea in her voice. 'Dammit,' she cursed under her breath, and pressed her lips together as she glanced towards the rapidly filling reception area.

She didn't have time to try to catch him now, but as soon as she got the chance she would tell him that her reaction hadn't been one of aversion—at least, not aversion to him as a person. She would have to find the words to explain that she avoided contact with everyone, regardless of the colour of their skin. Surely she could find some way of telling him without having to reveal the reason why. . .?

Over the next few hours Emma made several attempts to speak to Adam Wolf, but every time she went to approach him he managed to disappear. It was some while before she realised that his evasiveness was deliberate—that he was avoiding being anywhere near her.

As she gathered her belongings up, ready to go home at the end of her shift, she felt tired and dispirited.

The day's work had been no worse than that of any other summer Friday in a hospital situated close to a major motorway, but she was weighed down by a deep sadness that her unconscious body language had killed the first tender shoots of the fragile friendship which had been springing up between herself and the solemn Adam Wolf.

She had a feeling that he was as solitary as she was, and she could hardly lie to herself about the strength of the attraction she'd felt for him in spite of her usual wariness.

Now he believed that Emma had been repulsed by his revelation of his Blackfoot heritage, when nothing could have been further from the truth. She had been attracted to him as a man from the first moment she had turned and seen him standing in the office door-way—more attracted than she'd allowed herself to be in several years, perhaps in her whole life, and it wasn't just a physical attraction.

For the first time she had met a man who called to her on more than one level, someone who had challenged the cold stillness she'd cultivated inside herself ever since she had parted company with Richard two years ago.

For the rest of the evening she fought a silent battle with herself, vacillating between leaving the situation with the all too fascinating Dr Wolf just as it was and making an effort to try to set the record straight.

'He's only here on a three-month exchange,' she muttered as she ploughed through the hated pile of ironing. 'There's no point in letting myself get involved with him. He'll be on his way back to Seattle by the time we get to know each other. . .' She pulled a face as her heart sank. 'That's if he ever lets me get close enough to explain why I didn't want him to touch me.'

She drew in a deep, unhappy breath as she replayed the searing memories of the last time she'd tried to explain the unexplainable.

'That's always supposing that it's worth making the effort,' she grumbled later as she finally slid her feet under the covers and settled herself into bed. 'If I get the chance to tell him why, there's no guarantee that he'll believe me, and if he does and reacts the same way as Richard did. . .'

Misery settled over her as she imagined the intrigued disbelief if the rest of her colleagues were to find out what had been going on under their noses ever since she'd joined the staff at St Lawrence's. It had grown so bad last time that she'd moved out of the area completely, lucky to land her present job so quickly.

Was it worth taking the chance that she might have to move on again. . .?

Her tangled thoughts didn't allow her to sleep well, so that she was already awake the next morning when she was overwhelmed by a terrible feeling of hopelessness.

For the second time in as many days her control was shattered by a stranger's torment.

At first she fought to block the avalanche of emotion but the effort was useless, leaving her weak and trembling, her arms wrapped around herself as if she were trying to stop herself from flying apart into a million jagged pieces.

Finally she bowed to the inevitable and stopped fighting, allowing her body to relax bonelessly as she closed her eyes and concentrated on her sensations. Perhaps, now, two years on, she would be able to cope with them better; perhaps this time she could find some way to control what was happening. . .

CHAPTER TWO

SOMEWHERE, someone was fighting demons. Somewhere, far too close for comfort, there was someone being torn apart by the pull of two opposing forces.

Emma felt her own body being taken over by the overspill of emotions, her pulse rate and breathing accelerating as they reacted to the enormous tension.

Desolation.

Emma was overwhelmed by the terrible feelings of loneliness and isolation that she was picking up from this unknown person. Someone had a choice to make, and it was tearing them apart.

She concentrated fiercely. It didn't matter how hard she tried, she had no mental image of the person whose thoughts were invading her life, and no clear understanding of the nature of the awful dilemma they were facing.

It was so frustrating.

In the past she had been able to decipher enough about the people with whom she made a mental connection to at least have the satisfaction of knowing when their problems had been resolved. This time both the person and the nature of their dichotomy were a complete mystery to her.

Suddenly, as if someone had thrown an electrical switch, the connection was broken and Emma was left feeling as if she'd been hit by a bus.

She lay still for several moments as her breathing

steadied and her heartbeat slowed, then released a long sigh of relief.

'Gone,' she breathed in disbelief as she searched the corners of her mind. 'Completely gone.' And she finally allowed herself to relax.

'Well,' she murmured as she rolled over to the edge of the bed and sat up, 'whoever you were and whatever your problem was, I hope that's the last I hear of you.' And she padded through to the bathroom for a reviving shower.

Emma had been on duty for a couple of hours when the emergency call came through.

'RTA. Four. One critical,' she called over her shoulder, knowing that the rest of the team would swing into action with practised efficiency.

She could hear the various sounds which told her that the trauma rooms were being readied while she held the phone link to the paramedic in the ambulance with one hand and jotted notes as fast as she could with the other.

'MVA?' a deep voice queried as she put the receiver down, the dark honey of its accent pouring over her.

There was no way she could delay the inevitable, much as she wished that they could have had some privacy for this meeting, but privacy was a luxury not readily available in such a busy department.

'A what?' She barely remembered what she was asking as she turned to look up at his midnight-dark eyes for the first time in twenty-four hours, and found his gaze chillingly expressionless.

'MVA—motor vehicle accident,' he elaborated.

'RTA—road traffic accident,' she parroted, a sick

emptiness opening up inside her. 'Different terminology, same emergency.' And they turned simultaneously as they heard the sirens arriving.

'Are radiology on stand-by?' He was all efficiency.

Emma nodded. 'And the lab's ready for typing and cross-matching blood,' she confirmed just as briskly as they made their way towards the first patient, who was being wheeled through the doors.

'Male. Twenty-nine years old,' the paramedic began reciting as soon as they arrived. 'Blood pressure one-ten over seventy, pulse one-oh-eight, respiration twenty-four. Head-on collision caused impact with steering wheel. Chest pain.' He relinquished the upraised bag of IV saline to the nurse who took his place beside the patient.

Within seconds Emma was supervising the removal of the man's clothing to allow a closer examination.

'Mr Taylor?' She spoke above the escalating noise in the department. 'Do you hurt anywhere else than in your chest?'

'Knee,' he gasped through the clear mask covering his nose and mouth. 'Hit my knee. . .'

'OK.' She covered his hand with her own gloved one in a spontaneous gesture of sympathy. 'We'll take a look at it as soon as we've got your clothes out of the way. Is there anything else?'

He tried to shake his head, obviously forgetting that he was in a collar and strapped to a back-board, and groaned. 'Everything hurts,' he said in a muffled voice, 'but nothing else in particular.'

'Ribs,' Adam Wolf confirmed as his long fingers probed carefully over the man's chest and abdomen. 'No suspicious sounds from his lungs, no apparent internal damage. Patella's a mess, but it doesn't look as if any of the long bones are involved. . .'

In minutes the team had prepared Mr Taylor for the X-rays required to rule out spinal injury and for the set to be taken of his chest and knee.

Theatre was warned that he was on his way just as the sound of the second ambulance filled the air.

As the doors opened Emma had her first glimpse of the paramedic fighting with the occupant of the trolley.

'Mel? Where's Mel?' A blood-soaked arm flailed about as the young man tried to push himself upright. 'What have you done with Mel?'

'Mr Price.' The paramedic narrowly avoided having his clipboard sent flying as he tried to calm his patient. 'John, calm down. She's coming in a minute, I promise.'

The handover between the ambulancemen and the A and E staff was chaotic, with voices growing louder and louder to make themselves heard as they tried to pass on essential information over the patient's progressively violent language.

'Mr Price.' Emma ducked under the IV line leading into the back of his hand and positioned herself out of range at his head. 'Please, Mr Price, listen to me.' She laid one hand across his forehead and managed to catch his free hand in the other.

He was a big man with very well-developed muscles, and she doubted that she would have been able to hold him if she hadn't caught his injured arm. As it was, she tightened her grip and concentrated, dismissing everything from her mind except the need to calm him down.

'Listen, John.' She leant forward cautiously, keeping

a firm grasp on his wrist and allowing her voice to drop almost to a whisper, as if she were going to tell him an important secret.

'Listen,' she repeated softly, the word a soft susurration in the bustle of the room.

As if by magic, everyone else in the room lowered their voices too, no one wanting to miss out on what she was going to say.

'Can you hear it, Mr Price?' Emma whispered right beside his ear, her eyes suddenly catching Adam Wolf's dark gaze concentrating on her as she bent over awkwardly at the top of the trolley.

'Hear what?' The hoarse voice of the patient broke into her preoccupation with the grudging gleam of approval that she had surprised in Adam's eyes at the other end of the trolley.

'The ambulance siren,' Emma murmured confidingly. 'It's just arriving with Mel. Listen.'

While the patient was preoccupied with listening to the rapid approach of the distinctive sound Emma gave a nod to the rest of the team. With Mr Price finally calmed down, they could get to work on preparing him for the stitching up of the deep gash running down his arm from elbow to wrist.

'Nurse?' Worried blue eyes looked up at her as she kept her calming hand on his head, his macho bluster vanquished by the genuine concern on his boyish face. 'Will you find out what they're doing to Mel? It's her legs. . . She was trapped and. . .and I think she's hurt them pretty bad. . .'

As Emma watched, a single tear trickled into the dusty blond hair at his temple, and she shifted her hand on his forehead just enough to smooth the betraying dampness away.

'Only if you promise to behave yourself,' she bargained teasingly, giving his shoulder a squeeze. 'If you don't do what this lot tell you, I'll go off for a coffee-break instead.' She glanced up from her position at his head and received a brief nod from Adam as he completed his examination.

'Staff Nurse—' He addressed her formally in a normal tone of voice and Emma knew from her brief glimpse of his expression that it was for their patient's benefit '—when you see Mel, you can tell her that Mr Price will have collected an interesting scar but that everything else appears to be in working order.'

'Certainly, Doctor. At once.' She smiled down at her patient and, ducking out from behind the drip stand, walked swiftly towards the trolley just entering the trauma unit.

The young woman was strapped to a back-board and the white gleam of the collar surrounding her neck seemed to leach every vestige of colour from her face; her eyes were tightly closed above the clear plastic of the mask over her nose and mouth.

'Mel Price. Twenty-four-year-old female. Shunt injury. Both knees, possibly both hips involved. Blood pressure ninety over seventy, pulse one-eleven, respiration eighteen.'

'Hello, Mel.' Emma took the slender wrist between her fingers and monitored the pulse as soon as the back-board she was strapped to had been transferred off the ambulance trolley.

'Where's John?' Deep blue eyes flicked open to fix

insistently on Emma's. 'Is. . .is he all r-right? Have you s-seen him?'

'Calm down.' Emma soothed the fingers clutching frantically at her arm. 'He's here and he's safe.' She chuckled. 'In fact the doctor told me to give you a message when you got here.'

'A m-message?' The young woman caught her breath and winced as she was positioned ready for X-ray.

'Yes. He said to tell you that apart from a rather interesting scar on his arm—which, knowing men, he'll probably boast about for the rest of his life—everything else is in perfect working order.'

Emma watched the frightened young woman relax as the message sank in, and gave her hand a reassuring squeeze before she returned to business.

'Mel? We need to get a picture of you to make sure you haven't damaged your hips. Can you tell me the date of your last period?'

'Why. . .why do you need to know that?'

'It's a precaution we have to take, just in case you're pregnant. X-raying your knees isn't a problem but we need to take a picture of this area.' Emma gently touched the badly bruised area at the side of one hip and slid her hand across to the other side. 'And if you're in the early stages of pregnancy it can harm the baby.'

'I don't. . .I'm not. . .'

'Staff.' Adam Wolf's voice rumbled in her ear. 'Her husband says she's not pregnant. She's on the Pill.'

His voice sent a strange shiver up her back, to raise the soft hairs on the nape of her neck, but that wasn't the reason why she suddenly stiffened.

When he'd spoken, her hand had still been resting on Mel's slender abdomen, and now her eyes flew to meet the obsidian darkness of the tall man standing just behind her shoulder.

'Is he sure?' she murmured distractedly as she tried to concentrate on what her sixth sense was telling her. 'She hasn't had a stomach bug or...or taken any antibiotics recently, has she?'

'What are you thinking?' His eyes had sharpened on her, their gaze so intense that she almost felt as if he was trying to see into her head.

'Just...just double-checking.' She dragged her eyes away and bent towards the pale figure of their patient. 'Mel? Are you sure there isn't any chance that you might be pregnant?'

'I...I don't know. I...I might be...' The words were a breathy whisper as her cheeks gained a slight tinge of pink. 'I had an abscess under a tooth and the dentist gave me some tablets...'

'Antibiotics?' Adam demanded gently.

'I think so...' Her forehead pleated as she tried to concentrate.

'Right.' He straightened up decisively. 'We'll warn X-ray to use a shield, just in case you are pregnant, and then we'll take it from there.'

Emma studiously avoided his gaze as she took care of her frightened patient, but she couldn't help being aware that he was watching her, the impact of his dark eyes almost as potent as a physical touch.

She didn't need extra-sensory perception to know that he was wondering about her.

'Dammit!' she muttered under her breath as she saw the last victim from the crash leave the department for further treatment elsewhere in the hospital. Why did there have to be two incidents so close together and both of them when he was near enough to watch what she was doing?

It wasn't the first time she'd railed against the circumstances—accident of birth, fate, whatever it was—that had doomed her to go through life sensitive to people in a way few others were.

Most of the time she could almost forget about it— at least, she had been able to for the last two years. It was just her bad luck that she seemed to have lost her control over it just when they'd acquired a very keen-eyed doctor in the department.

If she wasn't going to find herself in a very uncomfortable position, she would just have to keep her fingers crossed for the next few days that nothing else happened to draw Adam Wolf's attention to her. The alternative didn't bear thinking about.

In the meantime, she decided, with a determined tilt to her chin, as she followed him towards the staffroom for a much needed cup of coffee, she had some unfinished business to settle with Dr Adam Wolf!

'Is there any water left in the kettle?' She directed her question at his broad back as she crossed the freshly polished composite floor, her soft-soled shoes almost soundless as she negotiated the informal groups of chairs on her way towards him at the kitchenette in the corner.

The delicious aroma of coffee struck her before she was halfway there and she drew it in with a deep breath of appreciation.

'I don't know about water in the kettle, but there's

an extra cup here if you'd like it.' He turned around to show her the carafe of dark liquid in his hand.

'Where did that come from? Did someone in the hospital hierarchy have a brainstorm and take pity on us?'

'No such luck.' His dark eyes glanced briefly in her direction. 'I brought this in myself as I seem to be spending more time here than at home.'

'So that's *real* coffee, is it?' she challenged, deliberately reminding him of their previous conversation on the subject.

'The real McCoy.' He poured a steady stream of the rich dark brew into one of the pottery mugs, raising one eyebrow at her as he held up the bottle of milk.

Emma nodded and watched as he added a thin stream and stirred it around for a second.

'Here.' He held the mug out towards her in one tanned hand. 'I'll forgive you the sacrilege of putting milk in it on the grounds that you don't know any better.'

To Emma's relief, the harsh expression he'd worn in her presence had softened slightly and she reached out to take the mug from him.

Without thinking about it, she curved her fingers around the top rim of the mug to lift it out of his grasp without coming into contact with his fingers.

'For God's sake. . .!'

His violent exclamation made her jerk her hand, nearly dropping the scalding liquid down herself. Only her quick reactions allowed her to step aside to allow the stream of coffee to splatter harmlessly on the floor.

'Did you burn yourself?' In one lithe movement he

was crouching in front of her, lifting the hem of her uniform to check her legs.

'No. It missed me—no thanks to you!' Emma subdued a shudder which was caused as much by the proximity of the powerful man bending down in front of her as it was by shock at her near escape. 'Why on earth did you shout like that? No wonder I jumped.' Her voice was shaky but the words were full of self-righteous accusation as she stepped back from him.

'I didn't shout *at* you.' He straightened up to glare down at her from his full height.

'You did—'

'It was your reaction,' he continued inexorably, totally ignoring her attempt to contradict him. 'That's the second time you've made a song and dance about going anywhere near me. Have you any idea how insulting it is?'

Emma gasped and her cheeks reddened as she found her horrified gaze trapped by the Stygian darkness of his.

'It wasn't. . .I wasn't. . .' she stumbled. 'Oh, Lord. . .' She glanced helplessly from his eyes down to the dripping mug in her quivering hand and back up again. She had wanted a chance to explain what had happened last time, had deliberately followed him in here to engineer a conversation, and it seemed as if all she'd done was make matters worse.

'Give me that.' He reached out for the mug. 'You'd better sit down before you fall down.' One hand wrapped deliberately around the curve of the pottery so that the lean length of his fingers wrapped over the slenderness of her own, taking her completely by surprise.

It was the shock, she told herself as a bolt of lightning shot through her at the contact. She wasn't in control of herself and *that* was why she couldn't block him out.

Years of practice were the only thing that helped her to keep her expression bland as she was flooded by the overwhelming reality of touching Adam Wolf for the first time, that same control allowing her to release her hold on the mug and begin to draw her hand away.

What she really wanted to do was snatch it out of his grasp and cradle it against her with her other hand, as if it had been burnt by the contact.

All the control in the world couldn't prevent her soft sigh of relief as he took the mug away and set it down on the coffee-table. Gratefully, she sank into one corner of the couch and tucked her shaky legs out of the way.

'Why?'

The single word emerged in the room almost as an accusation, his eyes never leaving her as he sat himself in the chair facing her seat, their expression emphasising the fierce control on the lean planes of his face.

Emma sat mute, her brain seething with a chaotic mixture of thoughts and feelings, none of them coherent enough to voice.

'*Is* it my colour?' The words were spoken as calmly as if her answer were unimportant, but Emma knew it wasn't; in spite of her determined efforts to block him out, his tension was reaching her in waves, each one stronger than the last.

'No.' She looked straight at him, fixing her silvery grey eyes firmly on the darkness of his as she filled the word with conviction.

His scepticism reached her then and she hurried into speech in an attempt to convince him, knowing without his having to say a word that this was an old wound.

'Honestly.' She held her hands out in a placatory gesture, leaning towards him as if to lend weight to her words. 'It's nothing to do with your colour or. . .or the fact you have long hair—'

'Then what is it?' he demanded, his low voice rough to her ears. 'Why do you shy away from contact with me as if I'll contaminate you in some way? What is it about me that offends your delicate sensibilities?'

'Nothing,' Emma declared earnestly. 'It's not you. . .' She shook her head while she tried to find the words to explain without revealing the full extent of her problem.

'Is it men in general?' he suggested. 'Were you attacked and it's left you frightened of the rest of us? Or—' a sudden thought struck him and he blinked '—do you prefer women to men?'

'No,' she shook her head in violent repudiation. 'It's nothing like that.' Her teeth worried at her lower lip as she realised that, far from being straightened out, the situation was growing more complicated by the minute.

'It's everybody.' The words finally escaped her precarious control. 'It's not just you. . .I can't touch anybody. . .!'

The ensuing silence was profound as his face registered his shock at her outburst.

'But. . .that's ridiculous!' The dark slashes of his eyebrows were drawn into a fierce frown as he focused his mind on her incomprehensible words. 'You're a nurse, for God's sake; you're touching people all day long.'

'That's different,' Emma said flatly.

'How?' he demanded. 'How is it different?'

'I. . .I don't know. It just is. . .'

'Have you been for any help? Perhaps a psychiatrist might be able to. . .'

Emma felt the familiar wave of revulsion sweep over her as she remembered the first time she'd been *persuaded* to see a psychiatrist, willing to try anything for the man she'd loved.

Perhaps it had been sheer bad luck that the one she'd seen had treated her like some sort of freak. . . 'All in the name of scientific research, of course. . .' he'd said. 'It will make such an interesting paper when it's published in the *Lancet*. . .'

Whatever the rights and wrongs of it—and she had found out during her nursing training that it had been very wrong—she had sworn that it would never happen again.

'Yes—' her voice was hard '—I've seen a psychiatrist, and no, it didn't help.'

'I'm sorry,' he said gently, his expression thoughtful when she caught his eyes on her white knuckles.

'Don't be,' she dismissed, with a shaky attempt at airiness, deliberately unclenching her fingers and leaving them to lie in her lap in a pretence of relaxation. 'I've worked out my own survival strategy and most of the time it works—'

'Doctor. . .?'

Diane West's head appeared around the edge of the door to inform him that he was needed, and Emma could have hugged her.

She knew that it would be only a matter of time before Adam Wolf's agile brain started analysing the answers she'd given and realised how evasive she'd been. All she could hope was that his concentration on his work would push the details of their conversation out of his head so that he couldn't remember exactly what she'd said. . .

'Emma?'

As if she'd conjured him up, he stepped back into the room again, his dark eyes finding hers with worrying ease.

For a moment she was certain that he was going to take their conversation further, and her stomach tied itself into a tight knot.

'You did well today in all that bedlam.' A rare smile lit his eyes with golden gleams. 'It was a pleasure to work with you.' And he was gone.

'Well.' Emma flopped back into the corner of the couch, surprise at his sudden compliment robbing her of all strength—and it wasn't just the compliment.

'That smile ought to be registered as a deadly weapon,' she murmured while her pulse registered its after-effects, which were like the tremors following an earthquake. 'It's potent enough to cause serious heart damage. . .'

As she forced herself to her feet she chuckled at her own silliness, her heart immeasurably lighter after their talk in spite of the prospect that the topic would probably be resurrected when he'd had time to think about it.

At least she'd been able to convince him that his Blackfoot heritage wasn't the reason for her aversion to contact. In fact, if she was honest with herself, it made him all the more attractive. . .

In the meantime she had several more stressful hours to go before she could afford time to daydream about a dark-haired, dark-eyed man who could send her pulse rate off the end of the scale with a single smile.

Her return to the department coincided with the arrival of several patients looking decidedly green.

'We think we've got food poisoning,' the spokesman said as he ushered the sorry-looking group in.

'What do you think caused it?' Emma led them through the department as quickly as she could because one of their number was growing paler by the second.

'Fish,' he muttered as he grabbed the bowl that Emma held out towards him, and made immediate use of it.

'Did you *all* have fish?' She counted eleven heads as she handed each of them a bowl.

'Birthday party for Grandad,' one of the youngest victims volunteered. 'He doesn't like prawns, so he's OK. They were the biggest ones I've ever seen—'

'Shut up, Tim,' one of the others groaned just before he too was violently sick.

'Where did you have the party?' Emma directed the question to the group as a whole. 'I need to know where the prawns came from.'

'Eagle Hotel, just outside town. Near the golf course,' someone supplied. 'We had to wait ages to be served and then this happens. . .'

Emma organised for extra chairs to be carried through and called Adam to check her findings.

'We need to notify the appropriate authorities so

they can send an inspector round to the hotel kitchen before the contaminated food can be disposed of,' he detailed in an aside to Emma. 'I'll leave it to you to sort that one out—you know the proper departments to contact in England better than I do.'

'Fine.' Emma smiled. 'In the meantime, I'm a bit worried about a couple of the victims. I think they're beginning to get dehydrated, and while they're still being sick we can't give them anything by mouth.'

'Let's work our way round the room to check each of them in turn. Any that are beginning to look a bit distressed can have an IV unit of saline to help them through. Luckily, this sounds far more like an outbreak of staphylococcal food poisoning than salmonella, so it'll be of a much shorter duration. Either way, we'll send some samples up to the lab for identification—the confirmation of the diagnosis can then be used in any prosecution against the hotel.'

'Let's just keep our fingers crossed that the hotel doesn't have any other parties booked while this lot are in residence here,' Emma muttered under her breath. 'It could end up looking like a scene from a disaster movie.'

For the next couple of hours there was a constant stream of patients between their makeshift ward and the nearby toilets as diarrhoea alternated with vomiting, and the nurses all took turns in ministering to the sorry party.

'Next time, I'll cook the food myself,' one of the women declared. 'I'd rather be worn out preparing a menu we'll all enjoy than exhausted by getting rid of food someone else has made.'

'And it cost more,' one of the men grumbled, prompting a weak round of laughter.

'Now I know you're getting better, if you've started griping about the cost rather than how bad you feel,' Emma teased, and received a few old-fashioned looks.

'Seriously,' she continued as she removed the last of the IV lines, 'as soon as you feel able to cope at home, it would be a good idea if you can ring for the members of the party who escaped all this, to get them to take you home. You'll feel better if you can lie down comfortably in your own home and, really, there isn't a lot more we can do for you here—you're all well on the mend.'

Within minutes one of them had ventured out with a list of telephone numbers, and the rest of them started gathering up their belongings.

'Thank you for looking after us so well,' one of the older gentlemen said. His face was still pale but his voice had lost its former tremor. 'You've all been very kind to us and we're grateful.' His smile held a touch of devilry as he continued, 'I hope you don't mind if we say that, in spite of your kindness, we'd rather not meet you again.'

'Uncle!' several voices remonstrated, but Emma smiled.

'As long as you don't mind us saying that we hope we never see you here again either!' And she shook their hands as they filed past her and out to the waiting cars.

Emma had no sooner returned the room to order than there was a warning that an ambulance was bringing in the victims of another poisoning.

'Suspected carbon monoxide. Two adults and two

children,' Diane relayed. 'I'm due off duty in a few minutes but I'll stay on if you need me.'

'Thanks, Di.' Emma glanced down at the time. 'If you can hang on until we see how bad they are. . .?'

The whole team was lined up and waiting as the ambulance drew up at the entrance. Each trolley was ready for the transfer of a patient, with a cylinder of one hundred per cent oxygen waiting with a non-rebreathing mask.

'Oh, my God,' Emma breathed when she saw how young the two unconscious children were. 'They're just little scraps.' And she supervised their immediate transfer to the larger trauma room.

'Can you spare enough nurses to cover each of them?' Adam's voice reached her over the hum and rhythmic bleeping of the monitoring equipment.

'Until they regain consciousness, certainly—barring a major influx of casualties,' she agreed, and detailed a nurse to each member of the family.

'Do we know how long they were exposed?' His murmur just behind her confirmed her feeling that he was nearby. It was almost as if her skin was sensitive to his presence, as if he was surrounded by some sort of force field that her body could detect.

'N-not really.' Emma scolded herself for her lack of concentration. This was hardly the time to be thinking about her reaction to Adam Wolf. 'The paramedic said it was probably the gas boiler they used for heating water. Apparently it was the only item in use.'

'Who raised the alarm? One of the parents?'

'No. A neighbour.' She chuckled. 'She came storming round to complain that their cat had come in through the wrong cat flap and had been sick all over their new carpet. When she couldn't get a reply in spite of knowing the family was home, she peered in through the window.'

'Sometimes it's quite frightening when you realise how important coincidence is in our lives.' His deep voice flowed softly in the muted bustle of the room. 'If the cat hadn't been affected, if it hadn't made it outside, if it hadn't gone in the wrong house, if it hadn't been sick, if the neighbour hadn't decided to go to complain. . .' He allowed the list to end with a shrug.

'When you look at those two—' Emma nodded towards the little bodies '—it doesn't bear thinking about.' She shuddered.

By the time she was ready to hand over to the next shift, all four members of the family were conscious and had been admitted for overnight observation.

Emma was glad. She would have hated to go home without knowing that they were all recovering well, especially the little ones.

She kicked off her shoes and flopped back on her bed. Her feet were throbbing with tiredness and her calves were tight and aching.

'Still, a good night's sleep and I'll be ready for another shift,' she announced to the ceiling as she tried to summon the energy to go to the bathroom.

Lazily, she unfastened her clothing and stripped it off without leaving the soft comfort of the bed. It was all going to go into the laundry basket anyway, so what did it matter that it was landing in a heap on the floor?

The warmth of the August sunshine still lingered in the room as she lay naked on the soft cotton cover of her duvet, and she glanced idly down at herself.

'Too skinny,' she muttered as she took in the angles and points of her ribs and hips. 'The legs aren't bad, though.' She raised one slender foot in the air and pointed her toes to admire the shape of her calf and thigh, then she winced as the muscles complained and let it drop back onto the cushioned softness with a thud.

'Heaven only knows where I got these from.' She cupped her hands around the abundance of her breasts. 'There's a very voluptuous woman somewhere out there who got the pair of bee stings I should have had!' She giggled at the mental image, knowing in her heart of hearts that she was rather proud of the unexpectedly beautiful bounty.

'Now all I've got to do is find a man to appreciate them. . .' She gave a snort. 'Except that's not the problem, is it? There are plenty of men who would want to get their hands on these if they were given half a chance—they just don't want the person they're attached to. . .'

Loneliness.

Emma jerked her hands away from herself in shock, her face flaming with embarrassed heat. The intrusion of another person's emotions into her head made her feel as if someone had just walked into her room and found her naked on the bed.

CHAPTER THREE

GET out!' Emma shrieked breathlessly as she scrabbled to cover her bare body with the duvet, pulling it right up under her chin just as if there really were an intruder in the room. 'Get out of my head!' And she pressed her fingers hard against her forehead as if she could force the thoughts away.

Loneliness. Longing.

The sensations poured through her like an avalanche, completely demolishing her puny defences. Whoever it was that kept breaking through her control, their problem hadn't been solved the other day. If anything, it was growing worse.

'I can't help you,' Emma moaned through gritted teeth as the familiar frustration gripped her. 'I can only hear you; I can't talk back. . .'

She remembered her attempts to communicate as a child, before she'd realised that none of her friends heard the same things she did. It had been some time before her mother had realised that her daughter had been afflicted with the family curse, and she'd tried to warn her what would happen—what had always happened to the women in her family.

Of course, Emma hadn't believed her. She'd felt bound to pass on the 'information' she received about lost children and injured neighbours, until the notoriety had forced them to move.

Eventually she had learned to be discreet. She'd

become more careful over whom she told and what she told them, but still she'd refused to believe that it could prevent her from having a normal life.

Until she'd met Richard and fallen in love. . .

Emma drew in a deep, shuddering breath. His rejection still hurt; his repudiation of her as a freak and his revulsion at the idea that she might be able to read his mind had left scars on her soul that might never heal.

Since then she'd been very cautious. Oh, she was friendly enough with people at the hospital, even joined in the occasional get-together for an engagement or a birthday, but she allowed no one any closer than that. Her mother had been right—it wasn't worth the heartbreak.

Isolation.

Why did she think of Adam Wolf when that emotion assailed her? He seemed a very solitary, self-contained person, it was true, but that could be because he was a newcomer in the department and his time among them was limited.

Need.

That certainly didn't make her think of Adam. She couldn't imagine him ever admitting to needing anyone. He was so strong—physically and mentally.

Unlike the poor soul crying out for contact.

How could she refuse? She knew that she couldn't reply, but, according to a child she'd 'heard' in a quarry all those years ago, he'd somehow known that someone was coming, known that someone was there.

Emma settled herself under the duvet and made herself comfortable. Hesitantly she willed herself to relax, not knowing quite what to expect.

'I'm listening,' she whispered into the growing shadows of the room. 'I won't fight you any more. . .'

She lay quietly, a feeling of calm drifting over her as she finally gave in to the inevitable. Whoever was 'speaking' to her must be desperate if they'd tried so often to make contact even in the face of her repeated rebuffs.

Alone.

Emma jerked with sudden awareness as, without her usual shield, the emotion hit her at full force. She drew in a deep breath and allowed it to trickle slowly away, taking with it all her tension. Later she might regret what she was doing, but, just for the moment, it felt right.

'Not alone any more,' she breathed softly, and waited to see what would happen.

Thank you.

She was bathed in an incredible mixture of warmth and light, which flowed around her, inside and out, until she was filled with it.

For the first time Emma felt the weight of her inherited burden lift.

'Morning,' Dave greeted her as she arrived in the department the next day.

'Gorgeous, isn't it?' Emma agreed, with a broad smile. 'No one would dare have an accident on such a lovely day, would they?'

'Optimist!' The accusation followed her as she went to deposit her bag and she chuckled. It was amazing the difference a good night's sleep had made to her outlook.

Not that she had expected to sleep well.

After her sudden capitulation to whoever had been plaguing her, she had expected to lie awake for hours. The last thing she had expected to happen was that she would drift off to sleep as easily as a newborn baby and wake with a smile on her face.

She felt good, she realised as she made her way back towards Reception with a spring in her step—and it wasn't just due to the beautiful weather either.

'Emma, are you half-day today or tomorrow?' Dave queried as she arrived.

'Supposed to be today. Why? Do they need me to stay on?'

'Not as far as I know,' he temporised. 'It's my own fault for leaving it so late, but I'm hoping to do a swap with someone for tomorrow.'

'Sorry. Can't help.' She turned away and walked straight into a living, breathing wall.

'Oops!'

'Sorry!'

Adam Wolf grinned down at her as they each took a rapid backward step, and Emma's pulse leapt. That smile was definitely a lethal weapon!

'Are we so quiet in the department that we're having to supply our own casualties?' he joked, and continued on his way.

'Wow!' breathed one of the junior nurses who had just started work in A and E that morning. 'He's yummy!'

'Careful, Jilly,' Emma laughed. 'You'll end up picking carpet fluff off your tongue if you don't put it away!'

'Staff!' Jilly's cheeks went pink. 'You can't tell me he doesn't get you going too. And that accent!'

Emma sent her about her duties without commenting because it was true. She *was* attracted to Adam Wolf—had been from the first time she'd seen him—but the more she got to know about him, the more she realised that there was a great deal more to the man than the fact that he was a good-looking doctor.

'Staff Nurse?' Emma looked up as she was hailed by the motherly woman at the reception desk, and altered her direction.

'Can I help?' She addressed the couple standing by the desk when the receptionist indicated them.

'It's Holly. She hasn't been well for a couple of days and we thought it was just a summer cold, but she's been ever so sick. . .'

'Bring her through here.' Emma directed them into the smaller trauma room and signalled for Adam to be sent in as soon as he was free.

While she was waiting for him to arrive she took a detailed history and helped Holly's mother to take her child's clothing off.

As she worked she kept up a soothing conversation with the parents, but her eyes kept straying to the doorway every time she heard a noise as she waited for Adam to come. She had a funny feeling about this one.

'Doctor, this is Holly. She's three years old,' Emma began the moment that Adam arrived, handing him a disposable mask and fresh pair of gloves as soon as he entered the room.

For a second he paused, one eyebrow raised as his eyes sought hers, then he gave a brief nod and donned the mask and gloves.

'Holly's had a slightly raised temperature and has

seemed as if she was getting a cold for the last couple of days,' Emma reported. 'About an hour ago she vomited and went very drowsy so her parents brought her straight in.'

'Well done. You did the right thing,' he murmured in a reassuring tone as he started his examination. 'Has she been in contact with any infectious illnesses like measles?'

'Not so far as we know,' her mother replied. 'She started playgroup about six months ago and she's had the usual sort of colds and tummy upsets, but nothing serious. Not until this morning. She said her head hurt.'

'Had you noticed this rash?' Adam flipped back the blanket covering the youngster and indicated the blotchy areas starting to show against her pale skin.

'No.' The poor woman glanced towards her husband for confirmation. 'We looked at her neck when she said it didn't want to bend but we didn't see a rash.'

'Have you any other children?'

'Not yet. Holly's our first.'

Adam glanced up at Emma across the width of the trolley and nodded. She could only see the part of his face not covered by the disposable mask, but the concern in his eyes was unmistakable.

'I'm afraid we need to do some tests on Holly,' he began as Emma watched carefully for the reaction of the little girl's parents.

'Do you know what's the matter with her?' the anxious father demanded. 'She's never been sick like this before and it happened so fast.'

'That's why we need to do these tests as quickly as possible to find out what's causing it,' Adam stressed. 'If you would go with Staff Nurse, she'll arrange for

you to go to a special waiting room, and a drink if
you'd like one. I promise I'll come to see you as soon
as I have something to tell you.'

'Can't I stay with her, Doctor?' the tearful mother
begged. 'She's so little. She's only three—'

'The fewer people there are in here when we do the
tests the better. It helps to cut down on the risk of
infection,' Adam explained kindly as he shepherded
them towards Emma at the door. 'Staff Nurse here will
be with her when the tests are done so she'll have a
friendly face to look at.'

Emma ushered them out of the room and beckoned
Dave over, passing on Adam's instructions as she
handed the shell-shocked couple into his care. A cryp-
tic explanation was enough to alert him to the serious
possibilities without the parents knowing.

'OK, Emma. Here we go,' Adam's brisk voice
greeted her as she returned to the room. 'I need one
of your best colleagues in here to assist us, and a tray
set up for a lumbar puncture as soon as you can.'

Emma sped to do his bidding, her heart going out to
the dainty little mite. Within minutes everything was
ready, and Janelle was helping to stabilise the little
body in position with pillows as Adam approached the
trolley. The poor child hadn't made a murmur, submit-
ting drowsily to whatever they wanted.

'Let me just do a final check that her shoulders and
hips are vertical to the bed...perfect. Now, Nurse,
keep her knees tucked up towards her chest until I tell
you to relax them.' Adam glanced across at Emma.
'Alcohol swab and local anaesthetic, please.' He
cleaned the skin over the child's lower spine, then held
out his hand again for the syringe.

Soon the area between the two vertebrae directly on the line he'd drawn between the tops of her hips had been numbed and he was able to position the spinal needle.

'Bull's-eye,' he muttered as the cerebrospinal fluid appeared on the first attempt. 'You can let her uncurl slightly now.' And he swiftly transferred about a millilitre of the cloudy liquid into each of the three tubes that Emma had readied.

'Get these up to the lab as soon as possible,' he directed as he completed the procedure. 'One for cultures, one for cell count and the third for chemistries. There's a blood sample to go up at the same time.' He pointed to the tube already on the tray.

Janelle left the room swiftly, with the samples sealed in a marked bag, her mask and gloves discarded carefully just in case they were dealing with a worst-case situation.

'In the meantime, let's get her first dose of intravenous antibacterial into her.' He turned to find Emma waiting with the prepared syringe and nodded his approval.

Then it was time for her to wrap their little patient up and wait for the results while Adam paid a brief visit to the waiting parents to let them know the tests had been done.

All too soon the results arrived, and he asked Emma to come with him while he broke the bad news to them, leaving Janelle to keep an eye on their patient.

'We've had the results of the tests,' Adam began as he sat himself in one of the low armchairs. Emma had noticed before that he was careful not to loom over patients. 'I'm afraid Holly's got meningococcal meningitis. . .'

There was a horrified gasp from the father and his wife collapsed against his shoulder and began to sob.

'Does that mean. . .?' He paused to gulp. 'Is she going to die?'

'We hope not.' Adam was being careful not to give any guarantees. 'You brought her in as soon as she became ill and we've already started treating her with antibacterial drugs.'

'Can we s-see her?' her red-eyed mother begged.

'Of course you can,' Adam confirmed. 'We're going to have her transferred up to the ward. You'll be able to see her as soon as she's settled, but she'll be in isolation at first.'

'How. . .how long before we know. . .?' The poor man couldn't continue.

'Usually the bacteria are cleared from the nose and throat within twenty-four hours of starting treatment, then, providing you follow the guidelines the staff give you, you'll be able to visit her.'

'How did she get it? Where did it come from?' the distraught mother demanded.

'We need to identify any close contacts your daughter has made in the last ten days or so,' Emma said.

'But none of them are ill. We would have heard.'

'Unfortunately, the disease can be passed on by carriers who aren't necessarily sick,' Adam explained. 'In any case, we need to check just in case Holly has infected any of her friends.'

'Oh, God. I didn't think of that.' The woman turned to her husband in horror. 'All those little ones in the playgroup. . .'

'Please don't upset yourself about it at this stage. It will help if you can start making out a list of names while you're waiting to go up to see Holly, then we can begin checking everyone. Any of them who are high-risk will have the chance of vaccination.'

Altogether it was a harrowing morning and Emma was delighted when she came to the end of her shift.

'Half the day left to relax and enjoy yourself,' Dave quipped as she went to retrieve her bag and change her shoes.

'Ha! You mean what's left of the day by the time I do my shopping and lug it home and put it away, then do a load of washing and clean the flat and cook myself a meal!' Emma accused. 'Not all of us have besotted girlfriends to run around after us—or boyfriends, in my case.'

'Just say the word and I'm all yours,' Dave hammed it up.

'No fear,' Emma hooted. 'That would be worse than ever because I'd have you to run round after as well!'

She left him chuckling as she made her way towards the big glass double doors, reaching them at the same time as a certain tall, dark-haired doctor.

'Are you off too?' Emma enquired, then could have bitten her tongue. Talk about asking obvious questions! The man was wearing jeans and a casual shirt and had a leather jacket slung over one broad shoulder, with not a white coat in sight.

'I think they've finally taken pity on me and let me out in time to see something of the area before I'm too tired to focus.' He pulled a wry face. 'All I need now is a guidebook or, better still, a human guide to show me around.' A raised eyebrow punctuated his words to make them almost an invitation.

'I'd be no good, then,' Emma admitted honestly, in spite of the temptation to spend time with him. 'I haven't been in the area long enough to know it well, and I haven't got any transport to take me outside the town.'

'Well, I've got the transport if you'd be willing to come exploring with me.'

A tiny voice inside her was saying, Yes! Yes! but caution was too much of a habit for her to ignore it so easily.

'I've got all sorts of chores to do—shopping and laundry and—'

'So have I.' He extended one hand in the direction of the glorious summer day in a clear invitation to walk with him. 'You can show me where the best shops are, and when we feel we've done our duty we can play hookey.'

'Hookey?' Emma found herself walking with him across the car park without a murmur of dissent, almost mesmerised by the fugitive glimmer of gold in his eyes.

'Ah!' he laughed, his teeth starkly white against the bronze of his sun-gilded face, blue-black gleams highlighting the darkness of his hair. 'An Americanism. Go AWOL. Take time out. Skip school. . .'

Emma nodded her understanding and laughed with him, her heart lifting like a balloon. That's just what it felt like—as if she was taking time out of her life just for herself. Time to spend with the most fascinating man she'd ever met. Time to learn a bit more about him before he disappeared out of her life for good.

*　*　*

It was fun.

For the first time in her life Emma found herself laughing and teasing her way through an afternoon without her old fears intruding.

What was it about Adam Wolf that made her let herself go? If anything, he was the most frightening man she'd ever known. His size and strength set him apart from any of the young men she'd gone out with when she'd still trusted herself enough to go.

Adam was a fully grown adult male in the prime of his life, his virility calling out to everything in her that was female.

Their errands completed, she glanced at him out of the corner of her eye as he strode along beside her, his paces deceptively smooth and silent, almost as if he were a hunting animal stalking his prey. . .

A shiver that had nothing to do with the fact that the sun had briefly disappeared behind a cloud snaked its way up her spine.

'Cold?'

The question surprised her. She hadn't realised that he was watching her so closely. 'Here's the car. You get inside in the warm. I'll just load up the bags and we'll be on our way.'

He deposited a handful of carrier bags at his feet, and leant forward to unlock the passenger door of the nondescript, mid-range car he'd hired for the duration of his stay in England.

As Emma slid into her seat she still couldn't get over her surprise at his choice of vehicle. Most of the doctors she knew would have chosen something far flashier, far more impressive, especially if they were single men on the loose in a foreign country.

Adam was different, though, she conceded as she obeyed his reminder to fasten her seat belt. He had no need of expensive cars to bolster his self-esteem. He seemed to be the most completely self-contained man she'd ever met, both in his work at the hospital, which was superb, and in his private life.

As far as she could tell from the hospital grapevine, he hadn't accepted a single one of the invitations he'd received—no matter how blatant. And yet he'd suggested spending an afternoon with her, shopping and doing their laundry, for all the world as if they were an old married couple.

The warm glow this thought started deep inside her was doused by a counterbalancing one, which reminded her spitefully that she obviously wasn't interesting enough to take on a proper date. . .

'Can I leave my laundry here until I bring you back later?' His deep voice broke into her musings as he drew up outside the drab building containing her minute flat.

'Later?' What was he talking about? she asked herself. Where was he going now?'

'When we come back from our voyage of exploration,' he explained as if she were simple. 'Don't tell me you've forgotten!'

That smile! Emma blinked. Much more of it and she'd be forgetting her own name.

'But. . .'

'But nothing! A promise is a promise. You can't expect me to find my way around when I'm having to drive on the wrong side of the road. . .and there's all that food to eat! Get yourself inside that house quick and dump everything. Time's wasting!'

Emma laughed and tumbled out of the car. This was a new side to the solemn Dr Wolf—an exuberance for life that was utterly contagious. She took most of the bags from the back seat.

'Back in ten minutes,' she flung over her shoulder with a smile.

'Never happen,' he taunted. 'No woman is capable of taking less than half an hour...' He slid himself down in his seat as though preparing himself for a long wait.

Emma blessed him for his tactfulness in staying in the car as she grabbed her belongings and sped inside. Her tiny rooms would never have coped with his overwhelming presence, especially as she would be trying to put her shopping away and change her clothes at the same time.

Nine minutes later Emma was still panting with the exertion of proving him wrong as she approached the car.

'OK, smart-ass! Apologise!' she demanded in an atrocious imitation of his accent as she stuck her arm through the open window to display her watch under his nose. 'Nine minutes!'

She leant forward to watch the expression on his face in the shadowed interior of the car, the hair she'd released from its professional-looking imprisonment tumbling forward over her shoulder to caress the side of her face.

Dark eyes gleamed at her from between slitted lids, then he moved suddenly to trap her wrist in fingers of steel, and before she could take evasive action he'd leant forward to plant a peck on the parted softness of her lingering, triumphant smile.

'Good. Hop in,' he ordered as calmly as if the sparks of electricity which had crackled over her lips at the contact had never happened.

Emma was silent as she sat beside him, her hand cradled over the warmth which lingered in her wrist where he had held her. She was lost for words after his totally unexpected action as he started the engine and pulled out into the traffic.

'Hey!'

The tone of his deep voice told her that it wasn't the first time he'd tried to attract her attention.

'Earth to Emma! Earth to Emma! Tell me which direction to take before we get to the end of this road or I might end up going round in circles!'

Jerked out of her daydream, Emma laughed at his nonsense and spread the large-scale map over her jeans-clad knees.

'Which way do you want to go? Is there anywhere in particular you want to visit?'

'Surprise me!' he invited, with a grin. 'This is my first time in England, the sun is shining and there's a beautiful girl in the car with me. Anything else is a bonus!'

'Ha!' Outwardly Emma scorned his flattery and set about giving him directions, but inside, where there had been no sunshine for years, a little seed had tentatively started to germinate.

'I know what's so different!' Adam's voice was filled with the enthusiasm of discovery after nearly an hour of meandering around the highways and byways to the north of the town where St Lawrence's was situated.

They'd crossed over the motorway soon after setting out and had caught sight of the build-up of holiday traffic going towards the West Country, but soon she'd directed him into the more rural areas, sending him down some turnings just because they liked the sound of the names of the villages.

'Different about what?' Emma demanded.

'Different about England,' he clarified. 'The horizon is much closer than it is back home.'

'It would be if you're driving down a lane surrounded by hedges,' Emma scoffed. 'I don't suppose the horizon is very far away in New York when you're surrounded by skyscrapers either.'

'*Touché*!' he conceded. 'But, if you'd ever seen Montana, you'd know what I mean.'

'Is Montana near Seattle?'

'Hardly!' Adam laughed indulgently. 'It's about four hundred and fifty miles as the crow flies, with a mountain range in between!'

'Oh.' Emma felt the heat in her cheeks at her ignorance.

'Don't sweat it.' There was still a chuckle in his voice. 'I've made some major blunders too, like asking Alec MacTavish what part of England he was from!'

'Oh, Lord, you didn't,' she chuckled.

'Then I made the mistake of calling him Scotch instead of Scots, and had a five-minute dressing down in the middle of Reception.'

'"Ye dr-r-rink Scotch, mon!"' Emma quoted wickedly. 'I've heard that speech several times in the last couple of years.'

'It certainly makes sure you never make that mistake again,' Adam agreed. 'But I noticed he didn't invite me to partake of any of it to fix it in my memory!'

Soon after that his stomach started rumbling and

they found a small patch of woodland for their impromptu picnic, the beech trees sounding almost like distant waves as the breeze rustled its way through them.

Unfortunately the light began to fade long before Emma was ready for the day to end, and she found herself moving slower and slower as they packed everything away into the car.

Finally it was time to climb back inside and, once seated, she twisted to locate the seat-belt point.

'Emma?' His hand settled over hers, preventing her from pushing the latch home, and she looked up to meet eyes gleaming darkly in the shadows. 'I hope you've enjoyed this as much as I have?'

The strange uncertainty in his voice barely registered in her brain through the overload of emotion that she was picking up through their physical contact.

Attraction.

Never had she been so aware of another person's reaction to her. Never had she realised how many facets there were to the magnetism between a man and a woman, and Adam Wolf seemed to be prey to all of them.

'Yes,' she whispered, totally overwhelmed. She didn't really know whether she was agreeing to her enjoyment of their afternoon together or to her own answering fascination with him.

For long moments they were still, gazing into each other's eyes in taut silence while a strange connection seemed to weave itself between them.

'Good,' Adam murmured in a husky voice as he finally released her hand. 'That's good.' He gave a

decisive nod as he turned back to secure his own seat
belt.

By the time he drew up outside her flat again it was
completely dark, only the intermittent circles of yellow
streetlights showing her where she lived.

'Hang on a second.' Adam released his belt at the
same time. 'I'll come with you to get my bags.'

'Don't bother. I'll bring them out to you.' Emma's
offer was ignored.

'No way, lady,' he drawled decisively as he unfolded
his long legs and straightened up out of the car. 'At
this time of night, I see my date safely to her door.'

A burst of raucous laughter punctuated his words
even as Emma was basking in the delight of being
called his date, and a ragtag bunch of youths spilled
out of an untidy house further up the road.

Adam had moved round to escort Emma across the
road by the time the group reached them.

'Hey, man. Look. It's a hippy nigger,' one called,
brave in the company of his friends. 'What you doin'
this side of town?'

Adam angled his body so that Emma was protected
behind him and straightened himself to his full height.

'You hear me, nigger?' The noisy youth strutted like
a bantam rooster, with his coterie around him. 'I'm
talking to you.'

Adam stayed silent, his hands hanging easily by his
sides as he watched the group coming closer, egging
each other on.

As Emma maintained a watchful position just behind
him she knew that there was little danger of violence —
Adam wouldn't let it happen while she was in his care.

The rowdy group only grew quiet when they realised that their target was totally unimpressed by them. Only *then* did they seem to recognise just how tall he was, how broad and powerful his shoulders were and how menacing he was in his utter stillness and silence.

Emma was aware of the moment when their puny nerve broke in the face of his sheer presence, and she could have laughed aloud at the panic-filled thoughts that she was picking up from them.

'Adam?' she murmured as the group finally slunk off, content with mouthing a barrage of insults once they were well out of reach. 'Shall I get your laundry?'

His chuckle came from deep inside his chest. 'I don't know if that's going from the sublime to the ridiculous or the other way round, but lead on.' And he finally ushered her over the road.

Emma fumbled for her key, suddenly far more nervous at the prospect of having Adam Wolf in the intimacy of her flat than she'd been of that group of miscreants a few minutes ago.

She swung the door open and switched the light on in the communal hallway as she entered, the hairs on the back of her neck telling her that he was following her inside.

'I'll wait here while you get my things,' he murmured, and she glanced back sharply to see him lean easily back against the wall and fold his arms across the impressive width of his chest.

With a muttered agreement, Emma flew up the stairs to her own rooms, her heart beating with a mixture of relief at the unexpected reprieve and disappointment that Adam hadn't been willing to come up with her.

'There you are.' She held out two bags of laundry as

she rejoined him moments later. 'I'll see you in A and E tomorrow,' she said brightly, proud of the casual way in which she was dealing with the situation.

Adam turned towards the door as if to leave, then bent down to deposit the bags against the wall before he resumed his original position, the leather of his jacket creaking as he folded his arms again.

'You were very calm out there.' He angled his head towards the road.

'I knew nothing would happen,' she said with calm conviction.

'Why? Do they do that sort of thing often?'

'No, it was the first time.'

'Then how. . .?'

'I knew you wouldn't let anything happen.' Her voice was only just louder than a whisper but it shouted her belief in him.

'Emma. . .' he groaned as he shouldered himself away from the wall and captured her hands to pull her into his arms.

CHAPTER FOUR

'STAFF!'

The call had more than a hint of panic in it and Emma responded swiftly.

'Yes? What can I—? Ah! I see!' The reason for the receptionist's urgency was evident as the young man in front of her doubled over again to be sick on the floor.

'Please, Mr Retallack, will you go with Staff Nurse?' Poor Mrs Burton sounded less than her usual unflappable self.

'Ring through to Domestic and get them to send someone straight up,' Emma reminded her, with a wry smile as she put her arm around the man's shoulders and led her distressed charge away.

'How long have you been like this, Mr Retallack?' Emma began her questions as soon as she'd provided him with a bowl.

'Coupla days,' he answered, his forehead dotted with sweat and his skin almost grey under the bright lights.

'Do you know what brought it on?' She took a chance and handed him a thermometer as soon as he was sitting.

'Thought it were eitherways food poisoning or stummick bug.' He closed pale lips around the cylinder, robbing Emma of her chance to hear any more of his wonderful accent.

When she retrieved it and confirmed her suspicions she handed him over to Penny. 'Will you help Mr

Retallack to take his clothes off if he can't manage alone, and then get him up on the table? I'll get the doctor to come and have a look at him.' She shut the door behind her and went in search of Adam.

'Mrs Burton? Do you know where Dr Wolf is?'

'He was on his way to Emergency Room One last time I saw him.' She smiled wanly at Emma as she presided over her newly cleaned domain. 'Sorry about the panic just then, but I thought it was going all over the desk any minute.'

'No problem,' Emma consoled her. 'Thank God for the domestics!'

'Hear, hear!' the older woman muttered with feeling as Emma took herself off down the opposite corridor.

She'd almost reached the double doors to Emergency Room One when they were pushed open by a trolley.

'Coming through,' a warning voice called, and she stepped nimbly aside. 'Grab the lift, will you, Emma? Going up to Theatre Four.' Dave was following the trolley with an armful of notes and X-ray plates.

Emma reached out to thumb the button and the arrow lit up. 'On its way,' she confirmed, and continued on her quest for Adam Wolf, holding one of the doors open to enter the room after the trolley was clear.

His back was towards her as the door swished closed behind her, his head bent forward as he concentrated on the voice on the telephone.

'Right.' His deep voice broke the quiet of the room. 'He should be with you in a couple of minutes. Good luck—I've a feeling you're going to need it with that one.' And he returned the receiver to the cradle.

He turned to face the room with a concerned frown

etched between his dark eyebrows, his mind obviously still on the patient he'd been talking about.

She had taken two steps towards him before her presence broke his concentration.

'Emma,' he said softly, and stood still, his expression almost wary.

'Adam.' She smiled, her pulse throbbing at the base of her throat as she fought the memory of the moments she'd spent in his arms.

'Were you looking for me?'

His voice had the same husky timbre as it had when he'd buried his face in the profusion of her unbound hair, and she had to fight the impulse to launch herself towards him and wrap her arms around the taut muscles of his waist.

'Oh! Yes!' His words finally penetrated the haze of memories. 'Can you come and take a look at a young man for me? His blood pressure's ninety over sixty, pulse ninety-nine between bouts of vomiting, respiration similarly variable. Rebound tenderness on the right. He thought it was food poisoning or a stomach bug, but I'm certain it's appendicitis and I've a feeling that it's just about to go—'

Before she'd finished speaking he was on the move, his long legs covering the ground effortlessly so that Emma had to work hard to keep up.

'Is he constipated or has he got diarrhoea? Did you manage to get a urine sample? When did he last have anything to eat or drink?' The questions were thrown towards her one after the other.

'Severe diarrhoea and pain on urinating, but he managed a sample and I took blood as well. He hasn't had anything since yesterday evening.' She answered each question in order, her brisk tone an exact copy of his own.

'Good.' His eyes met hers briefly as he turned to shoulder the door open, and he lowered one eyelid in an intimate wink. 'Let's see what we've got.' And he was all businesslike again as he reached for the container of examining gloves.

In a very short space of time Mr Retallack was on his way up in the lift, with a surgeon waiting at the other end of the short journey ready to perform an emergency appendicectomy.

'Well spotted,' Adam praised as he stripped off his gloves and disposed of them. 'If they get moving upstairs, they should get it out without it perforating.'

'Either way, he's out of our hands now.' She glanced up at the clock on the wall. 'I'll just go and check what else has come in, otherwise you might have time to get a pot of coffee going.' She gave him a cheeky grin as she left the room.

'You're very pally with the hunk,' a sharp voice commented as the door closed behind her, and Emma turned to see Marilyn Venning coming out of the opposite door. 'Organising private coffee-breaks with him now, are we?'

'Oh, yes,' Emma agreed, with a bland expression. 'So private that the whole of A and E can walk in at any time. . .' She just had time to see the slyly calculating look on the tall, voluptuous blonde's face when the doors burst open behind her.

'Emma, I need you.' Adam's voice was urgent and Emma's heart performed a spectacular double somersault in her chest as she heard Marilyn's gasp. 'There's been a major crash on the motorway,' he continued before she'd had time to embarrass herself.

'They need the team from St Lawrence's to attend and I was told you've been trained for it.'

'That's quite right.' All of a sudden Marilyn's pettiness was forgotten as she switched her brain into top gear.

'Equipment's kept ready, packed and labelled.' She took off in the direction of the ambulance embarkation point. 'Protective clothing's on board and we have radio contact and telemetry for transmitting electrocardiograms back to the hospital from the site of the accident.'

'Gotcha.' He raised a thumb as, with the rest of the group, they reached the vehicles. 'Give me a shove if I'm not where I should be.' His breathing was hardly altered by their dash along the corridor and Emma consoled herself with the fact that his legs were a great deal longer than hers—something he was proving as he tried to fold them as small as possible into a space between the packages of equipment.

'Hang onto your hats,' the driver called as he accelerated out of the bay, delaying switching on his siren only just long enough to avoid deafening them in the enclosed area.

He swung the vehicle into a tight turn and Emma slid across the seat, to land plastered against Adam's side, the long-wheelbase Citroën pulling away with a speed that still astonished her every time.

Her face grew warm as she shuffled until they were separated by a couple of inches, but the seat belt wasn't sufficient to prevent her from sliding just as helplessly

as they negotiated a roundabout before they reached
the slip-road onto the motorway.

'Might as well stay put and save your energy,' Adam
murmured in her ear as he secured his arm around her
shoulders; then he raised his voice for the benefit of
the two in front. 'I think our driver moonlights as a
stunt man.'

There was a burst of appreciative laughter from the
front seat. 'Nah! Far too tame after ambulance driving,'
he boasted. 'This baby will cruise at a hundred and
thirty miles an hour and still have enough under the
bonnet for a burst of real speed.'

The radio broke in with some rapid conversation
demanding their estimated time of arrival at the crash,
the voice on the other end sounding as unflustered as
if the whole thing was a practice exercise.

'ETA four minutes,' Don confirmed. 'One doctor,
one nurse and two paramedics on board.'

'Is that usual?' Adam blinked when he heard the
level of qualification of the other two in the vehicle.

'For *this* team, yes,' Emma said. 'Being so close to a
major motorway we need to have access to the best in
a hurry. As the personnel have to be able to double
for each other in a lot of situations, it makes sense if
the driver can work when he gets there, too.'

'Logical,' Adam agreed, with a nod. 'It sounds as if
the situation in the UK is developing in a similar way
to the USA. Thirty years ago there weren't any paramedics; now there are over fifty thousand.'

'Ah, but did you know that Belfast, in Northern
Ireland, was one of the first places in the world to have
the forerunners of the paramedics?' Emma challenged.

'We don't just copy American ideas, we're willing to pick up on anything worthwhile—'

'Here we go!' Don's voice broke in from the front seat and their eyes were drawn to the front windscreen and the terrible scene that met them.

The whole area was cordoned off by police and other emergency vehicles, their flashing warning lights incongruous on such a beautiful, sunny day.

The ambulance was directed to the side of the carriageway. By the time the vehicle drew to a halt all four doors were open and the team was exiting as fast as they could as voices and arms waved to them to hurry in several different directions, each one wanting their attention first.

'Lorry driver trapped. . .'

'Injured children in the car. . .'

'Motor cyclist. . .'

Emma was trying to look in all directions at once.

'Where do we start?' she said, horrified at the carnage surrounding them.

'With the first one we come to, in the absence of any other directions,' Phil said through gritted teeth as he swung a pack of supplies out. 'I hope to God someone here knows what they're doing and has started triage. . .' And he was away.

'Doctor!' A policeman was waving in their direction, obviously catching sight of the fluorescent markings on Adam's vest.

'What have you got?' Adam demanded as he reached the knot of rescuers, his bag gripped firmly in one gloved hand.

'You'd better have a look at him in the cab. He's losing a hell of a lot of blood. At this rate he'll run out before we can cut him out. We put a collar on him and he's got oxygen. . .'

It was a good job that Adam had long legs, Emma thought as she held his bag while he climbed carefully up the side of the shattered cab of the articulated lorry.

'Hey, man,' he said calmly as he reached in to make contact with the trapped driver, 'any room in there for another one?'

'Oh, God,' Emma heard the unseen man groan. 'Not another bloody American hitchhiker!'

There were several seconds of startled silence before Adam burst into full-throated laughter, the sound odd amid such carnage. 'I take it that's an example of never-say-die British humour,' he chuckled as he man-oeuvred gingerly to assess the extent of the man's injuries.

'Emma,' he called back over his shoulder, 'I need to get a temporary tourniquet above this while I sort out how to get a pressure bandage on it. If I had another pair of hands, I'd also put up an IV to start replacing lost fluids.'

'Coming right up,' Emma confirmed as she tapped the back of her hand against his leg, and he extended an arm back to have the items he'd requested placed straight in his hand without having to turn round.

'Dammit, I need to be an octopus,' he was muttering as he struggled to position the flat folds of a triangular bandage as a tourniquet and tighten it effectively at the same time.

'Will two more hands do on loan until you can have the grafts done for the rest?' Emma queried as she reached across from the other side of the cab to hold it in place.

'Emma?' He was frowning fiercely as their eyes clashed across the driver's body. 'What the hell are you doing in here?'

'My job,' she said sweetly, leaving him to continue his task as she tied a length of soft rubber tubing around the man's arm, swabbed the good, strong vein it raised and smoothly inserted the needle attached to the prepared macrodrop infusion set.

'I'll just get rid of my tourniquet, and tape this lot in position—' Emma was suiting her actions to her words '—then you can tell me where you need my hands.'

There was a choking sound from the driver and they both looked sharply at him to find that he was trying to stifle laughter. 'Doc, that was an offer you can't refuse!'

'Oh, yes, I can.' Adam smiled at their plucky patient. 'If I take her up on that sort of offer, it won't be in front of an audience!'

'*If*? What do you mean, *if*? Haven't you Yanks got any red blood in your veins?' he demanded, his voice gradually growing shakier.

'Quite a bit more than you have at this moment, so stop shouting the odds,' Emma scolded, her face still fiery from her realisation of her verbal gaffe. 'It's not a good idea to start insulting the man who's trying to stop you bleeding all over the place.'

'Sorry, Nurse,' he said, his voice apparently meek, but Emma saw the twinkle in his eye and the wink he gave her when Adam looked away.

Between the two of them Emma and Adam had managed to apply direct pressure over the site of greatest bleeding just in time for the fire-brigade team to take over.

They could safely leave him now that he was stabilised, knowing that the heavy-duty equipment would make short work of the structure of the cab and release the driver. After that, he would be loaded into one of the relay of ambulances which were ferrying the injured off to hospital.

They both jumped clear of the wrecked lorry and hurried in the direction of a motor cyclist lying between two cars.

In the few seconds it took for his long legs to eat up the distance, Adam's eyes were focusing on one damaged vehicle after another, checking to see how many people were still in need of help.

'It looks as if all the minor injuries have gone,' Emma said after her own rapid survey of the scene. 'This is probably the last of the bad ones, as far as I can see.'

Their second patient was still unconscious, and after they'd confirmed that his condition hadn't deteriorated since the initial taking of his vital signs it was decided that, once he was immobilised on a back-board, it would be better if he was transported to hospital for further investigation.

'Before we can touch him, we've got to stabilise his neck,' Adam muttered as he struggled to place the neck brace without disturbing the man's position.

'It wouldn't take me a second to get that helmet out of your way.' The helpful voice was accompanied by a pair of hands which were already reaching towards the brightly coloured dome.

'Don't you dare!' Emma's forceful voice rang out before Adam had a chance to speak, and the advancing hands froze instantly. 'I've actually seen a patient whose skull was shattered when he hit the road, and the only thing that was holding it together was the helmet. He walked away from the accident only to be killed by a helpful friend who pulled his helmet off.'

'Oh, God!' The young man's face turned quite green and Emma knew that that was one message he would never forget.

'Effective,' Adam muttered under his breath as they assisted in the young man's transfer to a back-board.

'It also happens to be true,' she replied softly. 'He tried to make a date with my friend in Casualty while he was waiting to be seen by the doctor, and five minutes later he was dead. . .'

'Rough,' Adam murmured, the single word conveying all that was needed.

'Doc! Quick!'

Adam's head went up as he tried to locate the caller amongst the noises and shouts all around them.

'Here, Doc!' Several arms waved him over towards the car and towing caravan at the heart of the tragedy.

Adam spared a last, quick glance at the deeply unconscious motor cyclist before he grabbed his bag to lope swiftly away. He knew as well as Emma did that the waiting ambulance crew were well able to take care of the man from this point until he reached hospital.

'What have you got?' he demanded as he reached the knot of rescuers.

'We've found another one. . .'

'We thought we'd got them all. . .'

'When the woman came to. . .'

Several voices broke in as one burly fireman, who'd been hunched down on the ground, turned awkwardly to reveal the tiny bundle, cradled in his huge hands as carefully as a piece of priceless Meissen china. Emma recognised what he was holding just as she was assailed by the agonising feeling of loss that she was picking up from Adam.

She watched silently as he dropped to his knees without a word and began checking the fragile burden, then she crouched down beside him, poised to supply whatever he needed.

'We didn't realise there was a baby in the car until the mother regained consciousness.' The many voices had resolved themselves into one spokesman. 'The driver was dead on impact and she was out cold. There was no safety seat or carry-cot restraint fitted so we had no reason to look. The baby must have been on her lap when it happened, and he ended up in the footwell under the dashboard. He hasn't moved or made a sound since we found him.'

The speaker was a seasoned veteran of many such scenes, but even *he* was unable to keep an emotional tone out of his voice.

There was a pause while the surrounding men almost seemed to hold their breath as they watched Adam checking the baby's vital signs.

'Is he going to be all right?' One man finally voiced the question on all their faces.

'I don't know.' Adam raised his eyes briefly from his task. 'He's had a blow to the side of his head and we won't know how much damage it's done until we do some more tests.'

Emma helped him start the IV line, the two of them simultaneously muttering imprecations under their breath as they searched for a vein big enough. Positioning an oxygen supply was just as precarious, and when they finally had everything regulated to his satisfaction Adam looked up at their audience, frowning darkly. 'Where's the mother?'

'In the ambulance.' A hand pointed. 'She nearly went mental when we took her away. Refused to be taken to hospital till we got the baby out. Will you travel back with them?'

'Unless you've got anything else?' Adam's words were clipped. The fact that the rich depth was missing from his voice was Emma's clue that he was searingly angry. It was to his credit that he didn't allow it to spill over into his dealings with other people.

'Well, thanks for your help with this lot. No doubt we'll be seeing you again at some stage...'

The rescue co-ordinator's words were following them across the intervening space as Adam gently bore the limp scrap of humanity away, Emma bringing up the rear with his hastily gathered bag of belongings.

'My baby! Did you save my baby...?'

Emma saw Adam's assessing glance go over the woman, noting her pale, shocked appearance and the angry knot on the side of her forehead, the collar that was protecting her neck making her movements awkward.

'We've got him out and he's still alive—at the moment,' he said curtly, and Emma gasped audibly as the baby's mother reeled back and nearly passed out, only Emma's quick reflexes saving her from crumpling in a heap on the floor of the ambulance.

'Doctor...' she muttered, with as much indignation in the word as she dared, her hand anchoring the woman's elbow while she straightened.

'Oh, God, he can't die,' the shaky voice rose in a wail. 'He mustn't die—I couldn't bear it!'

Emma reached for her again, this time her arm going around the slender shoulders as they shook with racking sobs.

'Shh now. Shh!' she soothed, glaring at Adam's stony face. 'You won't do the baby any good with this noise. What's his name?'

'A-Adam,' she choked, and sniffed. 'I called him Adam because it's a strong name. I thought it would help him when he grew up if he had a strong name. Do you think it helps?' She raised pink eyelids in appeal to Emma.

'Perhaps you should ask the doctor.' Emma turned to their silently brooding companion with a militant expression in her eyes. 'By sheer coincidence, his name's Adam too. He can tell you if it's made him strong.'

There was a long silence following Emma's pronouncement as the distraught woman turned her gaze to the powerful man holding her tiny baby.

'I don't know.' When the words came, his voice sounded almost rusty. 'I think we have to make the best of what we're given and just keep trying—' He stopped suddenly, his eyes flying to the tiny bundle, held so securely in his arms despite the fact that the ambulance was now travelling at full speed towards the hospital.

'He moved.' Emma saw his lips form the words and saw, too, the glimmer of hope in his eyes when he looked up at her. 'I felt him move and his eyelids just flickered. . .'

Emma felt the burst of uncontrollable emotion in him, wonder, caring, protectiveness. . .anger.

'If you love him so much, why didn't you take care of him?' he accused the cowering woman, his voice filled with anguish. 'Why wasn't he strapped in a carry-cot, safe on the back seat? Surely you knew that he shouldn't have been on your lap?'

Emma's arm was still wrapped supportively round the woman's shoulders, helping to brace her against the motion of the speeding vehicle, and she felt her slight frame stiffen, felt, too, her inner hurt at Adam's totally unexpected attack *and* sensed the second when it turned to rage.

'Yes, Doctor,' she grated through clenched teeth, 'I *do* know that he should have been in his carry-cot, and I *do* know it would have been safer, but *unfortunately* he arrived earlier than we expected and, instead of getting all that sorted out, my *husband* spent the week I was in hospital catching up with all his old drinking pals.

'Of course,' she continued relentlessly, 'the fact that we had a tiny baby didn't make *any* difference to the plans he'd made for his annual holiday, nor was he willing to stop at the services while I fed him, in spite of the fact that he started off this morning with a hangover and refused to admit he was falling asleep at the wheel. . .

'Oh, the bastard—the rotten, selfish bastard,' she wailed. 'If my baby dies, I'll kill him. I'll kill him with my own hands. It's all his fault. All his bloody fault. . .'

She finally ran out of words and breath and sat there, her eyes fixed on her infant son, ignoring the twin streams which flowed silently down her cheeks.

Horrified, Emma suddenly realised that the poor woman still didn't know what had happened to her husband. Her eyes flew to Adam's face and saw the same shocked expression as she knew was on hers.

Before she could think of a way they could break the news, they were drawing up outside the hospital and the opportunity was lost.

There was nearly another fight when Adam started to stride down the corridor with the unconscious child in his arms. The ambulanceman who was carrying the IV bag and oxygen cylinder was almost having to run to keep up with him, and Sister Noone stepped in to catch hold of the tiny child's mother to stop her following them through to the restricted area.

'No. Let me go.' She was tugging against the firm hold on her elbow. 'You can't stop me—'

'Please,' Emma intervened gently, and rested her hand casually on the woman's arm to make the important contact. 'You were knocked unconscious in the crash. You need to be checked over to make sure you're going to be all right.'

'But he's taking my baby away. I want to go with my baby.' Her tear-reddened eyes were full of fear.

'I promise you, Dr Wolf will be taking very good care of him.' Emma concentrated on projecting calm through her touch. 'He's hardly likely to do less than his best for someone who shares the same name. . .'.

The attempt at humour raised a weak excuse for a smile, but the mother seemed calmer and finally submitted to an examination after she was promised that she could join her baby as soon as the paediatrician had seen him.

While she was being taken to a cubicle, Emma

rapidly explained the circumstances to Barbara Noone so that she could pass them on to the senior registrar who would be seeing the woman.

Someone, somewhere along the line, was going to have to tell the poor woman that her husband had died in the crash.

'I'm just glad it's not part of *my* job,' Emma said that lunchtime, when she actually managed to reach the canteen for a snatched meal and ended up sitting with one of the junior nurses from Paediatrics.

'We still end up sitting in on enough of those types of interviews, though,' a charge nurse from Orthopaedics commented. 'We might not be the ones actually doing the telling, but we usually get left to do the mopping up when the big noises have gone.'

There was a general murmur of agreement.

'Perhaps. . .?' Emma paused in her train of thought.

'What?' the junior prompted.

'Well, I was thinking that perhaps we get the fallout because the patients or their relatives see more of us and feel they know us that much better.'

'You mean they know us well enough to be rude to us?' The charge nurse pulled a face.

'Maybe that's part of it,' Emma said thoughtfully, 'but I think it's more a case that they feel they can trust us because they see us doing our best for them hour by hour, and they know we'll understand what they're going through.'

'Hey, Emma.' Under the cover of the ensuing discussion, a staff nurse she recognised from Obs and Gyn muttered an aside across the table. 'Do you know a tall, dark-haired dreamboat with the most fabulous eyes? Because there's one at the table behind you who's hardly taken them off you since he sat down. . .'

Emma felt the heat steal up her throat and into her cheeks but refused to turn around and give rise to any gossip—the rumour mill in the hospital was bad enough without her providing any grist.

She'd known that he was there, of course. Her private radar had told her as soon as he'd entered the room, the prickle of awareness sending a shiver up her spine and raising the soft hairs on the back of her neck.

It had been her sense of self-preservation that had made her concentrate on her conversation with her colleagues around the table. Inside, every nerve in her body was screaming with the knowledge that he was looking at her, the touch of his eyes almost as tangible as a physical caress.

'You must be imagining it,' she murmured uncomfortably, wondering what on earth Adam would think if he realised that he was a target for such speculation.

Several people left the table, their allotted breaks over, and Emma silently sighed with relief. The fewer people who heard this conversation the better, she thought as her tormentor leaned towards her with a sly grin.

'You wait and see,' she said confidently. 'This one looks like the ultimate predator—a bona fide wolf in wolf's clothing. I think he's just sitting there biding his time until we've all gone so he can move in for the kill. Even *you* won't be immune to this one. . . Oh!'

'What's the matter?' Emma tried to sound innocent but she was struggling to control a smile.

'He's going!' The nurse sounded quite disappointed.

'Told you so.' Emma knew that she sounded disgustingly smug, but the temptation to say it was too much to resist, especially as her sensitivity to his presence had let her know that he was going before her companion had told her.

'Darn.' The grin was wry. 'I was really hoping I was going to be in on the start of some fresh gossip to liven up the tedium of bedpan time. Ah, well,' she sighed theatrically, and took her tray over to the collection point, waggling her fingers in a brief farewell before she left the canteen.

Emma lifted her coffee-cup and cradled it in front of her face between both hands to hide her smile.

'Is the coast clear?' Adam's deep voice murmured from behind her. 'Can I lure you away from the delights of the staff canteen with the promise of a mug of my *real* coffee?'

CHAPTER FIVE

'FOR a mug of *real* coffee, I'd follow you to the ends of the earth—or at least to the end of the corridor in A and E!' Emma laughed up at Adam as the cup of grey liquid she'd been cradling in her hands was deposited with the rest of the debris on her tray.

She couldn't help chuckling as he stuck his head out of the canteen door and ostentatiously looked each way with a shifty expression on his face.

'The coast is clear,' he hissed.

'I'm not afraid of being seen with you,' Emma hastened to assure him, momentarily worried that he might still harbour doubts about her feelings on that score.

'Ah, but if no one sees me spirit you away to my lair they won't know the wolf has you in his clutches.' He grinned a mock-predatory smile, his teeth gleaming whitely under the fluorescent lights of the corridor.

'Idiot,' Emma scolded. 'I gathered you'd heard what she was saying when you left the canteen.'

'We wolves have very sharp hearing,' he confirmed before his expression grew serious. 'Is it going to be a problem for you if people start linking us together? Will it put anyone's nose out of joint?'

'Yes,' Emma confirmed in a suitably grave tone, and felt a swift dart of satisfaction at the momentary disappointment which crossed his face. 'I'll probably get hate mail from every nurse in the place for attracting the attention of the dishiest doctor in the hospital.'

She was amazed to see the tide of red staining the high planes of his cheeks as he muttered an embarrassed disclaimer and hurried across the room to busy himself with the gadget in the corner, which was sending out its tantalising aroma.

'Adam?' Emma began tentatively when they were finally sitting down in adjoining chairs. 'There's something. . .' She paused, not knowing quite how to continue. All she did know was that it was important for her own peace of mind.

'What?' His eyes were shielded by thick dark lashes as he gazed fixedly at the mug between his hands.

'That can't possibly be the first time someone's paid you a compliment.' Her words sounded almost like an accusation. 'With looks like yours, you must have had women queueing up since you were in your teens.'

The colour returned to his face, darker than ever.

'Of course,' he agreed baldly, his eyes fixed on hers with a cold anger. 'Unfortunately, most of them viewed me as something in the line of an exotic pet — something to be displayed as some sort of trophy until the novelty wore off, when I would be discarded for a new toy.'

Emma had suffered from that once or twice herself and knew what it felt like. 'They don't realise how demeaning it is to be valued just for your entertainment value rather than as a person,' she murmured almost under her breath.

There was a moment of startled silence before he spoke again. 'I didn't think you'd understand — didn't think anyone who wasn't handicapped in some way —

physically, mentally or by their religion or colour—
would understand what it feels like.' There was a new
respect in his eyes.

'Not all handicaps are that easy to spot,' she muttered as the warmth of his approval melted a little of
the ice deep inside where she kept her own emotions.

Suddenly, she remembered their last tiny patient at
the site of the crash.

'How's your little namesake doing? What did
Paediatrics have to say?'

'"Wait and see."' He pressed his lips together in an
impatient line. 'Poor little sod. He's less than two
weeks old and he could end up brain-damaged or even
dead because his parents didn't care enough to make
sure he was safe.'

'That's not fair,' Emma objected, stung by his blanket condemnation. 'His mother cares.'

'Not enough to insist that her child's properly taken
care of,' he insisted. 'So much for mother-love.'

'You're very quick to set yourself up as judge and
jury, aren't you? Everything's so cut and dried, isn't
it?' she scorned. 'The baby should have been taken
care of, and she's the mother so it was her job to take
care of it—in spite of the fact that she had a Caesarean
delivery less than two weeks ago and her doctor told
her she shouldn't be going away, in spite of the fact
that she was only five feet two and weighed less than a
hundred pounds, wet through, and was married to a
rugby-playing, hard-drinking man of six feet who
weighed twice what she did. It was his baby too!' She
was almost panting for breath by the time she reached
the end.

'Point taken,' Adam said quietly into the fraught

silence which stretched between them, his dark eyes thoughtful as they rested on her heated face. 'But I doubt you'd have allowed it to happen to a child of yours, even if you were married to Goliath.'

Emma was heartened by the implied compliment. 'I would hope that whoever I chose to be the father of my child would love and care for him as much as I did,' she said, and was swept by a wave of mingled anger and pain emanating from the self-contained man who refused to let any trace of either emotion show on his face.

Someone had hurt Adam Wolf.

At some time in his past someone—probably a woman—had hurt him so deeply that his respect for women as a whole had been all but destroyed.

She found herself idly imagining what a child of his would look like, and was captivated by the mental image of a solemn-faced miniature of that handsome face, the lean planes softened by baby chubbiness.

A sad longing filled her that she would never know if she was right. The tentative friendship they were building was unlikely to last long after he returned to the other side of the world and got caught up in his own busy life.

Still, she thought, briskly banishing impossible dreams which had her cradling the tiny dark-eyed child to her own breast, he was here for three months, and at least she would have the memories of his friendship to look back on when he left.

'Back to work.' She glanced up at the clock and pushed herself to her feet. 'I'm amazed it's been quiet as long as this. Thanks for the coffee.' She saluted him with her cup as she took it over to the sink to rinse it out.

'Emma?'

For a minute she wasn't sure whether she'd heard the softly spoken word or imagined it.

'Yes?' She leant back against the edge of the sink unit and clasped her hands together.

'Will you. . .?' He paused and gave his head a slight shake. 'Have you ever ridden a horse?'

'Yes,' she replied hesitantly. 'I haven't been riding for years, but as a child. . .' She shrugged.

'If your day off is still tomorrow, would you come with me?' He seemed to have come to an important decision, his words firm and deliberate.

'Come where?' Emma sidestepped her immediate impulse to agree to anything as long as it was in his company. She couldn't afford the heartbreak that could bring.

'I saw an advert for some stables a few miles outside town, where you can hire horses by the hour. Would you like to come?'

'Yes, I'd love to,' she managed calmly while her heart was turning cartwheels round her chest.

'Great.' He threw her one of those lethal smiles and she began to wonder if her pulse would ever be normal around him. 'I'll pick you up about ten tomorrow.'

'No!' she yelped. 'I've got a load of laundry and an empty fridge to fill before I can go gallivanting off on horseback. If I don't do some chores I'll end up having to wipe my feet as I come *out* of the house, it'll be so dirty.'

'OK,' he conceded, with a nod. 'You shovel out the mess and I'll arrive at ten to take you shopping. Then we can set off as soon as we've stacked it in your fridge.'

It was an order rather than a suggestion but Emma hadn't the heart to point that out; the boyishly enthusiastic expression on his face was so appealing.

'OK,' she agreed in a tone of long-suffering. 'Ten it is.'

'Great!' He straightened up to his feet in one smooth surge of strength, his enthusiasm a balm to Emma's soul.

For the sake of her shattered concentration, it was a good job that the most serious injuries she had to deal with that afternoon were those of cyclist and a skateboarder who'd collided at speed and left several yards of skin on the road.

The whole time she was dealing with removing grit from bare arms and legs and cleaning and dressing their wounds, the two brothers were bickering about whose fault it was, and who had said what about which side they were supposed to cross of the slalom they'd constructed.

'Hey!' Finally Emma was moved to intervene. 'Why don't you do what the professional display teams do when they're setting up stunts?'

'Huh?'

'What?'

Emma nearly smiled at their astonishment that she'd actually said something non-medical, but she knew that at the first sign that she wasn't taking the whole thing as seriously as they were she would lose their attention.

'They practise a series of signals—such as hand movements—which only they know. Then, when they've practised over and over to get it really smooth, they can put on a performance and it looks as if they're reading each other's minds, because no one else knows what the signals mean.'

There were several seconds of blank silence while they gazed at her in awed amazement.

'Wow! Like a secret code,' said one, his surly expression breaking into a gap-toothed grin.

'Fantastic!' said the other, and for the rest of their stay in her care they were busily working together to sort out a plan of campaign for astounding their friends.

'Brilliant!' Sister Noone praised when Emma finally saw them depart. 'The noise was getting so bad in here that I was just about to come and ask if you needed a hand to negotiate an arms treaty to avert World War Three. I shall try a version of that trick on my nephews next time I get conned into babysitting!'

Although she was tired by the time she reached home, Emma wasn't nearly ready to go to bed. She was almost fizzing with anticipation at the prospect of spending at least part of her day off in Adam's company.

Even the dreaded chores didn't seem so bad when they were accompanied by thoughts of his open pleasure when she'd accepted his invitation, and she laughed aloud at his bossy organisation of her time — almost as if he wanted to spend as much of it with her as possible.

Whatever the reason, it was very flattering to have such a man eager for her company. It was a long time since she had allowed anyone, let alone someone from the male half of the species, close enough for them to feel that they wanted to go out with her.

Emma gave a little grimace as honesty forced her to admit that it was probably all her own fault, but she could hardly be blamed for her wariness.

She finally settled under the clean bedcovers in a pristine bedroom in a gleaming flat, with her hair freshly washed and her body sweet and clean in her prettiest cotton nightie.

Her mood was so buoyant that even the intrusion of her mental visitor couldn't dampen the bubbles in her blood, and she welcomed the unusually hesitant connection.

'Come on, then,' she murmured as she allowed her body to relax. 'I'm feeling so. . .so happy tonight that you can do your worst and it won't get me down. . .' She took a deep breath and released it, concentrating on filling her mind with positive, welcoming thoughts.

Hope.

The tentative emotion was the last thing she was expecting and she felt her breathing quicken.

Anticipation.

'Me too,' Emma murmured softly. 'Oh, whoever you are, I hope your problems are solving themselves. I know what it's like to travel down that long dark tunnel.'

Perhaps. . .things can get better.

Emma blinked as, for the first time, the feelings she was picking up almost seemed to take on words instead of being pure emotions.

Perhaps. . .we can learn to trust. . .to love. . .

A prickle of extra awareness made all the hairs on her body stand out, almost like a startled cat's fur.

This was uncanny. Eerie.

This was the first time anything like this had happened and she wasn't sure if she liked it. Was this how Richard had felt when he'd thought that she could read his mind? Because that was just what this mysterious person seemed to be doing.

Either that or the whole episode was some sort of wierd rebound so that she was picking up her own emotions. How else could she explain that the feelings she was experiencing from this other person mirrored her own so exactly?

Who else could possibly know her secret desire to trust Adam, her longing to be open with him, to share her thoughts and feelings in the hope that he was sharing the same growing feelings for her?

When the contact was broken Emma was left with a confused jumble of emotions of her own, but the thread which ran strongly through all of them was optimism. For the first time in years she was able to look towards the rest of her life with a feeling of hope.

The optimism was still there when she woke up in the morning, and she was smiling as she dressed in a well-worn pair of jeans in preparation for her outing with Adam. The shirt she chose had seen better days too, but she wasn't totally confident that she'd remember everything she'd learnt years ago and, if she fell off, didn't intend ruining a good shirt just so that she could impress Adam with her appearance.

The doorbell rang fifteen minutes early but she'd already been waiting impatiently for his arrival for an hour.

'Hi.' Adam's deep voice flowed through her like

dark molasses, his eyes gleaming with golden sparks as they travelled over her from head to foot.

'D-do you want to come in a minute while I get my bags from the kitchen?' It felt as if her heart was trying to climb out of her throat.

'Sure.' He shouldered himself away from his comfortable position against the doorpost and prowled past her.

Her eyes were riveted to the lean perfection of his hips and thighs, clad in jeans that clung even more closely than her own.

'Turn left,' she directed him hastily when she managed to drag her gaze away from the tight muscles of his bottom long enough to realise that he was nearly in her bedroom.

'It doesn't look in the least as if it needs a shovel,' he commented as he glanced around.

Every surface gleamed with cleanliness after her frenzied work yesterday evening, but she could hardly tell him that it was his fault she'd put in so much effort.

'It's small, but it's fairly near the hospital and it's affordable.' She shrugged diffidently.

'So, how long before you're ready to go shopping?' He tucked his hands in the front pockets of his jeans as if he didn't quite know what to do with them, his action stretching the faded denim across the blatant evidence of his masculinity.

Emma forced herself to look away and turned to grab the purse and shopping list she'd left ready on the top of her fridge.

'Ready to go,' she said brightly, hoping her lascivious thoughts hadn't shown on her face.

The shopping trip was fun, and she was able to buy

several things that she would have had to make a tiring second trip for if she hadn't had the luxury of transport.

'I could get quite used to the idea of having a chauffeur-driven car,' she teased as he locked the various bags and packages in the back of his car.

'Especially if it comes equipped with a driver with long enough arms to get the tins on the top shelves,' he taunted, reminding her of her attempts to reach the last of a special offer, which had rolled right to the back of a display.

'And with the muscles to carry it all back to the car,' she added as he unlocked the passenger door for her. 'Thanks, Adam. I don't remember when shopping was ever this easy—or this much fun.'

'You're welcome,' he murmured close to her ear, and helped her into her seat with innate courtesy.

It should have taken only a few minutes to unpack the shopping and put it away but Adam insisted on helping, so the whole exercise deteriorated into farce.

Two cups of coffee later they had finally recovered from their laughter enough to set off towards the stables that Adam had discovered, and Emma's stomach filled with a fresh set of butterflies.

'Can I help you?' an officious young woman called as Emma climbed out of the car, her tone coolly dismissive.

'I phoned yesterday evening,' Adam began in his distinctive American accent as he straightened up from locking the car.

'Oh, yes,' the woman breathed, her attitude completely different as her eyes travelled over him greedily from head to foot. 'Mr Wolf.'

Emma was torn between offering the woman a bib before she started drooling, or scratching her eyes out, but she bit her tongue and stayed silent.

'You said you had a horse trained for western riding?' he said calmly, as if he hadn't even noticed her reaction to him.

'Yes. I groomed him for you myself—'

'And the other horse has an English saddle?' he broke in briskly.

'Yes—' Her expression was growing distinctly frustrated as he prevented her from saying any more.

'And you were going to look out a large-scale map of the area around that hill.' He pointed to the tree-clad slopes which rose a little way behind the farmhouse attached to the stables.

'Yes. It's in the saddle-bag on the western saddle,' she confirmed, with a smile of anticipation.

'Well, if we could mount straight up, we'd like to get on our way,' Adam said politely.

'Oh, but. . .' Her avid face fell as she glanced up at the clock on the cupola above the entrance to the stables. 'I've got one girl off sick and some tinies coming in for a lesson soon, and the other girl hasn't come back with the other ride.'

'Is that a problem?' Adam enquired, his tone politeness itself.

'Well, it means I either have to cancel the tinies class or you'll have to wait until Debbie comes back,' she said, sounding quite flustered.

'Why should that make any difference?'

'Well, it means I'm not free to go with you.' She sounded almost tearful.

'Well,' Adam drawled broadly, 'that's no problem.

We'll just take ourselves off for a couple of hours and let you get on with what you have to do.'

'Oh, no. I couldn't do that—' she bleated.

'I thought you said the horses were—what did you call them?—bomb-proof. And I'm sure you said the land surrounding the hill was enclosed by stock-proof fencing.'

'Well. . .yes.'

'Well, I hardly think we're going to get lost, then, are we? So, if you'll just point our mounts out to us. . .'

By this time Emma was biting her tongue with a vengeance, and she was glad to leave the whole charade to Adam.

'But they're very valuable horses and I don't even know if you can ride,' the poor girl wailed.

'Well, you aren't likely to find out until you see us on them,' he argued logically, and she sighed heavily and gave in with bad grace.

The animal she led out first was an elegant-looking beast with a body the colour of polished conkers and a black mane and tail.

'That one looks like yours,' Adam commented to Emma as it was led towards them. 'Is that about what you were used to?'

'Pretty much,' she confirmed, liking the look of the animal immediately, and taking the time to introduce herself and let him get to know her before she checked the security of saddle and bridle.

'There's a good fella,' she crooned, her voice just above a whisper as she'd learnt from an old Irish horseman, and she smiled to herself as she watched his ears flicker back as he listened.

She was delighted to find that she'd lost none of her

old skill as she settled herself in the saddle and prepared herself for a thoroughly enjoyable ride with or without a chaperon.

'Is that the only western saddle you have?' she heard Adam enquire as a second horse was led out. 'I think it's more of a pony size...'

The horse wasn't a great deal larger than the one that Emma had been given, but he was powerfully muscled, with a characteristic spread of dappled markings, white on the dark coat over his rump.

Emma nearly choked at the incongruous sight of the diminutive saddle on a horse big enough for a powerfully built adult male and waited to see what would happen.

'I'll get an English saddle for you, instead,' the young woman offered.

'Don't bother.' Adam stepped forward and stripped the saddle off with the minimum of fuss. 'I prefer riding without, anyway.' And, after a similar introduction ritual to the one Emma had followed with her mount, he leapt easily onto the back of the powerful animal.

'Oh, my God,' gasped the young woman, clearly impressed with his skill, and a new expression crossed her face. 'I bet you're one of the actors working on that film—or a stunt man,' she guessed again excitedly. 'That's it! You're a stunt man, aren't you? I'm right, aren't I?'

Adam placed one finger against his lips and winked at her before he signalled silently for Emma to follow him.

Emma managed to hold onto her mirth until they were clear of the yard, then burst out laughing.

'I bet you're a stunt man,' she simpered, then reverted to her own voice. 'You're nothing but a big show-off, Adam Wolf.'

'Well, it meant we didn't have to have that empty-headed ninny coming along with us. I'd already told the woman on the phone that we were competent riders and that we were well insured.'

'You speak for yourself,' Emma demurred. 'You might be in practice, but it's years since I last rode, and as for insurance—'

'You ride well,' he broke in. 'You move with the horse as if you were part of him. Who taught you?'

'An old Irishman,' Emma said, a fond smile crossing her face as she remembered the first true friend she'd ever had. 'He'd broken so many bones in his life that he walked like a crab, but on horseback he was a magician.'

As she regained her confidence in herself and her horse she allowed her eyes to stray over the stunning picture that Adam made riding bareback. He was everything old Paddy had been and so much more, the empathy between him and the horse he encircled with powerful thighs evident in the proud carriage of each.

'Your heritage has never been more obvious than it is at the moment,' she murmured with open admiration. 'You look. . .right.'

There was a sharp question in his eyes when they met hers, but one glance was enough to tell him what she was thinking, and he smiled.

'I feel right too. It's too long since I've been on a horse and to find an Appaloosa of such quality in an out-of-the-way place. . .' He shook his head in amazement.

'They are native to America, aren't they?'

'Once they were introduced by the Spanish,' he elaborated. 'Ownership of horses was one of the measures of how well a plains tribe would survive, and the Blackfoot became known as superb horsemen. . .'

While they were talking they'd reached the track winding its way up the side of the hill towards the summit and entered the cathedral-like hush under the trees.

'I envy people who own land like this,' Emma murmured in a voice suitable for a church.

'To my people, the concept of owning land is alien. Land exists before we do, and will still exist after we go. We can't own it; we are merely caretakers of it for the duration of our time on it.'

Emma was silent for a moment while she thought about the concept. 'That idea makes a lot more sense than the one I've been brought up with, where everyone's intent on grabbing everything they can out of the earth for themselves. Your way means that everyone is bound to take care of the land for the next generation.'

The track was wide enough for the two of them to ride side by side, with a swath of grass up the centre, and for some minutes they rode silently, with bird song and the rhythmic crushing of last autumn's leaf-mould by the horses' hooves the only sounds to break the silence.

'Confident enough for a bit more speed?' Adam said, with a gleam of challenge in his eyes. He looked so at home on the animal he was riding, his body moving easily and naturally with every shift of gait, the powerful muscles of his lean thighs outlined by the worn fabric of his jeans.

'Define speed,' Emma demanded cautiously, dragging her eyes away from their blatant appreciation of his body to concentrate on the knowing expression on his face.

'Oh, just a gentle canter. . .for a start,' he suggested, and she saw the muscles in his legs tauten as he squeezed with his legs to signal to the horse.

Emma laughed aloud as her own mount responded to her instructions. 'This is great!' She shook her head as the breeze generated by their speed teased tendrils of dark hair from the controlling clip to curl around her face. 'He's got lovely smooth paces.' And she leant forward to urge him on, drawing up level with Adam's mount.

'Faster?' His teeth gleamed whitely in his smiling face.

'OK,' Emma tossed back, accepting the challenge, and their pace increased from the steady three beats of a canter to the faster double beat of a gallop.

The thudding of the horses' hooves on the packed earth echoed back to them off the trunks of the trees and reverberated up through her body like an extra heartbeat, the adrenalin pouring through her as the horses responded to the increasing angle of the hill.

The track widened suddenly and they emerged from the shelter of the trees into the sunshine of the wide, grassy area that sloped up towards the top.

'Whoa, boy. . .steady. . .' Adam gentled his mount into a slower pace and Emma did likewise until they were once more walking side by side. 'A couple of minutes to allow them to cool down, then we'll give them a break,' he said as they approached the summit.

'That was fantastic,' Emma panted as she watched

Adam jump lightly to the ground. 'I hadn't realised just how much I've missed it.'

'So you're glad you came?' Adam smiled up at her as he looped the reins of his own mount around his arm and reached two hands up to her waist to lift her out of the saddle.

The power of the reaction she felt as soon as his hands touched her was stronger than at any time before in her life, and her secret knowledge of the pleasure he felt as he held her body between his hands redoubled her own awareness of him.

She rested her hands on his shoulders to steady herself, and felt the taut, contained power in his muscles as he lowered her slowly, his breath warming her throat at the open neck of her shirt, then her face as her feet finally reached the ground.

'Fishing for compliments?' she said shakily, her heart racing faster than the echo of the horses' galloping hooves. 'Yes. I'm glad I came.' And she allowed her candid grey eyes to rise from the rapidly beating pulse at the base of his throat to meet the mysterious gold-shot darkness of his.

'Emma. . .?' Adam paused and his hands seemed reluctant to release her. 'Can I ask a favour?' he said hesitantly. 'You can say no if you think it's too much of a liberty. . .'

'What?' Emma was intrigued.

'Would you let your hair down?'

Emma's breath caught in her throat as she recognised the significance of the slightly hoarse tone in his voice, and her hands rose almost of their own accord to comply with his request.

At the last minute she paused and, keeping her eyes fixed on his, issued a challenge of her own.

'I will if you will,' she murmured huskily, and felt the jolt of awareness hit him.

CHAPTER SIX

'OK,' ADAM murmured, his voice soft and almost dangerous as he raised one hand to pull at the end of the leather thong that bound the dark strands at the base of his skull, his eyes focused on her as intently as lasers.

Midnight-dark silk spilled over his shoulders and he shook his head until it settled to frame the stark purity of his bone structure. As she feasted her eyes on the perfection of him his chin came up, the arrogant gesture throwing his jaw into prominence and accentuating the strength of his cheek-bones and the slightly curved blade of his nose.

'Your turn,' he growled, taking a step towards her, and, as she reached up to release the clasp that tried vainly to control the profusion of her hair he was already spearing his fingers through the strands as though he couldn't wait to touch them.

'Beautiful,' he breathed. 'It's so full of life. How can you bear to tie it in a knot like that? Hair like this should be free.'

His intensity almost took her breath away and her voice was shaky when she replied. 'I'm sure Sister would be well impressed if I came on duty with this mess hanging all over the place.' She flicked a dismissive hand at the dark curls spilling over her shoulders and halfway down her back.

'Mess?' He sounded outraged. 'This isn't a mess, it's

a glory.' And he buried his face in handfuls of it, smoothing it over the planes of his cheeks as though it were a priceless silken fabric.

'Come on.' He straightened up abruptly and drew in a deep breath as he released her hair. 'Let's settle the horses by some grass and sit down.' He turned, led their two mounts into the shade and tethered them.

Emma was glad that he'd taken charge of her horse, because she was having trouble staying upright, let alone walking, on legs that seemed to have forgotten how to support her.

When he beckoned her to join him at the summit she drew in a deep breath and took the first step, amazed that her knees remembered how to bend, and climbed the last few steps.

Gratefully she sank to the grass and wrapped her arms around her upraised knees, for the first time looking out at the view.

'Oh, Adam, it's fantastic,' she breathed as her eyes took in the vista spread out below them.

The gentle slopes of the valley were a patchwork of soft greens and the bleached gold of ripening fields of grain. The clumps of trees dividing them were in full summer leaf and they created dark patches of shade where sheep and cattle dozed out of the heat of the afternoon.

'How did you find this place?' she questioned, finally dragging her gaze away from the scene in front of her. 'Have you been here before?'

'No, but I looked on a map that showed contour lines to find it. Then, when I saw the advert for the riding school, everything came together.'

'But why were you looking for it in the first place?' Emma was intrigued.

'Wherever I go, I have to find somewhere like this.' He fixed his dark gaze on hers, his words sounding almost like a confession. 'I need the. . .recharging of batteries that this gives me.' He indicated the scene spread out before them with the wave of one lean hand.

'Have you always done this?'

'Since I was a child. It was something I was taught by my grandfather.'

'Didn't your parents do it too?'

'I don't remember them,' he said candidly without a trace of self-pity. 'My grandfather took care of me and taught me what I had to do.'

'He's Blackfoot too?'

Adam nodded. 'He's a tribal shaman—a healer.'

'So you're both healers.' Emma smiled her delight. 'He must be so proud of you.'

Adam was silent as a shadow passed over his face, and Emma picked up the echoes of a deep sadness.

'Wasn't he pleased when you wanted to train as a doctor?' she probed gently.

'He said that he had already taught me what my people needed me to know, and that if I went to learn white men's medicine I would end up knowing less as a man than I knew when I was a child.'

'That wasn't fair,' Emma objected. 'There are many things that his traditional skills aren't equipped to deal with. How could he do that to you—make you feel as if you had to make a choice?'

Adam smiled slowly. 'That's how I felt at first. I was angry with him, thinking that he had abandoned me.

Then I remembered how he'd taught me to think, to analyse, and I realised that he was making me think about my reasons for making the choice in the first place.'

'Was he disappointed when you chose to become a doctor? Did it cause a rift between you?'

'No. He still believes that I will return to the reservation to take his place before he goes.'

'How old is he?'

'Eighty-six—' Adam smiled '—but he would hate for me to remind him of it.' His smile faded as if he had just remembered something painful.

'What?' Emma prompted softly.

'I went to visit him just before I came over here,' Adam sighed. 'He said the same thing he always does—he's getting too old and when am I going to come back where I belong, where I'm needed the most.' He looked up at her with a deep sadness in his eyes. 'The trouble is, for the first time he sounded as if he meant it, and he seems to have suddenly grown frail.'

'Oh, Adam.' Her heart went out to him and, without thinking, she reached out a hand to rest it on his arm; the jolt of sensation stopped her breathing.

For several seconds they were totally still, her hand resting on the warm strength of his naked forearm, their eyes locked together as though neither of them wanted to break the contact.

'I need—' He broke off, his voice too husky to continue, and closed his eyes, finally releasing her from their spell so that she could remove her hand from the warm seduction of his flesh.

He cleared his throat before he spoke again but

Emma was sure that the words were different from those he had been going to say before.

'I need to switch off for a moment. Please, forgive me for being less than hospitable.'

She watched as he settled himself and drew in a deep breath, his chest expanding to stretch the soft knit fabric of his polo shirt over its impressive breadth.

'Is this something that your grandfather taught you too?' Emma murmured softly as she felt herself being enveloped by an aura of peace.

'From when I was very small,' he confirmed, his voice growing distant and low, almost hypnotic. 'I use it as a way of controlling myself when I can't control what's happening around me, a way of bringing myself back into balance...' The words died away on the breeze as she watched the tiny indications of tension leave his face as he relaxed.

Emma, too, made herself comfortable, crossing her legs tailor-fashion and allowing her hands to lie limply on her thighs in her own version of the yoga position, then she closed her eyes and allowed her mind to wander.

Gradually, through the usual kaleidoscopic jumble of images, she began to see a picture in her mind of a towering hill rising out of a tree-clothed plain. As she focused on the mental image she somehow knew that this was a very special place, a place of great power, and that it had a particular significance for Adam.

At first she thought that what she was seeing was an image like a photograph, but as she concentrated harder she saw something coming towards her.

It was several moments before she realised that she was looking at an animal—a large grey wolf whose golden eyes seemed, even in her imagination, to be fixed directly on her.

As she watched, mesmerised by the inner vision, she saw a shadow half-hidden behind the powerful presence of the big grey animal and she fought to see what it was, convinced that it was essential that she should be able to see it.

Eventually the shadow moved to stand beside the big male, and she could see that it too was a wolf but smaller and slighter, with great grey eyes, and she knew with utter certainty that she was the wolf's mate.

Later that night, after Adam had dropped her at home, Emma was still unable to decide what her vision had meant.

Adam had hardly spoken to her since he'd finally surfaced from their time of silence. He'd almost withdrawn into himself and Emma had known that it had not been the time to tell him what she'd seen or to ask him if he had an explanation.

Even so, she'd felt a strong sense of connection with him since their time together on top of the hill—even stronger than she'd had with the mystery person who had been invading her nights.

As she lay in her bed in the soft darkness she began to wonder if she had been wrong all this time.

Perhaps it was possible to gain enough control over this gift of hers so that she *could* lead a normal life. She now knew two men with whom she felt at ease in a way that she had never done before. Adam and her mystery visitor—and somehow over the last few days she had become convinced that the person with whom she'd connected *was* a man—each seemed to seek her company, either mentally or physically.

Maybe there were other people who would accept her for the person she was, without fear or disgust.

Perhaps *Richard* had been the one with the problem. Perhaps it had been *his* failing that he hadn't been able to cope with the fact that she was more sensitive than most to his feelings.

The more she thought about it, the more she realised that, in all the time he had known her, he had made no effort to find out about her gift but had tried to shut out all knowledge of it so that when an incident had occurred he'd reacted as if Emma had let him down in some way.

She curled up under the softness of her summer-weight duvet and realised that, if Adam hadn't been in such a strange mood this afternoon, she might even have found the courage to tell him about her secret.

Perhaps she was hoping for too much, just because she was so attracted to him, but she honestly believed that when she told him he would understand.

Anyway, a small voice insisted on adding, if she was wrong and Adam did turn out to feel the same way as Richard had, at least she knew that he would be returning to America when his three months were over, and she wouldn't have to cope with the trauma of trying to work with someone who despised her.

'Mr Demetriou? This is Staff Nurse Sullivan. . .' Sister Noone was trying to attract the attention of the man hunched over in his seat in the waiting area, his hands gripping the back of his skull.

As she continued he straightened gingerly and began to stand up. 'If you will follow her through to—'

'Catch him!' Emma shouted as the man started to go down like a felled tree.

Barbara Noone turned back just in time to grab hold of the lapel of his jacket, and between that and Emma's grasp of his elbow they managed to slow his fall.

'Trolley, quick!' Sister directed as she rolled him effortlessly into the recovery position. 'And grab a bit of muscle while you're about it.'

Emma took off, her pace just short of a run as she commandeered a porter and signalled Dave to come with her.

In no time they had the grey-faced patient on the trolley and he was on his way into the emergency room, with Adam Wolf following close behind.

'He staggered into the department under his own steam about fifteen minutes ago, complaining of a terrible headache which had come on very suddenly. He said he felt sick and the light was hurting his eyes and he was a bit confused, but, apart from a slight backache, there were no other obvious symptoms.'

While Sister had been filling Adam in on the presenting symptoms Emma had been noting down her initial observations of his vital signs, but it wasn't until she came to take his pulse that she received a frightening jolt.

Suddenly, counting his pulse was the least of her worries, and she swung to face Adam just as Sister left the room.

'Adam,' she said urgently, completely forgetting the proper form of address in the pressure of the situation, 'I. . .' She paused and swallowed hard in an attempt to control her fear. This was not the way she had wanted it to happen... 'Do...do you think this could be a subarachnoid haemorrhage?'

Inside, where she was sensitive to strong emotions, she felt the shock go through him at the same time as she saw the evidence of it cross his face.

'What on earth made you think of that?' The sharp words were accompanied by a rapid examination of the patient, Adam's forehead furrowed in concentration. 'Is there a tray ready for a lumbar puncture?' he directed over his shoulder. 'If there's blood in the cerebrospinal fluid—'

'You can't do that if his intracranial pressure's raised, can you?' Emma turned the essential words into a question, and earned herself another penetrating look and another knife-like stab of hidden suspicion.

'Let's put it this way.' His accent was very clipped. 'If I draw off fluid from his lower spine when the pressure is high in his skull, the imbalance could cause his brain to be sucked through the base of his skull and kill him.

'Now—' he turned to face her, fixing her with a stern gaze '—if you know something—anything—that could affect Mr Demetriou's chances of survival, you'd better tell me.'

Emma clenched her hands tight as she gathered her courage, and her nails bit into her palms as the words came out in jerky spurts.

'He's got a subarachnoid haemorrhage—a berry aneurysm at the base of his brain that's—leaking slightly and it's just about to burst.'

'Thank you.' One hand was already reaching out for the phone to alert Theatre and line up a surgical team.

Emma was still standing beside their patient, her hand holding his wrist.

'I don't know if they can get to it in time,' she murmured, her voice shaky with the strain of what she was doing. 'A small leak can repair itself, but this one is so big. . .'

Why did it have to be Adam who'd been in the room? With anyone else on the staff she could have found some way of bluffing her way through, trading on her reputation for lucky guesses, but she'd allowed him to get too close. . .

'How badly is he haemorrhaging?' he said in a low voice as they accompanied the trolley towards the lift.

'It's getting worse by the minute,' she returned almost under her breath as the doors slid closed behind them.

'Right,' Adam muttered, and slid one hand under their patient's neck, high up under his skull. As Emma watched in amazement he closed his eyes and grew still, a look of total concentration on his face.

There was a strange sensation in her fingers where they were still grasping Mr Demetriou's wrist and she nearly dropped it in surprise.

'Don't let go.' Adam's voice sounded strangely hollow and guttural. 'Help me. . .' And he was silent again.

Emma closed her eyes and concentrated on the sensations she was feeling through her hands and in her mind, analysing them carefully until she suddenly realised that Adam was trying to do something impossible—he was trying to control the man's blood pressure by some strange form of will-power, in an attempt to lessen the force on the weakened area of blood vessel.

Oh, she knew *why* he was trying to do it—if he

succeeded it would buy their patient a little more time in which the surgical team could operate to save his life. What she didn't know was what gave him the idea that it was even worth trying. What made him think that it was possible for one person to be able to control another's blood pressure by sheer will-power?

Impossible as she knew it to be, it was working. She could tell that the blood loss was slowing rather than increasing. . .

Deep inside, Emma felt the first stirrings of fear.

Who was Adam Wolf that he had such power? What other frightening powers might he be hiding?

The lift doors slid open and willing hands reached in to pull the trolley straight through for Mr Demetriou to be prepped.

In the general mêlée of people around the patient, Emma slipped silently away and returned to A and E, taking the long way down by the stairs to give herself a little time to think.

Except rational thought seemed to have fled. Nothing made sense any more.

For a moment she wondered if this were all a dream. In a few minutes, would her alarm clock ring so that she could laugh at the outlandish things she had imagined?

She pushed the door open at the foot of the stairwell just as an ambulance drew up outside the entrance to the unit, lights and siren going, and she knew it hadn't been a dream.

She shivered as all the hairs stood up on the back of her neck, and firmly shut a mental door on the events of the last half-hour. Later, when she was safely home in her little flat, she would think about it. Just at the moment, with a young motor cyclist bleeding from multiple injuries, she had far more pressing things to do.

That patient was the start of a hectic time, with a tide of injuries arriving faster than they could be treated, but Emma was grateful, knowing that it meant that there would be no time for Adam to speak to her alone.

She knew he wanted to—the glower on his face when he'd returned to A and E after seeing Mr Demetriou up to Theatre was enough to tell her that he was angry that she'd disappeared without a word. She didn't need any special powers to know that.

In the meantime, there was a patient with a violent allergy to peanuts, a lady with the back of her hand bleeding profusely from an accidental scratch by her dog, a child with a foreign body of some sort stuck up his nose, and a teenager who had developed a septic ear after a less than successful attempt at piercing his own ears.

'We gave her epinephrine to inhale and she's on oxygen via a nasal cannula.' The paramedic was completing his report as he wheeled the patient with the allergy reaction through.

'She apparently brought up most of the contaminated food before we got to her, just after she felt her face flush. She's got a large bore IV running wide open, and we've been picking up some tachycardia on the heart monitor. Her breathing isn't sounding good.'

'Emma?' Dave called across from the opposite room. 'I need you to take over here.'

She glanced in through the open door to see the

gory mess on the back of the dog woman's hand and nodded silently.

In a moment the two of them had changed places and Dave was positioning the allergy patient ready for intubation.

'Mrs Larkin? I'm Staff Nurse Sullivan.' She pulled on fresh gloves and checked that everything was ready for her to start work.

'Why did that young man want you to take over?' Her patient was obviously in pain, but there was nothing wrong with her powers of observation.

'If you'd ever seen the way he sews a button on a shirt, you'd know,' Emma said, with a smile. 'He's a very good technician, but he's the first one to admit that sewing up isn't one of his favourite jobs.'

'So how good are you at needlework?' The answering smile was a little wan, but she was definitely less tense than she'd been when Emma arrived.

'Pretty good,' Emma confirmed. 'Once I get this lot deadened, I can take my time and get it nice and neat.'

'Well, at least I know I haven't got to have a tetanus jab as well this time.' She averted her eyes as Emma prepared to inject along each side of the wound. 'Last time I missed the top step in the garden and gashed my shin. I swear the tetanus shot hurt more than the stitches.'

'I'll need to wait a couple of minutes to make sure that's good and numb, then I'll debride the edges to get a neat join. In the meantime, let's get you cleaned up a bit.'

Emma rinsed the surrounding area with saline before she finally started to draw the two sides of the ragged gash together.

'How on earth did you do this?' she asked, knowing that her patient needed to keep her mind occupied.

'I was playing with the dog and we both went to catch the same ball at the same time. Unfortunately, her tooth caught me right across the back of my hand where the skin's thinnest.'

'Is she a very boisterous dog?'

'Not usually. She's getting quite old and she's a wonderful guard dog, but so gentle. She was so upset when I shouted, and took herself off to her bed almost as if she was a child being sent to her room. I had to go and tell her I wasn't cross with her before I could come to the hospital.'

The suturing was soon done and her patient finally plucked up the courage to look at Emma's handiwork before she covered it.

'You've made a lovely job of that.' She released a deep sigh of relief and managed a more normal smile. 'The stitches are so small and neat and you've even joined the two halves of my freckle!'

Emma chuckled as she taped a dressing over her work. 'Keep it dry as long as you can so you don't slow the healing down or get an infection in it,' she advised. 'When the local anaesthetic wears off, you'll probably feel better with the hand raised and supported—just until it stops throbbing.'

'Oh, good. That means my husband will have to do the washing-up for a few days!' the woman chuckled, obviously feeling better by the minute. 'I had to come back a week later to have the stitches taken out last time.'

'Well, if you want a week without having to do the

washing-up. . .' Emma raised a teasing eyebrow. 'But
they'll probably be ready to come out after five days.'

She sent Mrs Larkin away in a much happier frame
of mind, with an invitation to come back at any time if
she thought the wound had developed an infection.

'What happened to the child with the foreign body?'
Emma asked as she went to find out what was next on
the list.

'Removed and gone,' Diane West confirmed. 'It was
the butterfly from the back of an earring. Fairly easy
to grab once we sat on the little eel to keep it still!'

'And the self-piercing job?'

'Still up for grabs. You can have him if you want
him,' she offered.

In the distance she heard the all too familiar sound
of Adam's voice and jumped at the chance to be busy
when he arrived down this end of the department.

Emma knew that she was being a coward but she
needed the chance to get her thoughts in order before
she saw him again. She knew that he was going to ask
her questions about her gift and she was prepared to
answer them—she had already decided that she would
tell him before today's traumatic happenings.

The thing she wasn't yet ready to do was find out
about the strange powers that Adam seemed to have.
She was well accustomed to the idea of being able to
pick up other people's emotions, rather like picking up
random stations on a radio. What she had never come
across before was someone who could actually direct
some energy, some power towards other people.

'Hello. I'm Staff—'

'I'm not going to have to have my ear chopped off,

am I?' the belligerent young man demanded as soon as
Emma began speaking.

'Not as far as I know,' she replied blandly as she
pulled on a fresh pair of gloves. 'We've got to have a
proper look at it to see what the damage is first.'

She beckoned for him to sit on the chair beside the
sink and handed him a stainless-steel kidney bowl.

'Hold this on your shoulder so it's right up against
your neck,' she directed, then began to explore. 'How
long ago did you do this?'

'About ten days— Ow!' He turned a little to glare
up at her. 'You're enjoying this, aren't you?' he
accused.

'Of course we do. That's why we become nurses—so
we can hurt people.' Emma concentrated on what she
was doing as she said the ridiculous words in a deceptively calm voice. She had the dubious pleasure of
watching his neck turn a dull red, the colour travelling
right up under his semi-shaven hairstyle.

'How many holes did you put in here?' she
demanded as she carefully probed the swollen lobe of
his ear.

'Six.'

'What sort of earrings did you put in? Gold
sleepers?'

'Nah. Studs.'

'Ah!' Emma knew what she was feeling now. 'When
did you take the studs out?'

'This morning. It was all swollen and I'd lost one of
them. . .'

'It's not lost,' Emma announced as she straightened
up. 'The flesh of your earlobe didn't heal up properly
around the hole you made and an infection started.

When it started swelling, there wasn't enough space between the stud and the butterfly on the back and they've burst into the lobe.'

'Oh, gross!' The young tough began to look distinctly green. 'Does that mean it's stuck in there?'

'No. It'll have to come out or the infection won't be able to clear.'

'How will you get it out?' There was no sign of the belligerence now. He had become just another apprehensive patient.

'I'll get the doctor, but I think he'll give you an injection to deaden the ear, then go fishing for it.'

'Will you be here?' He refused to look at her, but Emma was careful not to smile at the change in his attitude.

'Wouldn't miss it for the world,' she assured him breezily. 'You know how we nurses are into other people's pain.'

His head shot round towards her, his eyes wide with shock, and she threw him a grin and a wink as she went to organise the next stage.

Her luck was holding because, when she went looking for him, Adam was fully occupied in one of the emergency rooms and it was the senior house officer who came to retrieve the embedded jewellery.

Adam was still busy when she went off duty, and she arrived home with a sense of relief, locked her door behind her and collapsed in a heap in the corner of her slightly lumpy sofa.

She kicked her shoes off, and took the clasp out of her hair to relieve the tension headache which had been building ever since she'd realised what was wrong with Mr Demetriou.

She'd been glad to hear that he'd survived the process of repairing the damaged area of blood vessel at the base of his brain. Now his family just had to wait and see how much residual damage he would be left with.

She must have dozed off in spite of her less than comfortable position, because the evening shadows were filling the room when she woke up with a jump, all the hairs going up on the back of her neck.

'Who's there?' she whispered, her eyes darting about apprehensively. Was someone in her flat? How had they got in? She was sure that she'd locked the door when she'd returned from her shift.

CHAPTER SEVEN

ARE *you there?*

The sensation of her mystery visitor arriving in her mind unannounced had become familiar now, and she found herself relaxing as relief flowed over her.

'Yes, I'm here,' she murmured aloud into the quiet of her room, glad that it was only *his* presence she had felt and not some intruder's.

She let her head drop back against the high back of the sofa with a snort of disbelief. 'It's a good job no one can hear me. They'd think I was one sandwich short of a picnic to be sitting in the dark talking to myself.'

Even so, she stayed where she was and waited. After her fierce determination that she wasn't going to allow any communication with this intrusive stranger, she was surprised how welcome the contact had become.

She didn't know whether the knowledge that she was listening had helped him to feel less alone with his problem, but she did know that in a strange way the experience of making contact willingly had changed her.

Somehow, since she had given in to the inevitable and accepted his intrusion into her life, she had felt more at peace with herself and who she was...until today...

I need to speak to you. I'm so confused. I need some answers.

'Don't we all?' Emma muttered as she remembered again her growing fear at the sudden realisation that Adam wasn't what she had thought.

Oh, she'd known that he wasn't a man who let his emotions show. He spoke very little about himself during his hours on duty, working unstintingly to make his brief stay at such a centre of excellence for multiple trauma a learning experience in both directions.

In spite of all the offers he must have had from the various members of staff since he'd arrived at St Lawrence's, he had, she'd noticed, kept mostly to himself in his off-duty hours. When he had asked her to spend the day with him, her foolish vanity had made her believe that for some reason he had been attracted to her. She had wanted to believe that they were developing some sort of relationship—a friendship.

Now she realised that she hadn't known him at all. How could she, with her sensitivity to other people, have missed such a thing?

She couldn't forget the fear that had slid insidiously inside her when she had realised what he was trying to do for Mr Demetriou, and then the utter disbelief when he'd seemed to achieve it. Surely she must have imagined it? It just wasn't possible for one person to use his will-power to affect another in that way—was it?

And, if it was, what sort of person was he that he had such power. . .?

I'm afraid that I might be making a mistake. I might already have made a serious mistake. I need to try to sort it out, but I don't know if—

The sharp knock at her door broke her concentration and the connection was lost, leaving Emma frustrated. It was the clearest communication she had ever had with another person, almost as if she could hear him speaking directly into her head. Every word had been as clear as if he had been talking to her face to face, but, as well as that, she'd been picking up the emotions behind the words. . .

The knock came again and she glanced across at the clock on top of her television, peering through the gloom to decipher the hands.

It wasn't terribly late, not even ten, but she didn't usually have people calling at this time of night and her sense of self-preservation kicked in.

In stockinged feet she padded silently over to the spyhole in the door, to see who it was.

Adam. Her lips shaped his name soundlessly, and her heart leapt up into her mouth then sank like a stone. She wasn't ready for this confrontation and she certainly didn't feel comfortable that it should take place in her flat, where she would be totally alone with him. . .

'Emma.' His deep voice reached her through the door, his tone as soft as though he knew that she was only inches away, with her hungry gaze riveted to the stark planes of his face.

She felt a swift stab of sympathy when she saw how tired and drawn he looked in the dim light of the hallway. For the first time since she'd met him, his broad shoulders were slumped with weariness.

'We need to talk,' he murmured, his dark eyes focusing on the spyhole as though he could see her watching him. 'Please. . .?'

There was no way she could refuse him when she knew how much it was costing him to plead. He was far too proud a man for that to be easy. As if it was acting without her volition, her hand lifted to release the safety chain and turn the catch.

Wordlessly they gazed at each other for several long seconds before she stepped back to allow him to enter. As Adam went on into the lounge Emma closed and secured the door, the subdued rattle of the chain sending a little shiver up her spine, to tighten the skin on the back of her neck.

She was alone with Adam Wolf, locked in her flat with a man who frightened her—

Stop it! She gave herself a mental shake. That was sheer stupidity. She knew beyond a doubt that he would never physically harm her.

Her silent steps took her into the tiny lounge area, to find it still in darkness. Adam hadn't switched on the light but was standing at the window, looking out at the night.

'Would you rather I left?'

The deep voice travelled through the silence to wrap itself around her and, in spite of her fears, she felt herself relax. This was Adam, the doctor she worked with, who spent his days helping to save lives. Inside her, where she was ruled by instinct, she knew that he was a kind and caring man.

'No,' she sighed. 'Stay.' There was nothing to be gained by delaying this meeting.

'Would you like something to drink?' She reached out a hand to switch on a light.

'Don't.'

The single word held her hand poised by the switch and her head swung towards him to see that he was still facing out into the darkness.

'It might be more comfortable for both of us if we were allowed a semblance of privacy. We have too many things to say that might not stand the glare of light...'

Emma nodded even though he wasn't watching, and stepped across to sit down in the small fireside chair on the other side of the room, tucking her stockinged feet underneath her and wrapping her arms around her as if she was chilled.

'May I sit?' The request underlined his effortless courtesy in spite of the tension filling the room, and she smiled fleetingly as she held one hand out towards the sofa in invitation.

There was a longer silence once he had subsided into her own favourite corner and stretched his long legs out. She heard the squeak of leather as he crossed his ankles the way he always did in the staffroom, and she visualised the way he would then link his fingers together and rest his hands over the buckle of his belt.

'Are you still frightened?'

Emma blinked. It was the first time she had known anyone to be able to see behind her careful façade— but then she should have expected it. Adam Wolf was unlike any man she'd ever known.

'Not frightened, exactly...' She didn't know quite how to describe her emotions.

'If you weren't frightened, why did you run away from me?'

'I didn't—!'

'And why did you spend the rest of the day avoiding me?' He ignored her attempted denial.

Emma was silent for a moment. He was right, she admitted silently. She *had* been running away and she *had* gone to great lengths to make sure that she hadn't had to work with him for the rest of her shift. And what had it gained her? A few hours' grace, which had done her no good at all because she hadn't had a coherent thought since it had happened.

'I wasn't ready to talk to you,' she said honestly, her chin tilting up in a determined way. 'I needed time to think.'

'And are you ready now?' There was a roughness to his voice, a touch of gravel which revealed his own tension.

'No.' She shook her head. 'I haven't been *able* to think. It's as if my brain has blown a fuse or something and it can't make sense of what it saw...'

'Well, forget your brain. What do your instincts tell you?'

'To run,' she retorted, and he gave a soft huff of appreciative laughter.

'Point taken,' he conceded, and drew in a deep breath before letting it out in a sigh.

Silence fell between them again, but this time the tension was less.

'I feel guilty.' His words finally broke the stillness. 'I should have been able to warn you what I was going to try, but there wasn't time.'

'I probably wouldn't have believed you anyway,' Emma countered bluntly. 'If you'd said you were going to try to control Mr Demetriou's bleeding by mentally lowering his blood pressure—'

'I knew it!' His voice was quietly jubilant in the darkness. 'I knew you could sense what I was doing—I could feel it.'

'I had my fingers over his pulse.' In an automatic

reflex, Emma began to cover up the evidence of her ability, her pulse starting to race as it always did when there was danger of discovery and exposure. She couldn't bear to go through that again. 'I could feel—'

'No!' he growled. 'No evasions, no lies—not now. Not between the two of us. This is too important to play games.'

Emma subsided, the slender fingers knotted together on her lap the only outward evidence of her tension.

Finally, 'No, you're right,' she admitted. 'Denial at this late stage is a little pointless.'

'How long have you known?' he questioned.

'Known?'

'About my gift?' His tone was slightly impatient.

'I didn't. Not until Mr Demetriou. . .' She was surprised that he had to ask. 'That's why it was such a shock.'

'But. . .you've been picking up my thoughts for some time now—'

'No—' Emma hurried to correct him, the way she always had with Richard '—not your thoughts, just an impression of your feelings. I. . .it's happened ever since I can remember, especially when people touch me. . .' Her voice died away with the enormity of her admission.

The last time she'd spoken of it had been to the man she'd hoped to marry, and in the end it had caused him to turn away from her.

She was glad to be sitting in the dark now, as the shame she'd been made to feel all her life filled her face with heat. At least she didn't have to watch the expression on his face change as he realised what a freak she was.

'Which side of your family did the gift come from?'

She could hardly believe how matter-of-fact he sounded, as if he heard such things every day of his life.

'My. . .my mother's,' she stammered while she fought for mental balance. 'And it's hardly a gift,' she argued. 'In my family it's been more like a curse. It's ruined so many lives. . .' She was unable to prevent the bitterness colouring her tone.

'I get mine from both sides,' he said quietly.

'You. . .?' His words robbed her of breath.

'For generations my mother's family were shamans for one branch of the Blackfoot and my father's family held a similar position in a parallel branch.'

'And you inherited their skills?'

'I wish it had been that easy,' he laughed. 'I inherited their gift but I had to *learn* the skills.'

'What do you mean?' She was intrigued.

'I would rather have been taking part in the more active side of life, with my peers, but my grandfather was a hard taskmaster and insisted I must learn how to recognise the many medicinal plants and how to prepare them. Then there was the spiritual side of being a shaman. . .' He was obviously lost in memories.

'So the Blackfoot don't shun people who have our sort of inheritance?' The very idea was like a revelation. And how strange it felt to have someone to identify with. Apart from her mother, who had tried to obliterate all trace of the 'taint', she had never met anyone like herself before.

'Far from it,' he confirmed. 'Shamans have a very important place within the structure of the tribe both medical and spiritual.'

'Was it very difficult for you to reconcile what you already knew with what you learnt at medical school?'

'It wasn't as different as you might think. Oh, I had to do a great deal of book learning, where the shaman's teaching is mostly a verbal tradition, but, as far as dealing with patients is concerned, there is very little difference. One thing I recognised very early on is that the use of placebos in medicine seems to be universal, no matter what tradition you follow.'

The silence that spread then was a thoughtful one as Emma fought to alter all her preconceptions.

'When did you suspect that I had the gift too?'

'The first time you tried to cover it up.' She heard humour in his voice. 'You might think you're good at keeping a poker-face, but I knew immediately that you were hiding something.'

'Why didn't you say anything?'

'In case I was wrong. I *do* know about the sort of horrified reaction you've always met, but I was lucky enough not to come up against it until later in life, when I was already certain of the value of what I had.'

Emma envied him that certainty.

'Why did your grandfather teach you? Why not your parents?'

'When they were killed in a fire, trying to help others to safety, Grandfather took on the job of raising me. I was too young to know the difference.'

'Does your grandfather think you'd make a good shaman?'

'He complains that studying Western medicine as ruined all the work he put into teaching me the Blackfoot ways!' There was a wealth of love and respect in his words, but Emma wondered about the reality.

'Does he mean it? Does he resent the choice you made?'

'No, he's far too wise for that. He realises that we have become westernised over the years since the white men came and we are now prey to the white men's diseases.'

'In what way?'

'When we were dependent on hunting and gathering to supply our needs we had to stay fit and healthy or we wouldn't survive the hunt or the long, hard winters. Then we were confined to reservations, with insufficient food and nothing to do, and our numbers fell as we starved to death each winter because we were not allowed to leave the reservation to hunt.

'Now we still have many people living from hand to mouth in poverty, subsisting on welfare cheques, but we also have those who have become very wealthy and are suffering from obesity and heart disease, lung cancer, alcohol addiction, diabetes. . . The list goes on.'

'And, because these illnesses are so new in Blackfoot society, the shamans are still trying to deal with the new plagues?'

'Exactly. And in most cases it's beyond them, but they can't admit it. In times gone by, if a shaman had several patients in a row die, he was deemed to have lost his powers and he would be killed.'

Emma gave a startled laugh. 'It's a good job we don't apply the same criterion in Western medicine or some branches would soon be running out of practitioners!'

There was a stillness between them as though they had each managed to come to terms with what the other represented, and Emma was exploring the strange delight of knowing someone with whom she could speak about the problems and joys of something that she had only ever thought of as a curse before.

With this link between herself and Adam, perhaps he would feel moved to keep in touch with her even after he returned to America at the end of his three months.

'I'm thinking of extending my stay in England,' he murmured, as if he had been following the same train of thought. 'I'm due some holiday time and I was thinking of spending it exploring this area.'

'It's a beautiful part of the country,' Emma confirmed smoothly, not wanting to betray the leap of her heart at the thought that he might want to stay close to her for a while longer.

The cautious side of her nature was beginning to ring alarm bells. She had already realised that she was drawn to Adam—far more strongly than she had been to any other man. Even Richard hadn't been able to affect her as intensely as Adam did just by walking into a room.

The revelation that they had something so basic... so powerful...in common made the bond between them almost unique. She was becoming far too close to Adam Wolf—close enough that it would be like an amputation when he finally left.

'If I do stay on longer, would you be willing to spend your off-duty time with me?' His rich voice was so tempting, flowing around her in the still of her room.

She closed her eyes to concentrate her thoughts. Even the shadowy outline of Adam's broad shoulders and proud head were enough to distract her from the decision that she had to make.

'I don't know if that would be a good idea,' she said softly, an ache already beginning to gather around her heart at the thought of the time with him that she would be missing.

'Why not?' he challenged. 'I would have thought it would be an ideal opportunity for you to learn a little more about your gift from someone who could teach you how to develop it, how to turn it to good advantage after all this time of looking on it as a curse. You could turn it into a powerful tool to help you in your work.'

Perhaps, a stray thought suddenly popped into her head, she might even learn how to refine her skill so that she could communicate with her midnight stranger. At least that contact might go some way towards the loss of Adam's presence later on. Perhaps, if she became more skilled, she might even find other people with whom she could 'speak'.

'Can we be friends?' she suggested tentatively. 'I'd rather not spend time outside work with you if it can't be as friends.'

He was silent so long that she began to wonder if he was ever going to answer.

'Are you afraid that I'll try to force my attentions on you?' His voice was low and dangerous, as though she had accused him of something; as though she had insulted his honour.

'No!' The word was vehement. 'Never that.'

'Then why the stipulation?' he demanded.

'Because I'm afraid of getting hurt,' she said flatly, realising that only the truth would convince him. 'If we spend our off-duty hours together we can't help getting to know each other and growing close, especially as we're both basically lonely people.'

He made a sound of agreement.

'If we become more than friends in the time before you go, the loneliness will be worse than if I'd never met you. At least if we remain friends there will be something for me to remember with pleasure.'

'You don't think it would be a pleasure to become lovers?' His voice was like pure silk velvet, stroking over her skin until every nerve was quivering.

She was unaccustomed to sexual banter of this nature, and her embarrassment at his sophisticated taunt loosened her control on her tongue so that she abandoned diplomacy for bluntness.

'I've no idea, and I've no intention of finding out with someone who's going back to the other side of the world in a few weeks.'

She heard his sharply drawn breath but to her intense relief he didn't retaliate.

'If that's the way you want it,' he agreed quietly just as she was beginning to think that he would refuse. 'If you'll be happier that way, I promise that we'll just be friends while I'm over here.'

He left soon after that, refusing Emma's offer of coffee. The light in the hallway was too dim to show her any more than his usual self-contained expression, his eyes deeply shadowed and inscrutable as he made his goodbyes.

Emma delayed closing her door, surreptitiously watching his long legs eating up the distance as he walked away from her, until he disappeared round the corner.

'Adolescent nonsense,' she muttered disgustedly as she slid the chain into position and wandered through to her bedroom.

Having gained his agreement so easily, Emma couldn't understand why she felt so disappointed. Surely she should have been pleased that he had agreed to her wishes? Or, in her heart of hearts, had she secretly wished that he would refuse, that he would say he found her too desirable to contemplate a platonic relationship with her?

'Chance would be a fine thing,' she quoted her mother's favourite maxim as she got ready for bed. 'A man like that, as well qualified as he is and looking as fantastic as he does, could take his pick of willing women.'

Her cheeks blazed as she suddenly realised how presumptuous she must have sounded when she'd told him that she wouldn't have an intimate relationship with him.

'He probably hadn't even thought of asking me,' she moaned in an agony of embarrassment. 'Trust me to make an idiot of myself.' And she dived under the bedclothes to hide her face.

They were both due on duty tomorrow so she would soon know whether he still wanted to have anything to do with her. No wonder he hadn't been able to wait to leave this evening.

In spite of the way the evening had ended she couldn't regret the fact that he'd decided to confront her. They'd spoken about things that needed to be said and she'd learnt so much about him.

She fell asleep trying to imagine what he'd looked like as a child, his solemn little face breaking into that heart-stopping smile and his eyes gleaming with humour. . .

When her thoughts became dreams she didn't know, but she woke just before her alarm was due to go off, with her heart beating heavily.

'Adam. . .' she murmured, her voice husky with arousal, and slid one hand out across the wildly rumpled bedclothes. . .but there was no one there.

'Oh!' Realisation was slow, but eventually she woke up enough to realise that she'd been having the most erotic dream of her life.

She tilted her head back against the pillow to gaze at the ceiling while she willed her pulse to slow and her breathing to steady. It would take longer for the other evidence of her body's aroused state to disappear and she doubted if a cold shower would be the answer.

'How am I ever going to be able to look him in the face?' she groaned. 'Yesterday evening I almost accused him of lusting after my body, and I spent all last night lusting after his!' She shivered sensually as she remembered how she had run her hands over the smooth, warm copper of his naked shoulders and down the lean length of his back, until she'd cupped the tight curves of his buttocks in her hands.

'Stop it!' she wailed, and kicked the duvet onto the floor to scramble to her feet. The fine cotton of her nightdress untangled itself from around her body and slid down to cover her nakedness, the brush of the delicate fabric over her sensitised skin enough to make her moan with dismay.

* * *

Emma arrived at the start of her shift just as an elderly Mini came hurtling up the slope towards the main entrance.

'Nurse, help!' a voice shouted before the door was properly open. 'The baby fell in the bath—she's not breathing!'

Emma met the distraught mother halfway, grabbed the limp child and set off at a run towards the nearest emergency room.

'Call Dr Wolf,' she threw over her shoulder at the reception desk. 'Near drowning.' And she disappeared through the doors.

Before they had time to swing shut behind her they were thrust open again as a young nurse followed her through.

'I need to intubate,' Emma said between administering mouth-to-mouth resuscitation. 'The tube needs to be the same size as the child's little finger.' She concentrated on maintaining the rhythm of the resuscitation procedure while she listened to the sounds of equipment being gathered.

'Ready, Staff.' A gloved hand held the laryngoscope in her field of vision and Emma made short work of sliding the blade over the tongue and between the vocal cords.

'Hundred per cent oxygen,' Emma directed. 'Then we need to start an IV and get a nasogastric tube down to decompress the stomach.'

She was just suiting her actions to her words when the doors swung open behind her.

'How far have you got?' Adam's voice was approaching at speed.

'Intubated and receiving hundred per cent oxygen

on assisted ventilation, and that's the IV in and running.' She held her hand out and the young nurse
handed Emma the last of the prepared strips to tape
the IV tube in position.

'Good,' Adam muttered as he administered the
appropriate dose of sodium bicarbonate. 'Get that
blood sample checked for haemoglobin, blood gases,
electrolytes and urea. What's her temperature?'

'Thirty-six, rectal. Blood pressure eighty-five over
sixty,' she recited as she deftly threaded a nasogastric
tube into position. 'Ready to empty the stomach.' She
straightened up from positioning the bowl.

The atmosphere in the room grew tense as the
seconds ticked remorselessly away and their little
charge hardly seemed to be responding to their efforts.

Emma hated this side of her work, having to face
the possibility that they couldn't save all of their
patients all of the time, especially when they were little
children.

Suddenly, among the frantic bleeps and mutters
there was a choked cry of distress and little limbs
jerked in protest.

'All right!' Adam drawled the Americanism in a
voice full of relief. 'Welcome back to the world, little
angel.' And the tender way he smoothed the straggle
of blonde hair away from the child's pale, sweaty
forehead made Emma's eyes fill with tears.

'Who gets to give the parents the good news?' His
tone was definitely up-beat. 'Would you like to send
them in here, then arrange for her to be admitted
overnight for observation?'

Emma nodded, grateful for the few seconds to get a
grip on herself. If she wasn't careful, she'd arrive in the

little waiting room with tears running down her face
and the poor parents would believe that the worst had
happened.

The feeling of euphoria after little Sophie's resuscitation had spread right through the department like a
happy ray of sunshine, so the sudden warning of
impending multiple casualties was like a slap in the
face.

'There's been some sort of gang warfare out on one
of the housing estates. Probably a dispute about territory or something. About fifteen casualties with various
injuries, mostly from knives and coshes,' the message
came through. 'Probable involvement with drugs.'

'Right, people,' Adam warned, 'I don't know what
your usual system is here, but back home we assume
that everyone involved with the drugs scene is HIV
positive and take precautions accordingly. They are
our patients and we'll do our best for them while
they're in our care, but it's not worth risking our own
lives for them.'

It was a sobering message, but, even more, it was a
sign of the times they were living in, Emma thought as
she checked supplies of gloves, masks and gowns.

The first ambulance full of injuries was accompanied
by a couple of burly policemen.

'If you let us know where to go so we won't be in
your way,' the more senior one said to Adam, 'we'll
just make sure that they behave themselves while
they're here. Some of them will be taken away to be
charged as soon as you've finished patching them up,
but we don't want to risk them starting in on each
other again while they're here.'

'Fine by me.' Adam reached out one hand towards

the first of his charges. 'If you can identify the different gangs, perhaps you can line them up on opposite sides of the reception area.' He grimaced his sympathy at the policemen's task then beckoned Emma to follow.

The next two hours were filled with a stream of injuries bearing witness to the groups' fondness for knives and baseball bats.

'Do you think they used them because they wanted me to feel at home?' Adam quipped as he sent yet another set of ribs up for X-ray, and sat down with a fresh tray to begin suturing a vicious knife-slash across a teenage biceps. 'So far, we've had one fractured skull, two broken arms, one broken leg, assorted broken ribs, and more sutures than I like to think about.'

'Just like home, in fact,' Emma joked.

'Yeah, but I wasn't expecting to find it here,' he objected. 'I thought it would be what I call *real* accidents, not so many deliberately inflicted injuries.'

He finished the last of a neat row of stitches just as Dave Maddox stuck his head round the door.

'Doctor? Can you come and look at the one in Emergency Two? I think we've got some nerve damage where the injury crosses the palm.'

'If Staff Nurse will finish putting a dressing on my customer?' He raised a dark eyebrow.

'Fine,' Emma nodded and was reaching for the appropriate package before the door had swung closed behind them. 'Right, now, Shane.' With a professional smile, she turned to the shifty-looking young man and reached out for the package of dressings. 'Let's get this lot covered up and then you—' The words ended on a gasp when his uninjured arm came up to brandish a wicked-looking blade.

'Right, bitch,' he spat as he grabbed her outstretched hand and twisted it painfully, positioning the point of the knife at the side of her neck. He slid carefully off the side of the trolley until his feet met the floor, and gave an extra twist on her wrist to bring her hand right up between her shoulderblades.

'You're going to get me some stuff before I get out of here,' he hissed menacingly. 'The bloody pigs took everything I'd got except this.' He moved the cold steel against her skin and she felt the sharp bite of the tip as he pressed it harder against her.

CHAPTER EIGHT

'NOT a word,' the youth warned as Emma went to open her mouth, his voice too low to draw attention. 'You make one sound and I'll cut you. Understand? I ain't going to go cold turkey.'

Emma knew that he was referring to the traumatic effects of a sudden withdrawal of an addict's drugs, and understood that just the thought of going through it was enough to make him desperate.

She swallowed and felt the knife press a little harder, knowing that, whether he realised it or not, her assailant had positioned his weapon right over the carotid artery.

One false move and it wouldn't take many minutes before she died.

Everything inside her made her want to let out a blood-curdling scream, but logic told her that the young addict was already jumpy enough. If she gave in to her instincts, it would probably be the last thing she ever did.

Adam!

She closed her eyes and concentrated on her favourite mental image of him—his face filled with laughter as they'd galloped up the hill towards a meadow full of sunshine.

Why had she been such a coward? If she'd told him that day how she'd felt about him. . .

'Saying your prayers, are you?' the young thug

sneered as he gave her arm another yank upwards. 'Well, we haven't got time for that. Just get me some stuff and be quick about it.'

Emma felt sick as she picked up a mental image of the damage the young man had already done to himself with his drug abuse, her dread becoming outright terror when she realised that his craving meant that he was no longer rational.

Help me! Somebody. . .

She started to put her free hand down towards her pocket where the drugs key rested on the end of its chain. She didn't dare speak for fear that the edge of the blade might slice through those few millimetres which meant the difference between life and death, but, if she showed willing, perhaps she could persuade him. . . But before she reached her goal he stopped her.

'Hey, bitch!' he snarled close to her ear, giving an extra jerk on her captive wrist. 'What're you trying to pull? Ain't no one can do anything for you now—not till you get what I want.'

Drugs. He wants drugs.

She nearly laughed at the futility of it all. She knew that she couldn't speak to anyone, couldn't even open her mouth to call for help, and yet here she was trying to send a message by telepathy to someone she'd never met except in her head.

'Shane. . .?' She had to try to reason with him, had to try to calm him down enough to—

'Shut up, bitch.' He began to drag her over towards the row of cupboards, his hand tightening on the knife so that it angled even closer to that vital artery. 'Is this where you keep the stuff?'

If only the local anaesthetic would start wearing off, Emma yearned. He wouldn't be able to hold the knife so easily then, and she might be able to get away...

Hold on. I'm coming.

Emma stiffened with disbelief.

Somehow, for the first time in her life, she had actually managed to make contact. Her mysterious midnight stranger had heard her terrified messages and had found her. He was coming to help...

He's got a knife. Be careful...

She closed her eyes tight as she concentrated on visualising the scene in the treatment room. If she had been able to 'speak' to him, perhaps she could also 'show' him what he was walking into.

'Staff Nurse? Have you finished with that dressing?' Adam's deep, accented voice preceded him into the festering silence of the room as he pushed open the doors with his shoulder.

Adam! No!

Emma's heart was in her mouth as she stood frozen with horror. As she watched, mesmerised, Adam walked in without so much as lifting his eyes from the clipboard in his hand, and walked briskly across the room with all the assurance of a man at home in his own front room.

Get ready...

The voice of the midnight stranger spoke to her in the silence, electrifying every cell with the impossibility of his presence, but in the life-or-death situation unfolding in front of her there was no time for her brain to struggle with its confusion.

Her captor's grasp had tightened ominously as the intruder burst in on them, the knife gouging dangerously against the soft skin of her vulnerable throat. Emma felt the confusion pour through him as the big, white-coated man seemed totally to ignore his presence in the room, and he relaxed his grip slightly.

'Here. Catch!' Without warning, without even seeming to look in their direction, Adam flipped the clipboard towards the grotesque tableau formed by the motionless bodies of the two of them.

Automatically, they both reacted as it sailed towards the unprotected wound on Shane's injured arm— Emma to try to catch it, and her captor to duck out of its way.

Adam's long arm shot out to grab Emma's reaching hand just as her captor's grip loosened on her wrist, and she was dragged out of his grasp and swung across the room and out of danger.

'Bastard!' the young punk snarled, and lashed out at Adam with the knife.

He only had time for one sweeping blow before Adam's longer reach enabled him to deal a swift backhander to the boy's chin, which snapped his unkempt head back against the bank of cupboard doors.

From her position on the other side of the room Emma watched while, as if in slow motion, Shane slid down into a crumpled heap on the floor.

As he slumped into semi-consciousness he lost his grip on the knife, which landed with a metallic clatter at his feet, gleaming intermittently under the bright lights as it spun lazily to a halt.

'Are you all right?' Adam kicked the knife away and knelt down to check the young addict's vital signs just before the two policemen burst on the scene, his swift glance up at Emma's white face telling her that his concern was for her.

'Y-yes. I'm fine.' Her teeth were beginning to chatter as reaction set in. 'What about you? Did the knife touch you?'

Adam straightened up, with a slight grimace, to face the two uniformed men.

'The knife is over the other side of the room. Neither of us has touched it. He had Staff Nurse held at knife-point, demanding that she get drugs for him.' He glanced across at her briefly, his eyes glittering with anger. 'She has the mark of the blade on her neck.'

Directed by their gaze, Emma's fingers came up wonderingly to touch the sting at the side of her neck, and they came away sticky from the trickle of blood she encountered.

A mumble from the bundle of humanity on the floor drew their eyes away from her and she observed numbly as they hauled him to his feet, pausing for the few seconds it took to secure a dressing over his recently stitched wound before they unceremoniously frogmarched him out of the room.

'We'll need a statement from you, miss,' one of the policemen tossed over his shoulder as he let the doors slap shut behind them.

'Tomorrow will do,' Adam growled after them. 'She's in no state to do it today.' And he finally turned to walk towards her.

Unable to help herself, she allowed her eyes to travel over him, from the stern austerity of his drawn face to the broad shoulders and clenched fists and. . .

'Adam! You're bleeding!' She reached a hand out to

his side where bright red was beginning to stain the white of his shirt. 'He cut you!'

'It's nothing,' he dismissed as he reached out one hand to turn her chin gently to allow him to examine her own injury.

As soon as the contact was made she was instantly overwhelmed by a tidal wave of emotions, as his tender concern for her fought with blazing anger that she'd been hurt.

'Are you all right?' he repeated, his fingers tracing the curve of her jaw.

Were her teeth still chattering or was it his fingers that trembled against her? She couldn't tell. She didn't know anything any more. . .

'Oh, Adam—'

'Excuse me,' an apologetic voice broke in as the door opened again to reveal the younger policeman. 'I've come for the knife.' He held up a self-sealing plastic bag.

Emma took the opportunity to step back, breaking the contact with Adam's gentle touch without losing the incredible sense of connection.

'I. . .I'll send someone in to clean up in here,' she stammered, backing towards the door, not daring to meet his eyes for fear of what she might see, what she might learn.

'As soon as you've got that organised, come back in here and I'll check you over. You'll need a dressing on that knife wound.' There was a lingering huskiness in his voice which called to her, but she had to resist. She needed to understand what had happened between the two of them today before she could allow him to come any closer.

'As soon as you've had your ribs attended to,' she countered with a touch of bravado. 'My scratch might be in a more dangerous place but I'm not bleeding like a stuck pig.' And she made her escape.

She grabbed Dave between patients and got him to clean her neck of dried blood and apply an unobtrusive dressing.

'Looks as if you had a rather violent run-in with Count Dracula,' he commented, with an evil leer, then sobered. 'I feel terribly guilty, Em,' he confessed in a low voice. 'If I hadn't called Dr Wolf out to check on my patient it would never have happened.'

'There was no way you could have known what was going to happen. None of us did,' Emma tried to reassure him. 'He was very lippy and belligerent while we were sorting him out, but no one had any idea he'd flip like that—otherwise the police wouldn't have left him alone with us. They'd have been supervising him every step of the way.' She pulled a wry face. 'It was just unfortunate he decided I looked like a soft touch.'

By the time she had been cleaned up and patched up, Dave was looking more cheerful and Emma's shakiness had subsided, her recovery helped along by a large mug of hot, sweet tea.

When she reported back for the last hour of her shift, Sister commended her devotion to duty but insisted that she needed to go home and have a good night's sleep to help her get over the trauma of the day's events.

'Tomorrow morning will be quite soon enough to get back in the swing of things,' she said firmly. 'I can't have my staff neglecting their own health.' And she sent her off to collect her belongings.

As Emma slid her arms into a light cardigan she kept in her locker for emergencies, she could hear Adam's voice at the other end of the corridor and wondered if he had stopped to have his own wound attended to.

Every instinct she possessed made her want to be the one to take care of him herself, but she knew that she wasn't in a fit state yet to touch him without falling apart.

If she were to put her hands on his naked flesh, no matter how serious the reason, all she would want to do would be to wrap her arms around him and hold on tight, grateful that he hadn't been seriously injured by that slashing knife blow.

Her first priority when she returned home was to have a shower—somehow she just didn't feel clean after her close contact with Shane.

Luckily she was able to angle the shower-head so that she didn't soak the dressing on her neck—a hair-wash would have to wait—but it was wonderful to feel fresh and clean as she pulled on a pretty, matching housecoat over her nightdress.

Sister had been quite right when she'd said that it was better for her to take the rest of her shift off, Emma thought; but what she hadn't told her was how to stop her brain racing at a hundred and fifty miles an hour as it endlessly replayed the traumatic events.

She tried to block out all thoughts of the personal trauma involved—the shock that Sister hadn't known about, when the two men in Emma's life and heart had suddenly collided inside her head.

There was a knock at the door; Emma uncurled

from her position on the sofa cushion and padded silently out of the lamplit room to take the safety chain off and release the catch.

There was no point, this time, in looking carefully through the spyhole—she already knew who was waiting out there.

He was leaning back against the wall opposite her door, one foot crossed over the other and his arms folded across his chest to cradle a small bundle.

He was totally silent and unmoving, his face still and inscrutable as he waited for her to speak.

'Adam.' She stepped to one side as she opened the door wide to allow him to enter. 'Go straight through,' she invited, and closed the door behind him, taking a few seconds to re-secure the chain to give herself time to control her unsteady breathing and the galloping of her heart.

'Coffee?' she offered as she walked on bare feet towards the tiny kitchen. 'I bought some real beans.' She dredged up a smile but it wasn't returned.

'Oh, Emma.' His husky voice broke completely and he was across the room, hauling her into his arms, the bundle he'd been holding so carefully falling to the floor.

'I thought he was going to kill you.' The words were muffled as he buried his face in her hair and enveloped her so tightly against him that her feet left the floor.

'Adam. . .' After her initial shock at his uncontrolled reaction she couldn't help her hands coming up to cradle his head against her, her fingers spearing through the lush, straight silk of his hair, until she dislodged the thong that restrained it.

'Adam, are you all right?' She tried to lean away

from him, raking her fingers through the thick dark profusion to hold it away from his face as she tried to catch a glimpse of his expression in the subdued light. 'How badly were you hurt? Did you need stitches?'

'You talk too much,' he groaned as he wrapped his arms around her waist until she was hardly able to breathe. 'Just let me hold you. I need to feel you close to me.' And he rocked her in his arms as though she were a child.

Relief.

The sensation poured through her like an uncontrollable avalanche, as though he was unable to restrain it from overflowing, and Emma stiffened reflexively, reminded instantly that there were so many things that they had to talk about.

'Adam.' She pushed against his shoulders with both hands until he finally lowered her feet to the floor and loosened his hold.

She took a couple of steps backwards until his hands dropped away from her and the contact between them was broken. Her head tilting back, she met his darkly gleaming eyes.

'Did you know I was listening to you?' she demanded. 'How long have you known it was me?' In her agitation the construction of her sentences fell apart. 'Were you laughing at me, that I had no idea who you were?'

'No, Emma. No. It wasn't like that.' He ran his own fingers through the heavy fall of his hair, clenching them in its depths as though fighting with frustration.

'At first I had no idea *who* was listening to me. I hadn't expected *anyone* to be able to pick up my thoughts. The last thing I expected when I came over to England was to be able to communicate like that, even though the other person couldn't or wouldn't reply.'

He held his hands out to her in entreaty, pleading, it seemed, for her to understand.

'Then, when I discovered you were sensitive, I put two and two together. The chances of there being two separate people with that ability in the same small area. . .' He shrugged his broad shoulders as if his conclusion had been inevitable.

Emma shook her head in disbelief. When he put it like that it *did* seem obvious. How could she not have seen it for herself?

'I didn't realise that you and my midnight stranger were the same person until you walked through the door of the emergency room. I was so scared that Shane would accidentally cut me and panic and no one would find me until it was too late.' All the tormented thoughts of those endless minutes were tumbling out uncontrollably.

'When I heard the voice in my head telling me to hang on I was amazed that he'd been able to hear me, let alone how he'd found me.'

'Emma. . .?' His voice was tormented as he held out both hands to her, his expression full of entreaty.

Slowly she lifted her own shaking hands and reached out until she could place them in his.

Need. Longing. Desperation.

For the first time Emma was unable to tell whose thoughts belonged to whom, because each of them was consumed by the overwhelming relief that the other was safe.

'Oh, Emma. . .'

Suddenly, as if he could bear it no longer, he swept her into his arms and his lips met hers in a kiss of such overwhelming tenderness that it took her breath away.

'I need you,' he murmured between the kisses he scattered over her face. 'I need to make you mine.' And he took her mouth again, his lips parting hers, his tongue exploring her inner tenderness with an earthy eagerness that made her burn for a deeper possession.

'Adam, please,' she whimpered, her hands longing to explore his body without the barrier of clothing, her fingers plucking at his shirt.

'Ah, Emma, my Emma.' He captured both her hands in his and raised them up to kiss each finger. 'Are you sure?' His dark eyes burned with an inner fire as he gazed into hers. 'Is this just a reaction to the trauma you've been through?'

'Oh, Adam, no.' Emma knew that her heart was in her eyes as she gazed up at him. 'It's because I love you.' And she threaded her fingers through his hair to pull his lips down to meet hers.

The world spun and dipped as he carried her out of the room, finding her bedroom unerringly to lower her feet to the floor beside her bed.

Emma reached out to switch on the bedside light, the golden glow picking out the gleams of light in his eyes and along the dark strands of his hair where they framed his face.

'May I?' he requested formally as he reached for the tie to her housecoat, then slid the soft fabric from her shoulders to drape it over the foot of the bed.

His eyes travelled avidly over her and her pulse rate doubled as she realised that her nightdress must be all but transparent with the light behind it. . .

'May I?' Emma echoed, stifling her nervousness as she raised shaking fingers to unfasten the buttons of his shirt and pull it away from his body.

'Adam,' she moaned as the narrow, taped dressing was revealed, curving around the base of his ribs. She ran remorseful fingers lightly over it, hating the fact that he'd been hurt.

'It's not important,' he reassured her, shrugging his shoulders out of the shirt and dropping it over her housecoat.

'Oh,' Emma breathed when his torso was revealed in the subdued light. 'You're so beautiful. Like a bronze statue. . .'

She couldn't resist running her hands over the warm, naked splendour of his muscular shoulders, glorying in the satin smoothness as she stroked her palms down the lean length of his spine in an uncanny replay of her dream.

His leather belt was in the way when she tried to slide her hands inside the waistband of his jeans to find out if the rest of him lived up to her erotic imaginings.

'Help me,' she whispered, trying to unfasten it, fumbling as she manoeuvred the clasp.

'Ah, Emma.' He captured her hands again and brought them up to his lips. For long moments his eyes gazed deep into hers, as though he was making an important decision, then he nodded and drew in a cleansing breath.

'May I give you a gift, Emma? Something from my Blackfoot heritage to mark such a special day?'

Emma nodded, intrigued, as he raised one finger in the air and strode swiftly towards her sitting room,

returning almost immediately with the package he'd
been holding when he'd arrived.

'This was my mother's.' He held it out to her on his
open palms, his attitude almost reverent. 'After tonight
it will belong to you.'

Emma lifted it from his hands and unfolded it,
finding the fabric as soft as velvet and more supple
than anything she'd ever known.

'It's elk-skin,' he told her as she held it up to reveal
the simple shape of the robe. 'Will you wear it for me?'

'Of course.' Emma smiled up at him, knowing that
there was a special significance to his request. Later
she would ask him to explain. For now, it was enough
that he wanted her to wear it for him.

Unembarrassed, she slid her nightdress from her
shoulders and he helped to lower the robe over her
head.

'Perfect,' he breathed as he turned her to face the
mirror and ran his fingers through her hair to spread it
out over her breast. 'You see?'

Emma looked in the mirror at her reflection, but all
she could see was Adam standing behind her, his eyes
fiercely possessive as they watched her, the width of
his naked shoulders framing her slenderness, his
bronzed arms coming around her to pull her into the
shelter of his strength.

'Now, Emma,' he murmured as he leant forward to
lay his cheek on the crown of her head. 'Now you will
be mine.' And he turned her to face him.

As if she was infinitely precious, he explored her
face, outlining each of her features with gentle fingertips, seemingly committing them to memory for ever.

'So delicate...so perfect,' he whispered as he

anointed her with tender kisses, then took her lips with his own.

Emma had never known anything like the kisses she shared with Adam; the physical sensation of their lips meeting, parting and meeting again was intensified by her sensitivity to his emotional response.

Mine, she heard him say inside her head, while at the same time her ears heard the soul-deep groan which emerged from his throat when she opened her lips to him. *Mine*, she echoed as she began her explorations again, this time mastering his belt and pushing his last remaining clothes away.

'Ahh,' she breathed softly when, at long last, she saw him in all his glory. 'I *knew* you would look like this.' She heard the satisfaction in her own voice as her eyes travelled over his naked body, her hands totally unable to resist the temptation to explore his lean hips and cup the tight muscles of his buttocks.

'Dear God,' Adam gasped in a strangled voice. 'When did you learn to drive a man crazy?'

'When someone came into my head at midnight and taught me to dream,' she whispered just before he bent his head to ravish her mouth.

'Oh, Adam, it's not fair,' she moaned when he finally released her. 'I'm wearing too many clothes.' She brushed herself against his aroused body, the soft elk-skin robe abrading her aroused nipples and sliding over her sensitised skin.

'That's easily solved.' He bent to ease his hands up under the hem of the elk-skin to curve around the sides of her calves. The supple fabric gathered on his wrists as he slid his palms slowly up to her hips and then her waist, his eyes concentrating on each inch of her as it was revealed, his thick dark lashes throwing crescent shadows over his sculpted cheek-bones, hiding his expression.

When he finally drew the robe off over her head her hair was released to drift down around her shoulders and over the pale smoothness of her breasts.

'Like a priceless ivory statue,' he murmured as he put the robe aside, his hands returning to shape and caress her. 'But warm and soft. . .'

He bent to lift her into his arms, and placed her gently on the cool crispness of her bed before lying down beside her.

As if in a dream, Emma found herself responding to his every move and thought, her body growing heavy with arousal at the mental images that Adam was sharing with her.

He was patience itself as she took her time exploring his body, and she smiled with delight at his reaction when her nails came into contact with the deeper copper discs of his flat male nipples, tormenting them until they tightened into tiny buds.

Her roving hands travelled further—pale wraiths feathering their way over the earthy reality of his powerful body, until his ragged breathing and the sweat-sheened quiver in his tense muscles told her how much control he was exerting.

'Enough,' he growled when he finally reached his limits and rolled onto his back, pulling her with him so that she straddled his thighs.

'Adam!' she squeaked at the unexpected manoeuvre, steadying herself with a hand on each of his shoulders.

'Sit up,' he urged, propping his own shoulders against the pillows piled at her headboard. 'Sit straight and proud as you did when you went riding with me.' His hands outlined her shoulders and stroked down her arms while his eyes caressed the naked symmetry of her aroused breasts.

She had a mental image of herself and knew that it was coming from Adam's mind as he pictured the two of them in the shadowy light, her skin gleaming like pearl, the light fractured into glimmers in the tumbled profusion of her midnight-dark hair, her eyes shining silver, widely dilated with arousal.

In her mind she saw his image of her cupping her breasts in her hands and leaning towards him to offer them to him like ripe fruits, and found herself powerless to resist.

'Ah, Emma.' Never had his eyes looked so fierce as he accepted her offer, parting his sensuous lips to taste the bounty she was offering.

She hadn't realised the effect his ministrations would have on her until he suckled her strongly and, for the first time, she felt her womb contract inside her.

'Adam?' The sweet fire was spreading as he continued, his teeth and tongue intensifying the sensations until she was moving rhythmically, unashamedly. 'Adam. . .I need. . .I need. . .'

His hands were caressing her, shaping her, guiding her, but she felt so empty, a great ache building inside that she didn't know how to assuage.

'Ah-h-h. . .!' Her head dropped back and she groaned aloud as Adam finally filled the emptiness, the ache exploding into ecstasy as he made them one.

CHAPTER NINE

SUNSHINE was pouring in through the window when the alarm finally woke Emma early the next morning, and she lay still for a moment, wondering at the happiness that filled her.

'Adam,' she breathed as the memories flooded through her, and she rolled over under the rumpled duvet to find the bed empty.

For a moment she wondered if she had dreamed the events of the previous night the way she had before, but this time there was more than her aroused body as evidence.

This time she had the tell-tale redness of her nipples to prove that Adam had suckled them into arousal not once but several times in the long, passion-filled night. Her thighs, too, bore the evidence of more than one gallop on her tireless stallion.

She stretched lazily, sensuously, enjoying the lingering sensations in her body that told her she had been brought to ecstasy over and over again, and that her eager body was ready and willing for more of the same.

The night hadn't only been filled with the joys of the flesh.

Long hours had been spent in soft, intimate laughter as they'd discovered each other's pleasures, and in quiet conversation as they'd each spoken of their lives before they'd met.

Adam had told her of his tribe and the part of

349

Montana where they lived. He'd described Chief Mountain in the northern part of the state and told her of its importance in the spiritual life of his people. He'd explained the significance of the vision quest—a tradition which only survived in a few areas such as his grandfather's—and the journey he'd made as a young man to Chief Mountain.

He'd painted word-pictures which deepened the impact of the mental images, his voice resonant with conviction as he'd described the ritual of the days and nights of fasting and praying.

Finally he'd told her of the dream he'd had of the grey wolf who had become his spiritual guide and mentor and from whom he took his name.

While he'd been speaking, Emma had remembered the strange vision she'd had when she and Adam had sat side by side at the top of the hill the day they'd gone riding together.

She'd forgotten to ask him what he thought it might mean but now it seemed obvious—if he was Adam Grey Wolf, and she had dreamed of a female wolf joining the male, then that could only mean that she was going to be Adam's mate.

'Oh, Adam,' she groaned, and rolled over to bury her face in the pillow which carried the smell of his body. 'I need you here with me. . .' She wrapped her arms around the pillow but it was a poor substitute.

Pouting with disappointment, she made her way to the shower to start getting ready for work, the thought that she would soon be seeing Adam lending wings to her efforts.

Soon she and Adam—the man she loved; the man she'd given herself to body and soul without reservtion—

would find a space in their hectic timetables to sit down and make the important decisions which would shape the rest of their lives.

Too excited to stop for breakfast, Emma sped towards St Lawrence's, her brain going over all the reasons why Adam hadn't been able to stay until morning.

She hadn't heard a high-pitched bleep as the hospital called him in for an emergency, but then she'd been so exhausted towards dawn that she doubted whether she'd have heard anything short of a nuclear explosion. She certainly hadn't felt him leaving her arms and her bed, nor heard him dressing and letting himself out of her flat.

She smiled tenderly as she realised that he must have been concerned about her reputation and had made certain that he wouldn't be seen leaving her flat at an embarrassing time.

Still, she consoled herself, there would be other mornings—many other mornings—for them to wake up in each other's arms.

She smiled again as she remembered folding away the elk-skin robe, and wondered what special significance it had carried for Adam. Perhaps he would have time to tell her later today. . .

'Good morning, Marilyn,' she said cheerfully as she made her usual cursory check of the internal post rack.

The carefully groomed blonde head jerked up from its perusal of a letter and Marilyn's cheeks grew red as she quickly crumpled it in her hands and shoved it out of sight.

On her way to her locker Emma smiled to herself at

the thought that even an aggressive vamp like Marilyn had secrets she wanted to keep.

She'd been on duty for half an hour and Adam still hadn't appeared. She didn't want to draw attention to what was happening between the two of them before Adam was ready, but finally she had to ask someone.

'Isn't Dr Wolf on duty?' she asked, with what she was afraid was a rather transparent attempt at subtlety.

'He's not here any more,' Marilyn said as she replenished the supplies on a suture tray, her eyes never leaving her task. 'He's gone back to America.'

'He. . .?' The shock robbed her of breath so that it was several seconds before she could speak. 'When? When did he go?' There was a roaring sound in her ears and she held on tight to the side of the trolley, afraid that she was going to pass out.

'This morning.' Marilyn's reply was blunt, making it difficult for Emma to ask for details without giving herself away. 'Didn't tell you, did he?' There was a nasty slyness to her tone. 'Never did think you'd manage to land a big fish like that one.'

Emma hardly noticed when Marilyn left the room. Her brain seemed numb and her stomach was cramping as if she was just about to be sick.

Adam had gone. Back to America. Without a word to her. The disjointed thoughts were a mirror of the way her body was moving, her actions more suited to a robot than a human being.

Why? her heart was screaming. How could he, after the night they'd spent together? Hadn't it meant anything to him?

The notification of the imminent arrival of several

victims of a car crash was the only thing which managed to switch her brain to automatic pilot. For the rest of her shift she made certain that she was outwardly the same woman she'd always been—friendly, efficient, hardworking.

Only *she* knew that the person inside the familiar shell was mortally wounded, bleeding from a cut that went soul-deep.

Every time she heard a deep voice she went still until her foolish heart realised that it wasn't *his* voice—was unlikely to be *his* voice ever again.

Every time she saw a tall man with broad shoulders and dark hair her pulse doubled until he turned round, but it was never Adam—how could it be when he was half a world away?

For days she waited for a letter to arrive, either at her home address or at the hospital, to explain why he'd had to leave so suddenly. She imagined the words he'd use to tell her when he'd be coming back for her, or the invitation he'd send for her to join him for a new life in America—together.

It never came and hope began to die.

Slowly, over the next few weeks, she learnt that it was so much harder to cover up the emptiness once you had learned what it could contain. Slowly, she began to grow a callus over the wound so that it was less sensitive.

Eventually, she began to harden her heart against the man who'd known better than anyone how fragile her trust was and had still broken it.

She was so grateful that she had a job she enjoyed, a job she could immerse herself in for hours at a time without thinking of the handsome man who'd let her fall in love with him then stolen her heart when he went away.

It was nearly four weeks before the realisation dawned that she wasn't the victim of a lingering stomach bug.

'Adam's baby,' she whispered as she laid a trembling hand over her stomach. The paraphernalia for the home testing kit was staring at her from the side of the basin, the indicator an unequivocal positive.

For several terrified seconds she wondered how on earth she was going to manage to take care of a baby on her own. How was she going to provide for it and bring it up the way a child deserved to be brought up?

The problems were legion but they couldn't out-weigh the sheer joy at the prospect of carrying Adam's baby. In spite of her anguish at his betrayal, she was ecstatic that his seed was growing deep inside her and that soon she would give birth to his baby and cradle it in her arms.

Was it a boy, with his father's serious eyes and devastating smile? Would he grow up as tall and handsome as his father? Would he too become a healer? Or was it a girl safely nestled in her womb, her features the perfect female counterpoint to her father's masculinity?

It was so long before she would find out and she was already impatient, the secret knowledge putting a shine in her eyes and a spring in her step for the first time since Adam had left.

'You're looking happier,' Dave commented later that day, when Emma was teasing him about his failure to impress one of the new nurses assigned to A and E. 'Has he finally written?' he added softly, after a quick glance around to make sure that no one else was close enough to hear.

'He. . .?' For a moment Emma was genuinely puzzled. 'Who?'

'Adam Wolf.' Dave frowned. 'I thought it was a rotten trick to just disappear like that, but if he's been in contact—'

'No!' Emma's face grew pale and clammy as she suddenly realised what he was saying, and she fought to continue in a calmer voice. 'No. I haven't heard from. . .anyone.' She wouldn't. . .couldn't say his name aloud. 'What on earth made you think I was waiting for a letter?'

The question was sheer bravado and it didn't fool Dave. He'd known her too long and, in spite of his joking and playboy theatricals, he was a shrewd people-watcher.

'Come on, Em. I saw the way you were when he went back. If I'd been able to get hold of him I'd have—'

'No, Dave. It wasn't his fault. He didn't make any promises and I knew right from the first day that he'd be going back some time.' She shook her head and swallowed to give herself a second to get her voice under control. 'He hasn't written and I'm not expecting to hear from him.'

She'd managed to defuse Dave's anger, but he was still unconvinced by her assurances that she'd just had a nice surprise that morning which had given her a boost.

She went back to work, determined that no one should be able to detect how she was feeling from now on. She hadn't realised that she'd been wearing her heart on her sleeve quite so badly that everyone had guessed what had happened between herself and Adam Wolf. This time she couldn't afford to let anyone guess her secret.

In the quietness of her room she scanned the small pile of publications she'd gathered in her quest for another post. It had taken nearly half a day before the significance of Dave's observations had dawned on her, and she'd suddenly realised that it wouldn't be long before all her colleagues knew that she hadn't just been abandoned by Adam Wolf but that she'd been stupid enough to allow herself to get pregnant.

Ah, but what magnificent stupidity!

The abandoned papers slid unnoticed to the floor in an untidy muddle as she lay back against the pillows and rested both hands over her stomach. A smile softened the lines of tiredness as she visualised the tiny being resting safely inside.

'I don't regret it,' she vowed, hoping the little scrap would be able to sense the truth of her words. 'I don't regret a single minute of it. He was. . .' There weren't words to describe her memories of what had happened that night, and her voice faded away.

Her thoughts continued, though—and her memories of his gentleness and his passion; the pleasure he'd given her while he'd taken his own had been something she'd never dreamed of in her wildest imaginings.

And out of that overwhelming satisfaction had come this—her hand stroked slowly over the skin that would soon grow taut round the swollen evidence of their joining.

It was worth it, she told herself as she hugged her

secret to herself. It was worth all the heartache and loneliness she'd experience as she pulled up the few fragile roots she'd put down since she'd moved to St Lawrence's.

It was worth moving to somewhere where she knew no one and no one knew her, so that her pregnancy wouldn't be the source of avid gossip and her child would grow up untainted by vicious tongues.

With renewed determination she rolled over and retrieved the pages of adverts, the most likely ones already ringed in pencil so that she could start sending off her applications.

'It's just the two of us,' she murmured softly into the quiet. 'And we're going to do just fine.'

It took several weeks of writing and waiting, followed by a series of interviews, before she was finally able to hand in her resignation.

'We're very sorry to be losing you,' Sister Noone said when she was informed of Emma's impending departure. 'I'm only too pleased to give you a reference; you're an excellent worker.'

'Thank you.' Emma smiled with pleasure. 'I'm sorry to be leaving but...' She made a wry expression. She'd explained her reasons to Barbara Noone, knowing that she would understand the necessity. Everyone on the staff would soon be counting on their fingers... 'I haven't told anyone else why I'm going—just that it's a family matter. I've enjoyed working at St Lawrence's and I respect my colleagues too much to want to leave them with lies.'

Sister Noone's attention was briefly caught by someone waiting outside her door, but whoever it was

moved away at that point and she dismissed Emma
back to her duties.

There was no let-up in the pace of work, the usual
traffic providing them with plenty of casualties from
the motorway on top of the usual mixture of cases
from the circle of towns and villages they served.

Emma was glad to keep busy, her self-reliance coming to the fore again as she determined the new course
that her life was going to take.

Her new post was going to be very similar to her
present one at St Lawrence's, the Memorial being a
large hospital further north, built to cope with the busy
region between two major industrial areas.

They'd been delighted to find out that Emma had
plenty of experience working in a motorway-rescue
team, as they'd been hoping to expand their capabili-
ties further in that direction.

One of the older women at her interview had raised
a disapproving eyebrow when Emma had informed
them of her pregnancy, but, when Emma had pointed
out that it was the hospital's generous provision of day
care for staff children that had attracted her to apply
for the post, she'd appeared mollified.

Emma took the time when she was looking for
accommodation to explore a little further out from the
hospital, and found the biggest difference between
the Memorial and St Lawrence's would be the distance
she would have to travel to find a quiet hilltop.

Eventually, with the aid of a large-scale contour
map, she found one and toiled her way up in bright
sunshine to sit herself at the summit.

It would never be the same as the day she and Adam

had sat together but, when their baby was born, she would carry it up and explain the importance of listening for the voice inside him or herself.

Most of the time there would be nothing there and the solitude would only afford a measure of peace and tranquillity, but sometimes, when you least expected it, the voice would be there, loud and clear.

She walked slowly back down, her spirit calmed and strengthened by the time she'd spent there, and resolved that, once she had moved, she was going to haunt the local libraries until she managed to learn all she could about the life of the Blackfoot tribes.

Adam's child might never meet him, but she would make sure that it knew as much as she could find out about the uniqueness of his heritage.

Now it was just a case of moving herself halfway up the country and getting herself settled in. The rest of her life she would just have to cope with day by day.

Apart from the change in regional accents, there was very little difference in her work when she finally started at the Memorial.

The staff were the same as she would find in any hospital in the country, and the patients the same mixture of helpful and obstructive, brave and frightened.

Her first shift started off fairly quietly with a child cradling a broken arm after a fall off a kitchen stool.

'He wanted to get his own cereal packet down,' his tearful mother explained as Emma finished wrapping the plaster bandage around the slender arm, smoothing it into shape with the palms of her hands.

'I've told him and told him it's not safe to climb up there. . .'

'Well—' Emma smiled consolingly '—they do say boys will be boys. Just think how helpful he'll be when he's big enough to reach by himself.'

'If he lives that long,' came the wry comment. 'He's already fallen out of his cot and his high chair. Last time he tried to climb up on the kitchen stool he slipped and pulled it over and nearly knocked his teeth out.'

'Have you thought it might be possible to change your cupboards around?' Emma suggested. 'If you had the safe things that he can help himself to on a level that he can manage, perhaps he wouldn't go mountaineering to find them.'

'There'd never be any food in the house!' she laughed. 'It's obvious you haven't got any young children of your own to deal with. . .' She was still laughing as she led her son out, the young tough not looking in the least bit chastened by yet another visit to hospital.

Once they'd disappeared round the corner, with a cheeky grin and a wave of the uninjured arm, Emma's answering smile faded. No, she hadn't had any experience of young children, except for the patients she'd met in her job—but she soon would have.

She ran a surreptitious hand over the barely perceptible mound covered by her disposable plastic apron and smiled secretively.

Soon.

She pulled a face as she felt the gypsum drying on her hands, and started to clear up the bowl of milky-looking water. It was a messy job, but luckily it was one she was well-versed in and could do fairly quickly.

Her next patient was an ambulanceman who'd been assisting in the transportation of an elderly gentleman who hadn't wanted to go to hospital.

'He'd had a bit much to drink and fallen over. There was blood all over the side of his head, but you'd have thought I was trying to murder the old sod.' The young ambulanceman held out his hand for Emma to look at.

'Bugger bit me, right through my glove,' he complained. 'Thank goodness my tetanus shots are all up to date. It's bad enough having to take the antibiotic cover.'

He screwed his face up as Emma gave the wound a good soap-and-water scrub.

'There's no point pulling that face,' she chided. 'You know as well as I do that a human bite is much more dangerous than a dog bite. You wouldn't thank me if I just gave it a delicate dab of povidone-iodine and you ended up with a major infection.'

'You're right,' he groaned. 'Get it over with.' And he distracted himself by asking all sorts of getting-to-know-you questions, his eyes letting her know that he liked what he saw.

Emma glanced at his blond-haired, blue-eyed good looks and found herself totally unmoved. It seemed as if there was only one right combination for her, and she was unlikely to find it at the Memorial or even in England.

The more reading she did and the more she thought about it, the more she was coming to realise that she had a certain amount in common with wolves herself.

The book she'd borrowed from the library had painted a picture of wolves as faithful, family-orientated animals who chose a mate for life. It looked as if she

had learned too late that she held the same principles—
unfortunately the mate she'd chosen hadn't felt the
same way about her.

There was one decision she had to make that she
was putting off until later, although she knew it wasn't
going to get any easier. At some stage she was going
to have to get in contact with Adam to tell him that
he'd fathered a child. Logically, she knew that the
chance of his finding out accidentally was infinitesimal
and she could have kept the fact to herself for ever,
but she couldn't have lived with herself if she'd done
that.

Just the thought of writing such a letter was enough
to give Emma a bad case of the shakes.

What would he do when he found out?

Would he ignore the letter, believing it was a ploy to
bring him back to her? Or would he get a solicitor to
reply? Would he acknowledge parentage and then
ignore the child's existence from then on, or would he
insist that his child had a chance to get to know him?

There were so many possibilities that she could have
driven herself mad just contemplating them.

In the end she made her decision; she would wait
until the baby arrived so that she could send a photo
with a covering letter. That would give her a nice long
time to compose the letter and, at the same time,
would give her a good reason for delaying making
contact with him—a clear case of putting off until
another day the things she couldn't face doing today.

Emma went to bed early that night, exhausted by the
double strain of familiarising herself with a new place

of work and the drain on her body of the rapidly developing foetus inside her.

The tiredness had gradually been accumulating as, night after night, she'd fought to get a good sleep.

Oh, she hadn't been disturbed by intrusive voices; she didn't even seem to have any sensitivity to her patients any more, her gift apparently dormant for some reason. The biggest problem she had at the moment was dreams about the tall, dark-haired, broad-shouldered man with black eyes that gleamed with gold in the shadows of a bedroom.

No matter how tired she was when she went to bed, the memories were there waiting for her as her head touched the pillow, and she woke each day quivering with arousal, her grey eyes heavy with unshed tears.

'Why don't you get a prescription for some sleeping tablets?' Megan Jameson had suggested when Emma had confessed to sleeping badly.

Emma's first thought had been for her unborn child, but she hadn't been able to say so. There would be time enough for the news to get out. In the meantime, no matter what the books said, she wouldn't be taking anything other than vitamins and minerals while she was pregnant, and then only the ones prescribed by her obstetrician.

'It's probably just getting used to a new bed,' she'd said dismissively. 'Anyway, if I take those things, I'll sleep through my alarm like Rip van Winkle. I'd do better to go for a walk or take some exercise.'

'If you need to do some exercise before you're tired enough to go to sleep, you're obviously not doing enough work,' one of the charge nurses had called out. 'Give the girl another job to do.'

Emma had laughed with the rest of them, glad that she'd been accepted into the closed world of a hospital so quickly. For all that she didn't talk about herself, she'd begun to make friends and already had a couple of invitations to join groups going out to celebrate birthdays and exam successes.

If only her heart was in it, she'd thought as she'd cleared up after a particularly harrowing car accident.

She knew that she was doing her job well—her glowing recommendations from St Lawrence's meant that she would soon be contemplating taking on more responsibility as she continued her climb up the professional ladder.

Unfortunately it felt as if there was some sort of glass wall between herself and the rest of the world—as if her emotions had been put into storage when Adam had left her.

For now, she wasn't worried, knowing that she was doing her job well. Once the baby arrived everything would change. She could feel a deep well of emotion filling up, just waiting for the arrival for it to pour out.

Once the baby arrived...

She fell asleep with her hand resting on the barely perceptible evidence of that new life, a loving smile gentle on her face.

Loneliness.

Emma sat up with a jerk, her heart pounding as the echoes of an overpowering emotion eddied through her.

Pain.

Before she could block it the emotion slammed into her, almost robbing her of breath. What was happen-

ing? Who *was* this overwhelming her in this way? She'd
been so sure that these feelings had gone when Adam
had returned to America.

Anger.

There was such depth of feeling in the emotion that
she felt herself start to shake.

'Stop it!' She speared her fingers through her hair
and clutched at her head. 'Don't *do* this to me. I can't
bear it. . .'

The shock of the violence of the emotions, coming
on top of her pregnancy-induced tiredness and her
broken sleep, was enough to crack her self-control, and
she burst into tears.

'Whoever you are, get out of my head. . .please. . .'
And she sobbed as if her heart was breaking.

It was a long time before she calmed down enough
to go back to sleep, her thoughts drawn back to the
last time she'd had someone speak to her in the night.

Only one other person had ever reached her so loud
and clear, and when he'd gone she'd believed that she
would never hear anything like it again.

Now there was another one. Someone else with
troubles on their mind who wanted someone to share
them with. The only problem was that she didn't think
she could bear to go through it all over again. It would
bring everything back too clearly.

She was still tired when she woke up the next morning,
groggy from the lack of sleep and numb from the tears
she'd shed.

The bloom she'd heard that pregnant women
enjoyed seemed to have passed her by, she thought,

catching sight of herself in the mirror as she stripped off for a shower to wake her up properly.

Her hair refused to co-operate as she tried to skewer it into submission. She'd seriously contemplated having it all cut off to get rid of the constant reminder of Adam's delight in it, but when it came to it she'd only been able to allow the hairdresser to trim the ends.

The circles around her eyes were more marked than ever this morning, thanks to her tears in the middle of the night, her face seeming even paler by comparison. No one looking at her without make-up would believe that it was mid-summer. She looked like something that had crawled out from under a dark rock—all wan and etiolated.

'No more,' she muttered with determination. 'I've got to look after myself for the baby's sake...haven't I, Little Wolf?' She stroked the smooth, unmarked skin of her belly as she gave the child its nickname, longing for the first time when she would feel movement in there to make it real.

'From now on, we're going to do the right thing all the way down the line,' she said aloud. 'Eat right, sleep right, get lots of fresh air and exercise. You'll be so healthy when you finally arrive...' Her eyes gleamed with determination.

'Last night was just a minor hiccup.' She straightened her shoulders. 'Today is the start of a whole new regimen.'

By the time she was ready for the short walk which would take her to the accident and emergency department at Memorial, she'd had a proper sit-down breakfast instead of her usual coffee and toast held in either hand while she scurried about looking for tights and shoes.

There was a new swing to her stride as she walked swiftly through the maze of streets which took her to the huge complex—part Victorian, part brand-new—that was the Memorial.

Her head was up, her shoulders back and her carriage proud as she murmured with determination, 'This is the first day of the rest of my life.'

CHAPTER TEN

'ATTEMPTED suicide.' The trolley swung past Emma, narrowly missing her on its rapid way into the emergency room, the paramedic reeling off the vital information.

'Female, twenty-four years of age, found surrounded by empty drugs containers. Blood pressure ninety over sixty, pulse a hundred and eight. She was barely conscious when we found her, but she's out for the count now.'

'Do we know what she's taken?' Emma was supervising the patient's transfer off the ambulance trolley, hooking the bag of saline to a stand so that it could flow unobstructed into the IV set up *en route*.

'A cocktail.' There was a rattle as he turned out the contents of a plastic bag. 'We found empty containers of aspirin, codeine and paracetamol, and a number of tablets scattered on the floor by the body.'

'So she's taken two non-narcotic analgesics and one narcotic analgesic all available without prescription and all with a high rating for overdose. Do we know how long ago she took them?'

'Closest estimate is less than two hours ago.'

'So a fair number could still be in the stomach. I'll set up ready for aspiration of the stomach contents, and then we can administer activated charcoal.'

Gastric lavage was one of Emma's least favourite procedures and she was glad to be called out to another patient partway through, as her own condition seemed to be making her more squeamish than usual.

By the time she'd finished using cyanoacrylate glue on a minor head wound on a child who'd come up underneath a cupboard door, she had her stomach back under control again.

She returned to find the young woman awake and tearful, her face and hair spotted with the dark grey evidence of the charcoal she'd been given.

'Let me get you comfortable,' Emma offered, wiping her with a warm cloth.

'What's the point?' her patient said defeatedly, her voice hoarse from the treatment. 'I'm only going to have to do it all again. . .'

'Why?' Emma kept her voice gentle. 'What's gone so wrong that you want to do that to yourself?'

'I'm pregnant.' She began to sob. 'I'm pregnant and the father doesn't want to know.'

'Have you told him?' Emma probed.

'He walked out before I could. What am I supposed to do—go running after him?'

'Is he worth running after?'

There was a long pause before she answered.

'Yes,' she whispered.

'Well, then. Don't you think you ought to be deciding which outfit you're going to wear to knock his socks off when you go to tell him?'

There was a watery smile which disappeared as another thought struck her. 'What if he doesn't want it? What if he doesn't want *me*?'

'So what?' Emma made her voice brisk, although the whole conversation was striking far too close to home for her comfort. 'You don't need a man who isn't man enough to face up to his responsibilities, do you? There's plenty more fish in the sea.'

'But what about the baby?'

'Do you want the baby?' Her hand strayed towards her own waist and she linked her fingers together to keep them still.

'I don't know.' The pale blue eyes filled with tears again. 'I don't know how I'd cope.'

'That's one thing about pregnancy,' Emma said wryly. 'It gives you plenty of time to think about things. If you decide you can't keep the baby there are hundreds of people desperate to adopt. There are so many options. . .'

There was a soft cough behind her and she looked over towards the door to see a policewoman waiting.

'Is it all right for me to do my interview now?' The woman was pleasantly spoken, with a kind expression in her eyes.

'Are you feeling up to it?' Emma turned back to her patient.

'Yes.' It was hesitant but there was a new strength to the girl's voice. 'It's got to be done so I might as well get it over with.'

Emma was moving away to give the two of them some privacy when the young woman called her back.

'Thank you for talking to me — I feel as if you really understand what I'm going through.'

Emma smiled, her cheeks stiffening with the effort as she thought, If only you knew how well I understand! And she left them to their business.

The conversation kept playing through her mind at odd times during the day. She couldn't help remembering her own voice asking the young woman, Is he worth running after?

She was saddened to realise that, in all the weeks since Adam had left, it was the first time that the thought had occurred to her. She'd asked it of a complete stranger but she'd never thought of applying the criterion to her own situation.

Between dealing with an elderly woman with a strangulated hernia and a house painter who'd fallen off a ladder and had a suspected fractured skull, the answer become obvious. Of course he was worth running after! But, by the time she had contacted the appropriate secretary for an ophthalmic surgeon to see an amateur welder who had somehow managed to get his contact lenses stuck to his eyeballs, she was convinced that she had left it too late.

She was exhausted by the end of her shift. Not just because they'd had several casualties from a gas explosion, who'd needed a great deal of attention before they were stabilised and ready for transferral to the special burns unit, but because of the mental battle she'd been fighting with herself all day.

She stripped off her uniform and pulled on a simple cotton dress, grateful that she'd never been one for dramatic, clinging clothes emphasising her waist. At least her ordinary clothes would last her for some time after her shape began to change.

The cool water felt good as she splashed it over her face and she decided not to bother with make-up. She was only going to walk around the corner to her flat and she was unlikely to see anyone she knew—at least, not anyone that she wanted to impress.

She grabbed her bag, weighed down with copious

quantities of fresh fruit and vegetables in accordance with her new resolution, and made her way out of the hospital.

All the way back to her flat she was conscious of a strange sense of impending danger.

She looked over her shoulder a couple of times but there was no one there. She even searched through her other senses to see if she could find anything, but it was as if there were a blanket of cotton wool between herself and the rest of the world.

'It must be because I'm tired,' she muttered as she made her weary way along the last few yards to the main door of the converted house. 'I just need to lock myself behind my own front door and sit down with a hot cup of tea.'

'Taken to talking to yourself, have you?' a deep, accented voice said close to her ear as her bag was lifted out of her hand. 'Why don't you invite me in? I think I deserve a little of your conversation.' And he took hold of her elbow to hasten her steps inside the house.

'A-Adam!' For a moment she thought her knees weren't going to hold her up, and she swayed precariously as joy flooded through her.

'Keep walking,' he growled, 'or I might be forced to carry you. It's taken me long enough to find you, so you're not getting any chance to disappear until I get some answers.'

Suddenly she realised that Adam was angry—no, more than angry, furious.

Her confusion was so great that she didn't even think of arguing with him about his high-handed tactics, meekly allowing him to usher her through the tiny communal hall and into her flat.

He followed her closely across the room until she sank gratefully into a chair and kicked off her shoes; then, when she expected him to sit in the matching chair, he leant forward to grasp an arm of her chair in each powerful hand and loom over her menacingly.

'Why did you do it?' he demanded, his voice low and bitter. 'You could have told me.'

'Do what? Told you what?' Her head was twisted at an awkward angle as she tried to look up at him. She couldn't think straight while he was hanging ominously over her like a great dark thundercloud.

'Don't try to play the innocent.' There was disgust in his voice too. 'The blonde nurse told me—Marion Something, the man-eater.'

Emma allowed herself a wry grin at the thought of Marilyn's reaction to hearing Adam's description of her, but she was no closer to knowing what he was talking about. What on earth had the stupid woman been saying?

'I couldn't believe it at first.' He straightened up and turned to pace away from her, his long legs covering the tiny space between her and the chair on the other side of the room far too soon. 'So I went to Sister Noone and she confirmed it.'

'What?' Emma's frustration boiled over. '*What* did Marilyn tell you? *What* did Sister Noone confirm?'

'That you left St Lawrence's because you were pregnant with my baby.'

Emma was stunned. How on earth had *Marilyn* found out, of all people? She was certain that Barbara Noone wouldn't have told her...unless... A memory surfaced. Had Marilyn been the shadowy figure outside Sister's office when Emma had been telling her. . .?

'Was it true?' he demanded hoarsely, his hands clenched tightly into fists. 'Did you leave because you were pregnant?'

'Yes,' she whispered, knowing that this had been the last way she had anticipated breaking the news to him.

His shoulders slumped as though he'd been struck a mortal blow, and he sat down as though he'd lost all strength.

'Why did you do it?'

Suddenly she was able to feel the pain coming off him in waves, and she realised that until this moment he'd somehow been keeping a tight control on his emotions so that she couldn't read them the way she had before.

'Why did you kill it? I would have taken it if you'd told me—'

'What?' The word emerged as a startled squeak. 'What did you say?'

'It's not the first time,' he said, almost too quietly for her to decipher the words. 'Jaqui got rid of my baby before I knew she was pregnant. Said she didn't want a half-breed brat even if its dad *was* going to be a doctor able to earn a good living.'

The pain was years old but was still festering deep inside.

'Adam.' Emma took a deep breath and stood up, walking towards him on shaky legs. 'Please, give me your hand.'

She held out her own hand and waited, almost counting the beats of her racing heart as she willed him to comply.

Slowly he raised his head to look at her, his face drawn taut with torment, and she could feel his confusion.

She met his gaze fearlessly but couldn't manage the smile he needed for encouragement, so she settled for patience.

At long last she watched his knuckles regain their normal colour as he released his hold on the arm of his chair.

'Feel,' she whispered softly, her throat too tight for proper speech as she directed his palm over the slight roundness hidden by her dress.

Emma? She watched him form the word soundlessly as happiness filled his eyes like the sunrise after a long dark night. 'The baby's still there. Couldn't you go through with it?'

'I never had any intention of getting rid of it—that's why I moved.'

'But. . .?'

'If I'd wanted an abortion I could have had one without going through all the upheaval of changing jobs and moving,' she pointed out. 'St Lawrence's is less than an hour from several private clinics on that side of London. Anyway,' she challenged, 'what on earth made you think I wanted to have an abortion?'

'Your friend Marion.'

'Mari*lyn*'s *no* friend of mine,' Emma stressed. 'She's a self-centred bitch on the lookout for a wealthy husband.'

'But when I stopped off to leave the letter she said she'd make sure you got it. . .' His words died away as he saw her shaking her head. 'You didn't get the letter?'

A brief flash of memory reminded Emma of Marilyn's blush when she had caught her reading a letter which the girl had rapidly hidden.

'Not only did I not get the letter but my "good friend" opened it and read it.' She wrapped her arms around herself as the feeling of betrayal stole over her.

'Oh, God, Emma, I'm sorry.' He surged to his feet and took her in his arms, pulling her close until she rested against the warm security of his body, with her head tucked under his chin.

'I left early that morning so you wouldn't be the object of gossip, fully intending to set the record straight as soon as possible. Unfortunately, when I got to my place there was a message that my grandfather had been taken ill and I had to go straight away.'

'Oh, Adam. Is he all right?'

'He will be. He's too stubborn to die yet.'

'What was the matter with him?' the nurse in Emma couldn't resist asking.

'A heart attack. He's needed bypass surgery for some time, but kept refusing to have it done.'

'Why did he agree this time?'

'Because I told him about meeting you.' Adam's gaze was very intent. 'I told him about your gift and your incredible way with people, and I told him about the mental rapport between us and that I wanted you to marry me and bear our children.'

'If you told him all that, why didn't you tell me?' The words were a cry from the heart. 'I woke up in the morning after the most incredible night of my life and you'd gone.' She drew in a deep breath and held it, fighting for control.

'I wrote it in the letter,' he said simply. 'It was the

first love letter I've ever written in my life and you never saw it.' He wrapped his arms tighter around her and rested his cheek on her hair. 'I said thank you for the most wonderful night of my life. I told you that my grandfather was ill or I'd never have contemplated leaving you like that. I wrote my address and telephone number so that you could contact me and said I would be coming back for you as soon as I could. And I said I love you. . .'

He cupped her chin with one lean hand and tilted her face up to his, his eyes gleaming gold in the soft evening light. 'I love you, Emma Sullivan. You're the other half of my soul. Will you marry me?' And he lowered his head to brush his lips over hers in the tenderest of benedictions.

'Oh, Adam, I love you too.' Her hands slid over his shoulders to cradle the back of his head, her fingers dispensing with the leather thong so that his hair spilled over his shoulders as she pulled him towards her to deepen the kiss.

Within seconds the fire was blazing out of control as the weeks of loneliness were swept away by passion.

Clothing landed in haphazard piles on the floor between the sitting room and her bed, until finally they were once again naked in each other's arms.

This time they knew how to arouse each other swiftly enough for the sparks to fly. This time they made love with an urgency that bordered on compulsion, as though the time they'd spent apart had left them starving for each other.

I love you.

The overwhelming emotion needed no words as they

reached ecstacy together, their minds and bodies in perfect harmony.

'I'm sorry I couldn't come back any sooner.' Adam's voice was husky as he ran his fingers through her hair, spreading it out in an ebony curtain across the pillow.

'Once I'd got my grandfather to agree to the operation I had to stay until he was well on the way to recovery.'

'What did he say when you told him about me?' Emma was curious.

Adam laughed. 'He said it would be worth giving up the principles of a lifetime to be treated by Western medicine if it meant staying around long enough to meet the wolf's mate.' He cupped her cheek and turned her to face him. 'You are, you know.' His voice was serious. 'You're Grey Wolf's mate, and he mates for life.' The words were as binding as if they'd been spoken in front of a priest, and he lowered his head to seal the vow with a kiss.

It was a long time later before they spoke coherently again, but Emma had questions that needed answers.

'Where will we be living, Adam?' Her question was a tacit agreement that she would go wherever he wanted.

'I. . .I've decided that I can do most good if I return to Montana,' he said slowly. 'Some areas are heavily populated and the facilities are as good as anything you're used to, but some are far more remote and primitive and the people there have so little. . .'

He'd been lying on his back with one hand under his head, the other arm cradling her shoulders as she cuddled close to his side. He rolled over towards her until they were facing each other.

'Will you be disappointed that we're not going to Seattle? You would have been much sought after for your ER skills.'

'Emergency Room?' she guessed.

'Yes.' He smiled. 'You're almost bilingual already.'

She thought about the experience she could gain in one of Seattle's big hospitals, but the prospect paled against what Adam was offering.

'I'd rather be where you grew up,' she said quietly. 'I want our child to see the things you saw, learn the things you were taught.' Suddenly she remembered the vision she'd seen and told him about it.

'I was thinking about my visit to Chief Mountain when we were sitting on the hill, and I saw the female join the grey wolf too.'

'That was one reason why I was so upset when you went away,' Emma told him, and she knew that he could feel her pain. 'I knew I was falling in love with you and thought the vision meant that we were going to be together, especially when you told me about your vision quest.'

While she was speaking Adam's eyes were caught by something on the bedside cabinet, and he reached across to pick up a small pile of books.

'*Wolves*? *The First Americans*? *The Indians of the Plains*?' He read each title questioningly.

'I wanted to know about your people and your background so that I'd be able to tell our child.' She rested her hand over the slight curve and he placed his reverently beside hers.

'Now you won't have to read books about us; you're

going to be one of us and my grandfather can tell you what you want to know.'

'Does he know about the elk-skin robe?' Emma remembered the ceremony with which he'd given it to her. 'You said it was special but I haven't found anything about it in these books.'

'It's part of an old Blackfoot legend which tells of the grandson of the sun god being given an elk-skin robe. It was to be worn only by a virtuous woman who, once a year, would honour him in the sun dance so that the sick might be restored to health.'

Emma felt her cheeks grow warm at the implied compliment, her love growing for this special man with every hour she knew him.

Contentment.

They smiled at each other, marvelling at the difference a few hours could make in the course of a life.

'Do you think our children will inherit the gift too?' Emma's voice was growing sleepy.

'More than likely.' Adam's words had a husky undertone as he stroked her naked body, exploring the subtle differences her pregnancy had already made.

His fingers teased the pale globes of her breasts and she arched her back, her reaction telling him better than words that they were now even more sensitive to his ministrations.

'Ah-h-h, Adam, yes. . .' The sleepiness was disappearing fast as he began to make love to her slowly and thoroughly.

'I've been thinking. . .we shall have to do this often in the next six months,' he whispered against her rapidly tightening nipples, his hands already parting her thighs for his exploration. 'If our children do inherit the gift from both sides of their family, there's no telling when we'll be certain we can make love without having eavesdroppers. . .'

Emma laughed delightedly, the sound filling all the dark corners in the room. 'If ever I heard of finding a good reason for doing exactly what you wanted to do in the first place. . .' She smoothed her palms over his back to urge him closer, then grasped the tight curves of his buttocks explicitly.

'Far be it from me to deny my mate. . .' he murmured, and as they became one their simultaneous 'I love you' rang out loud and clear in the soft light.

The first few faint streaks of colour were lighting the early-morning sky when Emma opened her eyes, and her hand slid across the rumpled bedclothes to find an empty space.

There was a lingering trace of warmth which told her that Adam hadn't been gone very long, and she slipped her arms into the shirt he'd worn the day before to go to look for him on silent feet.

Their ranch-style house had more windows than walls, as befitted its location in a place of almost unlimited views. As soon as she'd seen it, Emma had understood Adam's long-ago comment about the horizon being so close in England. Here it seemed as if you could travel for ever before you ran out of space.

She came around the corner into the long, open-plan lounge and found another view of the sunrise, the colours growing stronger and brighter by the minute.

Silhouetted against the light was the familiar, beloved outline of her husband as he stood gazing out on his world. As she watched he bent his head and she realised that he held something in his arms—or rather someone.

Good morning.

She smiled as he communicated with her in a way that seemed totally natural now, neither of them needing to voice their joy in each other, neither needing to look to know when the other was near.

'Emma.' He turned partway towards her and held out one arm to welcome her at his side.

'What are the two of you doing up so early?' she chided. 'Weren't your beds warm and comfortable enough?'

Adam smiled in that familiar heart-stopping way.

'We were going to come back in a minute but I had to show him to the sun.' They both looked down at the tiny replica of the tall man holding him and saw that his dark eyes were fixed on the brightness outside the window.

'Don't you mean, show him the sun?' Emma smiled as she stroked the petal-soft skin of the baby's cheek with the tip of one finger.

'No. I'm following an old family tradition. When each new baby is born we show him to the sun and give thanks for the gift we've been given.' His arm tightened around her shoulders and he lowered his head to brush a gentle kiss over her lips.

'In fact—' he brushed his lips over the downy dark hair crowning his son's head '—I feel as if I should be here every day giving thanks for what I have—for what *we* have. . .'

Emma couldn't help agreeing. They lived in one of the most beautiful places on earth, doing jobs they loved, and they had found in each other the perfect other half. Now, with the birth of their son, already nicknamed Little Wolf, everything was perfect.

Without needing to say another word she wrapped her arms around her two men and gave herself up to a feeling of total contentment.

I love you. . .

I love you, my love.

For the rest of their lives the message would be loud and clear.

Sharon Kendrick had a variety of jobs before training as a nurse and a medical secretary, and found that she enjoyed working in a caring environment. She was encouraged to write by her doctor husband after the birth of their two children, and much of her medical information comes from him, and from friends. She lives in the historic town of Winchester. Sharon also writes for Mills & Boon® Presents. . .™

Other titles by Sharon Kendrick:

Nurse in the Outback
To Break a Doctor's
   Heart
A Medical Liaison
Specialist in Love
Seize the Day
Surgeon of the Heart
Short Story The Real
   Christmas Present

Casualty of Passion
Consultant Care
Taking Risks
Taking it All
Wait and See
All the Care in the
   World

CASUALTY OF PASSION

by

Sharon Kendrick

For the stars of Blood Transfusion –
the great Vera Hanwright,
and in fond memory of Eleanor Lloyd.

CHAPTER ONE

'I TELL you, it was *him*— I actually *saw* him!'

Kelly heard the disbelieving sighs which followed this intriguing statement and wandered round into the female clinic room of St Christopher's world-famous accident and emergency department, her curiosity aroused.

She grinned at the three nurses huddled there. 'Sounds interesting. Saw who?'

Two of the student nurses looked to their undisputed leader, Staff Nurse Higgs—a statuesque blonde with magnificent smouldering blue eyes, who had given Kelly a particularly hard time since she'd arrived as casualty officer just a month earlier, since she didn't take kindly to what she obviously saw as competition. Now she shrugged her magnificent shoulders and stared at Kelly as though she had just met her for the first time. 'We're talking about the new surgical registrar,' she said reluctantly.

Kelly blinked. 'Oh? We have a new surgical registrar on the rotation every couple of years. What's so special about this one?'

Staff Nurse Higgs's bosom swelled with excitement. 'This one——' she paused for dramatic effect '—just happens to be a lord!'

Kelly quickly picked up an ampoule of penicillin that was sitting on a dressing trolley and pretended to study it as a tiny shiver iced her skin into goosebumps beneath the white coat she wore. 'A lord?' she queried carefully, noting objectively that her swallowing reflex seemed to have gone to pot.

'Mmm!' said Staff Nurse Higgs, almost licking her scarlet lips. 'Lord Rousay—a real member of the aristocracy! And that's not all—he's young, he's bloody gorgeous, *and*——' there was a dramatic pause '—he's single! What do you think about that?' Her eyes narrowed, her instinctive ability to sniff out gossip alerted. 'Are you OK, Dr Hartley—you've gone awfully pale?'

'Yes, of course I'm all right,' answered Kelly briskly. 'Why on earth shouldn't I be?'

'You've gone as white as a ghost—and look, your hand's trembling.' The eyes narrowed even further. 'You don't happen to *know* Lord Rousay, do you?'

No, I don't know him, thought Kelly bitterly. I thought I did, but I was young, foolish, naïve. I was just a nobody he tried to take advantage of. She shook her head, but not one strand of the dark auburn hair in its constricting chignon moved. 'Know him? Now, why would I know him?' she said brightly. 'There happen to be over twenty medical schools in the British Isles, with thousands of students, and while I know that lords in the medical world are pretty thin on the ground. . .' She paused for breath, her voice unusually high, and as she looked at their faces she realised that she was completely over-reacting. 'No, I don't know him,' she finished lamely, not caring that she lied.

At that moment, she was saved by the bell. Literally. The sharp insistent peal of the red telephone on Sister's desk shrilled into their ears.

The emergency telephone: the one which never rang except in critical and life-threatening situations.

Nurse Higgs sped off, Lord Rousay temporarily forgotten, and Kelly followed her, her long and sleepless night shift banished by the rush of adrenalin which always accompanied a crisis. Life in the accident and emergency department was one long series of crises.

When she reached Sister's office, Nurse Higgs was just replacing the receiver. 'There's a child coming in,' she said succinctly. 'Aged two. Been savaged on face by a Rottweiler dog. Injuries extend to neck—the ambulance men are querying tissue damage to her airway. They're trying to intubate her, but there's swelling, apparently.'

'Bleep the duty anaesthetist,' said Kelly quickly. 'And can you send an experienced nurse into the resuscitation room to make sure the paediatric airway set is open? Did they say how bad the wound is?'

'No.'

'Well, when they arrive——' But Kelly's sentence was never finished because at that moment they heard the insistent sound of the ambulance's siren as it sped to the back entrance of the department.

'That's them!' said Kelly. 'Come on!'

Kelly ran out to greet it, Nurse Higgs hot on her heels. As soon as the back door was opened, Kelly climbed in, the blood draining from her face as she saw the extent of the child's injuries. No matter how experienced you were, it never left you—that feeling of helplessness when you saw someone who was terribly injured, especially when you were dealing with a toddler like this one.

The little girl was barely conscious. Shock, Kelly decided. Her breathing was stertorous but steady, and there was an airway *in situ*.

'We couldn't manage to intubate her,' said the driver, as he helped unhook the intravenous fluid bag from the drip stand before rushing the stretcher into A & E. 'You'll need an anaesthetist for that—the tissue is swollen.'

'He's on his way,' said Kelly briefly.

All the way into the department and along the short corridor to the resuscitation cubicle, she quizzed the drivers.

'What's her name?'

'Gemma Jenkins.'

Kelly bent her head and said softly into the child's ear, 'Hello, Gemma—I'm Dr Kelly. You're here in hospital and you're safe.'

Gemma remained unresponsive. Kelly turned worried eyes to the second ambulance man. 'When did this happen?'

'Only a few minutes ago, thank God.'

'Do we know how?'

The driver's mouth twisted with distaste. 'The dog belongs to the mother's boyfriend. He brought it round after a lunchtime session up the pub, rather the worse for wear. He disappeared into the bedroom with the mother, leaving the child to "play" with the dog.'

Kelly nodded. 'I see. Do we know where the mother is now?'

'She's following behind in a taxi. With the boyfriend.'

Kelly raised her eyebrows. 'But surely the mother wanted to accompany Gemma?'

'She's hysterical.'

'As well she might be,' said Kelly grimly.

'What she wanted,' said the ambulance driver, in the

kind of weary voice which indicated that he had seen too much of the dross of life not to have become a cynic, 'was to comfort the boyfriend. He's worried that she'll press charges.'

Kelly, too, had grown used to the vagaries of human nature: these days she was rarely shocked, but this comment left her momentarily speechless. She shook her head in despair. 'Come on—let's get her on to the trolley.'

To Kelly's intense relief, the anaesthetist arrived and began to intubate the little girl. If he'd been delayed, Kelly could have done it at a pinch but, unless you'd had specialist training, trying to get an airway down a child's tiny trachea was notoriously difficult, particularly if the area was as swollen as this child's. The most common mistake was to insert the airway into the oesophagus instead of the trachea.

While the anaesthetist was extending the neck, Nurse Higgs began taking pulse, respiration and blood-pressure recordings, while Kelly gently wiped the blood away from Gemma's face so that she could see how bad the wound was.

It was bad enough. A great gaping gash which extended jaggedly down the left side of her face, but which had fortunately just missed the eye.

Kelly glanced up at the anaesthetist. 'How's her breathing?'

'Stable. And she's coming round.'

At least with the child's condition stabilised the danger of respiratory arrest had been allayed for the time being, thought Kelly, and she turned to Nurse Higgs. 'She needs suturing. Can you bleep the plastics surgeon?'

'The *plastics*?' queried Nurse Higgs, and the hostility which she had been showing towards Kelly since she had started three weeks ago finally bubbled over. 'Aren't you going to do it yourself?'

Kelly frowned with anger at the implied criticism. 'Nurse Higgs,' she said quietly, 'I'm adequate enough at stitching, but not arrogant enough to play God. I'm not sufficiently experienced to do delicate work of this nature—a botch-up here could cost a young child her looks and leave her with an unsightly scar. Now, are you going to bleep the plastics man for me, or am I going to have to do it myself?'

Nurse Higgs's eyes sparked malicious fire, but she bustled out without another word.

The anaesthetist raised an eyebrow. He was a tall, pale man, infinitely calm like most of his profession. 'Trouble?' he queried mildly.

'Nothing that I can't deal with,' Kelly answered resolutely, as she dipped another piece of cotton wool into the saline solution and very gently wiped some dried blood away.

'Report her,' he suggested.

Kelly shook her head. 'I'll manage,' she said, and dropped the used piece of cotton wool into the paper bag which hung on the side of the trolley.

They worked in silence, until the glimpse of a blinding white coat out of the corner of her eye told Kelly that the plastics man had arrived, but before she could get a proper look at him, she heard a horribly familiar laconic voice.

'I'm here to suture.'

Kelly looked up briefly, her eyes flicking to his name-badge. 'Randall Seton, Surgical Registrar'. His title,

Lord Rousay—his still living father holding the title of Lord Seton, which Randall would one day inherit—was of course absent.

She swallowed, and looked down at the child again. 'I asked for someone from plastics,' she said. 'Not a general surgeon.'

He was already taking off his white coat and removing the gold cuff-links from his pristine pin-striped shirt. 'And there isn't anyone from plastics available,' he drawled, 'so you've got the next best thing. Me. Get me a pair of size nine gloves, would you, Staff?'

Staff Nurse Higgs had miraculously appeared by his side, like the genie from the lamp, and was staring up at him like an eager puppy. There was none of her delayed hearing problem in evidence today—the one which habitually had Kelly repeating her requests—and she sped off immediately to do the surgeon's bidding.

Kelly continued to clean the wound, her heart racing. She was professional enough not to let him know how much his closeness bothered her, woman enough to be unable to deny the potency of his attraction.

'Right,' he murmured. 'Let's have some local anaesthetic drawn up, shall we, Staff?'

The voice was the same. Centuries of breeding, the finest schools, the big, country houses, privilege from the word go had guaranteed that Randall would speak with that confident, beautifully modulated English accent, as precise as cut glass. But it differed from the popular conception of the aristocratic voice, because it was deeper, sardonic, mocking—worlds away from the popular idea of the upper-class twit. It was an exquisite voice—smooth as syrup and dark as chocolate, the kind of voice which sent shivers down the spine of every woman from sixteen to ninety.

The wound was almost completely clean, and he had gloved up and was ready to start suturing.

'Thanks,' he said softly.

Their eyes met for a fraction of a second, and the impact of it was enough to make Kelly feel as though she had been winded and bruised by an unexpected blow.

'I'd better go and talk to the mother,' she said quickly, but he didn't seem to hear her. He was too busy pushing a fine syringe into the damaged area of the child's face with delicate precision even to notice Kelly's departure.

Heart hammering, Kelly picked up the casualty card, rang through to the reception desk, and asked for the mother of Gemma Jenkins to be sent along to the doctor's office.

She sat down, noticing dispassionately that her hands were actually trembling. She had never thought that she would see Randall ever again, she really hadn't—or perhaps that had been wishful thinking. But even given the notoriously closely knit world of British medicine, she certainly hadn't considered that just the merest glimpse of him, just the sound of that seductive mellifluous voice would be enough to shatter her composure and make her feel like the insecure seventeen-year-old she had been when she'd first met him.

She sighed. Nine long years ago. Where had they gone? Nine years of study, study, study and work, work, work.

And she had imagined that she had acquired a little sophistication on the way, had thought that she had become a little more worldly-wise. Was she going to let just the sight of Randall rip away all the complex layers of emotional maturity she had carefully constructed over the years?

Like hell she was!

There was a soft rap on the door, and Kelly instinctively sat upright in her chair, pulling her narrow shoulders back and arranging her features into a neutral expression.

'Come in!' she called.

Gemma's mother had, predictably, brought the boyfriend in, clinging possessively on to his arm, as though he were the first prize in a raffle. He had lurid tattoos over every available inch of flesh and he stank of booze. Kelly swallowed down the feeling of revulsion, determined to remain impartial. She had been taught, over and over again, that emotionally involved doctors who made value judgements were simply not doing their jobs properly.

The mother could have been little more than twenty-two—a woman who looked little more than a girl herself. She's younger than me, thought Kelly, with a jolt of surprise. And yet there was a grimy greyness to her complexion which told of a life lived inside, in high-rise blocks far away from the fresh air and the sunshine. She wore cheap, ill-fitting clothes. Her legs were pale and bare and she had squeezed her feet into tight, patent shoes, obviously new, though they were spattered with mud. On her heels she wore plasters where the shoes had obviously cut into her flesh. Her blonde hair was full of gel with little bits spiking upwards like a porcupine's, and already the dark roots were an inch long. Stooping, sad and pathetic, she stared back at Kelly with blank, disillusioned eyes and Kelly cursed a society which could allow the cycle of deprivation which had made this woman into one of life's losers. And would now probably do the same for her daughter.

She schooled her face into its listening expression. 'Mrs Jenkins?' she asked politely.

'It's *Miss*!' interrupted the man. 'That bastard didn't bother marrying her when she had his kid.'

'And your name is. . .?' prompted Kelly.

'Alan,' he swaggered. 'Alan Landers.'

'How's. . .how *is* Gemma?' the woman asked, her voice a plaintive whine.

At last. 'The doctor is suturing her face now,' said Kelly briskly. 'Given his skill, and the fact that your daughter is young enough to heal, well—we're hoping for the best, but I have to warn you that she *will* have a scar, though the surgeon is doing his best to ensure that it will be as small and as neat as possible.'

She took a deep breath. The police would investigate, but the A & E department themselves would need details of what had happened. 'Just for the record, would you mind telling me how it happened?'

Mr Landers screwed his face up into an ugly and menacing scowl. 'Stupid kid was winding the dog up. That dog wouldn't hurt no one.'

Refraining from pointing out the obvious flaw in his logic, Kelly thought that if she had been a man and not a doctor nothing would have given her greater pleasure than to punch this ignorant lout on the nose, but even if she *had* done, that wouldn't have been the answer. He had probably grown up fighting violence with violence, and as soon as he was old enough had gone out and bought an aggressive dog as a kind of ferocious status symbol, supposed to demonstrate just how much of a man he was.

Kelly looked directly at the man. 'Did you witness the attack?'

'Nah.'

'But it was your dog?' persisted Kelly, her fountain-pen flying as she wrote on the casualty card.

'That's right.'

'And you weren't there when it attacked?'

'That's right,' he said again.

Kelly had to bite back the incredulous question of how someone could leave a big, violent dog alone with a small child. 'So where were you when the attack took place on Gemma?'

This provoked a raucous belly laugh. 'In the bedroom,' he leered, and his eyebrows lifted suggestively as his gaze dropped to Kelly's breasts. 'Want me to tell you what we was up to?'

'That *won't* be necessary, Mr Landers,' said Kelly crisply. She turned to the woman and her totally vacant expression.

'You do know, Miss Jenkins, that I'm going to have to call in Social Services?'

'Do what?' The grey-faced woman was on her feet at once. 'And get some nosy-parker social worker sticking their oar in?'

Kelly looked at them both sadly. Didn't they realise that if the child was deemed to be at serious risk she could be taken away from them? God forgive her, but in a way she wished that Gemma *would* be free of them, if she hadn't also known that often children in care suffered from a different kind of neglect. 'I am also going to have to report the injury to the police——'

'What for?' the man demanded belligerently.

Kelly put her pen down. 'Because this category dog is supposed to be muzzled, Mr Landers—as I'm sure you know. It certainly shouldn't have been left alone in a room with a toddler...' Kelly paused, recognising that, despite all her pep-talking to herself, she had done the unforgivable—she *had* sounded judgemental. But doctors were human too, and she wondered seriously whether anyone in their right mind could have stopped themselves from adopting a critical tone with a case of this sort.

But it was when the man stabbed an angry finger in front of her face that she realised that if she wasn't careful, he really *could* turn nasty. She had better let him have his say. Even in her three short weeks in A & E, she had learnt that 'verbalising your feelings', as one of the social workers put it, also tended to defuse pent-up emotions.

Mr Landers's face was contorted into an ugly mask. 'You listen here to me, you little bitch——'

'What's going on in here?' came a deep, aristocratic drawl.

The three of them looked at the door, where the tall, dark and rangy form of Randall Seton stood surveying them through narrowed eyes.

The man replied in time-honoured fashion. 'Push off, you stuck-up git!'

There was a silence of about two seconds, and then Randall moved forward, his whole stance one of alert, healthy and muscular readiness. He radiated strength and he spoke with quietly chilling authority; but then, thought Kelly somewhat bitterly, that was the legacy of privilege too.

'Listen to me,' he said softly. 'And listen to me carefully. Dr Hartley has just been caring for your daughter in Casualty. So have I. I've just stitched together the most appalling wound inflicted by an animal that I've ever seen, praying as I did so that it will leave as little scar tissue as possible. An anaesthetist is currently pumping air down into her lungs, because where the dog's teeth ripped at her throat it caused such swelling that if an ambulance hadn't been on the scene so promptly, her airway could have been obstructed and your daughter could have died from lack of oxygen.'

The mother gave an audible gasp of horror, as though the reality of what had happened had just hit her.

'She is shortly going to be admitted to the children's ward,' he continued, 'where she will be looked after by another series of staff. Now we've all been doing our job, because that's what we're paid to do and that's what we chose to do. What we do *not* expect is to be criticised or insulted for doing just that. Have I made myself perfectly clear, Mr—Mr——?' The dark, elegent eyebrows were raised in query, but there was no disguising the dangerous spark of anger which made the grey eyes appear so flinty. At that moment, he looked positively *savage*, thought Kelly, but he somehow managed to do it in a very controlled kind of way. But there again, Randall was the master of self-control, wasn't he?

'Landers,' gulped the man. 'Yes, Doctor. I understand.'

'Good.' Then the dark-lashed grey eyes swept over Kelly. 'Can I see you for a minute?'

Nine years, she thought, slightly hysterically, and he asks can he see me for a minute. Breaking up with Randall—not that such a brief acquaintanceship really warranted such a grand-sounding title—had been the best thing which had ever happened to her. But she had often wondered, as women always did wonder about the first man who had made them dizzy with desire, just what would happen if they saw each other again. What would they think? What would they say?

She had never imagined such an inglorious reunion taking place in a tiny and scruffy little office in one of London's busiest A & E departments, nor him saying something as trite as that.

He looked. . .

Admit it, Kelly, she thought reluctantly. He looks like a dream. Every woman's fantasy walking around in a white coat.

He was lightly tanned. Naturally, he was tanned; he was always tanned. In the winter he skied down the blackest runs in Switzerland, and in the summer he holidayed with friends around the Mediterranean on a yacht which he had owned since the age of eighteen. Nine years hadn't added a single ounce of fat to that incredibly muscular body, honed to perfection by years of rigorous sport. The hair was as dark as ever, almost too black—a gypsy ancestor had been responsible for the midnight gleam of those rampant waves, he had once told her—sure!—and it curled and waved thickly around a neck which Michaelangelo would have died to sculpt.

She stared into eyes the colour of an angry sea,

trying to equal his dispassionate scrutiny, trying to convince herself that it was just the shock of seeing him again which made her heart thunder along like a steam train. 'I can't,' she said. 'I'm afraid that I'm busy just now taking a history.'

He gave her a cool smile, the flash in the grey eyes mocking her. 'When you've finished, then?'

It would never occur to him to take no for an answer. 'I'm afraid that I may be tied up for some time.'

He shrugged the broad shoulders. 'In that case, I'll chase you up when I'm out of Theatre.' His eyes glittered. 'I can't wait.' It sounded awfully like a threat.

She wanted to say, Why bother? What was the point? Instead she shrugged her shoulders indifferently—a gesture which deserved to win her an Oscar. 'If you like,' she answered coolly. And picked up her pen again.

'And now, Miss Jenkins. If you'd like to give me a few more details. . .'

She didn't have time to think of him again during that shift; she was absolutely run off her feet. A middle-aged man came in on a stretcher with his leg badly broken in three places, and then a teenage girl was admitted with an overdose.

'How many has she taken?' Kelly asked her white-faced and trembling mother as she handed her the empty bottle.

'Only ten. That's all that was left in the box. She left a note. It said——' and here the woman started sobbing helplessly '—said it was to pay me back. I wouldn't let her go out last night, you see. Told her she had to revise for her exams, or she'd end up like me, Doctor, struggling just to survive.'

'Ssssh,' said Kelly softly, as she handed the sobbing woman a paper handkerchief. 'Try not to distress yourself.'

'She will be all right, won't she, Doctor?' asked the mother plaintively.

Kelly nodded, and answered with cautious optimism. 'I'm confident that she'll pull through. She's in good hands now.' Though it was lucky that the pills the girl had taken did not have any major side-effects.

She watched while the nurses, garbed in plastic gowns, gloves and wellington boots, put a wide tube into the girl's mouth and worked it down into her stomach. Then they tipped a saline solution into it, and waited for her to start retching. The physical ignominy of this uncomfortable procedure would hopefully make the girl think very carefully about attempting such an overdose again, Kelly hoped. Because what had started out as an angry gesture could have ended up with such tragic consequences.

She had been working in Accident and Emergency for just three weeks, but already she had discovered that her job was as much social worker as doctor—if she allowed it to be. And, frankly, she didn't have the time to allow it to be. The lives that people lived and the conditions in which they lived them sometimes made her despair, but there was little she could do to change anything, and accepting that had been a hard lesson.

It was seven o'clock by the time she finished, although she'd been due off at six. She had been held up with a cardiac arrest, and by the time she took her white coat off and washed her hands she was bushed, and could think of nothing she would like more than a

hot bath, a good book, and an early night, particularly
as she was not seeing Warren until tomorrow.

She set off for her room, through the winding corridors of St Christopher's—one of London's oldest and
most revered hospitals. The main corridor was particularly impressive at night, and the ornately carved marble
pillars dating back from a more prosperous time in the
hospital's history cast long and intricate shadows on the
well-worn stones of the floor.

Kelly heard a sound behind her. A sound she knew
so well.

Sounds echoed on this particular floor and footsteps
were normal in a hospital. Day and night, people
moved in endless motion.

But Kelly stiffened, then remonstrated silently with
herself. Of course she wouldn't be able to recognise his
footsteps. Not after nine years.

She turned round to face whoever was close behind
her, as any sensible female doctor would.

And it was him.

'Hello, Kelly,' he said, his voice a deep, mocking
caress, and Kelly felt herself thrill just to the sound of
him speaking her name. He managed to make it sould
like poetry, but he had always had the ability to do
that.

And as she stared into eyes as silvery and as crystal-
line as mercury, nine years seemed just to slip away,
like grains of sand running through her fingers.

CHAPTER TWO

NINE summers ago Kelly had been in the first year of her school's sixth form, studying science, and studying hard. When other students moaned about the rigorous demands of the syllabus they were expected to cover, Kelly did not. Her study had been hard fought for.

Not many students had to fight their parents to stay on at school—it was often the other way round—but Kelly's parents simply had not been able to understand why she didn't want to leave school at the earliest opportunity to start 'bringing a bit of money in', as they put it. Which, loosely translated, meant—certainly in the culture which Kelly had grown up in—to help boost her mother's already meagre income, made even more meagre by her father's liking for a drink and a bet on the horses. What they had expected for Kelly was a local shop or factory job. But Kelly refused to be condemned to a life of drudgery before getting married to a man like her father and having to scrimp and save and hide her money from him.

Kelly had tried to hide her bitterness at the lack of ambition in the Hartley household, knowing that any hint of rebellion would seal her fate. And she was lucky in two respects. The first was that she had been born with an outstanding intellect, and the second was that she had an absolute champion in her chemistry teacher—a Mr Rolls. Not only did his passion for his subject inspire her to work as hard as she possibly could, but through him she learned really to love the discipline of science.

If Mr Rolls had never achieved his full potential, he was determined that Kelly should not follow the same pattern. In his late thirties, he had never married, instead devoting all his energies to his students. It was Mr Rolls who spoke to Kelly's dazed parents, told them that it would be a crime if she were not allowed to pursue higher education. It was he who allayed their financial fears by telling them that all sorts of grants were available for gifted students these days, and that they would not be asked to provide money they simply did not have. The only thing he did not discuss with them, at Kelly's behest, was her ambition to become a doctor.

'Time enough for that,' Kelly told him firmly.

'But why?' He was genuinely non-comprehending.

She stared back at him, her large green eyes already wise beyond their years, in so many ways. 'Because it will honestly be too much for them to take in all at once,' she told him gently. 'To tell them that I want to become a doctor would be like telling them that I want to fly to Venus!'

But she had felt as though if she spread her arms she really *could* fly to Venus that August evening, as she walked up the gravelled drive of the enormous country house for the summer school in science which Mr Rolls had insisted she attend. He had even arranged for the school governors to sponsor the trip.

'And Seton House is in the heart of the country,' he told her smilingly. 'Do you good to get out of London for a bit—put a bit of colour in your cheeks.'

Kelly had never seen such a beautiful place in all her

life as Seton House. It was not *quite* as impressive as Hampton Court Palace, which she had visted on a trip with the Brownies years ago, but it came a pretty close second, with its sweeping manicured lawns in the most dazzling shade of emerald, and its carefully clipped yew trees, and its parklands.

She stared up at the house, slightly fearful of knocking, when at that moment the vast door opened and a man in his early twenties came running lightly down the steps, saw her, stopped, and smiled. He had thick, black hair and the longest pair of legs she had ever seen.

'Well, *hello*!' His eyes were sparkling—fine grey eyes with exceptionally long black lashes—as they looked Kelly up and down with open appreciation.

That summer she had grown used to the stares from men; it had been a liberating summer in more ways than one. She had grown her hair, so that it rippled in dark red waves all the way down her back, and the faded jeans and T-shirt which every student wore emphasised the slim curve of her hips, the gentle swell of her burgeoning breasts. If men ogled her, she soon put them in their place. But somehow she didn't mind this man looking one bit. It gave her the chance to look at him, and he was, without exception, the most delectable man she had ever set eyes on. 'Hello,' she answered. 'Who are you?'

He grinned. 'Well, actually I'm wearing two hats this week.'

Kelly blinked. 'Excuse me? Your head is bare.'

His eyes narrowed, and he laughed—the richest, deepest, most mesmerising sound she could imagine. 'Sorry. What I mean is that I'm one of the medical students running the course, and I. . .' And then his gaze fell to the cheap and battered old suitcase she was clutching, and his eyes softened. 'Come inside. You must be tired after your journey. Here, let me carry your bags for you,' and he took them from her without waiting for her assent. 'Come with me. I'll show you to your room. You're the first to arrive. We weren't expecting anyone until this evening.'

'I—caught the early train,' faltered Kelly, as she followed him up the steps leading to the house. The cheaper train, the bargain ticket, planning to kill time looking around the village of Little Merton. Except that when she had arrived in Little Merton there had been absolutely nothing to see, so she had come straight on up to the house. 'I can always go away and come back later,' she ventured.

'What to do? There's not a lot to see in Little Merton!'

'So I noticed,' remarked Kelly drily, and he turned his head to stare down at her again, giving her another of those slow smiles. She wondered if he knew just how attractive those smiles were—he *must* do!

Kelly followed him into the vast entrance hall, with him still holding her bags. No one had ever carried her bags for her before; in her world, women struggled with the heavy items, like pack-horses for the most part. She rather liked this show of masculine strength, and of courtesy. It made her feel fragile and protected, and rather cherished.

She stared around the hall. She had never imagined that a place could be so large and so beautiful, without being in the least bit ostentatious. There was none of the over-the-top gold scrolling which had abounded in

Hampton Court. Instead, just an air of quiet loveliness, and the sensation of continuity down through the ages, of treasures being treasured and passed on for the next generation to enjoy.

'It's quite perfect,' said Kelly simply.

He looked down at her. 'Isn't it?' he said quietly. 'I'm glad you like it.'

It didn't occur to her to ask why. She just assumed that, like her, he had an eye for beautiful things.

He showed her upstairs to her room, decorated in a striking shade of yellow with soft sage-green fittings. It was just like being at the centre of a daffodil, thought Kelly fancifully.

'It's rather small, I'm afraid,' he apologised. 'But we've put some of the boys in the larger rooms, sharing.'

Small? Kelly gulped. It was palatial! She had spent the last fifteen years sharing a shoe-box of a room with a sister whose idea of tidying up was to chuck all the mess into an already overflowing cupboard! 'It's lovely,' she told him, wandering to the window. 'And oh——' her gaze was suddenly arrested by the tantalising glitter of sunlight on water in the distance '—is that a lake I can see?'

'Mmm.' He came to stand beside her. 'We have black swans nesting there. Very rare and very beautiful. I'll show you later if you like.'

'I'd like that very much.'

He smiled.

She was suddenly very conscious of just how tall he was, how broad his shoulders; aware too of the powerful thrust of his thighs, similarly clad in denim more faded than her own jeans. She wasn't used to being alone in bedrooms with strange men, she thought, her heart beating hard, but he seemed unconcerned by his surroundings. But then, why should he not be? He was a medical student, and about twenty-four, she guessed. He would not look twice at a seventeen-year-old schoolgirl.

All the same, she felt that it was probably wise to establish a more formal footing.

'Which medical school are you at?' she enquired politely.

'St Jude's. I'm in my final year. How about you?'

'Another year of A-levels, then I'm hoping to get a place at St Christopher's.'

He frowned. 'So you're—how old?'

'Seventeen— *just*!' she smiled, disconcerted to see an expression of disquiet pass over his features. 'There's nothing wrong, is there?'

He shook his head. 'I somehow thought that you were older than that. Most of the students here are just about to go up to medical school. Some are even in their first year. You must be very good to be here.' The grey eyes were questioning.

Kelly smiled, not falling into the trap of false modesty, knowing her own worth and ability as a student. 'You'll have to be the judge of that,' she answered coolly.

Their eyes met, his giving a brief but unmistakably appreciative flash, and she found that she could not look away, that his face seemed to be at the centre of her whole universe right at that moment. She became aware of other things too, things that up until now she had only read about in biology text-books: the sudden drying of her mouth and the hammering of her heart.

The tightening of her breasts, as though they had become heavy and engorged with blood. And the sudden rucking of her nipples—exquisite and painful and highly disturbing.

Kelly wasn't stupid. She had grown up in a neighbourhood where girls experimented sexually with boys from as early an age as fourteen, and up until now she had always been disapproving and highly critical of such behaviour. Now, for the first time in her life, she acknowledged the dangerous and potent power of sexual attraction.

She turned away, wondering if he had seen the betraying signs of that attraction in her body. 'I'd better unpack,' she said awkwardly. 'Thanks for showing me to my room. . .' She hesitated. 'I don't even know your name.'

He paused for a moment before answering. 'It's Randall,' he told her. 'And yours?'

'Kelly. Kelly Hartley.'

'Because your eyes are Kelly-green?' he hazarded.

She shook her head and laughed. 'My mother says I was named after Grace Kelly, but my father disagrees. He says it was Ned Kelly—the bandit!'

He laughed too, then stayed her with a light touch of his hand on her forearm as she moved towards the tatty suitcase which looked ridiculously out of place amidst the restrained elegance of the room. 'Don't unpack now—there'll be plenty of time for that later. It's such a glorious day. Why don't you let me show you something of the countryside? We could have lunch somewhere. That's if you'd like to?'

She would like to very much, although the sensible, studious Kelly could think of all kinds of reasons why she shouldn't go gallivanting off to lunch with someone she had barely met. But something in the soft silver-grey of his eyes was proving to be impossibly enticing. He was not the first man to have asked her out, but he was the first one she had ever said yes to.

She grinned. 'I'd love to. Do I need to change?'

He shook his head. 'You look fantastic. Do you have a ribbon or something?'

Kelly nodded. 'Why?'

'Bring it, you'll need it.'

The reason why was a small, gleaming scarlet sports car which was garaged in an area he called the 'old stables'. Kelly's eyes widened. Brought up with frugality as her middle name, she said the first thing which came into her head.

'How on earth can you afford a car like this as a student?'

He seemed surprised by her frankness. 'It was a twenty-first birthday present,' he told her as he opened the car door for her. 'From my parents.'

'Generous parents,' commented Kelly wryly, as she climbed into the car.

He moved into the seat next to her, and turned the ignition key. 'Oh, they're certainly generous,' he said, in a voice which sounded strangely bitter. 'That's to say, they find it very easy to buy things.'

She stole a glance at him. 'What's wrong with them buying things?'

The silver-grey eyes were direct; disturbing. He shrugged. 'It doesn't make up for them never having been there, I suppose.'

'Doesn't it? I have exactly the opposite problem with my parents,' answered Kelly, giving a rueful little smile, wondering if anyone was ever contented with their lot.

'Then I guess we'll just have to comfort one another, won't we?' he said, his voice soft, mocking, having the power to increase her pulse-rate just with its deep, velvety caress.

Suddenly shy, Kelly quickly gathered her thick red hair up in the black velvet ribbon, afraid he might notice that she was blushing like crazy.

He turned on the ignition, and the little car roared off down the drive, spitting out pieces of gravel in its wake, and Kelly sat back in the seat to enjoy the drive.

It was one of those afternoons which stayed in the memory forever—the most perfect afternoon of Kelly's life. He drove her to a country pub for lunch where they ate crusty bread and great slabs of farmhouse cheese, washed down with local beer. After that, they walked. And talked. They didn't seem to stop talking. She told him all about the tiny terraced house she had grown up in, about the shared bedroom and the thin walls where the neighbours' arguments were broadcast so loudly that they might have been in the same room. She told him of her burning ambition to be a surgeon, and his eyes had narrowed.

'It's tough enough, anyway,' he observed. 'Even tougher for a woman.'

'I know,' she said passionately. 'And I don't *care*! I'm going to defeat all the odds, you wait and see!'

He had smiled then, his eyes soft. 'I can't wait,' he murmured.

She blushed again, realising that she had been monopolising the conversation; he was so incredibly easy to talk to. 'Now tell me about you,' she urged him.

'What, everything?' he teased.

'Absolutely *everything*!'

And Randall painted a picture of his own world, so very different from hers. Kelly's heart turned over when he described being sent away to boarding school at the tender age of eight.

'Cold showers and cross-country runs,' he said, and shuddered theatrically.

'Did you really hate it?' she asked sympathetically.

'I *loathed* it,' he said with feeling, then grinned. 'Don't look so tragic, Kelly—it was a long time ago,' and he took her hand in his. She didn't object; her head was spinning, as though he had intoxicated her just with his presence.

The afternoon flew by and it was almost six when they arrived back at the house. There were several cars parked in front of the house, and a woman, small and matronly, stood on the steps, talking to a group of people, most slightly older than Kelly, and whom she assumed were other medical students.

When the little sports car came to a halt, the woman came hurrying over to them, barely looking at Kelly, her face reproving. '*There* you are, my lord!' she exclaimed. 'Everyone's been looking for you. Five medical students and no one knows where to put them.'

Kelly stiffened. *Lord*!

'Calm down, Mary,' he drawled in a voice born to giving orders, and Kelly watched while the older woman softened under the sheer potency of all that charm. 'I'll sort it out. Mary—I'd like you to meet Kelly Hartley. Kelly—this is Mary. She lives here and provides food to die for.'

But Kelly knew instantly from his proprietorial tone that Mary 'lived' here purely in the capacity of staff. She felt somehow betrayed. They had shared intimacies, swopped secrets—and yet he had left out something as fundamental as the fact that he was a member of the flaming aristocracy! Her cheeks were hot with anger, but she managed to keep her voice relatively calm. 'Thank you very much for lunch,' she said crisply. 'I'll leave you to it—you're obviously terribly busy.'

'Kelly——' he began, but Kelly had jumped out of the car and run past the staring group and upstairs to her room before he could say anything more, or stop her.

And when the peremptory knock came on her door about half an hour later, she was not surprised, though she was tempted not to answer it.

She pulled the door open to find Randall leaning with languid grace against the door-frame, his grey eyes narrowed. 'Why are you angry?' he asked calmly.

'Why do you think?'

'If I knew that, I wouldn't be asking.'

'Why on earth didn't you tell me that you were a lord?' she demanded.

'Oh, that,' he said casually.

'Yes, *that*!' she retorted. 'I suppose that you actually *own* this house too?'

He shrugged. 'Guilty as charged. Although on a technical point, I won't actually own it until my father dies.'

'Damn you and your technical point!' she fired back. 'Why didn't you tell me?'

He came inside, closed the door firmly behind him

and took her by the shoulders. 'Because I didn't want you to know. Not then.'

Kelly's eyes widened. 'Why ever not?'

'Because people can be intimidated by the title, and I suspected that you might be one of them.'

She took a step back. 'Why, of all the most *patronising*——'

'And because sometimes the baggage which comes with all that stuff,' he interrupted coolly, 'just gets in the way of what really matters. . .you know?'

She shook her head, angry and confused. 'No, I don't know.'

'Yes, you do,' he said softly, and bent his head to kiss her. 'Of course you do.'

After that Kelly spent every moment she could with him, and for the first time in her life found it difficult to concentrate on her studies. He had put her in his tutorial group, and she really had to make an effort not to run her gaze dreamily over every glorious inch of his body, and to listen instead to his lectures, which she wasn't at all surprised to discover were absolutely brilliant.

Randall was the undisputed star of the course, and it was pretty obvious that every girl fancied him like mad, but he seemed to have eyes only for Kelly. At the end of each day's session he would take her off somewhere in his little sports car and they would walk for miles, arriving back only just in time for dinner.

'Should you be leaving them alone like this?' Kelly asked him, as the little sports car came to a halt and she tried to drag the brush through her tangled hair.

He smiled. 'Relax. There's plenty for them to do—

I'm not playing nanny to them. Now come here and kiss me before we go inside.'

Kelly was quite certain that she was in love with him. But it was more than just the completely over-whelming physical attraction she had been aware of from the very beginning, because he gave her a great sense of her own worth for her intellect, as well as a woman.

Thoughts of him disturbed her nights, and she tossed restlessly as she relived how his amazing grey eyes would darken with passion every time he took her into his arms. She suspected that she would willingly have gone to bed with him, except that he behaved with a restraint which she found admirable, given that even with her total inexperience she recognised just how much he wanted her.

And then came that last evening.

First there was dinner, cooked as usual by Mary, and then someone had laughingly suggested charades. So they all filed into the room which was known as the red library, but after a time Randall took her by the hand and led her quietly from the room. She didn't know whether anyone noticed that they had left, and, aware that she was leaving the following day, she no longer cared. Silently she went up the staircase with him, her heart beating like a wild thing when he led her straight to her bedroom and closed the door quietly behind them.

He stared at her for a long, long moment. 'I'm going to miss you, Kelly,' he said softly. 'Very, very much.'

She could have drowned in the intensity of that silver-grey stare. 'Are you?' she whispered.

'More than you could ever imagine.' He took her

into his arms, his face dark and unreadable, the light from the moon emphasising the aristocratic cheek-bones, the sculptured perfection of his mouth. He bent his face so that it was very close to hers. 'And I want to see you again—you know that, don't you?'

Kelly nodded silently, shaken by the fervour in his voice, which matched some spark deep in her soul. She wound her arms around his neck, and her body seemed to melt into the hard sinews of his, her unspoken surrender apparent in the kiss she returned so sweetly.

He gave a low moan as he ran his hands through the thick, silken texture of her hair, then let them fall to her waist, to gather her in even closer, so that they were moulded together and she never wanted to let him go. Never, never, never.

Her breasts tingled as he stroked them over the cotton of the simple white dress she wore, and she gave a little sigh, her eyes closing as she felt the warm river of desire flood her veins with sweet potency.

Still kissing her, he slid the zip of her dress down and she let her arms drop to her sides so that it glided down over her hips and pooled on the ground around her feet. He raised his head then, his eyes narrowed as they studied her. Her breasts were so small that she wore no bra, and she was clad only in the smallest pair of bikini briefs, her body silvered by the pale light of the moon, the thick waves of her hair tumbling down over her small, high breasts. Suffused with love and longing for him, Kelly felt exultant as she saw the expression on his face as his gaze slowly covered every inch of her, filled with an elemental and very feminine fire as she revelled in the power of her body, that *she* could inspire that look of ardour on his face.

'You're so beautiful,' he told her. His voice sounded unsteady, almost slurred with desire, as he started to unbutton his shirt, letting it fall to the ground as carelessly as her dress had done.

'So are you,' she whispered, and she heard him give a low laugh as his hand moved to the belt of his trousers.

Kelly felt shy at her first sight of his arousal, almost dazed and daunted by her ability to do that to him, but her shyness evaporated as he slid her tiny bikini pants down over her thighs, then, naked, pulled her down on to the bed with him and began to kiss her over and over again.

It felt so good. It felt so right. She was drowning in delight, each touch and each kiss making the pleasure escalate until she could hardly bear it any more, almost going out of her mind when his hand moved over the flatness of her belly, to teasingly stroke tiny provocative circles there. She began to move restlessly, and he gave another low laugh as his hand slid down between her thighs to tantalise her even further so that she made an instinctive little pleading sound at the back of her throat.

'Do you want me?' he whispered huskily.

'Oh, yes,' she shuddered ecstatically as he stroked her skilfully.

'Really want me?'

'Yes!' Oh, God, yes—more than she had ever wanted anything in her entire life.

He moved to lie on top of her. She was ready for him, gloriously and deliciously ready for him; ripe and hot and moist. She pressed her lips to his shoulders, eager for him to fill her, thrilling as he gently parted her legs, when a stark and elemental fear pierced through the mists of her desire with frightening clarity, as the dreaded phrase of her childhood came back to mock at her.

'That girl's in trouble.'

In trouble. . .

Kelly remembered Jo Grant at school, only fifteen, but now prematurely aged as she pushed the pram up the hill every morning.

'Randall,' she whispered urgently.

He lifted his head from her breast, his voice thick with passion. 'What?'

'You won't—'

'Oh, I most certainly will, my darling,' he murmured.

'—make me pregnant, will you?'

The silence which filled the room was brittle, electric. She felt him tense, heard him stifle some profanity, before he rolled off her, and, with his back to her, the broad set of his shoulders forbidding and stiff with some kind of unbearable tension, began to pull his clothes on.

Kelly was filled with hurt and confusion. She had meant. . .had meant. . .that they should. . .

'Randall?' she whispered tentatively, and when he turned, in the act of wincing as he struggled to zip up his trousers, she almost recoiled from the look of frustration on his face, which quickly gave way to one of bored disdain.

'You certainly pick your moments,' he drawled cuttingly. 'Couldn't you have said something earlier?'

'Well, what about you?' Outraged and indignant, she sat up, her hair tumbling to conceal her breasts, and she saw a nerve begin to work in his cheek. 'You didn't seem inclined to discuss it either. Don't you think that you have some responsibility too?' she demanded.

'That's just the trouble, Kelly,' he said, in a bitter, flat and angry voice. 'I wasn't doing any thinking at all.'

And without another word he slammed his way out of the room, leaving Kelly to spend the most miserable night of her life.

The next morning she had risen early, hoping to get away before anyone else was up, and yet trying to suppress the foolish and humiliating little hope that he would still want to see her. She quickly packed her few belongings into the suitcase and went silently down the stairs.

Mary was placing a pile of newspapers on a tray, and looked up, her eyes hardening with disapproval when she saw Kelly.

'Will you be wanting breakfast, miss?' she asked grudgingly.

Kelly shook her head. 'No, thank you. I—I'd like to get away just as soon as possible. Will you please——' she swallowed. She must be courteous; she still had her pride '—thank Randall for his hospitality?'

'Yes, miss. Though I don't know when I shall be seeing him next.'

'I'm sorry? But he'll be down for breakfast before he goes back, surely?'

'Oh, *no*, miss.'

Kelly's heart started thundering with the implication behind the cook's triumphant statement.

'Just that Lord Rousay's already gone back to London. Left here at dawn, he did. Driving that car of his as though the devil himself was chasing him.'

'Oh, I see,' said Kelly, in a small, empty little voice, as the fairy-tale disintegrated.

And she had never set eyes on him again.

CHAPTER THREE

UNTIL NOW.

Kelly stared at Randall, her features schooled into the coolly indifferent look she had perfected over the years because that passionate and impetuous creature who had offered herself so willingly to Randall Seton had gone forever.

'You've gone very pale—you look as though you could use a drink,' he observed. 'Let me buy you one.'

Kelly almost exploded with rage. Did he imagine— did he have the termerity to imagine—that he could simply walk into her life nine years on and calmly ask her for a drink, and that she, panting eagerly, would accept? 'No, thank you,' she answered, her voice iced with pure frost.

He was blocking her path. 'Kelly—this is crazy. We need to talk.'

She frowned, looking perplexed. 'Do we? I can't think why.'

'Because we go back a long way. Don't we?' He smiled, so sure of its effect, so sure that the grin which creased his handsome features would have her eating out of his hand.

'Hardly,' she murmured. 'We were little more than acquaintances a long time ago. Let me see—it must be eight years, surely—or was it seven? I can hardly remember.'

'Nine,' he gritted, and then a wry and reluctant look

of amusement spread over his features. 'OK, Kelly—
you've made your point with stunning effect, but I still
want to talk to you, and I don't particularly want to do
it in this draughty corridor. Not when I can think of so
many more attractive venues.'

'I'm *sure* you can,' she bit out crisply. 'But the fact
remains that I really can't be bothered talking to you.
I've had a busy day and I'm very tired. What I want is
a bath and an early night. Now have you got that,
Randall—or would you like me to spell it out in words
of one syllable for you?'

He carried his assurance like a badge, and Kelly
realised with a gleeful feeling that he was finding it
very difficult to cope with her refusal. She would lay a
bet that he had never had to cope with rejection in his
charmed life. A look of frustration crossed over his
face, to be quickly replaced by one of narrow-eyed
perception, and Kelly wondered whether she had gone
just a bit overboard on her hostility towards him.

Because he wasn't stupid. Far from it. He could
probably put two and two together and come up with
another theory of relativity. If she carried on sniping
quite so vehemently, might he not guess that he had
broken her heart, hurt her so much that she had vowed
never to let a man get so close to her again?

She sighed. Indifference was a far better shield to
hide behind than anger. Anger symbolised emotion,
and she had buried emotion a long time ago. She
glanced down at the slim gold watch on her wrist.

'Sorry.' She stifled a yawn, and gave him a polite
little smile. 'I'm just very tired, that's all.'

'Then you need a drink,' he said firmly. 'Where

would you like to go? There's a bar in the mess, isn't there?'

Kelly bit her lip. That was the last thing she wanted, to be seen with him in the doctors' mess. Hospitals were a hot-bed of gossip, and word would be bound to get back to Warren if she was seen out with the hospital's newest and most eligible bachelor.

'Yes, there is,' she answered grudgingly. But since the alternative would be to offer him a drink in her room, and she certainly was not going to do that, there seemed to be nothing to do except give in gracefully. 'OK,' she shrugged. 'But just a quick drink.'

He knew the way to the mess. They walked in silence along the echoing floors, and Kelly was reminded of just how tall he was, and how striking, since every nurse they passed looked him up and down with blatant appreciation.

The doctors' mess was a largish room, built on the lines of a pub, though the prices were subsidised. It was only half filled, with small groups of doctors, and the occasional table of nurses. Kelly's heart sank as she spotted Staff Nurse Higgs chewing at a cherry on a stick, the movement frozen when she spotted Randall, her blue eyes widening, and then a frown knitting her arched brows together as her gaze alighted on Kelly by his side. I might as well have taken a full-page advertisement out, thought Kelly on a sigh, as she followed Randall over to an unoccupied table.

'What would you like?' he asked.

'Any kind of juice, thanks.'

He raised his eyebrows. 'You don't drink?'

'Of course I do, but only in the right company,' she

replied sweetly, and his mouth twisted in anger as he turned away from her and made his way to the bar.

He returned, carrying two tall tumblers of pineapple juice and a saucer of black olives.

He sat down opposite her and his grey eyes regarded her steadily.

Under that cool appraisal, Kelly was hard put to find something neutral to say. 'You're not drinking either?' she queried.

He shook his head, took an olive and bit into it. 'I'm on call tonight. A young lady I operated on this afternoon may need to go back to Theatre, and I've a very sick patient in Intensive Care. It's a busy rota.'

'So I believe.' Under the cover of picking up her glass and sipping at the juice, Kelly was able to observe him surreptitiously from beneath her long lashes. She had thought that he hadn't changed but, close to, of course he had changed. She saw tiny lines which fanned at the side of his amazing grey eyes and they had not been there nine years ago. His face was leaner too—it had lost that youthful fullness. He had been twenty-four when she had first met him, and he had to be—good grief, she thought—he would be almost thirty-three now. Her eyes strayed to his hands.

'No, I'm not married.' A mocking voice disturbed her thoughts.

Kelly froze. She gave him a steady stare. 'I *beg* your pardon?'

He looked completely unrepentant. 'That's what you wanted to know, wasn't it?' The grey eyes swept over her own bare hands. 'And neither are you, I see. Married, that is.'

Kelly looked at him with dislike. 'How you do jump

to assumptions, Randall,' she said, in her most chilly voice. 'Lots of women copy men and don't bother to wear wedding-rings these days.'

'And are you one of those women?' he asked softly.

There was a pause. 'As a matter of fact, I'm not married. Although I fail to see what business it is of yours?'

'Do you?' he mocked, imitating the stilted tone of her voice, then leaned back in his chair to study her. 'You've changed,' he said suddenly.

If he started reminiscing—if somehow he had the ability to remind her of the glorious week they had shared, the memory of which even its inglorious ending could not destroy—then she would be lost. And vulnerable. And she had vowed never to be that vulnerable again.

She gave a brittle little laugh. 'Well, of course I've changed, Randall,' she said, rather in the manner in which a schoolmistress might scold a child. 'What did you expect, that I would stay exactly the same person?'

'I rather wish you had,' he said quietly. 'There's a restraint about you now, a brittleness which is totally at odds with the girl I once knew.'

Kelly put her glass down on the table with such force that a group of doctors and nurses on the other side of the mess turned to look at her curiously, but she didn't care—she was past caring. 'How dare you invite me for a drink and start insulting me? And how dare you speak with such authority about my character, when you don't even know me—and *you never did*?'

'Didn't I?' he mocked. 'I'd say I knew you pretty——'

She interrupted him before he could utter a word as

damning as 'intimately' and have her face burning shamefully with the memory. 'Well, you're wrong!' she bit back vehemently. 'I was just a little carried away that week—it obviously went to my head,' and she slipped into a brilliant parody of a cockney accent, 'to have his lordship take notice of a humble little schoolgirl. . .'

She didn't know whether it was the dart about her youth or about his title which caused that tight look of rage to twist his mouth into an ugly line, but she was glad, yes, *glad*. If she could cause Randall Seton even a moment's discomfort, then so be it—for it wouldn't cause him an iota of the pain he had caused her. She got to her feet and stared down at him. 'I knew that this drink would be a bad idea. You should have listened to me. Goodbye, Randall.' And she walked swiftly from the mess, aware of curious eyes on her, realising that their voices must have been raised and knowing that news of their little contretemps would be all round the hospital by lunchtime tomorrow.

It was when she was unlocking the door to her room that she realised he had followed her, and she turned to find him behind her, hearing the quickened sound of his breathing and seeing the look of anger which distorted the exquisite features. And still she did not have the sense to leave well alone.

'Still here?' she queried insultingly. She raised her eyebrows. 'Tell me, Randall, did you enjoy it so much—*slumming* it with me? Is that why you won't go away and leave me alone?'

And then she knew she had gone that little bit too far, as she saw the broad set of his body tense up as though for fight. The anger had all but disappeared, leaving a cold and cruel mask in its place, and Kelly knew a little shudder of apprehension. 'You little bitch,' he said softly, and his mouth swooped down to claim hers in a harsh and heavenly kiss which was just stamped with sexual domination.

As his mouth began a hot and erotic penetration, Kelly almost swooned against the open door, and she might have fallen had his arm not gone out to encircle her slender waist in a steely grip. He pushed her inside the room, his mouth plundering hers with a sweetly rapacious invasion all the time, and Kelly felt her breasts tingle into life, uncaring that he had pushed her against the wall, and that his hips were moulded into hers, demonstrating with sweet and daunting clarity the measure of his arousal. She felt his hand push her white coat away from her breasts, before he lightly brushed the palm of his hand over each aching and tumescent peak, and Kelly held on to him tightly, her eyes closed helplessly, a small cry of frustration and pleasure torn from her lips. And sorrow, too—that only Randall could do this to her. She fought to catch her breath, fought for control, and he released her mouth then, leaving her bereft and longing for the taste of him again.

'Such a pity to have to tie all that glorious hair back,' he observed, as his grey eyes lazily surveyed the stark hairstyle she had adopted for work. And she heard the amusement in his voice. A hateful, mocking amusement.

His hand moved before she could stop it, and he had deftly removed all the pins at the nape of her neck, so that the rich, dark red waves tumbled down around her face. Over her shoulder she caught a glimpse of herself—the green of her eyes almost completely obscured by the black, glittering pupils, her mouth all red and pouting and swollen from the pressure of that kiss which had seemed to go on and on, and yet be over far too quickly. But it was the hair which really seemed to symbolise her surrender. Cascading unusually all over her snowy white coat, she looked nothing more nor less than a wanton. A wild and sensual creature.

Lips trembling, she turned to him. 'Get out of here,' she said on a whisper.

'Quite sure?' he mocked her. 'I can stay if you want me to. The pleasure would be—my oh, so responsive Kelly—all mine.'

'Either you get out now or I slap your arrogant face.'

He grinned devilishly. 'Kelly, *darling*,' he drawled arrogantly, 'you've become so *aggressive*.'

Summoning a deep, deep breath, Kelly marched over to the other side of the room, where the old-fashioned black telephone sat. 'Or,' she said calmly, 'I can ring the authorities and tell them——'

'Tell them what?' he interrupted. 'Tell them that I kissed you, and you kissed me back? That if I hadn't stopped we'd be lying in that bed now, doing what we should have done all those years ago?'

Kelly lifted the receiver. 'Get out,' she said shakily, but as he complied, and the door closed on his tall, white-coated figure, it brought her nothing but a disturbing feeling of emptiness.

Randall resisted the urge to slam the door hard enough to shatter it to pieces and walked briskly away from her room, towards one of his six surgical wards.

God, how he wanted her! *Still* she possessed that ability to send all reason flying from his mind, to be replaced by an all-encompassing urge to make love to her.

It took an effort to smile at the nurse who greeted him so enthusiastically when he arrived on Cedar ward.

'Hello!' she said, unable to conceal her pleasure. '*You're* early tonight—you usually do your late-night round when I've gone to first break!'

Briefly, Randall tried and failed to imagine Kelly responding to him with such delight. 'I just wanted to see how the patient I operated on earlier is doing.'

'The emergency perforated duodenal ulcer?' queried the nurse.

'The very same.'

The nurse looked down at her Kardex. 'Mr Mulligan. He's making a good, uneventful recovery. He's fully conscious and his observations are stable. Would you like to see him?'

'Please.'

Mr Mulligan looked pale, but cheerful. 'Evening, Doctor,' he said hoarsely, as the nurse drew the curtains around the bed.

Randall smiled. 'Hello. How are you feeling?'

'My throat's a bit sore.'

'Nothing else?'

Mr Mulligan pointed to his abdomen. 'And here—just a bit.'

The nurse pulled back the sheet and Randall bent over to examine the wound. 'That looks fine,' he said, straightening up. 'Your sore throat is probably due to the anaesthetic—it's only temporary. And I'll be back tomorrow to deliver my usual stern lecture about the adverse effects of smoking, drinking and a poor diet!'

Mr Mulligan shrugged philosophically. 'Anything you say, Doc—just so long as I don't have to go through all this again!'

'Now that's gratitude for you!' joked Randall as he stood aside to let the nurse pass, wondering why it should irritate him when she laughed far more loudly than his feeble joke merited.

He meticulously went to see every patient on his firm, then visited the intensive care unit to assess the man with the aortic aneurysm he'd operated on earlier that day. He had sewn a patch graft in place, but the man was by no means out of the wood yet.

Randall looked down at the white figure hooked up to the confusion of lines and tubes, than glanced at the nurse. 'How is he doing?'

Her face gave nothing away. 'He's stable. Just.'

But she spoke too soon. The aneurysm ruptured while they stood there, and although a highly qualified team of them battled to save the patient, it was to no avail.

It was very, very late when Randall went back to his room in the mess.

And in the quiet and stillness of the night, he could not get Kelly out of his mind, or the ache for her out of his body, and the long, cool shower he took before eventually turning in did little to dampen down the heat in his blood.

CHAPTER FOUR

AFTER a night spent chiefly drinking cups of coffee and staring sightlessly down at a textbook, Kelly crawled in to work the following morning feeling like something the cat had dragged in. She rarely made her face up for work; this morning it had been an absolute necessity to try to cover up the almost translucent pallor of her cheeks, and to attempt to conceal the dark shadows which were smudged beneath her eyes.

She thought she might have overdone it a bit when she saw Piers Redding, the casualty officer she was taking over from, give a double-take and make an appreciative little whistle beneath his breath.

'Wow!' he exclaimed. 'You look amazing!'

At least fifty of St Christopher's nurses would have adored such a compliment from Piers Redding—not so Kelly. 'Well, I feel like death,' she answered wryly. 'I didn't sleep a wink last night.'

Piers grinned. 'Which begs the usual question, but, being the gentleman I am, I'll refrain from asking it!'

Kelly's cheeks coloured. The cause of her sleepless night could so easily have been what Piers was teasing her about. Oh, lord. How she wished Randall Seton a hundred miles away from her! She picked up the two casualty cards which were lying on the doctor's desk. 'Who have we got?' she asked.

They bent over the desk together, their heads very close—she could even smell Piers' aftershave.

'Cubicle one's a fractured tib and fib waiting to go up to the orthopaedic ward. Cubicle two is a woman with query obstruction. I've bleeped the surgical registrar, and he's on his way down. Oh-oh, speak of the devil!' He looked up. 'Hi, Randall—there you are!'

Kelly stared at him.

He was wearing his theatre greens beneath his white coat, there was the dark shadow which covered that fabulously strong chin to show that he had not had time to shave, and he too didn't look as though he had got very much sleep the night before. 'Thanks,' he said briefly, and held his hand out towards Kelly, his eyes cold, his mouth hard.

She blinked at him, shocked by his weary appearance, even more shocked by the blatant hostility which was emanating from that lean, muscular frame. They had parted on bad terms last night, yes, but she had somehow expected that, during work hours at least, Randall of all people would have behaved in a civilised manner towards her. It seemed not.

'The casualty card, please, Doctor!' Randall bit out tersely, finding the way that she stood so close to the other casualty office almost unbearable.

Kelly handed him the card.

'And can I have a nurse to chaperon me?' he asked.

Kelly was finding it very difficult to think what she was supposed to be doing. 'I've—only just come on duty,' she told him, finding herself caught up in the cold gleam from the grey eyes.

'How absolutely *scintillating*,' he answered sarcastically. 'And now perhaps you'd see about finding me a nurse?'

Kelly glared at him.

'Don't worry, Mr Seton,' cooed a voice of treacle from behind him, and Staff Nurse Higgs, her blonde cap of hair gleaming like a halo, smiled up at him. 'Here I am!'

'Thanks, Nurse——' he glanced at her name-badge '—Higgs.'

'Call me Marianne,' answered the statuesque blonde immediately.

He smiled, and Kelly felt a murderous rage envelop her.

'Marianne,' he agreed easily. 'Come on then.'

Kelly watched them go, hating the way that Nurse Higgs was simpering up at him, and hating herself even more for feeling that way. She sighed as she picked up the phone and dealt with one of the local GPs who wanted to send a child with a query appendicitis into Casualty. Kelly wrote down the details and replaced the receiver.

Avoiding Randall wasn't just going to be difficult, she recognised, it was going to prove downright *impossible*. As the surgical registrar, he would need to be called down to Casualty every time a surgical emergency came through those doors, and every time that *she* was on duty as casualty officer, she was going to have to be the one to call him.

Hell!

What a nasty little trick fate had played in bringing Randall Seton back into her life, she thought, as the emergency telephone began to ring and she grabbed at the receiver.

The morning was so hectic that she didn't get a chance to think about anything, other than how to try to save the life of a twenty-eight-year-old man who had shot some very impure heroin into his body.

They battled for almost an hour, and when Kelly transferred him up to Intensive Care he was hanging on to life by a thread, his kidneys badly damaged.

There followed a stream of admissions, some to medical and some to surgical wards, and a small queue of surgical admissions built up since Randall was busy in Theatre, operating. Consequently, every time that Kelly walked near to the waiting area she was accosted by irate people, wanting to know why their relatives had not been seen.

'I'm very sorry,' said Kelly patiently, thinking that if she could have a penny for each time she had had to repeat this phrase she would be as rich as Croesus! 'But the surgeon who needs to see them before thay can be admitted is operating at the moment.'

'Then why can't we see another doctor?' demanded one woman, rather forcefully.

Kelly sighed. Now was not the time to start a discussion on hospital economics or government policy; patients, in her experience, did not like to be told that there simply were not enough doctors. 'Because I'm afraid that there isn't anyone else available,' she told them, with a bright smile which was supposed to allay their fears. She could see the receptionist waving a fistful of cards at her. 'Now, if you'll please excuse me, I must get on.'

On very little sleep, Kelly was thoroughly exhausted by the end of her shift, and there was barely time to do more that eat half of the salad sandwich for lunch which one of the student nurses had fetched for her. No wonder she'd lost weight since starting this job.

The consultant in charge of Casualty had devised a series of twelve-hour shifts for each of the three casualty officers, with an overlap on Friday and Saturday nights when the department was usually full to bursting.

At ten to six everything was quiet, and Kelly glanced at her watch. Ten minutes to go before Harry Wells was due to relieve her, and, knowing Harry, he was more likely to be ten minutes late than ten minutes early!

She stifled a yawn. Maybe she would be able to grab an hour's sleep before getting ready to go out. Warren wasn't collecting her until eight o'clock.

She had been dating the hospital administrator of St Christopher's for almost two months, though they rarely saw each other more than once or twice a week. He was intelligent, good-looking, and good company in a lot of ways. A bluntly spoken northerner, he seemed to approve of the fact that so far she had refused to let him do more than give her a brief goodnight kiss, saying, smilingly, that the best things in life were worth waiting for, and that he would 'give her time'. Secretly, she wondered if that time would ever come. Warren's kisses were pleasant, yes, she enjoyed them very much—but there was no way that they turned her into the wild wanton that Randall's kisses did. Perhaps that was a good thing, really. She wasn't sure that she liked the person she became in Randall's arms.

She certainly didn't respect her.

At precisely two minutes to six, and with no sign of her relief arriving, the red telephone began its shrilly insistent pealing, and with a resigned grimace Kelly lifted up the receiver, her face growing pale with shock when she heard the ambulance driver's terse statement.

'Gunshot wound to abdomen. Youth of seventeen. Condition critical. ETA three minutes.'

She got one of the nurses to put out an emergency bleep for Randall and for the crash team, then, running into the resuscitation-room, she pressed the emergency buzzer. Three nurses came running.

'Can you set up the resuscitation-room?' asked Kelly breathlessly. 'And get on to the blood bank—we've a gunshot wound on its way. I'm going out to the double doors to wait.'

She didn't have to wait long. The white-faced boy lying critically injured on the trolley looked so young. So very young. Kelly shuddered as she pulled the sheet back to see a gaping hole in his lower abdomen which had left some of his internal organs showing. They pushed the trolley straight into the emergency room, and to her relief she saw Randall waiting. But no crash team.

They lifted the boy over to to the trolley. 'I've bleeped the crash team,' said Kelly.

'They're answering another call,' said Randall frowning, his long fingers expertly assessing the extent of the injuries. 'Let's get some saline up.'

'What are his observations doing?' asked Kelly.

'BP eighty over thirty and falling,' answered the nurse, obviously frightened. 'Pulse a hundred and forty. And rising.'

He was in deep, deep shock. Kelly glued the pads of the heart monitor to the boy's chest, her heart sinking as she looked up at the screen to see the bright green but erratic tracing.

'He's going,' said Randall, and at the same time as he said it the monitor gave its high, monotonous shrilling which meant that the heart had stopped beating. Randall swiftly and sharply brought down the flat of his hand on to the boy's chest, while Kelly began to breathe into the mouthpiece, but they conducted the task knowing that it was doomed to failure; the boy was losing far more blood that they could possibly pump back in, and Kelly could see that the extent of his injuries was far worse that she had first thought.

'Let's get some more fluid in!' ordered Randall urgently.

But when the straight line, with its depressing long bleep, had been showing for five minutes, Randall straightened up and shook his head. 'That's it. I'm afraid we've lost him,' he said, his deep voice sombre, obviously as deeply affected as they all were. 'I'm very sorry, everyone.' And he peeled off his gloves and dropped them into the bin.

'Relatives?' Kelly asked the nurse shakily, when her boss, Mr Chalmers, the casualty consultant, came in, closely followed by the crash team, who took one look at all the debris of half opened packages which surrounded the dead body on the trolley, then turned and silently filed out again.

'I'll see the relatives, Kelly,' he told her. 'The police will want to speak to you and Randall. Are you OK?'

She nodded, glad that she had a boss sensitive enough to know how much death could still hurt, no matter how many times you saw it. She found Randall staring at her, the grey eyes soft with comprehension, and she swallowed the lump which rose in her throat.

'Where the hell *is* Harry Wells?' demanded Mr Chalmers.

'He *has* just had a new baby, sir,' said Kelly quickly.

'You mean his wife has just had a baby,' corrected Mr Chalmers drily. 'Harry's a damned sight too fond of the squash court. Oh, there you are, Wells.' He gave the gangling casualty office a disapproving stare. 'There's an RTA coming in in ten minutes—and make sure you're on time tomorrow night. Dr Hartley's had a rough enough day without you adding to her stress levels.' He turned to Kelly and Randall. 'The police are waiting for you in my office.'

Kelly nodded and walked over the sink to wash her hands, Randall joining her. How intimate it seemed to be sharing the same washbasin, thought Kelly suddenly, as he dolloped some antiseptic solution on to the palm of her hand without being asked.

He was frowning as he looked down at her. 'Are you sure you're OK?'

She nodded. 'It was pretty awful, wasn't it?'

'Yeah.' There was a pause. 'You never really get over the shock of seeing something like that.'

'Not even you?' she asked quietly.

He shook his head, a wry expression on his face. 'No, not even me. It's no different for men, Kelly. We hurt just the same, and nothing can make you immune to it, nothing. You don't suddenly find that you wake up one day and it doesn't affect you any more. And if you do, then you're in the wrong job.'

'And there was nothing we could have done?' She knew that, he knew that—but always there was the need for reinforcement, the need to dispel the quite unnecessary guilt you always felt when a life, and particularly a young life, just slipped away.

He shook his head. 'Nothing.' His grey gaze flickered over her. 'Do you get a lot of gunshot wounds around here?'

'That's the first I've ever seen. There are plenty of stabbings, though, and a fair bit of mugging. It's one of the reasons why I chose to live in the mess. I didn't really fancy walking home at all hours.'

'No,' he said thoughtfully. 'I don't blame you. Come on, we'd better go and give our statements.'

The statement-giving was mercifully brief, and they both emerged from the office wearily. 'I'll walk your way,' said Randall. 'Unless you've any objections to that, of course,' he added sardonically.

Disappointedly, she simply shook her head. When he had been interacting with her as a fellow professional, everything had been fine. Now, it seemed, he was back to responding to her as a woman. She was too tired to retaliate, but curious anyway.

'I don't want to take you out of your way.'

'You won't be,' he said abruptly.

Kelly's eyebrows rose. 'But surely you're not living in the mess as well?'

'Why not?' His mouth was twisted into a cynical half-smile. 'You do.'

'But you're. . .' She hesitated, as their steps fell in line.

'I'm what, Kelly?' he enquired softly. 'Where did you imagine I'd be living? In some bloody great mansion up in Knightsbridge? It's all that excess baggage again, remember?'

The excess baggage which went with his title. Yes,

she remembered. She gave him a rueful look as they reached her door. 'Sorry.'

'Mmm,' he said absently, but he was staring down into her face as though he had not heard her.

The grey glitter of his eyes drew her gaze inexorably towards his, as lost as some poor sailor lured by a siren on to the rocks. She did not know for how long they stood there, but somewhere she heard a clock strike the half-hour. Bang goes my sleep, thought Kelly dazedly, as she realised that she was staring up into Randall's face, and that there was a curious half-smile on his mouth, a strange gleam in his eyes.

'You look absolutely exhausted,' he observed.

'So do you,' she said, aware that a strand of hair had fallen out of the tight chignon. She brushed it behind her ear.

'And tense,' he added. 'Am I the cause of that tension, Kelly?'

Kelly shook her head. 'Not at the moment. It's been an exceptionally busy day, and I found all that, just now, in there——' she jerked her head in the direction from which they had just walked '—it was. . .horrible,' she finished starkly.

He raked a hand through his thick, dark hair. 'I know. And part of the trouble with this infernal job is that we take so much on board, and we never let it out, and somehow we're expected to cope with it.'

Her wide mouth quirked into a smile. 'You think that there should be counselling for doctors dealing with trauma?'

'Don't you?' he countered.

'Resources, resources, Doctor!' she chided, and realised that she was grinning, and that he was grinning

too, and that his eyes had darkened, and—oh, lord—
how could a smile set your senses singing, start a weary
body zinging? And Randall had gone very still, very
tense. Had her body somehow communicated its fascination for him?

'God, I want to make love to you,' he said suddenly.

Kelly's lids dropped down to shield the disappointment in her eyes. Of course he did. She opened her
eyes and gave him a chilly smile. 'Should I be flattered
by such a remarkably direct statement, Randall?
Because I'm not. And I really don't think that my
boyfriend would like to hear you saying things like
that.'

He stiffened and his eyes narrowed. 'Your
boyfriend?'

She felt an intense kind of rage at his incredulous
tone. Just what did he imagine? That she was incapable
of sustaining an adult relationship? Or that she had
been pining away for *him* for all these years? She gave
a brittle little laugh. 'I'm sorry you seem to find that
peculiar——'

'Who is he?' he demanded, and his voice sounded so
odd and so savage that Kelly involuntarily took a step
back.

'Who *is* he?' he repeated.

She saw no reason not to tell him. If he realised that
Warren worked in the same hospital, then it might
make him leave her alone. 'Warren Booth,' she told
him. 'The——'

'Hospital administrator,' he finished grimly.

'You know him?'

'I've met him,' he said, still in that same grim tone.
'You surprise me, Kelly.'

'Oh? And why's that?' she queried coolly.

The grey eyes became shuttered. 'I value my career far too much to give you an honest answer to that particular question. Let's just say that he isn't my kind of person,' he answered tersely.

'I can imagine,' said Kelly, with an acid smile.

He glowered at her. 'But I find it rather difficult to trust anyone who happens to be in management.'

'And it's that kind of attitude,' she bit out, realising as she said it that she was doing nothing more than echoing Warren's very own words to her, 'which creates divisions between management and staff!'

'The divisions exist,' he told her quietly, 'because they have conflicting interests. All the management are interested in is saving money by cutting staff.'

'How simplistic!' she mocked. 'While all doctors are interested in is saving lives, I suppose?'

'Actually, yes,' he answered, very quietly, and his grey eyes glittered. 'At least, I am. Aren't you?'

With that clever sharp tongue, he had made it sound as though she was saying something very different from her intended defence of Warren. And why was she bothering to defend Warren to Randall anyway?

'Oh, that isn't what I meant at all and you know it, *damn* you, Randall Seton!' she snapped. 'I hate you!' she finished, and made as if to move away from him. But though her words sounded authentic, her heart knew the truth as she stared into that heart-stoppingly handsome face.

His mouth twisted in the parody of a smile as he caught her by the waist, imprisoning her there, though less by the force of his hands than by the enchanting silver dazzle of his eyes. He stared down at her for a long moment before he dropped on to her soft mouth a cold, cynical kiss which, though brief, none the less left her trembling helplessly in his arms before he let her go, his hands falling to his sides, his fists clenched white, as though he were going to punch somebody.

'You may hate me,' he ground out, 'but you still want me, don't you, just as much as I still want you? And I'm giving you fair warning that I intend to have you, Kelly.'

And he turned and walked off, leaving Kelly staring blankly after him, shaking with some unnamed emotion, her fingertips touching her mouth, as if by doing that she could preserve the brief memory of his lips on hers forever.

CHAPTER FIVE

WITH her heart hammering like crazy, Kelly closed the door behind Randall, trying to rid herself of the yearning which his kiss had produced.

She began to undress, her hands still shaking as she wrapped herself in a towelling bathrobe and went down the chilly corridor to shower. She was back in her room drying her hair when the telephone rang.

It was Warren, saying that he was running half an hour late. 'Pressure of work,' he complained.

'It doesn't matter,' said Kelly, wishing that she felt a bit more enthusiastic about going out.

'Can you dress up a bit, darling?' he asked her.

Kelly's heart sank. That didn't sound very much like the quiet dinner for two she had been hoping he would suggest. 'Why? Are we going somewhere special?'

'Fairly. One of the consultants is having a drinks party. He's invited me—and a guest, of course.'

'Which consultant?'

'Dr Berry—the physician.'

'Tonight?'

'Yes.'

'That's a little short notice, surely?' asked Kelly rather crossly, knowing that Warren would have walked to the end of the planet for something like a consultant's party. 'Were they short on numbers or something?'

'It's an honour to be asked,' said Warren firmly, an

unmistakable note of disapproval in his voice. 'It's usually only the clinical staff who get invited to these affairs. So run along, darling, and I'll see you in half an hour.'

Kelly found herself irritated with his remark. For goodness' sake! She seemed to be irritated with everything today, and she knew who had instigated her niggly mood.

Half an hour later she opened the door to Warren's ring on the bell, to see him blink at her slightly disconcertedly. He was dressed, as usual, in a conservative grey suit with a white shirt, and a dark blue tie bearing the hospital crest. Kelly hated that tie; she had bought him a wildly coloured silk one for his birthday, but so far he hadn't worn it.

'Good heavens!' he exclaimed, as his eyes skimmed quickly over her slender form.

She gave a twirl. 'Don't you like it?' He had never seen the outfit before. She was dressed in an exquisitely cut dress of tawny silk which brought out the auburn lights of her hair, which she had left loose to ripple all the way down her back. Her high-heeled black shoes made her slim legs seem endless, and she had deliberately worn seamed silk stockings instead of her usual tights, wanting the feel of some soft, sensual material on her thighs for a change. She had not stopped to ask herself why.

Warren gulped. 'It's—er—er. . .' He cleared his throat. 'Do you think it's really *suitable*, Kelly?'

Kelly knew that she was not in a good mood, and the sight of Warren tugging anxiously on his earlobe was not doing anything to improve it. 'What's wrong with it?' she demanded, and he raised his fair eyebrows when he heard her mulish tone. 'Don't you like the dress?'

'It isn't the *dress*. It's. . .'

'What then?'

'Your hair.'

'My *hair*?' she asked in disbelief. She had just washed it and spent an age drying it. 'What's the matter with my hair?'

'You usually wear it up.'

A forbidden, tantalising memory of Randall loosening the pins to set it free invaded her mind with persistent and exacting detail, and she tried desperately to brush it aside.

She stared at Warren—so tall, so fair, so smart and reliable in his grey suit—and willed the feeling of rebellion to go away.

It didn't.

Kelly sighed. 'I know I usually wear it up,' she said. 'And I fancy wearing it down for a change. OK?'

She smiled, and at the sight of her smile he relaxed. Kelly saw the little glint in his pale blue eyes.

'Actually,' he said, and his voice held a new, possessive note, 'I prefer it up. Am I allowed to have a preference?'

This was getting out of hand, Kelly decided. 'Of course you are,' she said crisply. 'But tonight it's staying like this.'

'I see.' Warren hesitated. 'It just doesn't look so. . .'

Kelly waited. 'So what?'

'Neat.'

The vision suddenly horrified her. Was that what she had become? A neat, tidy person, with her neat, tidy boyfriend? She put her chin firmly in the air, and the

thick, chestnut waves rippled in Pre-Raphaelite disar-
ray. 'I'll tell you what, Warren,' she said, her green
eyes sparking with unaccustomed fire, 'I'm really not
in the mood to be told how I can or how I can't wear
my hair, and I've had a bitch of a day, to be perfectly
frank. So why don't you go to the party on your own?
OK?'

A frown appeared, just visible beneath Warren's
blond fringe. 'What's got into you all of a sudden?'

Randall has, thought Kelly. And shuddered.
'Nothing. I'm sorry. I'm tired. You go.'

He shook his head with that calm yet emphatic air
he had perfected, the one she used to find comforting,
safe, reassuring, but tonight she found irritating. 'And
miss being seen with the best-looking woman in the
hospital on my arm? No way!'

Too tired to argue, and since she hadn't eaten a
thing and there was no food in the fridge, Kelly let him
lead her down to his brand-new family saloon.

She sat in the passenger seat, clasped her hands in
her lap and tried to smile, and Warren leaned over and
lingeringly kissed her passive lips.

'Maybe we should see about giving you my famous
cure for tiredness,' he whispered meaningfully. 'It's
never failed me yet.'

Kelly swallowed, realising that just the thought of it
left her completely cold. 'Warren, I——'

'We'll discuss it later,' he promised, in a husky
whisper.

Kelly stared sightlessly out of the window, feeling as
though all her chickens were coming home to roost.
Was Warren planning a big seduction tonight? And if
he was, then it couldn't be more ill-timed if he had

tried. She tried to relax as he put on some soft music while the car gathered speed, but it was difficult.

Dr Berry lived in a predictably large and comfortable house some distance from the hospital. In the driveway were other newish, and rather more opulent, cars. Inside, they were greeted by the eminent physician, and his well-preserved wife, who looked Kelly up and down with sharp eyes.

'Nice to see you both!' said Dr Berry. 'Come and get a drink! Warren—I've just the person I want you to meet.' He waved his hand in the direction of the chairman of the hospital trust, and Warren drew in a breath of excitement. 'Do you know Charles?'

Warren almost drooled at the sound of the physician using the chairman's Christian name. 'I've met him, of course, but——'

'Come and talk to him.' And Dr Berry led Warren away.

'There are drinks inside,' said Mrs Berry, but her eyes were elsewhere, distractedly scanning the room for more important fish to fry than a mere casualty officer.

'Thanks,' said Kelly, feeling somewhat redundant as she took a glass of white wine from one of the waitresses who were circulating the room with trays of drinks. She stood sipping it, until a haematologist she knew only very vaguely came over to chat to her. He was pleasant, if not the most exciting company in the world, and he obviously found Kelly very attractive. He started telling her about an article on platelets he'd just had accepted by the *British Medical Journal*, and Kelly found herself drifting off into a little world of her own.

'So would you like to?' he was saying.

Kelly blinked. 'Sorry?'

'Have dinner with me one night?'

But she scarcely heard him; the room swayed, tipped off balance as Randall walked in.

And though it was crowded, his grey eyes found her immediately, as if compelled to do so, and her heart began to beat painfully hard in her chest as his gaze deliberately swept over every inch of her.

It was a candid, sexual appraisal, and he took his time, his mouth softening into the sweetest caress of a smile as his eyes lingered on the swell of her breasts the longest. Unlike Warren, Randall obviously found the sight of her very pleasing indeed.

She had to get out of here.

'Please excuse me,' she managed to croak to the haematologist, and pushed her way through the small groups of people, away from Randall and that dangerous stare of his.

But she went with the resignation of someone walking the plank, knowing that it was inevitable he would follow her.

The plants in the garden were a mystery to her, but she pretended to look, even while every sense she possessed waited. Anticipated. She bristled as she heard the soft tread behind her, and she closed her eyes, afraid that he would read in them the glittering need to feast her gaze on him too.

'You can open your eyes now, Kelly,' came an amused, dry voice. 'And stop trembling like a Victorian heroine. I'm not planning to eat you.'

She kept her eyes shut. 'Go away.'

'Why?'

She opened them then. Why did he have to be so attractive? 'What is it with you?' she demanded. 'Why won't you leave me alone?'

He raised his eyebrows. 'Stop over-reacting. Let's go for a walk.'

'So you can try to seduce me?'

He smiled. 'If you like. But I was rather hoping we might talk. We used to talk a lot, you and I.'

'It's a pity we didn't stick to talking,' she said, on a bitter note.

'Come on. Let's look at all these plants.'

'I don't know anything about plants.'

'I know that,' he said patiently.

'How?'

'I remember you telling me, city-girl.' He saw her look of disbelief. 'Don't look so surprised. I remember everything about you, Kelly. Truly.'

She shook her head, trying not to warm to his charm. 'I'm here with someone.'

The curve of his smile became a derisive line. 'I know. With Warren, who is at present almost genuflecting in front of Sir Charles Ledbury.' He held a bottle of champagne aloft. 'Come on. Let's go and share this. We're both off duty.'

'How did you get hold of that?' she asked curiously.

'I batted my eyelashes at one of the waitresses,' he told her shamelessly. 'Look, there's a table down there, beneath the stars. Come and drink this champagne, and I give you my word that I will behave with the utmost decorum.' He gave a mock bow—superbly executed, thought Kelly reluctantly—and some glimmer of amusement which lurked deep in the grey eyes made her unable to repress a giggle in response.

He stared down at her for a long moment. 'Thank God,' he told her on a sigh. 'I actually thought that I'd lost my ability to make you laugh.'

Vexed and flattered by him, seduced by the potency of his charm, and the scent of the tobacco plants and the warm, seductive embrace of the sultry evening air, Kelly found herself following him down to the bottom of the garden, to where a white, wrought-iron table gleamed out at them from the dusk.

He pulled her chair back for her and she sat down, accepting the glass of champagne he handed to her.

'So, what are you doing here?' she asked coolly.

'The same thing as you, I should imagine. Perhaps not. You're here accompanying Warren, who sees the object of this party as some kind of PR exercise. Am I right?'

Damn him and his perspicacity! 'These affairs which involve work are never entirely social,' she countered. 'Don't tell me you're here with the sole intention of having a good time?'

'Not at all. I came here with the sole intention of finding you.'

Her hand threatened to tremble; she took another sip of the cold, fizzy wine, and it flooded her stomach with a welcome warmth. 'Oh? Should I be flattered?'

'I wouldn't have thought so,' he said wryly.

'What do you want to talk to me about?'

'Your career.'

Kelly was astounded. Admit it, she thought—she was expecting—hoping for?—yet another proposition. Work had been the last thing on her mind.

'Why my career?'

'I'm interested.'

'What exactly do you want to know?' she asked curiously.

He sipped his champagne, his grey eyes studying her over the rim of his glass. 'Fill me in. I assume you're doing the casualty job as part of your surgical experience?'

She had said the words so many times, to her tutors, her peers, her parents, yet still it hurt to have to say them again. She carefully schooled her face into the nonchalant expression she had chosen to accompany these particular words. 'No. I'm not going to be a surgeon.'

Randall was about to take another sip of his wine, but seemed to change his mind, and he put the crystal glass abruptly down on the table. '*What*?'

'I don't want. . .' But that was just too big a betrayal ever to pass her lips. 'I'm not going to be a surgeon,' she said firmly. 'I'm going to be a general practitioner instead.'

He frowned. 'I don't believe it.'

'It's true,' she said quietly.

'But that was your thing! That was your ambition. God, you were so passionate about it—you slayed me with your passion.'

She saw the look of disbelieving censure on his face, and now she felt like Judas. 'I was seventeen at the time, Randall,' she reminded him. 'A lot of people back-track on their youthful dreams.'

'Not you.' He stared at her thoughtfully. 'You won the St Christopher's gold medal in surgery; got a distinction in your finals too. Didn't you?'

Kelly's heart pounded. 'How on earth do you know that?'

'Oh, come on, Kelly, the results are published in some of the medical journals.'

'You looked my results up?'

'Sure.'

'Why?' It came out breathlessly.

'I was interested.'

Some eager little hope fizzled out, like a spent match. All those years, all those nine long years, he had known where she had been studying. And not once had he bothered to come and see her. She wanted to throw her glass of champagne in his face and run back inside, demand that Warren take her home. But she knew that her legs would not carry her, and that Warren would be merely peeved if she interrupted his talk with the precious Sir Charles. Instead, she managed an empty, almost bored smile. 'So now you know.'

He shook his head. 'No, I don't. Just tell me why, Kelly? Why did you welsh out on your ambition?'

Frustrated, bitter and angry, she turned on him, slamming her glass down to join his. 'OK, I'll tell you why. Because I'm a woman—it's as simple as that!'

His eyes narrowed. 'And what's that supposed to mean?'

She glowered. 'Don't be so obtuse! It means exactly what it says! Think about it. Surgery is a powerful speciality, and it's run by very powerful men. Because that's what it is, essentially—a men's club. Jobs for the boys. Women aren't welcome, in exactly the same way that lots of golf clubs have rooms which won't admit women. But in surgery it's much more insidious than that. There are laws which say that women mustn't be discriminated against——'

'And you're saying that you've been discriminated against?'

'It's more subtle than out-and-out discrimination. It's having to prove yourself, not twice as good as the next man, but ten times as good! And even then, it's still not good enough! After a while, that kind of attitude wears you down. And if you don't believe me, then look around. Look at the drop-out rate of women in surgery. And the further up the ladder, the harder it gets, especially if you've got family commitments. How many women consultants of surgery do *you* know, Randall, hmm?'

He said nothing for a moment, just continued to look at her with that dark, unreadable expression on his face, but Kelly felt confident that he, of all people, would understand. He had hurt her badly when she was young, yes, but professionally he had been her champion. Randall would understand.

His mouth curved disdainfully. 'You disappoint me, Kelly. I thought you had more guts than just to throw it in at the first hurdle.'

The disapproval which glittered from the angry grey eyes was almost unbearable. 'What do you know about it?' she demanded. 'You're a——'

But he cut across her ruthlessly. 'Don't bore me with all that "you're a man" stuff! We're not talking about me, are we? We're talking about *you*! Yes, you're a woman—an intelligent and gifted woman! A woman who defied all the odds to get to medical school in the first place! A woman who drew the recognition of the medical establishment to win half the prizes of her year!' He was on his feet now, had moved to stand in front of her, towering over her, his face dark with rage.

'A woman with no family commitments in her way, who could get right to the top of the bloody tree— *effortlessly*! And what does she do? She convinces herself that she's a victim, and she damn well gives it up!'

Kelly was on her own feet now, his words stinging her so bitterly because she recognised the truth in them. 'Have you quite finished?' she demanded, white-faced.

'No, I have not finished! I haven't even started!' And he hauled her into his arms to crush his mouth down on to hers.

She felt the anger flooding hotly from him to her; her own anger pulsed through her veins with its fiery heat, but within seconds there was no longer anger but a crazy, aching need to make love which had smouldered for nine long years and never gone away.

'Randall,' she whispered helplessly against his lips as he moved his hand to cup her breast with such fervour that the nipple peaked into immediate life against his palm through the thin silk of her dress. She felt her knees weaken, felt the hot, heavy rush of desire, as thick as honey, as intoxicating as strong liquor.

'Randall,' she whispered again, making no move to stop him as he pushed her behind the concealing wall of a rhododendron bush, covering her mouth all the time with that sweet, penetrating kiss. 'We shouldn't,' she managed, on a breathless note of wonder, coiling her long fingers into the thick black hair, her actions making mockery of her words.

'Oh, yes, we should,' he said huskily. 'Darling, we must, you know we must. . .'

He was pulling up the flimsy silk of her dress, sliding

his hand all the way up over her silk-clad leg, until he found the bare thigh which lay above the lacy rim of her stocking-top, and he made a murmured sound which was midway between a groan of pleasure, and a protest. 'Dear God!' he exclaimed. 'Why the hell did you wear stockings?'

Through the hazy whirlpool of desire, Kelly whispered foggily, 'Don't you like them?'

'Kelly, Kelly, Kelly. . .' His voice was frantic, urgent. 'Every fantasy I've concocted about you over the last nine years features you wearing stockings, me peeling them off. Dear God, I want to lay you down on the grass and make love to you right now, right here,' he said on a note of frustrated despair.

Kelly never knew what might have happened next had she not heard her name being called. She didn't ever dare to try to imagine, because the ignominy of being discovered making love in the grounds of Dr Berry's house was too much to contemplate.

'Kelly!'

With a stifled profanity, Randall immediately smoothed down her skirt, raked his hand through the thick, dark waves of his hair, moved away from her, picked up his glass of champagne, and downed it in one.

'Kelly!'

It was Warren. Her face burning with shame, Kelly quickly emerged from behind the bush to see Warren walking down the garden towards them, his head darting from side to side as he searched her out.

'Leave this to me,' said Randall curtly.

'*No!*' she turned on him angrily. 'You've done enough for one evening——'

'Have I?' he mocked, and her colour heightened further.

'I'll deal with it,' she said coldly. 'So go.'

But he didn't go. He just stood there quite calmly as Warren approached them.

'There you are, Kelly.' Warren's shoulders stiffened. 'Oh, good evening, Lord Rousay.'

Please, Warren, don't kow-tow to him, prayed Kelly silently, despising herself for what she had almost allowed to happen.

'I'd rather not use my title for work, if you don't mind,' said Randall curtly. 'And I'd like a word with you, please. In private.'

'Randall, *no!*' beseeched Kelly. 'I'll deal with it.'

Warren looked from Kelly to Randall, suspicion finally dawning in his eyes. Something ugly entered his face. 'I've got a pretty good idea what it is that you want to say,' he sneered. 'And I would have thought that you'd be able to find your own woman, without encroaching on someone else's property. Come, Kelly. We're going.'

Randall frowned, his face hard. 'You don't describe this woman. . .*any* woman, for that matter—as your property,' he said in a harsh voice.

Kelly had also bristled at the implication that she was Warren's property, but her sole intention was to dissolve the whole ghastly affair without causing a scene. She gave Randall a beseeching look, then turned and preceded Warren, walking towards the house, her head held high in the air, not even glancing again in Randall's direction.

*   *   *

Warren didn't say a word all the way back to the
hospital, and Kelly took one look at the forbidding set
of his jaw, and kept her silence also.

He walked with her to her room, and she hesitated,
utterly ashamed of herself. 'Would you like some
coffee?' she asked tentatively.

'I could use a drink,' he said shortly.

She poured two whiskies, and he drained his in one,
then turned to face her, his face white, an odd look in
his blue eyes. 'Warren, I'm so sorry——'

'Don't bother to try to apologise or try to explain,'
he cut in, and even his voice sounded unfamiliar. 'I'm
not a fool. Either you were just kissing Seton or he's
taken to wearing lipstick.'

Kelly's fingers fluttered up to cover her bare lips.
'Oh, God,' she whispered.

'Save your prayers!' he sneered, then helped himself
to another whisky without asking, drained that too,
and an ugly flush invaded his cheeks. 'What is it about
him, huh? That you act like some kind of tramp in his
arms?'

'I didn't——' she protested feebly.

'Really? That's why the two top buttons of your
dress just happen to be undone, is it? Why him, Kelly—
just tell me that? Is it the title? Is that what turns you
on? Do you imagine for one moment that anything will
come of it? If you're holding out hopes of becoming
the next Lady Rousay, I wouldn't bank on it.'

'Warren,' she said quietly, 'please don't say any
more.'

But he ignored her, ranting on like some fanatic on
a soap-box. 'We could have had it all, Kelly, you know
we could! We're alike, you and me—the same kind of

background, the same kind of struggles. We *understand* each other. It could have been us against the world.'

Kelly stared at him in bewilderment. 'But I never said——'

'Oh, no, you never said,' he interrupted bitterly. 'I thought I'd give you time to say it. I thought I'd wait, hold back, play the gentleman. Well, more fool me, when all the time you couldn't wait to drop your——'

Kelly whitened. 'That's enough, Warren! You've said enough!'

There was a high, disturbing pitch to his voice. 'I haven't said nearly enough! That's all he wants, you know. He's only after one thing, and once he's got it, he'll——'

'Get out,' she said, in a low, appalled voice. 'Get out, Warren, before you say anything else you might regret.'

But he didn't move, just looked at her, his eyes wild and unfamiliar, bright with whisky. 'Yes, maybe you're right, Kelly. Maybe the time for talking's over. Maybe I did a little too much talking, when all the time I should have just given you what you're obviously crying out for. . .'

And he lunged for her.

Caught by surprise, unbalanced by a strength emphasised by his determination, Kelly half fell on to the carpet, her eyes wide and frightened. 'No,' she whimpered, as she saw the expression in the pale eyes. 'Please, no. . .'

'Oh, *yes*,' he sneered, and he pushed her to the ground, falling on top of her, pushing all the breath out of her lungs as his mouth, reeking of whisky, began to cling slackly on to hers, his knee brutally pushing her thighs apart.

But the contact only lasted seconds, because the mouth was removed almost as soon as it had clamped itself on to hers, and Kelly turned her terrified gaze upwards to see that Randall had bodily picked Warren off her and was holding him by the shoulders, his face a study in naked rage. There was a stunned silence as Warren's eyes focused on the dark face above him. Don't hit him, thought Kelly, as she saw the grey eyes harden with contempt.

'I think the lady said *no*,' Randall said, in a voice tight with anger, showing the restraint he was obviously exercising over his temper.

And Kelly surprised a look of such malicious fury on Warren's face that she shuddered, and realised that by letting him off Randall had done the wrong thing entirely. For Warren came from a culture where men fought over women, where women were second-rate. If they had fought, they could have shaken hands, gone off and had a beer together.

'You'd better go, Warren,' she whispered.

'Yes, go,' said Randall tightly, 'before I tear you limb from limb. And if you ever come anywhere near her again I'll do it anyway. Do I make myself clear?'

There was a quiet, intimidating flavour of menace in his last gritted sentence, and Kelly could see the fear in Warren's eyes.

'Do I?' he repeated ominously.

'Yes.' And fixing them both with a final baleful stare, Warren stumbled out of the room without another word.

After he'd gone, neither she nor Randall spoke for

a minute. He was standing very still, with his fists clasped into whitened knuckles by his side, and she could see that he was having difficulty holding on to his temper.

'Are you OK?' he said, and his voice held a kind of tremor.

She gave him a blank, bitter kind of stare. 'What do you think? Yes, I'm OK. I don't know about Warren though.'

'Warren?' His brows flew up incredulously. 'For God's sake, Kelly. How the hell can you protect him, after what he tried to do to you?' he exploded.

'I'm not trying to protect him, I'm trying to understand him! And what do you think we tried to do to him?' she demanded, her voice wobbling as reaction set in. 'Humiliate him? Make him crawl?'

'Of course we didn't. What happened between us in the garden——'

'Forget it.'

He ignored her. 'Shouldn't have happened——'

'I said *forget* it!'

'No.' He came to within two feet of her. 'I'm not going to forget it. I can't. Can you?'

She turned away but he momentarily caught her by the arm, and even that brief touch of his hand made her blood race with excitement.

'Listen to me, Kelly. I didn't plan what happened. I certainly didn't expect it to get so out of hand, so quickly. I'm sorry if Warren was hurt, but you know, and I know, that he was the wrong man for you. But even given that what we did was wrong, that does not excuse his behaviour here. What on earth do you think would have happened if I hadn't walked in when I did? He could have *raped* you, for God's sake!'

'If it's plaudits you're after, then jolly well done,' she said tiredly.

'What I want is for you to make a complaint against him. He should be reported to the police. And you know that.'

Just the thought of re-enacting what had happened before a third party filled Kelly with a nameless kind of dread. 'No!' She tossed her head vehemently and the waves shimmered in a copper haze. 'I want the matter dropped,' she said fiercely. 'Do you understand, Randall? Dropped and forgotten.'

His grey eyes were very serious. 'And what if he comes back?'

'I don't believe he will. And I have a lock on my door.'

He was standing only inches away, with the soft line of his sculpted mouth within kissing distance. She still wanted him. Would she never be free of the torment of wanting him? Sick at heart, she turned away, and this time he did not stop her. 'And now, if you've quite finished, I'd like to get to bed.'

'Darling——'

It was the final straw; soft words could tug with such power at her resolve. She turned on him, her eyes fierce, shaking inside at the almost tender way he used the endearment. '*No*, Randall! No! I don't want to hear what you've got to say! Every time you come into my life you turn it upside down and ruin it, one way or another, and I don't like it. Neither do I need it.'

There was a long silence, broken only by the sound of their breathing.

'Do I make my point?' she said, in an empty little voice.

He stared at her for a moment before he shrugged his broad, elegant shoulders in an gesture of acceptance, but his eyes were now cold and as hard as metal. She had never seen him look like that before, she realised, her heart inexplicably sinking.

'Crystal-clear,' he answered icily. He turned and walked out of the room, and Kelly turned the key in the door behind him, the tears beginning to slide down her cheeks at last.

CHAPTER SIX

THE following morning the alarm-clock shrilled into harsh and unwelcome life at five a.m., and Kelly struggled to wake up.

Rubbing her eyes, she sat up in bed, her tousled hair falling all over her bare shoulders, her body cool and naked beneath the sheets, and she felt a slow heat rise in her face as she remembered Randall kissing her so passionately in the garden, and of her frightening response to his ardour. And the ghastly conclusion to the whole evening, with Warren leaping on her like a man possessed.

But it had happened; now it must be forgotten. She had decided to ignore what had happened, and she still had to work with both men. What it essentially boiled down to was that Warren had been both hurt and a little worse for wear, and that was why he had behaved so aggressively.

But she shuddered as she stood beneath the shower, and she tried not to think about what *could* have happened if Randall had not walked in when he had done.

She showered and dressed, then, putting her stethoscope and pager into the pocket of a clean white coat, she set off to the canteen for some breakfast.

The first person she saw was Randall. He was seated by one of the windows, scanning the pages of a textbook which was propped up against the salt and pepper pots, while he ate an enormous plateful of bacon and eggs. His hair was ruffled, and there were dark shadows beneath his eyes.

He glanced up at her, his eyes flicking briefly over her, and he gave her only the most cursory nod before turning back to his book.

Kelly turned away and moved like a robot over towards the counter, frozen by the indifference in that cold, grey stare, her hunger gone, but just to have walked out would have been a complete giveaway.

It hurt.

It hurt like hell.

But that had been what she had wanted, wasn't it? She had asked him to leave her alone, and now it seemed as though he was complying with her wishes. She found herself remembering his devastatingly critical words to her last night, when she'd told him that she did not intend pursuing surgery.

'Morning, ducks!' beamed the woman behind the counter. 'Cooked breakfast for you?'

Kelly shook her head. 'Just toast and coffee, thanks.'

The woman gave her a reproving stare as she put two pieces of toast, butter and marmalade on to a plate. 'You'll waste away, Doctor! There's nothing of you as it is!'

'I eat enough!' protested Kelly.

She carried her tray through the room, her head held high as she deliberately sat on the opposite side of the restaurant to Randall, but he didn't even look up from his book.

He left before she did, and she allowed herself to watch his retreating frame. Heavens, but he had the most amazing body she had ever seen. Tall and rangy and musuclar. And with the broadest shoulders.

Angry with her obsession with the man, she pushed the half eaten piece of toast away, and walked down to A & E.

She went straight in at the deep end, because, as Harry Wells was handing over to her, a middle-aged man was rushed in with chest pain. He was white and sweating and very anxious, and his wife was hysterical, which was only compounding his fears.

'He's not going to *die*, is he, Doctor?' the woman demanded frantically, grabbing hold of Kelly's arm.

Kelly gently but firmly disengaged her, and caught a student nurse's eye. 'We're doing everything we can for him,' she said gently. 'Nurse here will take you into the relatives' room and give you a cup of tea, and you can see him very shortly.'

Kelly went back into the cubicle and bent down to speak to the patient. 'Have you a lot of pain, Mr Dance?'

He nodded, his hand indicating the top part of his chest. 'Yes, Doctor,' he gasped. 'It's like a ton of bricks crashing down on my chest, and the pain goes down my arm too.'

Kelly quickly wrote up some intra-muscular morphine and some oral aspirin, and handed the drug chart to the nurse. 'Let's give him these as quickly as possible,' she said.

The drugs were administered, and as the nurse recorded Mr Dance's pulse, respiration and blood-pressure, Kelly started fixing the ECG electrodes to his chest.

This will help us to get a good look at your heart,'

she told him, but the morphine was already taking effect and Mr Dance was in a hazy state of euphoria.

''S'nice,' he mumbled dreamily.

Kelly finished the ECG and bleeped the medical registrar, and was just studying the tracing when he arrived and glanced at the trace-out over her shoulder.

'Hi,' he said. 'How is he?'

'Calmer. I've given him a shot of morphine,' replied Kelly as she showed him the ECG. 'There's definite ST elevation on his electrocardiogram.'

He nodded. 'Mild infarction by the look of it. We'll get him up to CCU as soon as possible for observation. Though I'll have to transfer someone to the medical ward before I can arrange a bed. I'll do that now.' He picked up the receiver and dialled the coronary care number.

'Right,' said Kelly, and went to find a nurse to stay with Mr Dance until he could be admitted.

She was then called to see a middle-aged man who was complaining of a sore eye.

'Looks like a classic case of conjunctivitis to me,' confided the staff nurse.

Kelly picked up the casualty card and looked at it. 'We'll see,' she said.

The eye *did* have the familiar redness of conjunctivitis, Kelly decided, and she was unable to see any foreign body when she examined him with an ophthalmoscope. Nevertheless, she took a full history with her usual thoroughness.

'Have you suffered any injury to the eyes, Mr Marshall?' she asked.

He shook his head. 'No, Doctor.'

'Can I ask if you've been doing anything which might have inadvertently damaged your eye?'

'Can't think of anything.'

But Kelly had noticed a plaster on the man's finger. 'What have you done to your finger?'

'Oh, that's just a blister,' he replied. 'Been doing too much hammering.'

'Hammering?'

'Aye. Been putting an extension on to the back of the house for the missus.'

An idea had occurred to Kelly. 'I'm going to send you upstairs to have your eye X-rayed,' she told him.

Half an hour later he was back, and Kelly stood in the office with the eye surgeon, looking at the X-ray.

'You see——' he pointed at the film '—there's a sliver of metal at the back of the eye which must have shot in there while he was hammering. Easily missed. You did well, Kelly. We'll remove it later under general anaesthetic.'

And Kelly blushed with pride when the eye surgeon smiled at her and said very quietly, 'Well done, my dear, you've probably saved that man's eye.'

It was rare moments like that, she thought, which made being a doctor absolutely unbeatable.

The department was then relatively quiet for a couple of hours, and Kelly spent it usefully employed in reading the job advertisements in the *BMJ*. She was doing her own training scheme for general practice. She needed to do six months each in four different specialities before she could qualify as a GP. After A & E, she was required to do medicine, psychiatry and obstetrics and gynaecology. She *had* intended to do all her jobs at St Christopher's, the hospital where she had trained and been happy, but now she recognised that she would no longer be able to do that. Not if Randall was going to be working here for the next two years. . .

Her reverie was interrupted by Staff Nurse Higgs, who had just arrived on duty, her cold blue eyes narrowing as she saw Kelly. 'Oh, it's you!' she said ungraciously.

Resisting sarcasm, Kelly summoned up a smile. 'Good morning!'

Ignoring the pleasantry, Nurse Higgs fiddled with her fob watch. 'There's a patient in cubicle four.'

'With?'

Nurse Higgs dropped the casualty card on the desk in front of Kelly. 'Top of the finger chopped off. She brought it in wrapped up in a handkerchief. We've packed it in ice.'

'How's the bleeding?' asked Kelly crisply.

'We've stemmed it.'

'Good.'

Nurse Higgs gave a sly smile. 'Shall I bleep the surgeon for you?'

'I'll do it. But I'd better take a look at her first,' said Kelly firmly as she got to her feet.

Nurse Higgs raised her eyebrows. 'Of course, you *would* want to ring him yourself, I suppose.'

Kelly drew her eyebrows together at the tone in the nurse's voice. 'Sorry?'

'Mr Seton—the surgeon.'

'Yes, I know that Mr Seton is the surgeon,' answered Kelly impatiently. 'I just don't understand what point you're trying to make.'

Another sly smile as Nurse Higgs shrugged her

shoulders. 'Just that you were seen at the party together last night.'

'Yes?'

'*Kissing*. Kissing Mr Seton, that is.'

Kelly flexed her fingers deep in the pockets of her white coat, and fixed the staff nurse with a steady stare, hoping that she wouldn't ruin everything by blushing like a schoolgirl. 'And since when has kissing been a crime?'

'Well, just that you arrived with Mr Booth——'

'Listen,' Kelly cut across the girl firmly. 'I'm here to do a job, Nurse Higgs, and so are you. That job happens to be the care of patients, not swapping idle hospital gossip. So if you'd like to come and help me in cubicle four, I can get on.'

'Certainly, *Doctor*,' answered Nurse Higgs mulishly.

It's nothing more than a personality clash, Kelly told herself, as she pulled back the curtains of cubicle four. It happens. But it was difficult to deal with the sort of insidious insubordination the staff nurse displayed towards her. Infuriatingly, she found herself wondering what Randall would do.

The patient in cubicle four was an ashen-faced girl in her twenties. There was a rough pressure-dressing covering the index finger of her left hand.

'How did you do it?' Kelly asked, as she gently picked the girl's hand up.

'Chopping up a cucumber—I'm a chef. Can you sew it back on, Doctor?'

'How long ago did this happen?'

'Only about ten minutes. My boss brought me by car straight away.'

Kelly took a look at the severed tip of finger. 'Well,

you've done the right thing by bringing it in, and so promptly. I'm going to get hold of the surgeon right now, and hear what he says.'

She had him bleeped.

'Seton here,' came the clipped, deep voice.

Kelly took a deep breath. 'Hello, Randall—it's Kelly.'

There was a pause. 'Yes, Kelly?' he said indifferently. 'What can I do for you?'

'I've got a young girl in Casualty who's chopped off the tip of her finger. I think you might be able to sew it back on. Any chance of doing it now?'

'I'll come down and have a look, and tack her on to the front of my list if I think it's viable.'

'Thanks.'

'OK.' He hung up abruptly, and Kelly tried to convince herself that she didn't care.

She saw him only briefly when he came into the office to pick up the casualty card from the desk at which she was working. She glanced up with an automatic smile, her face stiffening as he threw her a look of sheer indifference. Yes, she had told him she didn't want him in her life, but was there really any need for him to be quite so unpleasant about it?

Her face was pink with anger as she finished filling in an X-ray form, and she was glad enough of the diversion when she was called to examine a five-year-old boy who had a skin tear to his forearm.

He was screaming his head off even before Kelly had gone near him.

'Sssssh!' urged Kelly softly, as she walked over to the trolley. 'What's your name?'

'Go *away!*' he retorted, and aimed a kick at Kelly's abdomen.

'No kicking, please, Caspian,' said Kelly firmly, reading his name off the casualty card. 'Start cleaning the wound so that I can examine it, would you please, Nurse?' She turned to the thin-faced woman in the green waxed jacket who sat beside him. 'Are you Caspian's mother?'

'Yes. Oh, Nurse, *please*,' the woman twittered, as the volume of Caspian's shrieks increased. 'He's a *very* sensitive child. Would you mind treating him more gently?'

'Nurse is trained to be gentle,' said Kelly smoothly. 'But it's bound to hurt a little bit. Tell me, is Caspian up to date with his tetanus injections?'

Caspian's mother looked appalled. '*Tetanus* injections?' she queried, in a shocked voice. 'Most certainly not! His father and I are not into *conventional* medicine, I'm afraid, Doctor.'

'Well, he's going to need a booster,' said Kelly firmly, as she peered down at Caspian's arm. 'It's a filthy wound.'

Caspian shrieked.

'And I'm going to have to suture his arm, I'm afraid,' said Kelly calmly. 'But I'll give him some local anaesthetic first, and he won't feel a thing.'

Pandemonium reigned as Caspian's mother passed out on hearing this, and hit her head on the side of the trolley. She then needed a skull X-ray and was put in the adjoining cubicle for neurological observations before being pronounced fit enough to go home.

'The only good thing about it,' laughed Kelly to the nurse in the office afterwards, 'was that the surprise of being upstaged by his mother actually shut dear Caspian up, so that I was able to stitch his arm without getting my eardrums shattered!'

The ringing of the telephone interrupted them, and Kelly picked up the receiver. 'Dr Hartley,' she said crisply.

It was Warren. 'Kelly?'

Kelly nearly dropped the phone. He had been the last person she would have expected to hear from after last night. 'Hello?' she answered cautiously.

'Can I see you?'

'I don't think that's a good idea.'

He hesitated. 'About last night. . .'

She froze. 'I don't really want to talk about it.'

'Will you——' he hesitated; he sounded nervous '—be taking any further action?'

Kelly swallowed. 'I've decided not to.'

'Thanks——'

Her voice was tinged with disgust as she cut him short. 'Don't thank me, Warren. I'm doing it to spare myself the humiliation of having to recount the whole sorry experience. But I know what you did, and so does Randall——'

'Oh, does he?' he sneered. 'Did Randall get lucky after I'd gone? Did you get laid?'

In a minute she would put the phone down, but not before he knew the strength of her resolve. 'Listen to me,' she said, very quietly, 'while I tell you that if ever there's a repeat of what happened last night, if I ever hear that you've tried something like that on with another woman, then I'll go straight to the police. And that's a promise.'

'Oh, don't worry, Kelly,' and there was an odd,

strained quality to his voice. 'The situation won't arise again. You've taught me a lesson that I don't think I'll ever forget.'

But it was not relief which she felt as she replaced the receiver, and her hand trembled very slightly as she realised that she was unnerved and unsettled by the conversation she had just had, by the strange threatening tone in Warren's voice.

At six she finished her shift, taking the long way back to her room through the hospital gardens. She tried to relax, but the events of last night left her with a nasty taste in her mouth. Above her, the sky was the cloudless blue of late summer, and she knew that she could not face going back to her small, anonymous room in the doctors' mess. She needed to get out, just get away from the hospital.

On an impulse she took a bus to Hammersmith, and just over an hour later she found herself walking slowly up the dusty pavement towards her parents' house. The little terraced houses were tightly packed together, their windows masked by net curtains, though here and there Kelly could see that some of the old-fashioned front doors had been replaced by pine. There were even a few window-boxes, with blue lobelia and pink busy lizzies bravely blooming in spite of the dust which had coloured all the houses grey.

'Kelly!' Her mother opened the door with a surprised smile, and then a worried look crossed over her face. 'There's nothing wrong, is there?'

Kelly shook her head and grinned. 'No, of course not. Why should there be?'

'It's just that—well, you never really call without phoning.'

'I can go away again,' teased Kelly.

'Of course not! Come inside and I'll put the kettle on. Oh, it *is* nice to see you.'

Kelly stepped into the gloom of the narrow hallway. 'Where's Dad?'

'Guess!'

'At the pub?' Kelly hazarded, as she followed her mother into the old-fashioned kitchen.

Her mother nodded as she took her apron off and hung it over the back of the chair. 'But he's better than he used to be. Only has two at the most.' She paused. 'You'll never guess what he's done?' She put three teaspoons of tea into the warmed pot.

'What?'

'Given up smoking!'

'You're joking!'

'I'm not. That's all thanks to you, that is. The way you kept on to him about it. He says he feels much better for it too.' She handed Kelly a cup of the steaming, strong tea.

'You're looking very peaky yourself, dear. I can make you a bacon sandwich, if you like.'

Kelly hadn't eaten since toast at breakfast, and that seemed a very long time ago. 'I'd love one, Mum.'

Ten minutes later Kelly was eating the most delicious sandwich imaginable, with heaps of bacon layered between two doorsteps of buttered white bread. A dietician's nightmare, she thought in amusement. And a dieter's dream! 'Thanks, Mum,' she sighed, and put the empty plate down.

Her mother eyed her shrewdly. 'So are you going to tell me what's troubling you now?'

Kelly narrowed her eyes. 'How do you know that something's troubling me?'

'I can tell. You've got that look about you. It's something in the eyes—you've always done it—even as a little girl. It's not work, is it? Changed your mind about what you want to do again?'

Kelly sighed. 'No, it's not work. Well, in a way it's work.' She saw her mother's puzzled expression. 'It's a man,' she said.

'A man!'

Kelly pulled a face. 'Well, there's no need to sound so surprised, Mum! Lots of women have men worries.'

'But not you. You've never been interested in any men. Except for. . .'

Her voice tailed off. Kelly stared at her interestedly. 'Except for who?'

Her mother hesitated. 'The student. All those years ago. Had a funny name.'

'Randall.'

'Randall. That's right. Used to cry yourself to sleep every night after you got back from that summer camp.'

'He's back,' said Kelly slowly. 'Randall's back.'

Her mother listened. 'And you feel the same about him?'

Kelly thought carefully as she searched around for the honest answer to her mother's question. 'Yes,' she whispered softly. 'I do. Oh, I've tried to tell myself otherwise, that I don't, but—in my heart of hearts—he still means more to me than any other man I've ever met.'

Mrs Hartley's eyes narrowed. 'And? He's not interested?'

Kelly bit her lip. 'That's just the thing. I think—he is.'

'So what's the problem?'

'Years ago—all those years ago—Randall and I grew very fond of one another, but then the night before I was leaving, he...' She hesitated, not wanting to give too much away to her mother about how intimate they had almost become when she had been just seventeen. 'Walked out. And he went back to London. He never phoned me or contacted me. I never saw him again until the other day.' She put her teacup down. 'You see, he hurt me very badly,' she said.

'I know that.'

'And what sort of guarantee have I got that he won't do it again?'

Her mother shook her head. 'Unfortunately, life doesn't come with those kind of guarantees, Kelly. And relationships certainly don't. Otherwise we'd never make any mistakes. But, while playing cautious is always the safe option, it's not always the best option.'

Kelly recognised the wisdom in her mother's words as she twisted her hands in her lap. She realised too that this was the first time she had ever confided in her, and in thinking that she would not understand she had done her mother a great disservice all these years. 'There's something else I haven't told you, Mum.'

'And what's that, dear?'

How could she say it? 'Randall—he's...' Heavens— it sounded so ridiculously pretentious; it sounded unreal. 'He's. . . Well, he's a lord, actually. His name's Lord Rousay.'

Her mother looked momentarily abashed, then nodded. 'So?'

Kelly's mouth fell open in astonishment; her family was being full of surprises this afternoon. Her father had given up smoking, and now her mother was calmly accepting Randall's aristocratic status as though she were being confronted with this kind of problem all the time! She shrugged her slim shoulders. 'It's a bit like the prince and the showgirl, don't you think? Him and me?'

'No, I don't. You're a doctor and so is he, that's equal enough. And from what you tell me, you seem to like each other—so that's really all that matters.'

Kelly laughed aloud. 'I thought you'd. . .'

Her mother's eyes twinkled. 'Tell you that you were getting ideas above your station? If I'd believed that, we'd never have supported your ambition to be a doctor in the first place. I would have liked your opportunities myself.' She sighed as she poured them both another cup of tea. 'But things were different in our day.'

'You mean you didn't want to leave school at fourteen?'

Her mother gave her a funny look. 'Of course I didn't! But we needed the money, and when I say *needed* it, I mean it. There were no grants around in my day.'

'I was very lucky,' said Kelly in a low voice, deeply moved by what her mother had just told her, aware that to a teenager everything seemed so black and white, which was not always necessarily the case. She would never have imagined for a moment that her mother would have liked to go on to further education. 'Thank you for everything.'

Her mother beamed with pleasure. 'We're very proud of you, Kelly, don't sell yourself short. If he's not bothered about the differences between you, then why should you be?' She hesitated. 'You say he just walked out of your life?'

Kelly nodded.

'And did you never ask him why?'

She shook her head, so that the auburn hair rippled in fiery waves all the way down her back. 'No.'

'Then why don't you?'

Kelly's eyes widened. 'I couldn't do that!' she protested.

'Then you aren't being fair,' said Mrs Hartley firmly.

'You mean to him?'

Mrs Hartley shook her head. 'Not to him. To yourself.'

Kelly stared into space, her green eyes troubled.

'Perhaps I'm not,' she murmured slowly, thinking what a simple solution it was, yet wondering if she had the nerve simply to confront Randall and ask him outright why he had left her.

CHAPTER SEVEN

KELLY thought and thought about what her mother had said, about asking Randall for an explanation.

Of course she had not asked him why he had walked out on her all those years ago. He had had nine years to find her if there had been a reasonable explanation, and he hadn't bothered. And now he was back, and obviously still as attracted to her as she was to him, probably thinking that if she was as compliant as she had been before, that he might as well have an affair with her.

An affair which would bring her nothing but heartache.

So what was the alternative to an affair? Was it possible that they could bury desire, and become, if not best buddies, then at least friends?

But you could not be friends with a man who was frostily polite to you, who deliberately excluded you from his life as Randall now seemed to be doing, as he so crushingly demonstrated one day in A & E.

Kelly was standing behind the curtains of a cubicle, trying to get a history from a woman who spoke only French, when she heard Randall talking to his houseman outside the cubicle.

'Come and have a drink later in the mess—there are a few people coming.'

'What's the occasion?'

'My birthday.' Randall's voice was wry. 'Not the

venue I'd normally have chosen for such an auspicious occasion, but—typically—I'm on call.'

'Your birthday, Mr Seton?'

Kelly cringed as she heard heard Staff Nurse Higgs' syrupy tones.

'That's right.'

'I just *love* birthdays,' cooed Nurse Higgs.

Kelly bristled as she heard the indulgent tone in Randall's voice. 'Want to come for a drink in the mess later?'

'Just try to stop me!'

Kelly felt sick. He could have gone out with *anyone*. Surely he was not going to start dating the awful staff nurse who made being obvious into an art form!

'*Docteur! Docteur! J'ai mal au ventre! C'est terrible, Docteur!*' The woman on the trolley was gripping Kelly's hand tightly. And then she slipped into a torrent of totally incomprehensible French.

'*Attend, s'il vous plaît*,' stumbled Kelly in her absol- utely appalling schoolgirl French. '*Je trouverai une personne qui. . .*'

'Having problems?' came a deep drawl from close by, and the curtains were swished back to disclose Randall, his grey eyes resting innocently on her flushed face.

Fancy blushing like an idiotic schoolgirl! 'I need a fluent French speaker to take this patient's full history,' she said stiltedly.

'Will I do?' he drawled.

It was little things in life that could rile you so much that you felt like screaming. Like the fact that he had invited everyone for a drink except her. And that the arrogant show-off just *happened* to be fluent in French!

'Only if you have the time,' she said stiffly.

'*Bien sûr!*' he mocked, and leaned over the patient. '*Bonjour, madame.*' He lapsed into flawless French with an impeccable accent, while the patient virtually fainted with pleasure at the sight of the tall Englishman with the spectacular dark-lashed eyes who was speaking her language with such fluid ease.

Angrily, Kelly turned to leave.

He lifted his head, some unreadable light in the depths of the steely eyes. 'Won't you stay to chaperon me?'

'I'll send a nurse instead,' she said tartly. 'I'm sure that Nurse Higgs would be only too *delighted* to assist you.'

As soon as the words were out, she regretted them, and she didn't need the quirk of amusement which lifted the corners of his mouth to tell her that she had succeeded in sounding jealous. How *could* she have done?

'I'm sure you're right,' he murmured, still smiling, his fingers lightly resting on the patient's pulse.

Kelly walked back into the office, where Nurse Higgs was perched on the edge of the desk, chatting to the houseman and swinging her shapely legs like a pendulum. 'Would you mind going to assist Mr Seton, please, Nurse?'

Nurse Higgs wriggled her bottom off the desk, her look of rapture quickly being replaced by one of triumph. 'I'd be delighted,' she purred, then added to the houseman, 'See you tonight, then, Damian, at *Randall's* party.' She couldn't resist a triumphant glance over at Kelly, but Kelly lowered her head and doggedly carried on writing on the casualty card.

She wouldn't let it bother her, she just wouldn't. He could go out with whom he liked, and they were welcome to him. She, for one, was well rid of him.

With a determination to put Randall out of her mind, Kelly picked up a set of notes which were awaiting the arrival of a GP admission, and began to read them.

She managed to lose herself in them so completely that she didn't hear Joe, the male nurse, come in until he cleared his throat and grinned at her.

Kelly looked up and smiled back. Joe was in his mid-forties, and the longest-serving member of the casualty staff. 'Hi,' she said. 'Got something for me?'

Joe nodded. 'A young woman with acute, severe abdominal pain.'

Something in the way he said it made Kelly give him a sharp look. 'But?'

Joe hesitated. 'There's something you should know.'

'Mmm?'

'She's known to us. She's given a false name, but I recognised her. She's in our black book.'

'Oh. I see,' said Kelly slowly.

The black book.

Most casualty departments reluctantly kept one. In it they listed persistent abusers of the system, such as drug addicts and faked illness in order to obtain strong painkillers.

'What's she in the black book for, Joe?' Kelly asked quietly.

He pulled a face. 'Münchhausen.'

'Oh,' said Kelly again as she followed Joe towards the cubicle, her mind scanning over what she knew about Münchhausen's Syndrome. She'd read about it, naturally, but this was the first case of it she'd actually encountered in four months of working in A & E.

Named after Baron von Münchhausen—proverbial teller of tall stories—Münchhausen's Syndrome was a disturbing psychiatric disorder of unknown aetiology. Patients became addicted to hospitals, and to hospital treatment. Hospitals somehow gave their usually miserable lives some meaning and importance. In a bizarre form of attention-seeking, they often endured many major surgical interventions before their condition was diagnosed.

Kelly pulled the curtains open and looked at the overweight and pasty young woman who lay doubled up on the trolley.

'Hello,' she said gently, as she put her fingers on the girl's wrist. 'What seems to be the trouble?'

The girl was hyperventilating. 'Just give me something for the pain!' she gasped. 'Please, Doctor!'

'You'll have to try and give me a bit of your history,' said Kelly quietly.

'I've got Crohn's disease, but this pain is worse than anything I've ever had before! I feel like it's going to kill me, Doctor! For God's sake, can't you give me something for the pain?'

Kelly shook her head. 'I can't give you anything just yet. I need to examine you first. Now will you show me exactly where the pain is?'

'Here,' the girl muttered, and as she lifted her arm to point to her abdomen, Kelly caught sight of the tell-tale multiple scarring on her wrists which indicated self-mutilation.

Kelly examined her. Her abdomen was covered in old scars, and the list of operations she cited was truly astonishing. Eventually, Kelly straightened up. I'm going to ask a specialist to come down and take a look at you,' she said, and indicated to Joe that he should follow her.

Back in the office, she frowned. 'I don't *think* there's anything physically wrong with her. Her abdomen is certainly rigid, but I got the feeling that she was controlling that herself by holding her breath. And if she *has* Crohn's disease, then the level of pain she was demonstrating would be indicative of a perforation, but her observations certainly didn't tally with *that*. It's a psychiatric referral we need,' she said, in a low voice. 'But we need to get hold of her notes, and I'd better get her checked out by the general surgeon just in case. This might just be the first genuine medical crisis of her life, and I'm not prepared to take that risk.'

She bleeped Randall, who said he would be down straight away, and, true to his word, he appeared almost immediately.

'How sure are we it's Münchhausen?' he asked Kelly.

'Pretty sure. Her wrists and abdomen are riddled with scars. Joe recognised her immediately. She has a history of visiting this department, using various aliases. I've sent for her notes, but of course there may be more than one set floating around.' She lifted her eyes to his. 'But I have to be sure that she doesn't have a *genuine* surgical problem before I can give her a psychiatric referral.'

'Sure.' Randall nodded, took the casualty card from her and went off with Joe to examine the patient, but he had returned within minutes, a rueful expression on his face.

'She's gone,' he said succinctly.

'Gone?' Kelly frowned.

'Mmm. Done a runner, as they say. She obviously guessed that you suspected her.'

'That was pretty stupid of me!' Kelly threw her pen down on the desk crossly. 'How on earth can we help her if she goes off like that?'

Randall gave her a curiously sympathetic look. 'But you know that we can't help her anyway, Kelly, not if she doesn't want to help herself.' And he gave her a brief smile before he turned and was gone.

Kelly was absolutely exhausted by the time her shift had finished, but the prospect of an evening alone didn't fill her with joy, particularly if she had to play witness to the sound of the tip-tapping of feet as they wended their way to Randall's birthday drinks in the mess.

She decided to ring the hospital squash club, and luckily found herself a partner for that evening, a girl called Penny, one of the nursing sisters from ITU, whom Kelly had partnered on a number of occasions.

Kelly played a vigorous game but was completely thrashed, and afterwards, both panting for breath, they shook hands.

'You weren't concentrating!' scolded Penny, her face all pink and shiny. 'You're normally much better than me! Not that I'm complaining,' she added, with a grin. 'I really enjoyed winning!' She rubbed a towel at the back of her neck. 'What are you doing now? Anything?'

Kelly shrugged. 'I hadn't planned anything.'

Penny's eyes narrowed. 'You've split up with Warren Booth, haven't you?'

Kelly had to try very hard not to shudder at the mention of his name; she had managed very successfully to put the memories of Warren completely out of her mind. 'Yes,' she said. 'We have. But it actually wasn't serious.'

Penny laughed. 'That's not what the gossip said. Rumour has it that Warren was seen prowling around jewellers' shop windows at the dead of night!'

God forbid, thought Kelly, wondering how she could have been so blind and so insensitive as not to have seen that he was so keen on her.

Penny zipped her squash racquet into its case. 'Well, if you're free, do you fancy coming for a drink? There's a crowd going down to the doctors' mess.'

'No, thanks, I——' The automatic words of refusal froze on Kelly's lips as she realised what had prompted them, and indignation reared its head. This was *her* hospital, after all. She had trained here, worked here since qualifying. And she *did* quite fancy a drink after a hard day's work and her game of squash. So was she going to let her confused feelings about Randall change her life to such an extent that she could no longer even go out for a friendly drink with a girlfriend?

'Actually, yes,' she amended quickly. 'I'd love to.'

'Great! Shall I meet you there in about half an hour?' asked Penny. 'That gives us time for a shower, and to slap a bit of make-up on.'

'Fine. See you there.'

Kelly showered and dressed simply in a pair of old jeans worn with a simple emerald-coloured body, which brought out the deep green of her eyes, but her nerve almost failed her as she stood outside the mess, listening to the raised voices of laughter which were coming from inside.

There was a split-second silence when she walked in, and then there were shouts of 'hello' from several people who knew her.

She knew exactly where Randall stood in the room, and though she heard him talking, laughing, she immediately became aware that his attention was fixed on her. The grey eyes were following her with their intense, spectacular gaze, and that knowledge filled her with a heady excitement which was immediately dampened down when her gaze came to rest by chance on Nurse Higgs.

Marianne Higgs was looking stunning. Her silky blonde hair streamed all over her magnificent bosom, and she was wearing a short, tight T-shirt dress which showed a great deal of bare, brown thighs. But it was her coldly hostile look which unnerved Kelly, and she shook her head a little to dispel a sudden, irrational fear. Because for a moment there, the other girl had glowered at her as though she really despised her.

'Hello, Kelly,' said Penny, who had appeared by her side.

Kelly forced her attention back to her squash partner. 'Hi!' she said. 'Feeling better for that shower?'

'You bet!' Penny looked at her and gave a rueful smile. 'How on earth can you look so good just wearing a pair of jeans and a body? Half the room can't keep their eyes off you.'

Kelly shook her head, and the auburn waves rippled down her back. 'You look great too.'

Penny looked down at her flower-sprigged dress.

'I'm much too short and curvy. I certainly couldn't get away with wearing *that* outfit!'

'Some men like curvy women,' smiled Kelly.

'So they tell me. I'm still waiting to meet them! Come on, let's get a drink. Loser pays!'

'OK,' laughed Kelly, and they walked up to the bar.

They bought two glasses of beer and Kelly reached into the back pocket of her jeans for some money.

'It's already paid for,' came a deep voice behind her.

Her heart began its wild and familiar dance. She turned round slowly to face him, almost drowning in the dazzle of that grey, speculative stare. Suddenly it was difficult to speak. 'You—don't have to do that.' Did her voice sound hesitant, stumbling?

'It's my pleasure,' he insisted, with a smile.

Aware that Penny was standing silently by her side, Kelly quickly turned to her squash partner. 'Do you two know each other?'

Penny's eyes were fixed on him with frank admiration. 'Oh, yes, I know Randall,' she said, sipping her drink. 'He's a regular face in ITU. I think I could quite like him if he didn't send us so many patients! Thanks for the drink, Randall—cheers!' and she lifted her glass up to him.

He raised his mineral water in silent toast and then the cool grey eyes were turned on Kelly.

With an effort she lifted her glass to him, hostility and the years forgotten as she lost herself in that devastating smile. 'Happy birthday,' she said in a quiet voice, hardly realising that she had said it.

The dark eyebrows were elevated. 'Why, thank you, Kelly,' he murmured, and an undercurrent of sardonic amusement transmitted its way towards her. 'But I wasn't aware that you knew it was my birthday?'

Of course he wasn't—because she had been shamelessly eavesdropping at the time! Of all the crass things to do! 'I—er, er—overheard you telling someone earlier.'

He was staring very deliberately at her mouth, as though he wanted very much to kiss it, and Kelly put her glass down with a hand that was in terrible danger of trembling.

Penny was looking from one to the other of them with a bemused expression on her face. 'I think I'm a little *de trop* here,' she said drily, and then, with an obvious sigh of relief, 'Oh, look, there's some people from ITU, you must excuse me. Great game, Kelly, thanks!'

'Let's do it again soon,' said Kelly from between parched lips, as she watched Penny go. 'I must go too, Randall.'

'Don't.' He put his hand at the small of her back, at the most delicious spot, as though he were about to massage it, and she had physically to force herself not to wriggle back against it luxuriously.

'I haven't eaten.' Her voice sounded strange, even to her own ears. As though she had forgotten how to speak, because the dryness of her mouth and the blood thundering to her temples was utterly distracting.

'Neither have I. We'll get a Chinese meal delivered, if you'd like it.'

'Randall?'

His voice was very soft. 'What?'

'I must go. I don't know why I came.'

'Yes, you do,' he demurred. 'It's pointless fighting it any more, Kelly. It's inevitable.'

He made it sound as though they were doomed; doomed to be swept away into a mad sea of their own passion, and she wondered whether they would sink, or swim.

'Come and have some champagne with me?' he suggested.

'In your room, I suppose?' she answered bitterly.

'Well, yes.' He sighed. 'Hell—don't look like that! I happen to be on call, so I can't leave the hospital, which leaves us with a number of alternatives. We can postpone this talk which we're long overdue to have until tomorrow night, but frankly, you're so damned elusive that I'm extremely reluctant to do that.'

'And don't I get a say in all this?' she countered, but her breathing was erratic.

'Only if you agree with me,' he said softly.

She stared at him, momentarily flummoxed and rendered speechless by his effrontery, his flattery.

'So,' he continued, still in that deep, seductive drawl, 'we can stay here where everything is getting rowdier by the second. . .'

Kelly glanced up, frozen once again in the malicious ice which glittered from Marianne Higgs' eyes. No, she certainly did not want to stay here.

'Or we can do the sensible thing, and go somewhere quiet to talk——'

'Like the hospital canteen, I suppose?' she put in drily. 'Or the library?'

He gave her a sweet smile and a feeling like a flock of butterflies tumbled about exultantly in the pit of her stomach. 'Perhaps not private enough,' he murmured, and there was no disguising the sensual glimmer which lay behind the question in the silver-grey eyes.

She tried to tell herself that it was because she wanted to straighten things out between them, but if she put her hand across her heart she knew that was not the reason. The reason was love—plain and simple. She'd loved Randall at seventeen, and she had never stopped loving him. There had never been another man to match him for wit, or charm, or charisma or irresistible sex appeal.

She would ask him why he had left, and if the answer he gave her did not satisfy her—then she would walk away and never look back. Because she would never respect herself if she did anything different.

She became aware of the hostile daggers of Marianne Higgs' glance. 'But won't I be cramping your style?' she enquired, somewhat waspishly.

'What?' And he saw the staff nurse looking over at them.

'Oh, I see. No, of course you won't.'

'There's no "of course" about it. She's glaring over here as though I'm poaching on her territory.'

'Well, you're not, and forgive me for saying so, Kelly—but *you're* the one who is sounding a trifle put out. One might almost say jealous?'

'I'm not jealous,' she whispered, wondering if he could read the lie in her eyes.

'I think we're rather going round in circles here,' he said softly. 'So are you coming with me, or not?'

Nine years on and she had become a strong, independent woman in everything. Except this. Him. 'Yes,' she sighed.

He grimaced. 'There's no need to sound as though I'm leading you into a den of lions.'

'Probably safer,' she retorted.

He laughed. 'No comment. Wait here while I go and tell them to leave a tab at the bar.'

'That's very expansive of you,' she commented.

'Oh, but I'm feeling very expansive—quite extra-ordinarily so,' he murmured, and his gaze travelled lingeringly all the way down her body, causing her to tremble helplessly under that slow, seductive scrutiny.

He strode over to the bar, his tall, rangy dark figure attracting the attention of every woman in the room.

Oh, this is hopeless, thought Kelly. He's a walking dream-machine. Elusive and gorgeous—and who in their right mind could ever expect to hang on to Randall Seton?

'Everyone's watching us,' she observed, when he came back from the bar.

'Of course they are. All the men are envious as hell of me, and all the women are wishing they looked as beautiful as you do tonight.'

'Don't try to flatter me.'

'I'm not,' he smiled. 'I pride myself on a candid tongue.'

Compliments from Randall could turn a girl's head, and she forced herself to be prosaic. 'And it'll be all round the hospital tomorrow.'

He was staring at her very intently. 'What will?'

'Us. If we leave together.'

'And do you mind?'

She stared into the dark, handsome face which had haunted her dreams and her waking hours for so many years, and realised that no, she *didn't* mind. More than

that—Kelly felt almost reckless with an anticipation
and excitement she had not tasted for years.

'No,' she answered quietly, 'I don't think I do.'

She waved goodbye to Penny, and walked out of the
room, with Randall following closely behind her, but
she was aware of the excited buzz of chatter as they
left. They walked in silence along the corridor to his
room, and she found herself wondering how she would
view her recklessness in the morning.

He shut the door behind her and she half expected
him to pull her into his arms and kiss her, but he didn't.
Instead he walked to the opposite side of the room,
away from her, and gestured towards the fridge.
'Champagne?' he asked, and he sounded almost
distracted.

'I thought you said that you were on call.'

'I am. I'm not having any—but you can.'

'Don't open a bottle just for me.'

'Oh, for God's sake!' he exploded, and his face was
a mask of tight, angry lines. 'Nine years of wanting and
waiting and we're standing making inane comments
about what we are or what we're not drinking, like two
people who've just met at a cocktail party!'

She found his savagery exciting, perplexing, but disturbing too. She realised suddenly, for the first time,
that deep, dark, angry emotions ran beneath the outwardly urbane sophistication which was Randall's
trademark. She did not know what she had expected
when she came here tonight, but it had certainly not
been anger. 'Perhaps I'd better go,' she said curtly.
'You brought the subject up, after all. You offered me
champagne, but I don't really care if I have any of not.

I was under the impression that you wanted to talk. However, if you *don't* want to talk——'

'No,' he whispered, and his eyes glittered with dark, devastating fire. 'You're quite right—I don't want to talk, Kelly, In fact, talking's the last thing on my mind right now. Because I want to make love to you. All night long, and every other night of my life. You must know how much I want you, Kelly. How badly.'

She felt her body react instantly to the raw passion in his words. She felt the hot sweetness of desire, the full flooding to her breasts as he spoke.

'You *do* know that, don't you, Kelly?' His voice shuddered on a sigh, but still, to her surprise, he had not moved. And thank God he hadn't—for after that stark avowal of need that had thrilled her to the core of her body, would she have been able to resist him if he had come to her; taken her into his arms; kissed away her doubts and replaced them with fire and with passion?

She sat down in an armchair and made her mind focus on one of the water-colours on the wall. It was not hospital issue; he had obviously brought it with him. There were several more by the same artist. She liked them very much, and then she saw, with a tearing wrench of her heart, that one depicted his family home. Seton House.

He followed the direction of her gaze, then let his eyes fall on her white cheeks, her widened eyes. He came to kneel at her feet, to take both small frozen hands in his own.

'Yes, I know,' he said. 'That beautiful summer.'

But the tears, refusing to be suppressed any longer, had risen up in her throat, sparkling saltily in her big green eyes. She forced the question, knowing that if it was never asked, then any future with Randall would stop right here.

'Why did you leave me like that, Randall?'

His mouth twisted, as though he were in pain, as he expelled a breath of air on a long, long sigh. 'Because I was in love with you——'

His words made her so angry that she tried to get out of the chair, but he would not let her; the firm pressure of his hands was just too restricting.

'Don't lie to me,' she said huskily, a tear trickling down her cheek. 'Say what you want, but don't lie to me. I haven't come here to listen to your lies.'

He frowned. 'It was no lie. You knew how I felt about you. Everyone did—it was as obvious as life itself. And I knew what you felt about me——'

'Oh, yes,' she interrupted bitterly. 'You loved me so much that you ran off and left, without a word to say why.'

'But don't you realise why?' he asked softly.

'No. I don't.'

He glanced down at her hands, enclosed so warmly in his, then looked up into her face again. 'Let me tell you then, Kelly. I'd met hundreds of beautiful women in my life, but at twenty-four no one had ever remotely touched my heart. And then I saw you, and. . .' He gave a slow smile as he remembered. 'For someone who bordered on cynicism, who didn't believe in love at first sight, it came as something of a shock to me. Because when I saw you, that was it. Lights, stars, fireworks—the whole business.' He paused, as if searching for the right words. 'But everything was against it, us——'

'You mean that I wasn't an Honourable-something-or-other?' she put in caustically.

He shook his head. 'Darling, I really don't care about my title; I never have. Most of the time it's been a hindrance instead of a help—and certainly in medicine it's done me no favours at all. I told you. People tend to have preconceptions about you. Some women find it a turn-on, but how could a man respect a woman who was interested in him solely because he happened to have a title?'

'Which, presumably, was why you didn't tell me about it at first?'

He frowned. 'You know what the reason was. Not because I thought that it would attract you. I knew as soon as I looked into those beautiful big green eyes, that you weren't the kind of girl to be influenced one way or another. I didn't tell you because I didn't want you be intimidated by it—it *can* be intimidating,' he emphasised. 'And that *isn't* supposed to be patronising. I wanted one afternoon with you where all we needed to be were the people we really were. Underneath.

'And we had it. If I thought I'd fallen in love with you when you stood so wide-eyed and gorgeous carrying that ridiculous old suitcase, then I was certain after I'd spent the afternoon with you.' He shook his head slowly as he remembered. 'You were so bright and so passionate and so sweet. Very, very sweet. Unaffected.'

She let her eyelids flutter down to hide the confusion and the suggestion of tears which still threatened to fall, touched by the poignancy of his words, reluctant to let herself believe them.

'When I said I wanted to see you again, I meant it. I imagined us going out together while you went through medical school. And then, that night, when we almost made love, you said something which completely freaked me out.'

She stared at him in confusion, racking her brain to know what he meant. 'What?'

'You said, "You won't make me pregnant, will you?" Don't you remember?'

Yes. Come to think of it, she did remember. She had been haunted by a vision of someone she had been to school with, prematurely old and pushing a pram. 'Yes,' she affirmed. 'I remember. But——'

'It brought me to my senses,' he said savagely. 'And how! I thought about what we'd so nearly done. You'd told me all about your struggles to get your study taken seriously, how difficult it had been to persuade your parents to let you go to university, when none of your friends were going. I thought of all the sacrifices that they had probably had to make; would continue to have to make. And here was I, supposed to be a responsible medical student. Yet I almost made love to you, unprotected, without a thought for the consequences, because I was enraptured by you, so crazy for you. With a single act, we could have put your career to death before it had even begun. Didn't you realise that?'

'But that doesn't explain why you left without a word of explanation. We could have. . .' Her voice tailed off.

He understood immediately. 'Yes, we could have sorted out some contraception. We could have followed my original plan and continued to see one another when we were both back in London. But. . .'

'But?' she prompted, and she was now no longer afraid to look him in the eyes; something in his voice told her unequivocally that the words he spoke were true.

'I knew that if we did, the chances of it lasting were small. All the odds were against us. You were still at school; I was working hard at medical school. Romance would get in the way of study—not just yours, but mine too. And then I would have qualified, perhaps been sent to a hospital miles away, working a one-in-two, giving us little opportunity to spend time together. I could see all those things whittling away at our relationship, and I didn't want to risk it. You see, it was too precious to me. You were too precious to me, and I simply didn't want to risk losing you.'

Kelly felt some languorous flame of relief invade her body, like sweetest fire. 'Don't stop now,' she urged as he fell silent, the grey eyes studying her intently.

He gave her a sad smile. 'And so I decided to let you do what you'd always wanted to do—to succeed as a doctor, without bringing any undue pressures to bear on you. And then, only then, would I come back to find you.' He frowned. 'Kelly. Don't you realise that it wasn't just coincidence that brought me here to St Christopher's? I came here to find *you*.'

He had missed out on an obvious point of logic.

'But what if I'd met someone else along the way?'

He shrugged. 'That was a risk I had to take.' Then he gave her a wickedly arrogant smile. 'I was pretty sure you wouldn't.'

Her mouth twitched. 'What an ego!' she whispered in mock disbelief; but he was right and, what was more, he knew he was right. 'And what about you? What if you'd found someone else?'

His eyes were very soft. 'I knew I wouldn't.'

'Oh, Randall,' she said helplessly.

'What?'

Her mouth curved into a totally new and over-whelmingly exciting smile, that of a woman who had rediscovered her sensuality, and was about to have it awakened. 'Let's go to bed,' she whispered.

He murmured something sweet, profound and essen-tially shocking beneath his breath, and the raw words thrilled her. 'Kelly—you are an amazing woman, do you know that?' But he did not wait for her answer as he pulled her to her feet, put his arms round her and kissed her with a passion so intense that she felt she could die from the heady pleasure of it.

'Oh, my darling,' he whispered against her mouth. 'Do you know how many nights I've dreamed of this moment?'

'Yes,' she sighed helplessly, all reasoned thought deserting her as her fingers reached up to coil them-selves in the thick waves of his dark hair, then fell to rest possessively on the broad, powerful breadth of his shoulders. 'Oh, yes!'

His hand immediately slipped the body down from her shoulders to cup and smooth her bare breast with shocking and devastating intimacy as though he could not wait to caress her naked skin, but she did not care—they had both waited far too long for this—and she didn't want to wait a second longer. She wanted him now. Right now.

She began to tug impatiently at his tie, when a deafening alarm echoed through the room. They both froze in horrified disbelief as his emergency bleep shrilled with its persistent and ear-splitting sound from the pocket of his white coat.

CHAPTER EIGHT

'*HELL*!' exploded Randall, and swore softly and explicitly beneath his breath, but with an effort he got his breath back and picked up the telephone immediately, giving Kelly a rueful and frustrated glance as he waited.

She brushed her hand back through her ruffled hair, her own pulse starting to slow down to normal as she gazed on the ruffled black splendour of his hair, and the way that his tie was all awry. Oh, God—how she loved him!

'Seton here,' he said, then listened.

Kelly could see at once that whatever he was being bleeped for was serious, because he slammed the receiver down in its cradle and headed for the door. 'Sorry, darling,' he said swiftly. 'They're bringing an RTA into A & E.'

The shorthand of hospitals, so familiar. RTA—road traffic accident—one of the more horrific abbreviations. Kelly winced. 'Bad?'

He nodded, his expression tight. 'It seems so. Four teenagers. The fire brigade are cutting them out now.'

'Oh, God.' Realising from the way he was looking at her that she was still in a state of partial undress, Kelly glanced down and immediately pulled the body back up over her naked breasts, her eyebrows creased together in a frown as she realised that, because it was a week night, there would only be one casualty officer

501

on duty. And that meant that there would be insufficient cover if the accident was really bad.

'You go on down,' she said to Randall briefly. 'I'll get my coat. I might as well come and help.'

'OK.' He gave her a brief, warm smile before he was gone, and then she ran out of his room and into her own, slipping into a sweater and some flat, comfortable shoes and quickly pulling on her white coat.

She ran down the corridor to A & E. For once running was permissible, since the old hospital rule still carried: Never run except in cases of fire or haemorrhage—and with four kids being cut out of a car by the fire brigade, there was sure to be haemorrhage. . .

Kelly arrived in the department, which seemed abnormally quiet, and the first person she saw was Harry Wells—automatically in charge of the department since he was the casualty officer on duty.

'I've come to help,' she said immediately.

He nodded. 'Randall told me.'

'What do you want me to do?'

'We're waiting for the ambulances to get here. Can you see if the night sister has arrived yet, and ask her to organise some extra nurses? We're going to need someone to cope with relatives. Then come and help deal with the casualties.'

'OK,' said Kelly. She sped off and relayed Harry's message to the duty night sister who had just arrived. 'It's going to be pretty bloody in there, so make sure that the relatives are kept well away, won't you, Sister?' she said quietly. 'And could you ask the receptionist to put out an announcement that all minor injuries may have to wait some time?'

'Sure. You can bet that all the minor injuries will be up in arms, though,' said the night sister cynically.

Then Kelly went swiftly back towards the resuscitation room just as the eerie blue light heralded the arrival of the first ambulance, and she immediately ran forward to join a small group of doctors who were at the door to greet it, stopping when they saw the expression on the ambulance man's face.

His face was white with an almost sickly green tinge, the sombre expression in his eyes conveying some of the horror he must have witnessed that night. And suddenly Kelly realised that the accident was very bad. Ambulance drivers were among the bravest and hardest working of the paramedics. The things they saw would make most people sleepless for a month. Kelly knew this particular officer too. He had been on the job for almost a decade, with a reputation for being calm and unflappable. And yet tonight he looked as shocked and appalled as the newest recruit.

'Who's the casualty officer?' he said blankly, and Randall and the others began to move away, aware of what was coming next.

Harry stepped forward. 'I am.'

'There's a. . .' His voice tailed off. He swallowed. 'DOA in the back. If you could. . .certify her, Doctor— then I can take the body straight down to the morgue. I feel I should warn you that. . .' His voice lowered; he looked around, as though afraid that relatives might be within earshot, even though he knew that all relatives were banned from this area of the department. 'She's been decapitated.' His voice broke then. 'Only about seventeen, and she's been decapitated.'

Harry went straight out and climbed into the back

of the ambulance, and Kelly instinctively put an arm on the driver's shoulder. He was shaking quite badly. 'Go and get some tea,' she urged, 'after you've driven to the morgue. Don't go out on the roads until you've had something for shock. Do you understand?'

'Yes, Doctor,' he mumbled, like a polite child, and went back to his waiting vehicle.

And then came the sickening cacophony of noise which meant that more than one ambulance was pounding its way towards them.

After that it was mayhem and afterwards Kelly was only able to recall fragments of the long night.

People running around. People calling urgently to one another as trolleys with blood-stained sheets were being brought in.

Perhaps an outside observer might have found it all fragmented and disorganised, but every doctor and every nurse was rallying together as they had all been taught, to work at full stretch, with only the most essential words being spoken.

As Kelly helped push a trolley into the resuscitation room, she could see that already two grim-faced policemen stood, waiting for the all-clear from the doctors before they could interview any of the passengers.

Kelly looked down at the stretcher as they ran, trying to assess visually any obvious injuries before she had the chance to examine the patient. Amid the long, tangled hair and the caked blood she could see a girl of painfully tender years. She looked barely sixteen, her face almost colourless, the eyes closed, but with the strange, indefinable cast which differentiated sleep from unconsciousness. Kelly's face paled as she saw the crimson flowering of blood spreading ever wider on the sheet.

They bundled her into the large room, just as another trolley was brought in close behind.

'Over here, please!' Kelly said to the porter, and together they pushed the trolley into a spare space. Randall was already in there bending over another trolley, his houseman and a nurse by his side, all working urgently, their faces intent, disturbed.

The night charge nurse came straight over to Kelly's trolley. 'Can you do her observations, please,' she said, automatically pulling on a pair of latex gloves, since they all had it drummed into them night and day not to expose themselves to possible infection by blood.

Although the situation was grave, it was also very simple. In an emergency of this type, only the bare essentials of life-saving were relevant. It was necessary to maintain a clear airway, to stop haemorrhaging, and to replace the volume of fluid already lost before the body went into irreversible shock.

'Have the crash team been bleeped?' called Kelly.

'They're on their way,' someone called back.

At that moment, an anaesthetist from the crash team arrived. 'Someone else is on their way—who needs me most?'

'I do!' called Kelly. 'This girl needs intubating.' She allowed him access to the patient's head, and meanwhile she stripped the sheet off to seek the source of the blood. It was not difficult. Immediately a great red gush pumped out of a long gash in the arm, its bright colour and the force at which it was expelled meaning that it could only come from an artery.

'Get me some suction and an artery clip,' said Kelly

quickly. 'And can someone else try and find a vein to get a line in?'

By now the rest of the crash team had arrived, and behind them, the orthopaedic team. The room was bursting with people.

'Any fractures?' called the orthopaedic registrar.

The charge nurse working with Kelly nodded. 'Here,' he said. 'Her leg's lying at an awkward angle.'

The orthopod strode over and ran his gaze over the limb with an experienced eye. 'Classic compound tib and fib,' he muttered. 'How's her general state?'

'Not brilliant,' admitted Kelly, as she pushed the suction catheter out of the way. 'She's lost a lot of fluid and—oh, *good*—I've got the clip on! Now let's get some fluid into her, and can we do some neuro obs on her, please?'

But one crisis averted soon made way for another.

'Cardiac arrest!' called Randall's houseman urgently, as the boy's heart went into ventricular tachycardia.

The crash team went into action.

Drugs were drawn; injections given.

'He needs shocking! Everyone stand back!' ordered the medical registrar as he clamped the paddles on to the boy's bare chest.

They all waited while the boy's body was jerked upwards by the electrical current, and Kelly heaved a sigh of relief as she watched the monitor and saw the wavy erratic lines of ventricular tachycardia give way to a normal sinus rhythm.

Randall, who had been quiet, now spoke urgently to Damian, his houseman. 'This boy's bleeding internally. Can you ring Theatres? We're going to have to get him up there right *now*.'

'Right.'

'And ring ITU. Tell them we're going to need at least two beds. We hope,' Randall finished grimly.

Kelly did not know how long it took for everything to go back to normal. Patients were removed one by one, two to Theatres and one to the ward. The other lay cold and silent in the hospital morgue. Nurses began to clear away the debris—the bloodied sheets, the discarded needles, the empty syringes and used intravenous bags.

Tiredly Kelly made her way to the cloakroom where she scrubbed at her hands and her face, and tried to put the whole incident out of her mind.

It was easier said than done. One dead; one had almost died. The girl she had looked after had a badly broken leg and a wounded arm, but hopefully would recover. With Randall's case of internal bleeding, a sure diagnosis was never possible until the patient had been opened up in Theatre, assessed and then operated on.

She was just coming out of the cloakroom when she almost bumped into Harry, a grim look on his young face.

'I was waiting for you,' he said, without preamble.

'Why?'

'I wanted to—thank you. You didn't have to come in.'

Kelly shook her head. 'I'm glad that I could be of help.'

'Kelly,' he said slowly.

'What?'

'Can I ask you a—favour?'

'That depends on what it is.'

'Come here.' And he led her into an empty office, shutting the door firmly behind them and turning to face her once inside. 'That girl I certified, in the ambulance.' He swallowed. 'Her parents are waiting in the relatives' room.' He paused, and then it all seemed to come out in a rush. 'Kelly—can *you* tell them about their daughter?'

Kelly shook her head, her eyes bright. 'Don't ask me to do this for you, Harry. Please.'

'*Please*,' he said starkly. 'I know what you're probably thinking—that I'm asking you because you're a woman, and that relatives take this news better from women. But it isn't that. I've never shirked anything like this before but, so help me, I can't tell them. Kelly, I just *can't*! I can't face them. But you can. You didn't . . .have to. . .*see* her. . .' He swallowed convulsively; he was actually shaking. 'But I did. And I don't want them to know—how—what it was like,' he finished in a rush, almost in tears.

Kelly dropped her head in her hands, understanding Harry's dilemma immediately. It was true, she hadn't seen the girl; there would be no horror or revulsion on her face. Nothing which would intensify the grief of the parents even further. She knew, as they all did, that it was well recognised that how bad news was broken was tremendously important in how relatives managed to come to terms with their grief.

She nodded, her heart heavy, as she prepared for the very worst that the job could throw at you. 'Very well,' she said quietly. 'I'll go and do it.'

Kelly let herself into her room after midnight, glancing at Randall's door as she did so; but there was no light beneath it, and she assumed that he was still in Theatres, operating. Inside her room she immediately went to pour herself a small glass of brandy, swallowing it in one, the fiery liquor bringing a little warmth back into a body which felt frozen like ice.

It had been one of the worst experiences of her life, to have to tell those parents—themselves still only in their late thirties—that their only daughter, their pride and joy, lay dead. All because a foolish car journey in a high-performance vehicle which had been stolen by the daughter's 'friend', had ended in tragedy. The driver had been going hopelessly fast down a narrow country lane. And, according to blood tests, he had been drinking. But of course Kelly had not told the parents *that*. Thankfully, that was not her task—that particularly onerous burden was left in the hands of the police.

Instead, in words which were heavy, carefully and painfully spoken, she tried to convey, in the best way she could and as she had been taught, that their daughter was never going to be coming home to them again.

Best? Derisively, she kicked off her shoes, not caring where they fell. How could *any* way of telling them be the *best* way? A young life snuffed out, and for nothing. Kelly thought that she would remember the terrible keening sound that the mother had made for the rest of her life.

By the time she had showered and got her hair dry it was late, and she yawned, looking at her watch to see, without surprise, that it was past one o'clock. She really ought to think about going to bed, and yet she needed to see Randall, quite badly.

She slithered into a pair of jade-green satin pyjamas, put some Chinese embroidered slippers on her feet, and padded along to his room. It still lay in darkness, but it was unlocked, and she remembered that he had left for A & E before her, and she had run out without thought of security in the face of a medical emergency.

He could be a minute; he could be an hour. She yawned again, before deciding that she might as well be comfortable while she waited for him. So she climbed into his bed and wriggled around a little, burying her nose in the pillow, like a dog hungry for its master's scent. And she *could* discern that particular heady, masculine aroma which was all Randall—soap and lemons, with some seductively musky undernote. A scent long-forgotten and tonight rediscovered in his arms.

Hurry up, Randall, she thought sleepily, but her lids were growing heavier and heavier. She would close them just for a minute. . .

When she woke it was starting to get light. The recognisably pale and cold light of dawn filtered through her still-closed lids, and she could hear a faint sound in the room. She opened her eyes by a slit, to see Randall standing over the sink, shaving, and that the sound had been the faint rasp of the razor over the dark shadow of his chin. He was wearing nothing but a pair of trousers, his chest bare. Through the mirror she could see the dark whorls of hair which grew there. His back was brown and broad and muscular and, oh, she could have lain in bed for a year just feasting her eyes on him.

'Hello,' he said, a smoky note of amusement in his voice.

She sat up, her mouth relaxing into a soft smile as she realised that the horror of the night was over; the new day was just beginning. 'How did you know I was awake?'

He turned round. The grey eyes were soft, the expression in them thrilling her to her very soul. 'I could tell—your breathing changed, almost imperceptibly, but I noticed. And in sleep your face goes very, very soft. Do you know that your eyelashes actually brush your cheeks, they're so long?' He said this as though it were the single most fascinating subject in the world.

'What time is it?'

'Five.'

Five! She had to be at work in an hour! 'And I have to be at work at six,' she said mournfully.

'I know.' He came to sit on the bed, but he kept his distance, she noted, and began to wonder if last night in his arms had in fact all been just a dream.

'What happened to your patient?'

He grimaced. 'He died on the table about two hours ago.'

'I'm so sorry,' she whispered.

'Yes.'

She suddenly felt a fool for being here; he had not touched her. 'What time did you get back?'

'At about three-thirty.'

Her cheeks went pink. He hadn't...got into bed with her?

'No, I didn't join you,' he said, with a tender smile,

as though she had actually spoken her thoughts aloud to him. 'I've been watching you instead.'

'Watching me?'

'Uh-huh.'

After nine years, coyness was a slight waste of time. 'So you didn't want to get into bed with me?' She couldn't mask the disappointment in her face.

'Of course I did, you foolish woman—but what I *didn't* want was my damn bleep going off at a crucial moment after all this time! I've waited nine years for you, Kelly. I can wait a little longer. And we'll take just as long as you like.'

She couldn't think of anything worse!

She pushed the thick waves of dark red hair off her face. 'So what happens now?'

'You get up, because you're on duty any minute. I'm going to leave you to get dressed——' his eyes gave a rueful glint '—because I don't think I quite have the control to witness you doing *that* impassively. And tonight I'm taking you somewhere spectacular.'

'OK then,' she murmured demurely and pushed the bedclothes back, but she saw the dramatic darkening of his eyes as he watched the unmistakable outline of her breasts and long thighs beneath the jade satin which clung to every soft curve of her body.

'On second thoughts,' he said, in a voice which held the husky note of desire, 'come here.'

'Why?' she asked innocently.

'Why do you think?' he groaned, and pulled her on to his lap, his hands tangling in the rich cascade of auburn hair, before bending her head down to kiss him.

And the kiss obliterated every dark and dreadful

thing, leaving her almost mindless with delight as he pushed her back down on the bed, coming to lie beside her.

They lay there for exquisite, timeless moments, kissing with such fervour, as though they were trying to make up for all the long years apart, until she was moving restlessly against him, aching with frustration, feeling from the tension in his body that he felt just the same.

'Shall we,' he murmured, 'get beneath the covers for a little while?'

'Yes,' she whispered, her heart racing out of control.

But once in bed, it seemed very difficult for Randall not to start undoing the buttons of her pyjamas, one by one, and stroking her breasts with a sweet skill which made her moan softly. And then he was sliding the pyjama bottoms off, and her hands seemed to be on the belt of his trousers, pulling frantically at the zip, until all their garments were kicked out of the bed, and he was naked and glorious and he moved to lie on top of her, his eyes dark as night with passion.

'You witch,' he groaned. 'You beautiful, tempting. . .' But the sentence was never completed because he had started to make love to her in a way which surpassed every dream she had ever had about him. And he did not need to finish the sentence for Kelly to understand, because she knew that—in his own delectable way—he had been telling her that he loved her. . .

CHAPTER NINE

'DARLING! Wake up!'

It was a sexy voice, a deep voice. Through the mists of her heavenly dream, it sounded awfully like Randall's voice. Consciousness seeped back into her body and she came awake to find a pair of beautiful grey eyes looking down at her.

'Hello,' he said softly, and bent his head to kiss her.

'Hello,' she said, smiling—widely, foolishly, and idiotically most probably, but who cared? She felt the amazing, unfamiliar aching deep inside her, which somehow seemed to be what her body had been waiting for all her life.

'You've got about ten minutes to get yourself dressed and down in A & E,' he reminded her softly.

'*Hell!*' She kissed him quickly and jumped out of bed, hunting around the room for her pyjamas and beginning to scramble back into them.

He lay on his back, just watching her, his head resting in the cradle of his palms, his eyes narrowed with appreciation. 'You know,' he murmured, 'I think I shall always have to make you run late for work, if it means that you're going to run around the room naked like that.'

She threw him a look. 'I'll make you pay for that, Randall Seton!'

'I can hardly wait!' he laughed.

She reached for the door-handle. 'I must go.'

'Kelly?'

'Mmm?'

'What would you like to do tonight?'

She grinned. 'The same as you, I shouldn't doubt.'

He laughed again and she glowed inside at the richness of the sound. Heavens! Were all women as soppy as this when they fell in love?

'Bye,' she said softly, and opened the door.

'Oh, Kelly?'

She turned round. 'What?'

'Do you know how much I love you?'

She smiled, never as happy in her entire life as she was at that moment. 'I think I have a pretty good idea,' she whispered, soft colour stealing into her cheeks at the way he was looking at her. 'Since I feel exactly the same way. And now I'm going,' she said firmly, appalled at the way she wanted to do nothing more than go back to his arms and spend the day in bed with him.

She dressed in record time, and made it to A & E with seconds to spare, only to see Harry looking extremely surprised to see her there.

'I thought you'd be late,' he protested. 'I was quite prepared to cover for an extra couple of hours.' He paused. 'I owe you one, after last night.'

'Thanks very much for *telling* me that last night,' said Kelly ruefully, thinking that she *could* have spent, if not the day in bed with Randall, then at least an extra couple of hours.

She sipped the coffee which Harry handed to her, her cheeks going pink as she remembered Randall's reaction when she had told him that there had been no other lover; that he was her first. He had gone very quiet, and said, 'I wish that you were mine.'

At which point she had whispered, 'Well, I don't. Because you probably wouldn't be so good at it.' And he had kissed her so deeply in answer to that. But afterwards she had not been able to stop herself from weeping a little bit, saddened by all the years they had been apart.

She was woken out of her daydream by the arrival of a male nurse who poked his head around the office door apologetically. 'There's a back injury in cubicle one,' he said, and Kelly immediately put her half drunk coffee on the table and followed him down the corridor.

The patient was a young man aged seventeen. He was lying flat on the trolley, his neck constricted by an orthopaedic brace, his brown eyes wide and worried.

Kelly went and bent over him, so that he could easily see her. 'Hello.' She smiled. 'What's your name?'

'Gary,' he replied. 'Gary Webber.'

'Well, Gary——' Kelly's fingers rested lightly on his pulse '—what have you been doing to yourself?'

He grimaced. 'We were playing with a frisbee—me and a few mates. It landed on the roof of our shed. I climbed up to get it down, and I sort of lost my footing, and slipped.'

'And how high was the shed, do you think?'

He said. 'Dunno. Twelve feet, maybe?'

Kelly nodded. 'And when you fell, did you hit your head?'

'Yeah. I put my hand out to save myself, but I caught the side of my head on the barbecue.'

'Did you lose consciousness?'

'No.'

'Good. And did anyone move you?'

'No. One of my mates said I should stay still until the ambulance arrived. So I did.'

Kelly smiled. 'Sounds as if you've got a very sensible mate, Gary.'

Kelly heard the fear in his voice as he asked the question. 'Am I going to be paralysed, Doctor?'

It was always one of the most difficult things to answer, especially before you had examined the patient. 'I don't know,' she replied honestly. 'We're going to have to do a few tests to find out what you've damaged.'

He winced. 'Can I have something for the pain?'

'Not yet,' said Kelly. 'We need to do some neurological observations first. Even though you didn't actually lose consciousness, we still have to be sure that there's no swelling in the head. Or indeed any fracture to the skull, so I'm going to order a skull X-ray to rule that out. You also need an X-ray to your spine.' Kelly took a pin from the pocket of her white coat and held it up. 'And I'm going to do a couple of tests of my own. I'm going to prick the sole of your foot with this pin. I want you to tell me whether you can feel it. OK?'

'OK.'

Kelly lifted the sheet and pricked his foot.

'Ouch! *Ouch!*'

She smiled. 'That's a good sign,' she remarked, as she then took the patella hammer from her pocket. She scraped the pointed end down the length of Gary's foot, pleased to see the big toe jerk upwards—a sign that there was no spinal damage, although not conclusive. An X-ray would be needed to confirm that.

Kelly scribbled out an X-ray form and handed it to the staff nurse, then bent over Gary again.

'We'll get you up to X-ray as soon as we can and, in the meantime, will you promise me that you'll continue to keep as still as possible?'

He gave her an engaging smile, encouraged by her gently confident manner. 'You bet!'

Kelly was just suturing an elderly man's head when the nurse informed her that Gary was back from X-ray, and Kelly grinned widely as she read the radiologist's report on the X-rays to his skull and spine.

She went into cubicle one, where Gary's mother and girlfriend were now seated on either side of the trolley, both looking extremely anxious. They glanced up as she walked in.

'Good news,' she told them straight away. 'You've sustained a hairline fracture to one of the vertebrae in your neck, Gary, but due to the quick thinking of your friend, by not moving you, there's been no damage done to your spinal cord.'

Gary's face broke out into a relieved smile. 'Does that mean I can go home, Doctor?'

Kelly shook her head. 'Oh, no. Sorry. You'll have to be admitted. It's strict bed-rest for you, my lad, for at least a month, I'm afraid.'

Gary groaned.

Kelly smiled at his mother. 'The other good news is that his skull X-ray was fine——'

'You mean it showed that he's got nothing between his ears?' queried Mrs Webber acidly, and Kelly laughed as she bent over the trolley once more.

'Just one other thing, Gary,' she said, her wide mouth twitching into a smile.

'What's that, Doc?'

'Why don't you take up marbles next time?' And Kelly gave his hand a squeeze before going off to examine a child who had lodged a bead up his nostril.

His mother was babbling nervously.

'He knows never to put anything up his nose, *or* ear!'

'It happens more often than you think,' said Kelly. 'What's his name?'

'Luke.'

'Hello, Luke!' Kelly smiled down at the wide-eyed toddler, noting that his right nostril was running with slightly blood-stained mucus.

' 'Lo!' he answered cheekily.

'Been putting things up your nose?'

'Lucy's bead——'

'Lucy's his big sister,' explained his mother.

'Just the one bead, was it, Luke?'

'Yes. 'Cos Mummy shouted.'

'I'm not surprised!' laughed Kelly. 'Are you going to let me take it out now?'

He nodded. 'Luke brave boy!'

Kelly grinned. 'I can see that! Well, I promise to be very quick. Could you fetch me the nasal tray, please, Nurse?' The nurse disappeared and, putting her hand into the pocket of her white coat, Kelly took out a tiny, fluffy white teddy-bear, and held it out towards Luke. 'This is Harry,' she said. 'Once he got a bead stuck in *his* nose, so he knows what it feels like. Would you like to hold him for me?'

Luke nodded, and his plump little hand clutched the toy immediately.

When the nurse returned, Kelly dilated the nostril

with some nasal prongs and, once she had located the bead, she slipped a slim pair of forceps up the nostril and withdrew the foreign body easily.

Luke's mother breathed a huge sigh of relief. 'Oh, *thank* you, Doctor! Thank you!'

'OK, Luke?' asked Kelly, as she pointed to the bright yellow bead which now lay in the kidney dish.

'Luke keep Harry!' he asserted, and hugged the teddy into his chest.

'*Luke*!' reprimanded his mother, but Kelly shook her head.

'Let him keep him,' she said, then lowered her voice. 'I keep a job lot of them for occasions just like this!'

The mother beamed. 'Got any of your own, Doctor?'

Kelly blinked. 'Sorry?'

'Kids! You're very good with them!'

'Oh, heavens, no—I'm not even married!' But to her horror, Kelly found herself blushing furiously, and she didn't dare stop to analyse why.

Life, she decided, had settled into a blissful, if somewhat erratic, pattern. She spent every moment she could with Randall, though these moments, frustratingly, proved not enough for either of them, since their duties often seemed to clash. Randall's senior registrar was on holiday for three weeks and, due to hospital economies, the management did not get a locum to replace him. Consequently, Randall's workload was about to be almost doubled.

So he reported back to Kelly, his face tight with anger, after a confrontation with Warren Booth in his office,

'Half of me wonders whether this isn't personal,' he

told her, as the waiter poured them both a glass of Bardolino in the small Italian restaurant they had come to think of as 'theirs'.

Kelly paused in the act of chewing a bread stick. 'You're not serious?'

He shrugged. 'Aren't I? He knows we're seeing one another, and I don't think he's ever forgiven either of us. Believe me, Kelly, there's a way he has of staring at me with those pale, mean little eyes of his.' He shuddered. 'I really think he's a man with problems.'

'I'm sure you're imagining it,' said Kelly. But she remained slightly uneasy, wondering if there wasn't a kernel of truth in what Randall said.

And besides, she too had had her fair share of hostility, because if Marianne Higgs had been rude to her before she had started going out with Randall, then she was now doubly worse. But the staff nurse was very subtle, and her rudeness was never in front of anyone else; indeed she was actively over-zealous in being polite towards Kelly when they had an audience. And Kelly didn't know how to cope with it; she wasn't sure that the nursing officer would believe her if she complained. After all, it was only her word against Marianne's. And there was also something defeatist about a female doctor complaining about a nurse, especially when none of the male doctors had any complaints. Little whispers of bitchiness tended to fly around the place.

She told Randall, of course, but he brushed off her concern, in the same kind of way she had brushed off his about Warren. 'You're only working there for the next four months,' he pointed out, quite reasonably. 'What harm can she possibly cause you in that time?'

And, speaking of the next four months, Kelly still hadn't fixed herself up with a job to go to for the next part of her GP training scheme. That was something else she intended to discuss with Randall...that she was having second thoughts about giving up surgery.

One night Randall was so busy on call that he did not get to bed at all, and only managed to get back to the room at six a.m., his face tired, dark shadows beneath the grey eyes.

She woke up immediately, holding her arms open to him, and he came over to the bed and gathered her in his arms, stifling a yawn as he did so.

'Thanks!' she teased. 'Are you bored with me already?'

His answer was to kiss her so thoroughly that she was left in no doubt whatsoever about his feelings for her!

'Come to bed,' she murmured huskily.

He shook his head regretfully. 'Can't. I'm due up in Theatre in ten minutes.'

'Damn!'

He gave her a hint of his devilish smile, but she could see how weary he was. 'Never mind. We'll go and have an early supper, then come back here and find something to do,' he finished, on a murmur.

Kelly gave a little grimace. 'We can't.'

'*Can't?*'

'I'm working. Remember?'

He said something very explicit beneath his breath, then sighed. 'No. I'd forgotten.' Then he gave a wry kind of smile. 'Do you know, someone really ought to do a bit of research into whether the birth-rate among married doctors is lower than that of the general populace.'

Kelly looked perplexed. 'Why?'

'Because they never get a chance to have sex together,' he said ruefully, as his bleep went off. 'That's me due in Theatre. See you sometime tomorrow, darling. Save me an hour, won't you?'

And during these snatched moments, they met each other's parents. It had been Randall's idea.

'Why?' Kelly asked stubbornly.

'Don't be dense, Kelly,' he teased. 'Because that's what one does when one is in love.'

'*One*?' she teased back.

She took him to the tiny terraced house in Hammersmith where she had grown up, casting him little glances as they walked hand in hand together up the dusty pavement, just daring him to make any kind of caustic comment.

But of course he didn't.

He was charming and courteous as he stepped into the best 'front' room, rarely used by the family, but opened up for Randall's visit, with the smell of furniture polish so strong that it was almost overpowering.

Randall demolished a whole plateful of egg and cress sandwiches, much to her mother's obvious delight, and then proceeded to do justice to the old-fashioned seed cake she had baked. They sat and rather stiltedly made small-talk until the arrival of Kelly's sister, Jo, who was clearly curious to meet Kelly's highly connected boyfriend. She came with her two small children, which immediately broke the ice, and the next hour was spent wiping noses and removing small china ornaments from their sticky fingers.

Randall—naturally—charmed both children, sitting them on a knee each and making up an outrageous story about the circus which had the two little boys giggling like mad. And when Kelly's father arrived, Randall accepted a glass of bitter with alacrity, and Kelly's mother even had a glass of sherry, so the whole affair ended most satisfactorily.

Until they got outside.

'You seemed to get on very well with them all,' said Kelly, as he unlocked the door of his car for her.

He caught her by the shoulders and gently turned her to face him. 'You don't sound very pleased about it,' he pointed out.

She hated herself for having the suspicion, but if you couldn't express your doubts and fears to the person you were in love with, then who else could you tell? 'You weren't—patronising them, were you?'

For a moment he looked extremely angry; a muscle worked in his faintly tanned cheek. 'No, Kelly, I was not,' he said quietly. 'And it rather sounds like *you* patronising me, if you have to ask questions like that.'

It was their first small disagreement, made worse by the fact that she was as nervous of meeting Randall's parents, who had agreed to see them on a flying visit on their way back from the Canary Islands.

Seton House looked magnificent in its autumn hues and when Kelly and Randall arrived there were two gardeners gathering up the fallen leaves. Against the sky she could see little puffs of smoke and the air held the smoky nostalgic tang of autumn, but more than that, Kelly felt as though she had been catapulted back into another age.

'It's such a different world,' she said in a low voice, but he heard her, and squeezed her hand tightly.

'I agree, darling. It is. But it isn't *our* world.'

But one day it would be, thought Kelly, as she went into the grand drawing-room to meet Arabella and Gideon Seton. One day Randall would inherit all this, and the house in France as well as the complex in New York.

Arabella Seton was blonde, ethereal and still beautiful, even though she was now in her late sixties. She had delicate bones and fine skin which was almost translucent. A thoroughbred of a woman, thought Kelly suddenly, feeling like a carthorse.

She looked Kelly up and down before giving her a glacial smile. 'Come and have some tea,' she said carelessly. Then, frowning, 'Do you ride?'

'No,' said Kelly stiffly. 'I'm afraid I don't.'

For a moment, Randall's parents both looked utterly shocked, as though Kelly had just admitted to some dark, dreadful secret. 'Oh, what a shame!' said Gideon Seton eventually, his ruddy complexion showing his own love of the outdoor life. 'Randall's quite brilliant in the saddle.'

Arabella patted the sofa beside her. 'Come and sit beside me, Kelly, and tell me all about yourself,' she said, then gave a delicate and perplexed little frown. 'Randall told me all about your people, but I don't believe I actually *know* them?'

It was torture; and as Kelly observed their cold demeanour she could scarcely believe how Randall had turned out to be such a gorgeously well-balanced man with parents like that.

Afterwards they drove home in Randall's sports car

in virtual silence, and it was not until they had parked
at the hospital that he turned to her.

'Are you going to speak to me now?' he asked
quietly.

'If you want,' she said, without looking at him.

'Kelly,' he said patiently.

She turned to face him, her green eyes dark and
huge in the gloom of the car.

'What is it?' he persisted.

'Don't you know?' she demanded. 'Can't you guess?'

'It's my parents?' he hazarded.

'Yes, it's your parents! Or rather—it's not. It's me!
They hate me!'

'They don't hate you; they hardly know you. It's
just——'

'Just what, Randall?' she asked dangerously.

He sighed. 'You're just not what they expected, I
suppose.'

'Or hoped for?'

'Probably not,' he agreed. 'But it isn't they who are
in love with you; it isn't they who are asking you to
marry them.'

'*What*?' she said disbelievingly.

'It's me,' he concluded softly.

'You want to get married?' she squeaked. 'To *me*?'

There was an unmistakable look of irritation on his
face. 'Of course I want to marry you!' he exploded.
'Just what did you *think* was going to happen? For
God's sake, Kelly, will you stop investing me with
some of the qualities which my ancestors might have
had! I am not exercising my *droit de seigneur*, you
know—spending every spare minute of my time making love to you before dumping you in order to marry

someone who's suitable! That is not,' he said grimly, 'what I am about. It has never been what I'm about and the sooner that you damned well accept that the better!'

She had never seen him so angry. They went to his room, where he almost ruthlessly took her clothes off and proceeded to make love to her with a skill which nearly had her weeping with pleasure, bringing her to the brink time and time again before he finally allowed her to collapse trembling into his arms. Afterwards, neither said anything, and Kelly stared at the ceiling thoughtfully for a long time after Randall had fallen asleep, bitterly ashamed because she knew that every word he had said was true.

He opened his eyes to find her studying him.

'What is it?' he asked.

'I'm sorry,' she whispered.

He shook his head and smiled. 'Don't be sorry, darling, just don't be silly. We love each other, that's all that matters.' He propped himself up on an elbow and looked down at her, smoothing back the thick waves of auburn hair from her forehead. 'You're tired,' he observed with a frown.

'Comes with the job,' she smiled, and with a gentle finger touched the skin beneath his eyes. 'And speaking of tiredness, what are these great shadows underneath your eyes? You're tired too.'

'Yes,' he yawned. 'I guess we ought to get some sleep, then?'

'I suppose so.'

But his hands were on her body, stroking her so that she moved ecstatically beneath his fingers, thrilled to the sweet plunder of his lips. Sleep was a long time in coming.

But over the next few weeks, their off-duties rarely seemed to coincide, and though they both tried very hard not to grumble about it, it put a strain on both of them.

One evening, Kelly was an hour from finishing duty when she had an emergency admission of a fourteen-year-old boy, whose GP was querying meningitis.

The boy was slightly dazed, but, other than that, showed none of the classic symptoms of meningitis, leading Kelly to believe that his GP was simply being over-cautious.

'Does your head ache?' Kelly asked him.

'God, yeah,' he muttered. 'Like hell.'

'Any neck stiffness?'

'No.'

'There's no sign of any rash on his trunk, and he doesn't seem to be at all photophobic,' observed Kelly to Joe as she shone her pencil torch in his eyes. 'Still, I'm going to get the medical reg down as soon as possible. He'll probably want to do a lumbar puncture anyway, to exclude——' But her sentence was never completed, for suddenly and without any warning, the boy collapsed and had a cardiac arrest.

Kelly pressed the emergency buzzer, and she and Joe immediately started resuscitation.

The crash team arrived, and they worked on the boy for an hour, but he was obviously very, very sick with septicaemia, and when at last they managed to transfer him up to ITU, there was very little hope that he would pull through.

Kelly could have wept with the unfairness of it, as she slowly made her way to Randall's room.

She sat down on the edge of the bed and kicked her shoes off, close to tears.

Minutes later in walked Randall. He came over and kissed her, his eyes taking in her pinched, pale expression. 'What's up?' he asked.

Kelly shrugged. 'Oh, just one of those awful, unrewarding days. You know.'

He sat down on the bed beside her. 'No, I don't know. Why don't you tell me about it?'

'Just that we had a fourteen-year-old sent in by his GP with some awfully vague symptoms. I didn't think there was much wrong with him at all—thought the GP was panicking. Then——' she let out a troubled sigh '—he went off—really quickly. One minute he was talking to me, and the next he'd arrested. We worked on him for an hour before we transferred him to ITU.'

'What was it?'

'Meningitis. The medical registrar had to tell the mother that there was only a twenty-per-cent chance of survival.'

'That's bad,' he murmured, his voice soft with sympathy.

She nodded. 'What's worse is that there's no follow-up, not for me anyway. That's one of the worst aspects about A & E. You treat people at the crisis point of their illness, and you never get to know what happens to them.'

'There's nothing to stop you ringing up ITU,' he pointed out.

'Do you think so?'

'Why not? He's your patient too.'

She thought about it. 'I'll ring tomorrow,' she decided. 'He's too close to crisis now, and the drugs will have had a chance to work by then.'

She hoped.

Randall was there the following day when she rang through to the unit and spoke to the sister in charge, and he didn't need to ask what the outcome was when he saw a smile like the sun coming up, lighting her exquisite face.

She put the phone down and hugged him.

'I gather that all is well?' he smiled.

She kissed him. 'Well, you know what they're like—cautious, but optimistic. But he's responding to the drugs they're giving him.'

Her worries abated, her attention was suddenly caught by the sight of a large cardboard box which was sitting on the floor underneath the window.

'What's that?' she enquired curiously.

He grinned. 'I thought you'd never ask!' And he walked over to pick it up, then handed it to her. 'Present.'

'For me?'

'That's right!'

Kelly looked up at him in bemusement. 'What is it?'

He smiled. 'To which he replies, "Why don't you open it and find out?"'

She took the top off. Inside were a pair of extremely sturdy brown leather boots. 'They're—er—lovely,' she ventured.

He laughed. 'Lovely they most definitely are *not*. What they are is functional.'

'And what are they for?'

'Walking.'

'Walking?'

'Mmm. There's a bank holiday next weekend. I thought I'd take you up to the Lake District.'

'Oh, Randall!' She threw her arms around his neck.

'Do I take it you're pleased?'

A long weekend alone with him, away from the hospital. It sounded like paradise. 'I can't wait,' she told him.

'Neither can I,' he agreed with a devilish glint in his eye, and slowly started to unbutton her shirt.

Marianne Higgs overheard them discussing their forthcoming trip the following day. Her blue eyes narrowed. 'The Lake District?' she asked. 'Whereabouts?'

She really was the nosiest girl, thought Kelly.

'Near Grasmere,' said Randall reluctantly.

Nurse Higgs tossed her splendid blonde head. '*Really*? Now that's a coincidence. My sister works at a hospital near Grasmere.'

Randall's eyes met Kelly's. 'I doubt we'll meet her,' he observed drily, 'since we aren't planning to go anywhere *near* a hospital.'

It was not until afterwards that Kelly was to remember those words, and be haunted by them. . .

CHAPTER TEN

I'M ABSOLUTELY *exhausted*!' Having just gingerly removed her sturdy walking shoes, Kelly collapsed back in the comfy sofa by the log fire which Randall was in the process of lighting.

'You look absolutely gorgeous,' he observed. 'Pink cheeks and sparkling eyes.'

'And I could eat a horse,' she said ruefully, idly reaching over to pull a red apple out of the bowl, and crunching into it. 'If you weren't such a slave driver, making me walk so far every day, I wouldn't be ploughing my way through such an enormous amount of food!' She sighed. Never had the prospect of returning to work seemed so gloomy. 'It's so heavenly here. I don't think I ever want to go back.'

The fire flared into life, and Randall sat back on his heels and watched her, the flames sending flickering shadows across his autocratic features. 'I know what you mean. I can't remember ever having enjoyed a holiday so much.'

They had been in the Lake District for three days, staying in the wonderful little cottage which Randall had rented. And it had been heaven. Days spent walking amidst some of the most beautiful scenery in the British Isles, and the evenings and nights spent making love. For the first time in her life, Kelly was actually dreading returning to work.

'It's hellish, us both being doctors, in a way,' she said

suddenly. 'We'll never lead a completely normal life. You do know that, don't you?'

He shrugged. 'What's normal? Anyway, there's not a lot we can do about it.'

'I suppose not.' Kelly sighed again. 'Unless I give it up.'

He frowned as he came and joined her on the sofa.

'You're not serious?'

The thought of not having to do a twelve-hour shift suddenly seemed awfully appealing. 'Why shouldn't I be serious? A hell of a lot of people go part-time.'

'Not women like you,' he said firmly. 'And besides, why should you *want* to go part-time?'

She kissed the tip of his nose. 'Men can be so dense sometimes,' she sighed. 'I'm talking about if we *do* get married——'

'When, not if,' he corrected her. 'And why on earth should that make you give up working, even if we have a family? You can always fit your work in around it.'

Kelly thought of all the juggling; remembered the last female consultant she had met, telling her how impossible it was to keep all the balls in the air at once and that something always suffered. 'One of us will have to compromise—and it'll probably be me.'

'And how do you propose compromising?' he asked quietly.

'As I said. By being a half-time GP, I guess.'

'You'll never get the intellectual fulfilment you need if you do that,' he pointed out. 'I thought so when you first told me you were switching from surgery, and I still think so.'

'Well, maybe there's more to life than intellectual fulfilment,' she objected.

'For some people, maybe; not for you.'

'Thanks for the vote of confidence.' She grinned at him and threw her apple-core into the fire with a perfect aim. 'It's just been great being with one another like this, rather than always having to snatch moments together. I don't relish going back to it. I—*ouch*!' She winced, her face whitening as her hand covered her abdomen.

Randall frowned. 'What is it?'

'Nothing. Just a pain. It's gone now.'

'Sure?'

She nodded.

'You shouldn't devour sour apples,' he teased.

'It wasn't; it was beautifully ripe,' she protested.

'Just like you,' he murmured, and pulled her into his arms.

But after they had made love, she felt odd—cold and trembly and then that sharp, bewildering pain stabbed again at her, but she did not tell Randall. There was little point in worrying him over what was probably nothing more than a touch of indigestion.

Randall cooked spaghetti for supper, but Kelly just picked lethargically at hers, and he saw her and frowned.

'So what happened to the gargantuan appetite you were boasting about earlier?'

'It's gone.' Her face felt pale; pinched.

'I can see that.' He laid his hand over hers, his eyes narrowed in concern. 'Darling, you are OK?'

She nodded. 'Of course I am.'

He sipped some wine, then put his head to one side and sat very still for a moment. 'How very odd.'

The pain had retreated. 'What is?'

'Listen,' he said softly.

Kelly blinked. 'To what? I can't hear anything.'

'Precisely. And what does that tell us?'

She gave him a rather wan smile. 'I give up!'

'Think what we've heard on other nights.'

No traffic drone, that was for sure. Perfect peace, apart from. . . 'The birds?' she guessed.

He nodded. 'Exactly. Remember we commented on how loud they sounded when they sang? But tonight there's nothing.'

'I'm the townie,' she smiled. 'I don't know if that's unusual or not.'

'Dramatically so,' said Randall quietly, and his voice had a quality of unease about it.

They were in bed when the storm started and Kelly never knew what woke her—the sound of the tree crashing to the ground in the garden of the cottage, or the pain in her abdomen which felt as though someone had ripped it open with a carving knife.

She opened her eyes to see Randall standing naked in front of the window, and became aware that there was a strange howling sound from outside the window, punctuated by another heavy thud of a falling tree. She wanted to get out and join him, but she realised that she could not move, the pain was so intense.

'Randall,' she croaked. 'What the hell is happening?'

'There's a storm outside and it's bad—very bad. I've never heard or seen anything like it in my life. We'd better sleep downstairs, darling. . .' He turned then, saw her face and was over by her side in seconds. 'Kelly? What on earth is wrong with you?'

She was trembling and sweating at the same time. 'I don't know. There's a pain—I, *oh*—Randall. . .'

He stripped the covers back. 'Easy, darling. Show me where.'

She let her hand vaguely brush at her side, then gripped her knees in an attempt not to cry out in pain.

With cool, expert fingers, Randall was carefully assessing and examining her.

With an effort she pushed her eyelids open, staring into his calm, impassive features. 'It's. . .appendicitis, isn't it?' she groaned.

'I'm afraid it looks that way.'

'Randall! What the hell are we going to *do*?' she wailed, for she knew that she would need an emergency operation which should not be delayed by a second if she were going to avoid the potentially life-threatening condition of peritonitis.

'You,' he said firmly, 'are going to be carried down on to the sofa, where you will stay and *not* worry. You will leave that to me, do you understand?' But his voice held some savage, grim note.

She felt weak; she felt helpless. 'Yes, Randall,' she said, knowing that if anyone in the world could right this awful situation, then he could.

He carried her downstairs, and a nauseating wave of dizziness swept over her and she was sick while he laid a cool hand on her forehead, then, afterwards, he picked up the phone, his features not altering as he listened. 'The lines are down,' he said shortly, 'as I expected.'

'Then what can we do?' she whispered.

'We wait.' He saw her face. 'Just until we are certain that the storm has abated. Half an hour will make little difference,' he said. 'But if we go out into the eye of the storm, then we risk something falling on us. As soon as I'm satisfied it's as safe as it can be, then we get you in the car and drive you to the nearest hospital. And pray that the roads aren't blocked by fallen trees.'

'But what if the storm—what if it doesn't stop?'

'Then we have to take the risk,' he said grimly, and put his long fingers on her wild and fluttering pulse.

But the storm did abate; that uncanny howling eventually died down and the horrible creaking and thudding were gradually no more.

Randall wrapped her up in blankets and carried her to the car.

She had no idea how long the journey took, of how many times Randall had to slow the car right down. Her only reality was the pain; the pain which just got stronger and stronger until it seemed to dominate her whole world like some malevolent demon.

It seemed hours later when she heard Randall mutter something beneath his breath, and the car pulled up to a halt.

Blearily, Kelly opened her eyes to see a bright sign saying 'Scanton Cottage Hospital'.

'At least they've got power,' said Randall, still in that strained, savage voice. 'Darling—wait right there.'

'I'm not going anywhere!' she managed to joke, then clutched at her abdomen again as the pain returned with a vengeance.

He was back within seconds, lifting her gently from the car, and the grim tense look on his face filled her with some nameless dread. 'Is everything OK?' she whispered.

'It's going to have to be,' he answered obscurely.

Everything became a blur; the pain eclipsed everything. A nurse came forward; a nurse with a familiar-sounding accent. Kelly stared up into blue eyes and frowned, puzzled, but then the pain came back and swamped her confusion. The nurse dressed her in a hospital gown and then she and another nurse were pushing her down the corridor on a trolley.

'Where is the porter?' croaked Kelly.

'No porters on duty tonight,' said the nurse.

Kelly didn't understand. Of course there must be porters—how else would they get patients to and from Theatre? And then they were wheeling her into the anaesthetic room and a very old man was smiling down at her.

'Don't you worry about a thing, my dear,' he said. 'We'll soon have you better.'

She felt the scratch of the needle on her hand, and then she saw the tall figure dressed all in green come into the room. He must be the surgeon, she thought.

He was so tall. He had broad, powerful shoulders. He looked familiar. The drug began to steal over her senses as the tall figure walked towards the trolley.

'Count backwards from one hundred,' instructed the anaesthetist in his kindly voice.

'Ninety-nine, ninety-eight,' she mumbled, her mouth falling open and stopping in confusion as she stared above the mask into the grey eyes of the surgeon.

Those eyes. . .

But it *couldn't* be.

Because those were Randall's eyes!

It was the worst experience of his entire life.

An operation he had cut his teeth on, like all medical students, a simple appendicectomy he could have done in his sleep. He had performed countless operations during his surgical career, operations far more difficult than this, and yet he felt like a complete amateur about to tackle the most complex micro-surgery imaginable.

'Is everything all right, Mr Seton?' asked the gowned and masked nurse at his side.

'Yes,' he said tersely, as he pulled on the pair of size nine gloves she had opened for him.

He held his hand out for the scalpel which she slapped into his palm, glancing up at the anaesthetist as he received it. 'Are you happy with her?' he asked him.

The anaesthetist nodded. 'Ready when you are.'

Knife to skin. . .

Randall lifted the scalpel and the blade flashed beneath the bright glare of the theatre lights. He felt the cold beads of sweat forming on his forehead, and instantly the nurse dabbed them away.

He felt the unfamiliar tremor in his hand as he prepared to make the first incision, trying to put out of his mind the fact that the area of flesh lying exposed and waiting was not the anonymous flesh of an ordinary patient. That was *Kelly* who lay there, *Kelly* whose very life depended on his skill and his impartiality.

He swallowed once more as he brought the scalpel down to make the first incision. . .

Randall's eyes, thought Kelly disbelievingly, as she swam back to life from her drugged sleep.

She blinked as she looked up to see the tall, dark figure of Randall Seton standing by the edge of her hospital bed, staring down at her, an unfamiliar expression on his face. He looked, she thought suddenly—distant. So remote and aloof, not like Randall at all.

Gingerly she put her hand beneath the bedclothes and lightly touched the dressing which covered her operation site.

'How do you feel?' he asked. But it was his doctor voice.

'Sore.' And her patient voice.

He nodded. 'You would do; it was a nasty appendix.'

'You did the operation,' she said quietly, and he gave a silent nod, his grey eyes narrowing.

'Randall—*why*?'

'Because there was no duty surgeon and the nearest hospital was over thirty miles away. There wouldn't have been time to get you there, even if the roads hadn't been all blocked—which they were. As it was, the only person who was available to anaesthetise you was the retired anaesthetist who fortunately lives very close to the hospital. He was, by the way, quite superb.'

'I see,' she said, very quietly.

'You're under the care of another doctor now.' He paused. 'Kelly, I'm going to have to go back to London and leave you here to recover properly. Do you understand?'

'Of course I do.' What she *didn't* understand was why Randall hadn't touched her; hadn't kissed her; and why he was standing with that cool and dispassionate look on his face which made him seem like a total stranger.

'I'm arranging to have you flown home, when they discharge you.'

'There was no need for that,' she said politely,

thinking that now they were even *talking* to each other like strangers.

'On the contrary,' he demurred. 'There's every need.'

He hesitated, as if he were about to say something, but when the word came out it only confirmed some niggling horrible fear which had just sprung to life in her heart. 'Goodbye, Kelly.'

She nodded. 'Goodbye, Randall.'

He was true to his word, and several days later Kelly was flown home on a private jet which Randall had hired, and taken by ambulance directly to her mother's house, where she was given her old bedroom.

She had not slept there for years, and it was very easy to cry herself to sleep, just as she had cried herself to sleep over him all those years ago. Because she knew without being told that it was all over between her and Randall. Something had died; she had seen that in his eyes the last time they had spoken, when he had stood over her hospital bed with that frosty remoteness on his face.

He did not come to visit her, not once, and Kelly was grateful for her mother's tactful lack of questioning as to why. She didn't know whether her miserable emotional state had anything to do with her slow rate of recovery, but it was a fortnight before she even *felt* like going back to work.

She left her parents' house and went back to the mess, where she bumped into Penny, her erstwhile squash partner who greeted her with the words, 'Are you better?'

'Much,' lied Kelly, not at all surprised by Penny's

next words, but profoundly shocked by them, all the same.

'Why did Randall leave so suddenly?' asked Penny curiously. 'Do you know?'

Kelly swallowed, the word invading her mind like an enemy. '*Leave*?' She spoke the word carefully, like someone struggling with a foreign language, but she needed to be clear that Penny heard it correctly, so that she could deny ever having said it.

Penny nodded. 'Yes. It was the talk of the hospital for days. He suddenly upped and resigned—left immediately. Don't tell me that you didn't know?'

Sick with grief and betrayal, Kelly shook her head. 'No, I didn't know. We didn't discuss it.'

'Was it all—over—between you then?'

Kelly nodded, willing the tears to stay at bay. 'Yes. It was.'

'And he operated on you, didn't he?'

'Yes. He did. Now, will you please excuse me, Penny? I really must go and lie down.'

Pushed under her door was a letter. She recognised the distinctive black handwriting on the envelope immediately. Wishing that she had the strength of character to bin it, she ripped it open with trembling fingers.

And she had been wrong; it was not a letter. For the envelope contained nothing more than a few words written on a piece of writing paper.

It said, 'One day, I will explain everything, Randall.'

'Oh, no, you bloody well w-won't, Randall Seton,' said Kelly aloud as she painstakingly tore the piece of paper into dozens of tiny pieces and let them flutter like confetti into the bin.

CHAPTER ELEVEN

KELLY glanced up at the video screen on the wall, and with great dexterity removed the gall-bladder through the sub-umbilical stab. Not for the first time in her career, she marvelled at all the great advances which surgery had made. 'Keyhole' surgery was fast and efficient, and left the patient with the tiniest of wounds, and she was one of its fiercest and most devoted fans.

'Thanks very much,' she smiled, as she completed the operation, glancing above her mask as one of the recovery nurses entered the operating theatre and approached the table.

'There's someone waiting to see you, Miss Hartley. A man. He's waiting in the staff-room.'

Kelly peeled off her surgical gloves and dropped them in the bin, then pulled the mask from her mouth and threw that away too.

'Any idea who?' she asked, as she left the operating theatre.

The nurse shook her head firmly. 'Sorry. He wouldn't give his name.'

'I hope it's not another drug rep?'

The nurse shook her head, then grinned. 'Oh, no. He certainly doesn't look like a drug rep.'

'Good. Well, would you tell him I'll be about ten minutes getting changed?'

'Yes, Miss Hartley.'

Kelly washed her hands, thoroughly exhausted but

exhilarated all the same. Life as a surgical registrar
took some beating! It had been a long list that afternoon, and what should have been a routine laparotomy
had developed all kinds of problems but, thankfully,
she had coped superbly.

Not for the first time, she marvelled at the dramatic
upturn of her life and her fortunes, astonished at how
satisfying she found her work these days.

In the two years since Randall had turned her life
upside down by leaving her for the second time, she
had worked, and worked hard, to achieve what had
always been her life's greatest ambition. And she was
now a surgeon, set on course for the top—or so her
boss kept telling her!

And if the one drawback was that once more she
had no one special in her life, she could only heave a
huge sigh of relief. She had been down that road, and
she knew now that she and love were totally incompat-
ible. Or rather, she and men were. She had resigned
herself to the fact that if she couldn't have Randall,
then she did not want anyone. A one-man woman, that
was her; it was just unfortunate that she had fallen for
the wrong kind of man.

She had missed him, of course. In the early days, it
had been absolute hell, trying to pretend that she did
not want to hear from him, yet desolate when she
didn't. But now the missing had become nothing more
than the occasional poignant pang of regret.

Only once, early on, had she tried to find out where
he was. She had been for supper with a pregnant
girlfriend, and had drunk almost all of the bottle of
wine they had shared. Egged on, she had telephoned
Seton House and someone who sounded awfully like

Mary, the cook, had answered. Swallowing her pride and knowing how much she was going to hate herself in the morning, Kelly asked if she knew where Randall was.

'Oh, *yes*, said the woman, and when she heard the familiar note of triumph in her voice, Kelly just *knew* it was Mary. 'Lord Rousay left for America almost a month ago. Was there any message?'

'No message,' Kelly had said tersely, replacing the receiver and breaking down in anguished tears.

Knowing that he had gone, there had seemed little point in pursuing her plan to go into general practice and so she had changed direction, channelling all her energy into her ambition, and managing to gain distinctions in both parts of her fellowship examination.

Going into the changing-room, Kelly quickly showered, then dressed in jeans and a silk shirt in softest coral. She brushed her hair vigorously, since the tight cap she had to wear all day to operate tended to flatten it. She had had her long hair cut to a more manageable shoulder-length, and it suited her. It was sleeker and more modern that the tumbling old style had been.

Snapping out the light, she walked slowly down towards the office, her thoughts miles away as she opened the door, when her startled eyes took in the tall, dark and elegant figure who stood facing her, the grave face still impossibly handsome. Like some betraying stranger, she felt her body stirring in response to the sight of him, and part of her wanted just to stand there and feast her eyes on him, like a starving man invited to make free at a banquet.

'Hello, Kelly,' came the deep, sonorous voice.

Her mind went into over-drive. She didn't want to hear what he had to say.

Did she?

She could go or she could stay. And half of her wanted just to run and run. But would running away not make him realise that he could still send her into a total spin, could still make her body ache and hunger for him, even after all he had done?

And what the other half of her wanted, she was horrified to discover, was very simple.

She wanted *him*.

It wasn't fair—it simply wasn't fair. She looked at him, lost in the silver-grey dazzle of his eyes, and realised that she wanted to find herself in his arms again, wanted his kiss, wanted him naked beside her, beneath her, covering her, filling her in the act of love.

She shuddered at her inherent lack of pride, determined that he would never know, and determined, too, to drive him away with a cool self-possession which would give him no hint of the turmoil of feelings he could still arouse in her.

'Hello, Randall,' she said coolly.

He gave her a long, slow appraisal, the silver-grey eyes telling her nothing whatsoever.

'I need to talk to you,' he said at last.

She managed to look faintly and superciliously surprised. '*Really*?' she queried. 'I can hardly imagine why.'

A frown appeared between the dark brows. 'Yes, you can.'

She gave him a condescending glimmer of a smile, pleased to have angered him. 'Well, I'm not going to get into a slanging match,' she murmured. 'So whatever it is that you want to say, why don't you just get it over with?'

He shook his head, his gaze taking in the bleak office. 'Not here.'

'Then I'm afraid that I won't be able to hear it, because I don't intend going anywhere else with you...' She started to turn away, when he moved quickly to catch hold of her, and she felt the hot tide of colour ride into her cheeks as she felt his touch on her skin.

'Don't you?' he mocked her, and didn't even give her a chance to answer, because he kissed her.

For a split-second she fizzed with resentment, and then her body yielded to him as surely as a sapling bending to the demands of the north wind. And the hard, almost brutal assault of his mouth immediately became transmuted into something softer and infinitely sweeter as he gentled the kiss, his tongue licking sensually at her lips until she gave a little moan.

The sound of that helpless little moan brought with it the mind-jarring crash of reality. She tore herself out of his arms, her eyes slitted with anger and spitting with green fire.

'How dare you?' she whispered. 'How *dare* you?'

'Quite easily.' He threw her a mocking glance. 'I enjoyed it and so, quite obviously, did you.'

Frustration and rage combined to make her lose her temper completely. 'You think that it's the answer to everything, don't you, Randall? Sex! You think that all you need to do is to kiss me and you'll have me eating out of your hand? Well, you're wrong! Oh, I might unfortunately still find you attractive. You're a very good lover, as I'm sure you've been told countless times. But it isn't enough for me!'

'What isn't?' he said quietly.

'I told you!' she glowered at him bitterly. 'Sex!'

'But I wasn't offering you just sex,' he said. 'I never have done. I'm offering you marriage.'

She lifted her hand to slap him, then froze with it mid-way to his face, staring down at it in disbelief that she had been provoked to violence by him, she who had never laid a finger on another soul in her life. So these were the depths to which he could make her sink. . .

'Just go away, Randall,' she said tiredly. 'Please.'

'No. Not until you've listened to what I have to say.'

'I don't *want* to listen! I don't trust you any more! I don't want even to associate with someone who says things they don't mean. Someone who goes away, and. . .' She broke off, aware that she was on the brink of tears.

'I had to go away,' he said quietly.

She met his stare full on, her chin lifted proudly in the air. 'And what was the excuse this time?' she asked sarcastically. 'More concern about my career?'

He nodded. 'That was one reason. There were, in fact, a number of reasons,' he told her.

Let him try and worm his way out of this one! 'Such as?'

He sighed. 'I'm trying to work out the best way to tell you, Kelly. And it isn't easy.'

She felt indignant that he even had the *nerve* ever to expect it to be easy! 'Oh, come *on*, Randall,' she taunted. 'You've never been stuck for words before!'

'Sit down,' he said curtly, and pointed to a chair, and then he added, quite gently, 'Please?'

His gentleness was her undoing, and she found herself sitting without thinking, watching him warily as he pulled over a chair and sat opposite her, just feet away.

He gave a long sigh as he remembered. 'When I arrived back here, leaving you in the Lake District, I was asked to go straight away to the hospital administrator's office.' His mouth twisted into a savage line. 'Our old friend, Warren Booth,' he said baldly.

Kelly blinked, then shuddered. Warren Booth. Good heavens, it seemed such a long time since she had heard her former boyfriend's name. And fortunately she had been spared the embarrassment of seeing him, since he had left St Christopher's shortly after Randall, under some sort of cloud, though she never did find out exactly what it was all about.

'And what did he want?' she asked reluctantly, her curiosity alerted by the serious expression on his face.

'He threatened to report me to the British Medical Council,' he said bluntly.

This was such a bizarre thing for him to say, that for the moment all Kelly's hostility towards Randall vanished. 'He did *what*?' she demanded incredulously. 'But *why*?'

'For operating on you.' His mouth thinned into a derisive line. 'He said that what I'd done was unprofessional, that I'd broken the laws of conduct, and that it was a flagrant abuse of power for a doctor to perform an operation on his girlfriend.'

'Good *grief*!' exclaimed Kelly in shock, as her mind tried to take in these astonishing facts. 'I don't *believe* it!'

He nodded. 'Oh, it's true all right.'

'But it isn't illegal to carry out an operation on a relative or a lover,' Kelly pointed out.

'Of course it isn't,' agreed Randall. 'But it can be open to legal action if it is thought that any impropriety has taken place. None had, of course, but that was the line of investigation which Warren was threatening to take.'

Kelly shook her head in bemusement. 'How did he find out that you'd operated on me?'

'You remember Marianne Higgs saying that her sister worked at a hospital in the Lakes?' he asked.

Kelly nodded speechlessly. Whatever next?

'Well, as fate would have it, it happened to be the one we ended up in that night. Marianne's sister actually happened to be the nurse who got you ready for Theatre; she even looked after you in the recovery room.'

Through the mists of memory, Kelly vaguely recalled seeing a pair of familiar-looking blue eyes.

'And she informed Marianne, who took it upon herself to let Warren know. It was a bit of a scoop to them both, since they were both bitter, Warren because of your relationship with me, and Marianne because I'd never taken her up on her numerous and frankly repugnant invitations to go out with her.'

What he had told her spun round and round in her head. 'But I would have died without that operation!' protested Kelly in a choked voice. 'We both know that!'

He nodded. 'Yes, we both know that,' he said quietly. 'And the road to the next hospital was blocked, so there certainly wouldn't have been the time or the means to transfer you to another hospital.'

She stared at him, not understanding. 'So why didn't you just fight it?'

'Because I didn't want to fight it. For a start, I didn't want to risk being suspended while it was all being investigated, or risk your career being affected by the accusation. And, yes, I would have won eventually, but mud sticks, Kelly,' he added quietly, if enough of it gets thrown about. I even spoke to a friend of mine on the Council, and he was the one who suggested that if I distanced myself from you for some time and let it all die down, then no one could say afterwards that there had been any kind of impropriety.'

Kelly had gone over and over that last dreadful meeting with him so often in her mind, that she could have repeated it word for word. Her eyes narrowed. 'But that day when you left me in the Lakes, when you came to see me—you were so cold, so distant. And that was before you say you were summoned to Warren's office. I felt that something had died between us.'

A look of regret clouded his eyes. 'And you were right, up to a point. Something between us had not died, but was in mortal danger,' he agreed. 'Which was another reason why I had to go away.'

Mortal danger? Kelly screwed her eyes up in confusion. 'I don't understand.'

He stared down at his long, surgeon's fingers for a moment, and when he looked up again, the grey eyes were rueful. 'It's just that the operation *had* changed something between us, and I was finding it very difficult to look on you as Kelly, the woman I loved and intended to marry. All I could see was the operation, playing over and over again in my mind. Of thinking that——' his voice shook a little '—that I was going to lose you. Of remembering what it felt like to actually *cut* you open with a scalpel,' he shuddered. 'And I didn't know if I'd ever be able to forget it,' he finished quietly.

Kelly nodded. 'I see. And were you—able to forget it? What am I now? Kelly the patient, or Kelly the woman?'

He smiled. 'You are Kelly, the living, breathing gorgeous woman whom I've missed with all my heart.'

And with these words, so honestly and beautifully spoken, Kelly felt the love which had never really gone away, burst into her her heart once more, and there was absolutely nothing she could do to stop it. 'Warren left shortly after you,' she said shrewdly. 'Did you have anything to do with that?'

'Not directly. But I let it be known that both you *and* I had had difficult dealings with him.' He saw her face. 'And, *no*, darling, I didn't go into details. I merely suggested that it might be an idea to keep a close eye on him. Which they obviously did. After all, someone who could use his position to achieve his own ends was obviously unstable. Not to mention what he'd tried to do to you,' he concluded grimly.

He leaned forward as though to take her hand, then paused, his eyes narrowing. 'But there was another reason for going too, even though on its own it wouldn't have been enough to make me leave.'

She nodded. She knew him so well that she had a pretty good idea what *that* was. 'Tell me,' she said softly.

'I felt there were still a number of issues we hadn't resolved. I could sense that you were regretting your decision to give up surgery and yet I also knew that you were reluctant to start on a course which would mean we had less hours together instead of more. It was your wish to be a surgeon battling against your wish to have a normal life. Ironically, I realised that all those years without you I had selflessly sacrificed——' he grinned '—to your career were about to be wasted, since you were considering chucking it all in just because we *were* in love. I remember that we spoke of compromise, and that you considered that you should be the one to have to make it, as women usually do. And I saw a way in which you wouldn't have to.'

She shook her head. 'I still don't understand,' she said, on a whisper.

'You will,' he promised. 'I suddenly realised that *I* could make the compromise. And that's what I set about doing. I've been in the States for the past two years, recruiting some of the finest research minds in medical science.'

She saw the passion and the commitment in his face, but she had absolutely no idea what was coming next.

'*Recruiting* them?' she echoed.

He nodded. 'I discovered that I had the answer to our dilemma. You may or may not know that I have a trust fund, set up for me by my grandfather when I was born. Piles of untouched money which I have no particular desire to spend, and which you've *certainly* got no interest in. So I've set up a research laboratory, which will be financed by my trust fund.'

'So you've just *given up* surgery?' she queried in disbelief. 'Just like that?'

He nodded and grinned.

'To administer a laboratory?'

He shook his head. 'No, Kelly, not to administer it. Someone else will do that. I intend to devote my time to pure research.'

'But what about surgery?'

'No.' He shook his head with determination. 'You see, I've had my *own* career crisis, and I'm afraid that I've had it with surgery. The more I did it, the less rewarding I found it. I felt like a mechanic, in truth. I wanted to start using my *brain* for a change, instead of my hands. And I'll be working much more sympathetic hours than you'll be doing. Research hours are regular, so if we have a family, then I can contribute a lot of time to the children.'

Now this *was* a lot to take on board. Kelly blinked 'Seriously?'

He met her eyes. 'Why not?'

'There's the famous male ego, for a start,' she observed drily. 'Won't you worry about what people think?'

He shook his head. 'Why should I? I'm brilliant and rich and handsome enough not to give a stuff about how other people perceive me.'

'You arrogant so-and-so!' she scolded, but she was grinning all the same.

His face went suddenly serious. 'I mean it, Kelly. I want our children to have the kind of life which I never did. I want them to have us, and our time and I don't particularly care which of us provides the *most* time. I want to be a hands-on father. I don't want them sent off to boarding school at the age of eight, miserable as sin and missing us like hell. Do you undersatnd that?'

She nodded, swallowing a lump in her throat as she tried to imaging his sterile childhood. Her own might have been poor in the material sense, but at least there had been plenty of love around.

'I'm so fired up by the research,' he continued, his voice vibrating with a passion and enthusiasm which was infinitely rare. And quite suddenly Kelly could easily imagine a future where Randall might make some discovery which would really *benefit* mankind, and she thrilled with incipient pride.

'I'm totally committed to it,' he finished quietly. 'And it's the second most important thing I've ever done in my life.'

She supposed that she was a fool for staring into those amazing grey eyes and asking, almost as though he was willing her to ask, 'And what's the most important thing?'

He gave her a soft smile. 'Why, not leaving here until you've agreed to be my wife.'

She looked at him. Wasn't trying to resist him the most pointless and stupid thing in the world? 'What would you do if I said no?'

He shrugged. 'I would persevere,' he said, in the distinctive deep voice. 'Using whatever means were available.'

Her heart beat a rapid tattoo. 'Such as?'

Had he moved his chair and pulled her to her feet without her noticing? Was that how she ended up in his arms, with his mouth searching hers? 'I've always found kissing pretty effective,' he murmured. 'Certainly with you.'

'Oh, really?'

'Mmm. Really.' And he proceeded to demonstrate with devastating effect.

She was out of breath and dismayed when he stopped. 'Oh!' she protested.

'One of your nurses just poked her head round the door and looked extremely shocked, to say the least, but you were past noticing. I think, my darling, that we really ought to go somewhere a little more private.'

Kelly blushed. So much for her staunch reputation in Theatres of not being interested in men! Oh, lord, how she *wanted* him! 'I guess we should.'

He tilted her chin up to look at him. 'So will you marry me?'

'Yes, Randall,' she sighed in delight, wondering if she should change her name by deed-poll to Cinderella.

'And will you object to being Lady Rousay?'

She thought about it for a bit, then shook her head.

'Like you, I don't intend using it at work. But you've done so much for me that accepting the title is a small thing—and it might just please your parents.' It would certainly annoy them if she *refused* the title!

'Good. And are you free this Saturday?'

Her mind scanned over her off-duty rota. 'Er—yes. I am, actually. Why?'

'Because I just happen to have a special licence in my pocket and I thought we'd get married.'

'A—special—licence,' she repeated slowly, and he nodded.

Kelly's eyes widened. 'And how did you manage that?'

'Oh—I persuaded your mother to give me your birth certificate.'

'But you can't just *do* things like that!' she protested.

'I just did,' he pointed out, with a complete absence of modesty.

Kelly shook her head, and giggled. '*You*,' she told him firmly, 'are the most outrageous man I've ever met.'

'I am also the most patient, my darling, but not for much longer. So can we please leave now, before I'm tempted to give in to my baser instincts and have my wicked way with you right here?'

And when a man loved you enough to rearrange his whole career for you—his whole *life* for you—there was really only one thing you could say.

'I love you, Randall Seton.'

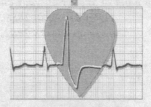

READER SERVICE™

The best romantic fiction direct to your door

Our guarantee to you...

The Reader Service involves you in no obligation to purchase, and is truly a service to you!

There are many extra benefits including a free monthly Newsletter with author interviews, book previews and much more.

Your books are sent direct to your door on 14 days no obligation home approval.

We offer huge discounts on selected books exclusively for subscribers.

Plus, we have a dedicated Customer Care team on hand to answer all your queries on
(UK) 020 8288 2888
(Ireland) 01 278 2062.